VECTOR

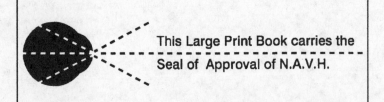

VECTOR

JAMES ABEL

THORNDIKE PRESS
A part of Gale, a Cengage Company

Farmington Hills, Mich • San Francisco • New York • Waterville, Maine
Meriden, Conn • Mason, Ohio • Chicago

LIBRARY OF CONGRESS CATALOGING-IN-PUBLICATION DATA

Names: Abel, James, author.
Title: Vector / by James Abel.
Description: Large print edition. | Waterville, Maine : Thorndike Press, a part of Gale, a Cengage Company, 2017. | Series: A Joe Rush novel | Series: Thorndike Press large print core
Identifiers: LCCN 2017029873| ISBN 9781432841515 (hardcover) | ISBN 1432841513 (hardcover)
Subjects: LCSH: Large type books. | BISAC: FICTION / Technological. | GSAFD: Suspense fiction.
Classification: LCC PS3568.E517 V43 2017b | DDC 813/.54—dc23
LC record available at https://lccn.loc.gov/2017029873

Published in 2017 by arrangement with The Berkley Publishing Group, an imprint of Penguin Publishing Group, a division of Penguin Random House LLC

Printed in Mexico
1 2 3 4 5 6 7 21 20 19 18 17

FOR JAMES GRADY
DR. NOIR

ONE

Kyle Utley received the first threat outside the New Post Pub, in Washington, a dark, cool bar on L Street near 15th, popular with *National Geographic* editors and local softball teams. Inside, on July 10, the White House National Security Team was celebrating a victory over the Senate Committee on Intelligence when the stranger appeared. The "Protectors" had overcome a 4–1 deficit to win the division championship. Twelve sweaty men and women sat drinking cold draft beer and eating the pub's famed Diplomat Burgers, reliving the game. Their come-from-behind victory had been so satisfying that for once no one talked shop.

Nothing about this morning's raid by FBI agents in Miami, where a gun battle and explosion had destroyed a small home. Three "foreign males," as neighbors described them, had rented the house, barricaded themselves inside, and blown them-

7

selves up rather than surrender. "All evidence was obliterated," the FBI report said.

Nothing about jihadist branches popping up in South America. Or the U.S./China face-off in the South China Sea. Just softball and gossip, until the cute Thai waitress bent over and told Deputy Assistant National Secretary Advisor Kyle Utley that a man needed to speak to him, outside.

"Tell him to come in."

"He says it is too noisy in here."

"Who is he?" Kyle asked, only half paying attention.

"He says he has big news," the waitress said.

Kyle left his cell phone on the table — mistake — and walked out of the bar. On humid L Street waited a trim, white, neatly bearded stranger wearing a wide-brimmed red Nats cap, blue tennis shirt, and Adidas. Utley, a former Army Ranger, noted the lower end of a Special Forces tattoo on the right bicep: a coiled snake on a knife hilt. Above that, but hidden beneath the sleeve, would be the skull, beret, and snake head on the muscled arm.

"Sorry to interrupt the party," the stranger said, not looking that way at all. "Nice home run in the seventh, by the way."

8

"What do you want?" Kyle was irritated at the coy, I-know-things-you-don't attitude, and the fact that the guy had been watching him. He noted the southwestern twang, alert posture, and smile that did not reach the mud-colored eyes. The man's slim frame rose to wide shoulders. He radiated fitness.

"Kyle, you have instant access to the President's Security Advisor. You're not important enough to have a bodyguard. Pass along a message, will you?"

"What message?" Utley asked, chilled despite the heat and understanding that a threat was coming. All threats — he knew — were to be taken seriously.

"That slush fund you guys run out of Ankara, Turkey? To pay off friendly warlords across the border? We're going to kill several hundred Americans in seventy-two hours if your bosses don't divert that money. On this paper is a list of charities. Three hundred million dollars is not a lot. Imagine if a few hundred million would have averted the World Trade Center attack. That cost trillions and the bill keeps rising. Pay and everyone stays safe. Plus" — he winked — "it all stays secret, with the convention coming up. Hey, the money's there already! Easy access!"

Utley stared into the eyes and saw intelligence and calm. His pulse had risen. His combat time in Afghanistan had destroyed any illusions about the depths of human violence. The stranger seemed rational, if that word could be applied to threats. Kyle eyed the paper and thin rubber gloves on the stranger, meaning no fingerprints.

"You sound American," Utley said.

"Then my language lessons were good."

"If you have a gripe about something, let's talk."

"We are."

"What's the money for?" Kyle asked, trying to delay, thinking, *five foot ten, mid to late twenties, no visible scars, gap in the front teeth, three freckles on the right lower lip.* He felt sweat on the back of his neck.

The man said, "Consider the payments reparations for Tol-e-Khomri."

"What was that name again?"

Darkness had fallen. Kyle had never heard of Tol-e-Khomri. A lone Volkswagen Jetta cruised past. Two wilted-looking *National Geographic* writers — the only other people on the block — brushed past, into the bar. Air-conditioning blasted out into the ninety-degree night.

Kyle held out the paper. "These organizations are not charities. They're fronts for terrorists."

The man smiled. "That can't possibly be right."

"You'll stop making demands if you get the money?" Utley said, not negotiating, just trying to keep the man there while he took mental notes, figured out what to do.

"Give us what we want and we go somewhere else."

"What exactly will happen if we don't pay?"

"Something terrible and unprecedented. *Bombs, but not bombs.* Panic, but no one will understand at first. It will occur in three cities. It will turn your world upside down. When America learns this warning was ignored, there will be consequences for your bosses. The third coming of wrath."

"You're not being clear."

"I think I am."

"I don't believe you."

The man shrugged. "Then wait seventy-two hours."

"How about if I call someone more senior than me." Kyle gathered himself to attack. He'd been trained in close combat, but that was years ago. These days he didn't even have time to work out in a gym. He said, changing stance so he could move fast, "This is not my area and I'm sure . . ."

"Stop!" the man hissed.

He'd stepped back. "I'm faster than you, Kyle. You've been out of the service awhile. Just call your boss. That's all you have to do. Then your part is over."

The man smiled. *What could be easier?* he seemed to suggest. Leftwinger? Right? Veteran who had suffered some injury and blamed the government? Kyle had been schooled in what to say if a threat ever came, although the lessons had always assumed a phone call, not a personal confrontation. *Try to control the situation.* What a laugh. He might as well try to fly.

The man said, "On 9/11 you had no warning. This time you have a choice." He turned and limped briskly up the block toward 15th. Utley began to follow. The man spun and raised an index finger. Kyle halted.

Kyle watched the man disappear around the corner. Kyle went to the corner. Somehow, the man was gone. That he could disappear so fast made his threat seem more real.

Kyle went back into the pub, where his teammates realized from his expression that something bad had happened. He retrieved his phone, walked back outside, and punched in the emergency number for the

President's National Security Advisor, who picked up immediately. He was at a barbecue in Potomac. Kyle heard men and women laughing in the background. Someone had made a joke.

"A nut," the National Security Advisor said, after hearing the story, but they both knew this was hope, not analysis.

After a beat, the NSA asked, "He actually said Tol-e-Khomri? Those exact words?"

"What's Tol-e-Khomri?"

"Never mind. Special Forces, you say? An American?"

"He had the tattoo. But anyone could have that."

"He knew about the special fund, eh?"

"Sir, everyone over there knows. It's the worst-kept secret in the Mideast."

"There's never been a situation where someone just walked up and made a threat outside a bar. And bombastic rhetoric is par for the course. They talk big. They bluff."

An hour later Kyle was at the barbecue, too, at the home of the White House Chief of Staff, on the patio, where a strategy session — how to handle *soft-on-terror* charges before the national political convention — had just been interrupted. He recounted the story, ice cubes melting in the tumbler of Maker's Mark in his hand.

By midnight, the heads of all major security agencies were on a conference call with the President, answering questions about ongoing alerts. There were no specific threats being investigated at this time. The three terrorists in Miami were dead. Nothing alarming intercepted over the past few days on monitored phones or e-mails. No particularly important national events scheduled within the next seventy-two hours. They tried to figure out what *"bombs, but not bombs"* meant.

"Like I said, someone wants to rattle us. If they really had something, they wouldn't give us a heads-up," said the head of the CIA.

"The third coming of wrath? Churchill called the nuclear bomb the second. What's the third?" That from the FBI.

"Pretty damn confident, bragging that they're here already. Usually they claim credit after," Kyle fretted.

"The *Tol-e-Khomri* reference bothers me the most," the National Security Advisor said.

The decision was not to pay, of course, or announce a potential threat days before the national political convention, but relevant agencies would try to track all spending by the "charities" overseas, even though the guess was that money trails would be dead ends, a traceless series of transfers, cash disappearing into black holes.

The national terrorism threat level was raised to red that night, but Homeland Security announced it was a drill. Police around the country increased patrols around public facilities. Army Reserve copters flew over major harbors. Homeland Security added staff at airports. The cost drained hundreds of millions of dollars, as usual.

Another drill.

"We don't bow to threats," the National Security Advisor told Kyle boldly, after the meeting.

We just did, he thought, at home on Calvert Street, unable to sleep. The seventy-two-hour deadline had shrunk to sixty-six. He had not told his wife what happened. On TV, sound off to let her sleep, he watched a firefight between U.S. Rangers and ISIS troops. Then came a segment about veterans being mistreated in VA hospitals. *Is it about this?* Utley wondered, each time the announcer detailed another gripe.

At that moment Amtrak's regularly scheduled Patriot Express pulled into Pennsylvania Station in New York City, and the fourth man who exited the quiet car no longer looked as he had at the New Post Pub. The blond wig was gone. The hair was short, thick, black, and curly. The limp was absent, the tattoo and freckles washed off. The man stood just on the tall side of average. The face, without beard or cheek plugs, seemed rounder, and the eyes, contact lenses out, were almost azure blue, with a slight bulge that made him look less intelligent. The look was deceptive.

Tom Fargo transferred to the New York City subway Two train, heading south, downtown. Even at this hour people were moving around the great city. College boys coming back from having sex with girl-friends. Pissed-off Yankees fans who had closed a Chelsea bar after the fiasco with the Red Sox tonight. A homeless man who snored and stank of urine. A Japanese tour-ist, too shy to ask directions. Any of them, Tom speculated, might be dead by next week, and the subway filled with panic-stricken people trying to flee the metropolis any way they could.

Tom Fargo looked around the car and hated these people with a vast, steady drumbeat that pulsed through his veins. *You are of them but not one of them,* Dr. Car-dozo had said. He had fought them overseas, in dry wadis and wet melon fields. He'd assassinated an American diplomat in a Rio shopping mall. Now he was back home.

The subway rocked, and he smelled cologne and garlicky sweat, French fries and cleaned-away vomit. These people lived in filth. They were so fat that they actually paid others to help them become thin, the natural hungry state of millions elsewhere. Their armies slaughtered while they occupied themselves with subway advertisements to cure toenail fungus. These people were as oblivious as the old fool who had taught him what to do tonight.

When you make a threat, Hobart Haines had told him, long ago, *you need to back it up with action. Hook them with easy cooperation. Then nail them to the wall.*

Tom Fargo was not afraid. Running over what was to happen next, he recalled that before boarding Amtrak he'd made a phone call from outside Union Station, used an encrypted cell, punched in a twenty-digit number, and the signal had joined a hundred thousand other calls shot gunning into space at that moment, to bounce off a commercial satellite in a flood of talk that overwhelmed monitoring. Even if listeners broke the encryption, which was virtually impossible, he spoke in code. He and Dr. Cardozo traded comments about soccer. Hundreds of miles above earth, words lived, money moved, plans coalesced. Their coded words had meant:

"Think they'll go for it?"

"Makes no difference. We do the same either way."

"Your suggestions were smart, Tom. *You* suggested sending two separate groups to America. *You* said to make the demands first, not after. *You* know how to talk to them."

"I had a good teacher."

At Borough Hall, Tom Fargo exited the train and walked up top and into an area housing century-old municipal buildings. He headed toward Brooklyn Heights. The night was sultry, the air so saturated with moisture that a light mist coated cars, the hulking courthouse, a neon-smeared falafel shop window. The city smelled of baking tar, coal-oven pizza, hundred-year-old brick, diesel fuel. At 3:45 A.M. even the muggers were asleep. The neighborhood was a high-income area filled with young professionals. His rented co-op was in a converted potato chip factory, across from the Brooklyn Bridge, down the cobblestone street from the popular River Café.

Tom Fargo pushed through a polished glass revolving door to enter the sparkling lobby, where the night doorman sat behind a large post, eyeing a portable TV on which a White House spokesman was telling a news announcer, "The President has kept us safe for four years."

"Good morning, sir," the doorman said.

"Call me Tom."

"Been clubbing again in Manhattan?"

Tom Fargo grinned and rubbed his thick hair as if happily woozy from drink. "The shop doesn't open until noon. Might as well have some fun before that."

The doorman sat beneath a framed black-and-white 1950s photo of Christmas shoppers on 5th Avenue: sleekly dressed executives, upscale tourists, wealthy leisure seekers. The shot caught the casual power and confidence at the heart of a great empire. People who knew they were safe. But Tom knew that within days the looks on those faces would change. It was too late to stop his first attack. He'd set it in motion before going to Washington. There was no way the Americans would capitulate to demands at this stage without proof.

The doorman was a forty-year-old Dominican, nine years in the union. He lowered his voice, as if to reveal a secret. He was a tall man with a tough face and sensitive disposition. He wrote poetry lyrics late at night, and listened to biographies of singing stars on DVDs.

"It happened again, sir."

Tom Fargo stiffened.

"She came down to walk the dog. Her face, sir. It was black and blue. It's not right."

Tom Fargo relaxed, because this wasn't about the FBI. But he was angry. The doorman was hoping Tom would call the cops on his next-door neighbor, a big, loudmouthed architect who chaired the building co-op board and relished his nickname, "Captain," and lived with his girlfriend. The doorman wouldn't make the call, fearing that if he did, he'd lose his job.

"Someone ought to stop it, sir."

Stay out of it, Tom Fargo told himself. *What happens to Rebeca is none of your business.*

"You're a good guy, Mauricio," he said.

Mauricio, disappointed, went back to watching the news.

The elevator had a TV in the wall — Americans needed them like drugs — that showed CNN news, something about an explosion in Miami. Four stories up the door opened into a freshly painted semipri-

20

vate foyer providing entry to only two apartments. There were framed lithographs of British jockeys and barristers on the wall, his neighbor's idea of class. He slipped the key into his top lock, then the dead bolt. Inside, the polished concrete floor threw back moonlight flooding in through floor-to-ceiling windows. The view of the Brooklyn Bridge was close and magnificent. The lights of Manhattan — even from across the river — drenched exotic artwork on his walls: jaguar head Day of the Dead mask from southern Mexico; tropical hardwood crucifix inlaid with Spanish gold links, from Peru; lacquerware bowl, 1859, Guatemala; Chacala rosary necklace that Tom's mother had picked up on a buying trip south, fifteen years ago, when she only owned one shop, not fourteen, scattered around the U.S., and an online shopping site, too.

Just the art that a spoiled trust fund artist wannabe — as his neighbors believed him to be — might display.

Forget Rebeca. Check the darkroom, he thought.

The darkroom — ground zero — had been installed by the owner, a photographer who was in China on assignment, and who had sublet the place to Tom for cash. He'd installed extra locks. Tom stood in a red glow, excitement building. The room was hot and moist. He could almost feel the vibration coming off the terrariums on the shelves, from a thousand *particles,* as he thought of them. He'd learned about particles from Hobart Haines when he was a teenager, in the high mountains, under a clear blue sky.

Bombs, but not bombs.

There was also $30,000 in cash here, and two perfectly good credit cards in other names. There were pistols and explosives, a microscope, a laptop, medicines and Clorox wipes, and, in a rack on the wall, bulb-shaped glass containers clasped upside down, and, stretched across each top, a thin membrane of elastic covering.

He was startled when his encrypted phone rang. It was not supposed to ring unless there was an emergency. His heart seized up. "Hi there," he answered, casually.

A half-drunken voice slurred, "Felix? Felix! It's Marty, man! Marty Bolton!"

"There's no Felix here."

The caller hung up, and Tom Fargo — in shock — took the SIM card from the phone. He smashed the card and phone with a hammer. He tried to control his racing heart. His plan had just changed almost before it started. *Felix* — said twice —

meant bad news. *Bolton* made it worse. *Marty* was a worst-case scenario. He understood instantly that the CNN report, the Miami explosion, meant that the other team here to carry out attacks was all dead.

Shocked, he went back into the living room, with its view of the high-rises, power centers, and apartments across the river, filled with enemy. Enemy extending across a continent; 350 million of them. He had always dreamed of facing long odds. Now he faced the longest.

The message had been: *You are the last one left. They will kill you if they find you. Good luck.*

Back in the darkroom the red light seemed to come from inside him now, pulsing into the air to saturate the glass containers and water pans, plastic cassettes, steel tweezers, and glass pipettes. As if fission was produced by intent, and *will* answered a scientific question, *will* was a formula that Dr. Cardozo jotted on his blue board. *Will = energy. Energy = destruction.*

Tom, filled with will, thought, *I can do it.* He was hot with rage but not fear. He'd lost that capacity some time ago. *I can fool them. I will make them think there are many groups here. I will finish this thing even if I have to do it alone.*

TWO

No one at the gold rush was interested in the missing American. They were too busy to care about my best friend. They were used to men being present one day, disappeared the next; dead from illness or murder, accidents or suicide. Miners died when rusty anchor cables snapped and their boats swept into jungle rapids. Rival crews cut cables on boats at 2 A.M., and turgid currents finished the job. Divers fought with knives in the darkness below the surface, sliced one another's air hoses and died clutching rubber tubing. Some got dengue fever, or keeled over in the 110-degree heat. They killed one another over prostitutes and $4 beer tabs. One man liked samba on a jukebox. Another wanted heavy metal. In the end, a body floated on the Madeira. Caimans ate it.

"The captain says that Dr. Nakamura was very sick," the translator told me. "Your friend was shaking with malaria. He was advised to go to the hospital in town, and Senhor Edward said he would. This is what the police told us also. I am sorry. The police gave up the search."

"Eddie never reached the hospital or our hotel."

"This happens," said Anasasio sadly.

"If he was going to town someone must have taken him. If we find that person we'll learn more," I insisted.

"Here, no one ever learns more."

Here was the Madeira River, forty miles from the Brazilian Amazon city of Porto Velho. From the deck of the mining boat I saw a ragged moonscape of bad possibilities: red mud that bred malarial mosquitoes, tin-roofed shanty bars where knives flashed at night, thick jungle. Rickety docks sagged in brown water. In mid channel were anchored two dozen mining boats, *dragas,* in calm areas between rapids. They were big as 1850s Mississippi riverboats, two-story-high herds of dumb animals belching smoke, pumps roaring, decks crawling with poor men come to seek their fortunes. They slept on hammocks on deck.

"Dr. Nakamura is tough," I said. "He would have found a way back."

The captain of the boat said something in

Portuguese, and Anasasio nodded with sympathy. "Tough is nothing against illness. He says sick men can be robbed or killed. They are weak and cannot defend themselves. They have hallucinations and wander into the jungle. The police said this same thing, Joe."

"Let's try the next boat."

"We've been here for seven hours."

"The police kept me in town for two days!"

"They checked your story thoroughly."

"You mean they grilled me. *Are you really a doctor? Are you involved in transporting drugs?*"

I'd told the Federal Police major, over and over, back in town, that we were here for pure research, science, a joint humanitarian project with their government and not any secret reason.

Which was a lie.

Eddie and I had been friends for over twenty years. We met in Marine Corps ROTC at UMass and went through boot camp together. I was best man at his wedding and godfather to his daughters. We served together in Iraq and shared more memories than a married couple. Now I was sick with apprehension. Eddie and I had split up three days ago for a day of studying

26

new malarias. I'd stayed in town, interviewing sick people in slum areas. Eddie was supposed to take a translator with him to the gold rush, but had not told me that the translator was sick, so he'd gone alone, hoping that his California Spanish might get him by, that he wouldn't lose a day of work. He'd planned to go out in the morning and come back at night. He had a road map and a rented jeep, which he'd paid a man to watch as he went out to the *dragas*. The police had found the jeep onshore.

"Where can I get a gun?" I asked Anasasio now.

"You cannot have one. I explained this. You are a foreigner. It is against the law."

"You said no one around here obeys laws."

"If the police know I gave you a gun, I will be arrested," he said stubbornly, in heavily nasal-accented English, reflecting the rough local Portuguese called *língua geral*. Anasasio looked like a cross between a thug and a dandy, tall and leanly muscled with a brush mustache — 1950s Madison Avenue style — and gleaming slicked-back hair. His shirt was blue silk, open to a Saint Christopher medal. His pleated Italian trousers were creased, but he'd rolled them up past his hairy knees, making them shorts against the heat. Baby-blue hospital booties

27

protected his loafers from mud, and a Beretta 9mm rode at his belt. He worked for the miners' union, a local partner for our health project with Columbia University. I was liking him less and less by the hour.

"We've visited ten boats already, Joe. Maybe Eddie fell out of a launch and drowned. On the highway are many accidents, not reported. Nothing here is reported. Give up."

But Eddie wouldn't have given up on me. He would have torn this place apart. I leaned over the gunwale and waved to hail a small passing outboard. These one-man ferries carried miners from *dragas* to shore, to bars, or for supplies: potatoes, meat, bullets, medicines.

Anasasio sighed, his ferret face shiny with sweat. "This is a tragedy."

"Not yet it isn't."

Anasasio had been confident when we left this morning. "I am a human lie detector," he'd bragged. "We will get to the bottom of things!"

Now he mopped his brow with a soiled handkerchief and said, "This place eats men."

My name is Joe Rush, and I grew up in the hamlet of Smith Falls, Massachusetts, in the Berkshire Hills, where there was no gold rush or malaria or 110-degree heat, not ten miles south of the Vermont line. My problem then was lack of challenge. There was nothing to do for a restless kid.

I was bored with our school board squabbles and Labor Day parades and hot dog cookouts. Bored even with my friends. I thrilled to commercials showing U.S. Marines storming ashore in foreign lands, saving lives, having adventures. So I left my girlfriend and parents and enrolled in Marine ROTC in college. I met Eddie Nakamura there. We competed — between us — to win best recruit, obstacle course, map use, range contest, until I edged him out and Eddie started calling us *One* and *Two*. As young lieutenants, in Iraq, we led our squads down a hidden tunnel and into a biolab where Saddam Hussein's scientists were experimenting on monkeys, trying to weaponize disease.

The experience changed our lives. The Corps paid for med school, and later we were seconded to a small, secret bioterror unit. Our records were sheep dipped, falsified so that even most high-level Marines never knew what we really did. The sections labeled EXPERT MARKSMAN and COMBAT EXPERIENCE AND ABILITY TO RUN FIELD

HOSPITALS remained; all true. But new parts, the killing of eight innocent Marines to save a thousand, the cooperation with an unfriendly intelligence service to murder a terrorist . . . were left out.

Eddie and I were sworn to secrecy without understanding what that meant. I don't think anyone understands the price of secrecy, even after you pay. I'm talking about more than the healed shotgun scars on my back, or my two amputated toes from a mission in northern Alaska. I'm talking about my wrecked marriage, and the way, a year later, my work led to the violent death of someone I loved very much.

These days, looking back at age forty-three, I realize that I would have made the same decisions. Looking forward, I've resolved to never put another loved one in danger again.

"How will you do that?" Eddie asked me on the plane that took us from New York to Brazil, three weeks ago.

"George Washington said it. No foreign entanglements."

"You can't spend your life alone."

"I'm not talking about forever. Just now."

Now Eddie lives in Boston with his wife and daughters. I live in the Berkshire Hills, back in Smith Falls, a tranquil place that I appreciate more than when I'd been growing up. Eddie and I have quit government employ and own a two-man biocure company, looking for microbes in the wild to help cure diseases. Good bacteria for a change, not bad. Little one-celled missiles to kill pancreatic cancers, or AIDS. We also work with the Columbia University Wilderness Medicine Program, heading down to New York on Amtrak two days a week to consult. And it was at Columbia, two months back, that I'd made the decision that led to Eddie disappearing now.

"You don't have to do what he wants," our boss, Dr. Stuart Harris, had griped that morning, glancing at his unwanted guest. He'd moved us from Harvard to Columbia some months before.

I pictured it as Anasasio and I rode a flying boat toward the last *draga*. I saw Stuart's cramped office two stories above Broadway, three blocks from Columbia's campus, where Wilderness Medicine shared a floor with researchers from NASA. The outer-space guys were addicted to popcorn, and the hallway smelled of butter. I saw the well-groomed, gray-suited man who occupied the steel chair by Stuart's desk, eyeing me with a businesslike smile. Eddie stiffened at the sight of the man.

"You know Ray Havlicek from the FBI," Stuart said.

Yes, I thought. *Ray thinks his fiancée is in love with me, and her daughter told me he's right.*

"Nice to see you, Joe," the new FBI assistant director said. "You're looking fit. Eddie, too."

"Whatever you need, the answer is no," Eddie said. Stuart brightened at that, but Ray concentrated on me.

"I understand you two are headed to Brazil to study frontier malaria," Ray said, crossing his legs.

Wilderness medicine means providing care to people in hard-to-reach corners of earth. Sometimes they are wealthy adventure seekers: shark divers in Ecuador, or bungee jumpers in Malawi. But more often they are the poor: impoverished settlers pushed from third-world cities into jungles where they have no experience with diseases, or natural disaster. Indonesian fishing villagers after a cyclone. Haitian cholera victims. Colombian peasants after an earthquake.

And *frontier malaria* is a new, resistant variety exploding through Amazon settlements. The mosquitoes that carry the disease have evolved to survive pesticides. The parasite is growing hardier, which makes mosquitoes the most deadly animal on earth; a nuisance in the United States, a tragedy overseas. Worldwide, fifty thousand people a year die of snake bites. Twenty-five thousand die of rabies. Two hundred fourteen million people caught malaria last year, and five hundred thousand died. So it was good to be working on preventing disease, instead of on weapons.

Ray said that day, "As long as you're going anyway, how about doing your old friends a little favor?"

I'd waited for more. Ray, Eddie, and I had served on a bio-attack task force a couple of years back. Ray was now promoted. And the bioterror world is small. The same people stay at the same hotel in Zurich, drink at the same bar in Port-au-Prince, run into one another at Defense Department conferences, birthday parties, or war games. Sometimes they fall in love. Ray was engaged to a woman we'd both worked with, and who had rejected him earlier. I had feelings for Chris Vekey but had never acted on them. Her daughter was my sixteen-year-old summer intern. I warned you that our world is incestuous. "Mom went back to Ray, on the rebound from you," Aya Vekey had told me, two months back.

"Nothing happened between your mom

and me, so how could there be any rebound, Aya?"

She'd answered with a teenager's irritating mix of innocence and objectivity. "When nothing happens between two people who like each other, they imagine the best. You only see bad stuff after you get to know someone."

"You're too young to be a cynic."

"Why? You're a cynic so it must be right. You should have tried with Mom. She gave up on love after you."

"There wasn't any *after,* Aya."

Eddie didn't trust Ray. I just felt sorry for him. It's tough to be the one in a relationship who loves the other person more. It wears you down. That wasn't my problem, though. It was Ray's.

But in Stuart's office Ray had remained professional, on the surface at least, as he unrolled a map of Brazil, the diamond-shaped fifth-largest nation on earth, after China. Most of the country was solid-green Amazon, with the megalopolis cities Rio and São Paulo far to the east. Ray's finger had poked down near the border with Bolivia . . . on the thin Madiera River in the west.

"We don't care about the malaria," he said.

34

"What do you care about, Ray?"

"Al Qaeda, ISIS. New fringe groups active there. We've heard rumors that they're planning something, possibly a run on a U.S. embassy in South America."

"Rumors? From who?"

"I can't tell you."

"Then we can't do it, Ray."

"Brazilian Federal Police," Ray said smoothly, as if he'd not refused to answer seconds before, "recovered a laptop in a raid in Rio, while arresting gold smugglers. Hezbollah and Al Qaeda are not listed as terrorist organizations in Brazil, and they're active in smuggling there. In the laptop was a file referring to a project in the Amazon, probably a training camp. Problem is, we can't send people officially because Brazil is touchy about interference. They claim they'll take care of it. But their Federal Police are riddled with corruption. Their own people in Brasília don't trust the ones out west."

It made sense to me. The Amazon was far from the Mideast, but the whole modus of terrorist organizations is that they pop up where you don't expect them. Hunt them in Syria and they show up in Yemen. Send agents to Yemen and next thing you know, they're in Brazil.

35

"The world is crisscrossed by invisible highways," Ray continued, sensing a more receptive audience. "Don't think of them as routes for specific items but as toll roads. The road for illegal migrants will be used one day by arms merchants. Then cocaine mules. Cargo is interchangeable. Once a road exists, anyone can use it. If you're looking on Highway 90, they'll be moving on Route 66, and 66 goes through the Amazon. You've got new airports there. New cities going up. A population of millions. Think Wild West. Gold rush. Arms. Loose law enforcement."

What Ray wanted, he explained, Stuart having been asked to leave, was for us to *pay attention* in case anything looked off, *ask casually* about the presence of Muslim groups, *steer talks* with officials, look for any thread that might lead to a terrorist training camp in the jungle.

"You know how to do it, boys," Ray said.

"You've got a million other people to ask," Eddie said.

"But you two are the best," Ray said, concentrating on me. "You'll have my phone number, and I'll be available twenty-four hours a day. Ask a few questions. I trust your instinct. Just sign the nondisclosure agreement and . . ."

36

"No signatures," I interrupted.

"But, Joe . . ."

"Last time we signed something you guys almost locked me away in Leavenworth," I said, aware, with a sinking feeling, that I'd started negotiating. "You want a favor? Then if I want to pick up the phone and call the *Times* right now and tell them about the rumor, I'll do it. No lawyers. No signatures. We're civilians now. So our rules."

Eddie looked up at me, and you had to know him to see that his straight-on stare meant he was feeling betrayed. *One, you said we were finished with this stuff. It's not even an emergency, just a rumor. I don't trust Ray.*

My own look back meant, *I know. But what are we supposed to do if there's really a training camp there?*

Ray saw the looks. "Good. So you'll sign?"

"What did I just tell you?"

Ray stood and announced that would not do. *We had to sign.* If we wouldn't, his hands were tied. He shrugged and shook hands with Stuart, who had come back in, nervous, and with Eddie, who relaxed, and me. Ray and I experienced one of those *who-has-the-stronger-grip* moments, which guys do even if they are presidents. Vladimir Putin shakes Trump's hand. He squeezes.

So does Trump. They both smile. Babies-"R"Us.

Ray walked to the door. He turned back around, grinning. I had a feeling he'd just won some private bet.

"I told them you'd never sign. It's a deal," he said.

I snapped back to the present. Our outboard boat was closing the last ten feet toward the next *draga*, last chance to learn on the water about Eddie. The gunwale rode inches from the water. The temperature had to be 105. Sweat soaked my shirt, cargo shorts, armpits. *I'll never be finished with secrets*, I thought. In the water floated debris: soiled paper plates, floating orange peels, a splintery log, but as we drew abreast the log had eyes. The eyes blinked. The log dived, showing a nine-foot tail. *Caiman.*

"People come here with big ideas. They never last," Anasasio said, nodding as if he'd just imparted great and historic wisdom. His bottom front tooth gleamed, gold.

As we pulled up, Anasasio waved to the raggedy crew of six glaring down at us. They were a tough-looking bunch in cutoffs, sweat-stained black-and-white logo Botafogo team soccer shirts, and grimy tractor caps. Their bellies were swollen from beer or amoebas. The captain was an Asian Indian, with thick gray-flecked hair, goatee, and massive forearms. They all radiated antagonism, *Stay away.*

Anasasio called up to the crew, and I recognized Portuguese words for *doctor, important,* and *missing.* The captain shook his head. I heard *ouro,* which means gold, and *mercúrio,* which means mercury. Anasasio snapped a threat back. The argument raged as the crew stared. The captain fell silent, and Anasasio turned to me with a broad smile.

"He says we are very welcome aboard."

"That's not what it sounded like."

"Oh, that is because they are about to make the gold. But I said you would not interrupt. I said you are not here about the use of illegal mercury. In fact you will find this very fascinating. You will see the gold made."

"I'm not interested in gold."

"Everyone is interested in gold," Anasasio said, paying our driver in *real,* reaching for the rope ladder. "Watch your step. I would not want you to fall into the river. Piranhas have an undeserved reputation. Usually they do not bother people. But here they have had a taste of men."

THREE

"Every day, we get gold," the captain bragged.

I tried to hold in my impatience. I was in an agony of waiting and couldn't care less about stupid gold. It was almost impossible to hear him and Anasasio talking over the roaring of the pump. We stood on the vibrating aft deck, the captain pointing with pride to a python-thick rubber air hose snaking over the side and into the brown water. Thirty feet down, he explained while I pretended to pay attention, Miguel, the diver, wore a dry suit and helmet and stood on the bottom and held a vacuum attachment that sucked up mud.

"Professor Miguel taught math at the university. Here he earns one hundred times what he made in a month," Anasasio said.

Was Eddie here earlier?

The mud sprayed out behind us onto a floor-to-ceiling wooden sluice box, its ramp-like surface covered by a thick synthetic carpet. "The carpet traps gold and allows lighter water to run back into the river," Anasasio translated, as delighted as a boy at an ice cream factory, all thoughts of Eddie wiped away by proximity to gold. "They do this twenty-four hours a day. But now we will see what they have found."

Questions multiplied in my head as two twentysomething crew members stepped up to the sluice box. The engine stopped. The black water ceased pouring onto the carpet.

Is Anasasio eager to go back to town because he's tired, or involved? What if Eddie was taken because he asked questions about the wrong thing? What if there's really a training camp in the jungle, and he is a prisoner there?

"Two *dragas* can be next to each other," Anasasio explained as the deck rocked from a drill smacking into rock far below. "One brings up three kilos, worth one hundred twenty thousand U.S. dollars. The other . . . nothing. It is a miracle."

From the stories I heard, it's probable that Eddie caught malaria. He and I are taking different preventatives because he's allergic to one. He must have contracted a resistant strain.

A chubby, intent-looking redheaded man

41

in a soiled floral print shirt — unbuttoned to fat — waddled up with a glass jar, "filled with liquid mercury," Anasasio said. "This man is named Rooster." Rooster poured the silvery stuff into a cut-off oil drum as diesel smoke from the pump blew into our faces. "The mercury fuses with the gold," Anasasio said excitedly, over the roar.

Shoulders jerking like a pneumatic drill operator's, Rooster used a long-handled electric mixer to churn up the mercury, silt, and gold. The sense of movement never stopped. The deck rocked as the drill operator below punched into river bottom. The river rushed into rapids eighty yards away. The anchor cable quivered from the current as more "flying boats," as Anasasio called them, brought crewmen from the bars or whorehouses onshore to other *dragas*.

"Anasasio, ask the captain if . . ."

The captain snarled at me in Portuguese. I didn't need translation. "Wait for the gold!"

The redheaded crewman, Rooster, inserted a garden hose into the bucket. The water washed excess sand onto the deck and, through gaps in the planking, into the river. The crew stood transfixed. Anasasio had grown unnaturally still.

Gold fever was the paramount disease

here for ten thousand miners. Rooster poured the gold/mercury mix onto an old T-shirt and used the fabric as a strainer. He squeezed out the T-shirt, and silvery mercury ran out, into a flat pan. Anasasio said, "They will reuse the mercury."

When Rooster opened the shirt, an irregular ball, the size of a large marble, lay inside. It looked like clay, not like anything worth money.

"Now the best part," Anasasio breathed.

Get this over with so I can ask about Eddie.

The pudgy crewman carried the ball into a closet on deck and waddled out carrying a small portable oven on a tripod, with a spigot jutting out the top. He put the mud ball in a tin pan and the pan in the oven, and shut the door. He lit a fire with a match beneath the tripod. After two minutes steam oozed from the spigot.

"Mercury flies away," said Anasasio. "It will come back as rain."

Rooster opened the oven and, hands protected by thick mitts, pulled out the pan. The mud ball was gone. In the pan lay a pool of molten gold, with rainbow colors: crimson and emerald and cobalt rippling across the surface in the seconds it took to dry. The hardened mass was the diameter of a coffee cup and as thick and pitted as a potato pancake. Sunlight brightened the surface. It looked pure and clean. Rooster placed it in my palm. It was cool to the touch, heavier than it looked.

Anasasio told me, "Okay, Joe. Ask about Eddie now!"

Three minutes later — after the captain finished his story — Anasasio turned to me, looking stricken. He said too softly, "I think we have the answer."

His expression filled me with an agony of fear.

"The captain says that Dr. Nakamura was here. He was shivering, but working, asking about malaria. He left to go to another *draga*, the *Santa Catarina*. Many men were sick there. But, Joe . . ." He laid a hand on my shoulder. "The *Santa Catarina* is no more. Its anchor cable snapped. It went into the rapids. All aboard died."

I felt as if someone had punched me in the stomach. The heat filled my head and my vision shrank. I gazed toward the turgid foam marking the narrow rapids. There, on muddy shore, lay wooden debris left by smashed, destroyed *dragas*, pieces of boat, clothing, and cutlery that had washed up.

I'm going to have to phone Eddie's family.

The captain pulled at Anasasio's arm and began another explanation, pointing at the gold ball. The gold that could not bring back Eddie. *We'll walk along the river. We'll look for his body.* I felt a nudge at my side and found myself looking into the dirty green eyes of the miner named Rooster. But what I saw wasn't sympathy. It was something more urgent. The eyes slid left, toward the sluice boxes. Then Rooster moved that way — *come with me* — as the captain and Anasasio grew more animated in their talk. Eddie was forgotten. To them he was one more casualty of the rapids. The men would be on their favorite subject . . . gold.

Wait a minute! He knows I don't speak Portuguese. Does Rooster speak English?

My pulse fluttered to life. Anasasio's back was to us as we moved to the smoke-spewing pump. It looked about a hundred years old, its pistons chugging like some factory engine in the year 1900. The whole contraption seemed to be straining so hard it might tear the ship apart. Water rushed from the hose again, gushed down the screens and into the sluice boxes in the perpetual hunt for gold. Rooster pretended to adjust the hose. His English, when it came, was so nasal that there was a lag time between my hearing and understanding. He seemed to be talking through his nose.

"Your translator is lying to you."

I felt a surge of hope. "How do you speak English?"

"I worked as a tour guide in Bahia and came here when I lost my job. Those union people are thieves and liars. They take our dues and do nothing. They sell cocaine. That man is not telling you what the captain really says."

"Which is what?"

"Your friend did not go to the *Santa Catarina*. He boarded a flying boat to go to the hospital. He was very ill, like the other men who have disappeared."

"What other men?" Now my pulse sped up as I realized that the captain saw us talking. But the captain laid a hand on Anasasio's shoulder to keep him from turning. The captain wanted my conversation with Rooster to continue.

But why? Because Anasasio lied to me? Or because these miners are the liars and want to steer me away?

Rooster said, "The sickest men have been disappearing. They leave their *dragas* for the hospital but do not reach Porto Velho. They are being taken. This happened to my brother. I think your friend went north."

"Taken?" I stared into the chubby, earnest face and recognized fear and self-blame and saw that once again, retired or not, I had

46

returned to my old haunt, the land of liars.

"Where are the missing people being taken?" I asked.

"Upriver."

"Why kidnap sick people?"

"To sell them. I heard a story from the Indian who worked on the *Muito Ouro* and now is in town. He said there is a foreign doctor upriver, who lives on an island and pays money for sick men. He said the island has guards. But stories are easy to learn because half the time they are not true. Maybe you will find out if this one is."

"Why buy sick people? It makes no sense."

"The Indian said they keep them in a little house."

"And the doctor is foreign? From where?"

A shrug. "He said the doctor came a year ago, to help the old one already there. He said at first the new doctor helped villagers and Indians, but then more foreigners arrived, with guns. Then the sick miners began to come."

"How can I talk to this Indian?"

Rooster suddenly stepped back angrily, and his face told me to break off questions. *Anasasio must have turned around.* Rooster started yelling in Portuguese. He slammed his fist on the sluice box. He was a good actor. He shouted, *"Perigoso,"* which means dangerous, and he shoved me away from the apparatus. Then he spun and spat something at Anasasio. *Can't you control your gringo?*

Anasasio's eyes lingered on Rooster for a fraction of a second too long. Then they slid to me, and he said, shrewd speculation in his voice, "You got too close, Joe. You must not touch the machine, you know."

One of the other crew members joined in with Rooster, poking his finger at my face. It hit me that they all knew I'd not touched the machinery. That — when they'd looked unfriendly as we approached the boat — the anger may not have been directed at me, but at Anasasio. Their union rep.

They are scared of him. But why?

I felt a familiar clenching in my belly. This is what always happens. You fly into the new place. You are surrounded by strangers. Some are lying but you can't tell who. You can't judge by clothing or by income level. The rich man could be the enemy. Or the poor one. Or the smiling child. You must make choices and make them fast. This was tough enough in the days when I could call Washington for help; from research people, search satellites, our embassy. I'd tried already with Ray Havlicek. I'd called him days ago. He'd been sympathetic, but impotent.

"My hands are tied, Joe. Officially, you're not there. Maybe if you'd found the camp I might be able to push things, but Eddie getting sick is unrelated."

"Ray, just *say* it's related. Make up something!"

"You know I can't do that."

"Can't? Or won't?"

Welcome to civilian life, I thought bitterly, free of high-level interference, but also of high-level help.

I will find you, Eddie.

Anasasio told me that we were leaving. He steered me to the gunwale, and the captain grunted good-bye. The crew went back to work. There was no way to ask more questions. Rooster's back was to me. We might have never met.

"There are no more boats to visit, Joe. Let's go home. You could use some sleep."

I need a gun, I told myself. *There must be a gun here.*

My options had dwindled. I needed to find an Indian in town. If the guy even existed. But there were 400,000 people in town, and lots of them were probably Indians. "Town" consisted of at least fifteen square miles: slums, office buildings, shopping, a soccer stadium. I had no idea where to go, what to look for, if the Indian had gone back to his village, or what language he spoke. Or even his name. Rooster had called the Indian "he," so it was a guy. Old guy? Young guy?

I'll ask Anasasio to drop me off in town. I'll get a car and come back here on my own, like Eddie did, and get back on that draga and look for more answers.

But then there was no need to do that.

Because, on the way to shore, in the little flying boat, I found a clue.

FOUR

The first victim was an airline baggage handler named Mikaela Dehlman. On the night of July 11 she watched an unclaimed parcel from Flight 1264 out of Frankfurt, Germany, go around and around on a luggage carousel at Houston's George Bush Intercontinental Airport, twenty-two miles from downtown. She was unaware that the national terrorism alert level had gone to red.

The unclaimed package lacked a name tag, or even destination tag. They'd shredded. The box was rectangular, about eight inches long, but the wrapping had ripped, and a piece of wooden corner had splintered at the top.

All the passengers had left.

Mikaela picked up the package and, as instructed in a recent security advisory, took it to room 1002A where lost baggage lay, waiting, if not claimed by owner, for eventual X-ray and opening. Sometimes cargo stayed here for days. Mikaela noticed that the parcel had not started its journey in Frankfurt, but from Rio. Probably the package had been put on the wrong plane, sent to Europe by mistake.

It was really interesting looking, she thought, trying to peer inside. She saw plastic wrapping in there, and what looked like a small statue and a clay pot. It was probably artwork. And artwork can be worth a lot, she knew. She and Glenn had taken a walk around Houston's galleries a few weeks earlier, and she'd been blown away by prices. One little vase had been tagged at $8,000.

I told myself I would not steal things anymore, Mikaela thought.

With a backward glance at the package, and quick look at the broken security camera in the corner, she returned to the run-up area outside. For the next two hours she unloaded bags from other planes. But the package stayed in her mind. She knew that a few handlers stole things from expensive bags, owned, they figured, by people rich enough to afford losing a camera or a laptop computer or any valuables they'd been stupid enough to pack, uninsured.

Besides, expensive bags and artwork are

usually insured, she thought, *so no one loses money except insurance companies, and they're crooks anyway, sucking the life out of hardworking people like me and Glenn, who these days sits around drinking my paycheck away. But when he's working, he's a good man: kind, generous, fun.*

Without two incomes, Mikaela and Glenn were behind on the rent.

I promised not to do this anymore!

All unclaimed luggage, Mikaela knew, ended up at the national lost luggage center in Scottsboro, Alabama, where it was sold at bargain-basement prices to any stranger who showed up and took advantage.

I assured Father Neilly, and I will stick to my word!

Mikaela brought a lovely Samsonite bag that was supposed to be in Montreal to the lost luggage room. The Rio package was now in a corner, almost hidden behind duffel bags, valises, rolling suitcases, and a set of Ping golf clubs that should have been in Qatar. FestivaWest Airlines had the highest rate of lost baggage in the industry. That was one reason it was failing, due for a takeover any day.

Mikaela's mood worsened when she got back outside. It was raining, and wind blew off the Gulf of Mexico, slanting sheets of water into her face and down her poncho, soaking her shirt. Some days out here it was nice and sunny, and others, today, the salary didn't seem like enough for her to put up with the shit. Mikaela was a trim, strong woman who had no children. She and Glenn opted to have fun instead. They used Festiva's free passes to travel on weekends. Last week they'd first-classed to Las Vegas, gotten the airline hotel rate, and lost this month's food and clothing budget at the blackjack tables at the Venetian.

Maybe I could sell that little clay pot to the man who buys stolen computers and jewelry!

Mikaela unloaded a flight from Salt Lake City. There was a dog show at Minute Maid Park scheduled this weekend, and the animals coming down the ramp shivered with fear. Mikaela felt awful each time she had to unload a caged animal. She had grown up with four Labradors, and anyone who would lock up an animal in a loud, vibrating luggage bin had her contempt. The cages were filled with piss and shit. The howling was pitiful. She didn't mind engine noise, but wore earplugs to keep out the suffering of poor, dumb animals.

Something about the callousness of pet owners — and travelers in general — made her feel justified in what she thought next.

I'll just open that parcel and get a better look at what's there.

Mikaela went into the lost luggage room. A flush lit her face, and she felt a quickening in the blood, just like the one she experienced at age eleven when she stole Snickers bars from a local candy store, in Galveston.

She made sure that the green light was off on the "broken" security camera. Last month ten baggage handlers in Tulsa had been caught in a sting, breaking open luggage, unaware that "broken" cameras recorded them. Mikaela carried the luggage to a corner that the camera didn't cover for some reason even when it was on.

But when she pried open the package she cursed. The pot had broken. There were shards of pottery in there and bits of wood and lots of plastic and paper wrapping and . . . *shit* . . . all this fretting for no payoff. She rummaged quickly among the debris and —

Ouch!

Something had bitten her, goddamnit! An insect or spider must be in there and *ouch* — it came again and she yanked out her hand. There was a little red bump on her wrist. Two bumps. She peered into the mass of wrapping. She wondered what had bitten her.

She stuffed the paper back in and put the parcel on a shelf.

By the time her shift was over, three hours later, the bumps had reddened and swelled and kept itching. When she got home she smeared calamine lotion on the bumps. Almost instantly, the itching stopped. She felt better. *Maybe,* she thought wryly, *the bites were a warning for me to stay on the straight and narrow and not steal anything anymore.*

By the time Glenn got home from another day of failed job hunting, she'd forgotten about the bites, and she certainly wasn't going to tell him about breaking into the parcel. They ate a low-budget spaghetti dinner. In the morning the bites were down.

That afternoon, she felt slight pain in her knees and elbows when she went to work, and attributed the throbbing to the strain of carrying luggage. Perhaps she had twisted the wrong way.

By that evening, there was a tight band-like sensation in her abdomen, pressing in, like fists pushing her intestines together. As if the muscles were coiling, sending bile back up into her belly, and making her nauseous from pain in her chest.

She must have twisted her neck, too, while carrying luggage, because it throbbed. Eva, another baggage handler, gave her a massage in the locker room. A couple of the guys offered massages also, but she called them perverts and they laughed and went back to work.

The pains got worse that night.

Summer flu, she thought.

The apartment got cold. The air-conditioning system must be turned down low, she figured, but when she looked, it was set to the usual seventy-two degrees. So she took her temperature. It was down to ninety-six. That's why she was cold. So cold that she'd begun shivering. Mikaela piled on more blankets. But the blankets did no good. The cold seemed to be working its way into her knees and elbows. *Man, this is the flu.*

At 3 A.M. she went into convulsions, bouncing on the bed, heels slamming mattress, arms flailing. She had never been so cold in her life. Glenn woke, frightened, and he made her hot tea. She couldn't hold it in. Her stomach seemed to close in on itself. She felt twisting knives in there. As she lurched toward the bathroom she was losing vision at the edges, and she had to use the wall for balance. She made it to the toilet, at least, and for a long time, whatever she had eaten over the last day seemed to come out everywhere it could.

By 4 A.M. everything had switched and she was hot, drenched with sweat, like she was a human rag and gigantic fists squeezed liquid from her forehead, face, armpits. Sweat soaked the blankets. She threw them off. She tried to stand and fell. She was going to be sick again.

"I'm turning yellow," she said in horror, looking at her shaking hands.

That did it. Glenn got her to the car and drove fast to Houston Methodist Hospital. He told her not to worry when she'd voided her bowels on the way. He'd clean the car. But she was horrified in the emergency room when they got her clothes off and her urine was red, dripping on the floor. The nurse looked hazy. Mikaela's throat was hot and the pain was in her spine now, flowing up and down, like razor blades skimming nerves.

She screamed when a doctor touched her.

The doctor looked small and tiny, and she saw him from far off through a tube.

It was now thirty-eight hours after the threat had been made to the Deputy Assistant National Security Advisor, outside the New Post Pub, in the capital. Mikaela's accidental infection might have given authorities time to prepare for what was coming had they connected it to the threat, but no one did.

Mikaela was passing out.

A voice above her was saying, "The disease doesn't happen this fast. *It doesn't! It's impossible!*"

"Yeah? Then you tell me what this is, Doctor. It's bad. I've never seen it this bad, but it's not impossible."

Glenn was screaming, "That monitor! Look at the lines! What's wrong with her heart!"

Later, blood tests confirmed the cause of death, and a notation was made beside the name of Mikaela Dehlman and forwarded to the city health department. Under the national security advisory, suspicious outbreaks were to be reported immediately to Homeland Security and the Centers for Disease Control and Prevention, in Atlanta. But this case was not considered related to the advisory, so officials were not notified.

After all, Houston is a tropical city. It lies near many bodies of fresh water that can breed insects. In the summer, Houston is rife with mosquitoes. Over 30 percent of the city is foreign-born, many from tropical countries, and Mikaela worked at an airport, exposing her to foreign travelers. So what she had contracted was considered, quite logically, to be extremely rare but natural, conceivable, in this warm, humid place.

The parcel was transported to Alabama and locked away in a dark corner. Ninety days would have to pass before, by law, it could be opened or sold.

Mikaela's death, doctors thought, was a tragic rarity. They certainly did not regard it as a harbinger of things to come.

In their reports, notations read, *"Hemolysis, burst blood vessels in the urine. Acute kidney failure. Death from a lethal, unusual malaria."*

FIVE

"You know what you need? A woman," Anasasio said.

We were in the mining union Land Cruiser, heading back to town on the Amazon highway, the air-conditioning cranked up to arctic level, the world fractured and nonsensical.

Four more hours until eleven, and the secret meeting. I never even felt Rooster shove that note in my pocket, I thought.

The highway extended across a continent from Brazil's megalopolis of São Paulo over a thousand miles east, to Peru and the Pacific Ocean, over a thousand miles west. Porto Velho was in the middle. The two-lane road was new but already crumbling. We passed a new fifteen-foot-high overpass, except it was unconnected to the road, just plopped down as if from a spaceship, in the jungle.

Better drivers wove back and forth insanely, avoiding two-foot-deep holes. Anasasio steered around an enormous semi truck piled high with tropical hardwoods. "Cut illegally," he announced. He passed a refrigerated cattle truck, swaying like an accordion. "Yum! Meat!" We carried sloshing fuel in plastic jugs in back, as "gasoline sold on the highway is watered." The windshield wipers smeared mosquitoes. Eight P.M. was mosquito cocktail hour.

Three hours left until my meeting with Rooster.

"I wish we could have tracked Eddie through his phone," I said.

"It is probably at the bottom of the Madeira."

I thought, *Rooster's note in my pocket said,* 11 P.M. 32 Rondon Street. Do not bring Anasasio!

"You know the poem. A woman and cocaine dull all pain," Anasasio said. His hand was on my knee.

If Rooster is the liar, the meeting will be a trap.

Traffic thickened as we entered the Rondônia state capital. Twenty years ago it was a sleepy backwater. Now the road widened to four lanes, and we slowed into a traffic jam of old metro busses and smoke-belching trucks and new Mercedes cars. The outlying shantytowns, once rain forest, were masses of one-story-high tin-roofed shacks where trees were memories, the sky criss-crossed by pirated power lines: copper, TV wiring, anything that carried electricity. Anasasio laughed at the lawbreaking. "What do *you* do in *your* country when a law is stupid? You ignore it, of course."

I told him that I did not need him this evening as a translator. I lied and said that I'd stay at the hotel. We passed into the newer business area, banks, glass office buildings, even a "museum of nature" — museums being where civilized people like to keep nature — and paved residential streets lined with ranch-style, white-walled, stucco-roofed homes. Richer properties came with alarm systems. The difference between first-world and developing countries is the attention given public places versus privately owned ones.

"My friend, Joe. Let me take you along tonight. I know an excellent place on Rondon Street."

I tried not to show surprise on my face. I hoped the place on Rondon Street was not the same one where I was to meet Rooster. That Porto Velho was one of those towns where saloons, brothels, and gambling dens are located in a row.

"Just the hotel, Anasasio."

"No! Let us make another tour of the malaria hospitals. Perhaps your friend checked in while we were away! We must keep trying! You are right! Maybe he did not drown!"

Ninety minutes to go.

The "hospitals" were one-room clinics where dozens of victims lay looking half dead in beds beneath mosquito netting. Intravenous lines ran blue medicines into their arms. Malaria patients exhibit the rag doll attitude of the dead, when they are not shivering.

Suddenly I straightened and joy filled me! I saw Eddie, in a bed in the corner!

It wasn't Eddie. My spirits plunged.

Anasasio put his arm around my shoulder as we arrived at the hotel and main plaza. "The hotel of lost causes is well named. I'll see you in the morning. Sleep is what you need, Joe. Then a trip home. Good night."

The hotel of lost causes — the Ecológica — lay across the plaza from the Governor's mansion and cathedral and two-story-high barracks that served as state headquarters for the National Police. I'd been grilled there for hours when I'd reported Eddie gone.

Why are you really here, Doctor?

The hotel was the sort of remote bastion of idealism that Stuart usually booked for researchers: bright, clean, and filled with underdogs from the world over; German environmentalists trying to save the rain forest, New York Botanical Garden scientists seeking cancer cures in the treetops, leftist journalists chronicling rich ranchers fighting poor rubber tappers, and Indians, who got a cut rate at the Ecológica, discounts being the only benefit of contact, since half the Indians had been wiped out by "civilized" disease. The common cold.

There are many interesting foreign stamps in your passport, Federal Police Major Rubens Lemos had said.

The Hilton got the mining company execs, the Ecológica the miners. The Marriott got the hydroelectric dam builders, the Ecológica the grad students studying forest to be drowned when waters rose up, a year from now.

I walked in after Anasasio dropped me off, dreading the upcoming phone call to Eddie's family. The owner's son shook his head at me from behind the reception desk, *Sorry, no Eddie,* and held up a finger, meaning he had something to tell me, probably tonight's menu. I kept going. I was in no mood for

65

food. Ignoring him would prove to be a mistake.

The lobby was sunny with arched doorways and smelled of fresh coffee. It was tastefully decorated with Indian spears, baskets, and potted Brazil nut trees. Everywhere hung leftist political posters, in Portuguese, but between the clenched fists, marching peasants, and smiling spider monkeys, it was easy to get the messages. *Save the Forest!*

In my second-floor room — sunny, usually, balcony overlooking the plaza, rotating ceiling fan, latched door/windows — I called FBI Assistant Director Ray Havlicek, hoping that the new information might help. He listened, but seemed dubious. "An Indian? A bar? A rumor?"

"As I recall, Ray, you asked us to listen for rumors."

"Don't you think you're reaching for answers?"

"What happened to *call me anytime?*"

I hung up and called our summer intern Aya Vekey, in New York. She was a brilliant high school senior whose youth had nothing to do with her abilities. Adults underestimated Aya because of her age. Sometimes when I phoned her I felt as if there was a forty-year-old professor on the other end, and at other times, a kid. But I owed my life to Aya, and she was as much a member of the team as Eddie. She knew Eddie was missing, but didn't know the secret part of our mission.

"I've been reading more on Rondônia, Joe. Stay away from the police. Last year there was this report in *O Globo* about police helping cocaine smugglers there."

"Good work. Meanwhile, keep learning more about this place. Issues. Factions. Medical studies. Check the journals."

"Medical studies? Why?"

Because if someone is kidnapping sick people, I want to know why. "Just do it," I said.

"But why?"

"Aya, you're the intern. I'm the boss."

"I'll tell Mom to put pressure on Ray Havlicek. She'll *make* him help Eddie. He does what she wants."

"No. Not that way."

"Why? This is about Eddie, not you! She doesn't even love Ray! She only landed up with him because you wouldn't —"

I relented. The kid was right. If Chris could pressure Ray to act, if that would help Eddie, why the hell not?

I dreaded the last call, to Eddie's wife and daughters. I'd known Johanna Nakamura

67

for over twenty years, since Eddie had met her after boot camp. I'd attended birthday parties for Renee Nakamura, seventeen, and India Nakamura, eighteen, since they were toddlers. When I called, the receiver was snatched up after half a ring. I envisioned the women on extension phones, in Boston. Johanna and Renee accepted the risks of Eddie's profession. India's childhood affection for me had soured. She blamed me for Eddie's absences.

"I've got a lead," I exaggerated.

Technology made their voices seem two feet away.

"Stop lying, Joe," India snapped.

"India! Please," Johanna said.

"If it wasn't for him, Dad would be here."

I heard a sob and click, which would be Renee hanging up, hating arguments. India had been right, though. *Eddie came because of me.* Johanna tried to make it better, said she knew I was doing all I could, said that she knew I loved her husband as much as they did. She was going crazy, but still tried to make me feel better. She's that way.

"I have a feeling, Joe. He's alive."

I hung up feeling exhausted. It was time to go meet Rooster, but without a weapon, and in a place where my foreign language skills would be useless.

I was armed with a crumpled slip of paper with Rooster's purplish scribble on it, already half faded. Everything in the Amazon is wet. Moisture eats shoes. Paper. People. Ink. Even water seems wetter.

I rushed downstairs to find a cab — they usually idle outside the hotel — but the desk clerk again waved me over, more forcefully. *Muito importante!* This time I came. There was something urgent in his face.

"Did the woman find you, Dr. Rush?"

"What woman?"

"The beautiful one. The photographer," he said with admiration. His hands moved in an hourglass shape. "She said she thought she knew you. She was the one who sat at your breakfast table this morning."

I frowned. "No one sat with me."

"No? But I pointed you out. She said she was going over. Next time I looked, you were gone and she was there and your dishes were not even cleared away yet. Other tables were empty. So I thought you'd talked."

"She said she knew me from where?"

A shrug. "Last night she said she was going to knock at your door. Didn't she do that?"

I felt a tug in my chest, a faint ticking of alarm, but I kept my voice casual, as if I'd

69

missed a friendly opportunity. "I was out. Can you describe her?"

He put both hands to his heart, meaning, *Beautiful!* "Small and dark, like the Lebanese man who sells newspapers on the plaza, but not *that* dark. And copper hair, worn up. Very nice lips. And green eyes, like the dark green under the water at the reef in Rio Grande. She asked to see your passport photo, to make sure you are the man she knows. I did not let her, of course."

I grinned, but did not feel like grinning. "You sound in love, Tarsisio."

He smiled. *With her, that would be easy!*

"She's a photographer, you said?"

"She is with her brother, a very tough-looking man! They are taking photos of the *garimpeiros,* the *seringeiros,* the *índios.* For a book, they said. A big one for the table on which you place coffee."

Photographers go everywhere, talk to everyone.

"Are you sure I can't see her passport photo, Tarsisio? Maybe it will help me remember her."

He looked sad to turn me down. "We respect privacy."

She sat at my table immediately after I left? She chose my table when others were open? Why?

70

I opened my wallet to offer cash, but Tarsisio looked pained. Apparently bribery was not allowed in the hotel of lost causes, honesty being a virtue that came with access to this normally pleasant, throwback place.

"Joe. Please," he said, reddening. "Izabel Santo is in room 215, and her brother is in 311. They are not there now. Maybe you will see her later."

"Tarsisio, one last question."

"Anything." Clearly, he felt guilty at disappointing me by not taking the bribe.

"Would you know if any cutlery or glasses were missing from my table this morning, after breakfast?"

He drew himself up and frowned. "Did you see someone take things?"

No, but I think someone did, for my DNA or prints.

"Just curious."

He looked relieved. "Everyone who works here has been with us for years. They are honest."

I hurried from the lobby, into the night heat, where three ethanol-powered, battered taxis waited. I climbed into the first and handed the driver the slip of paper with the address that Rooster had given me. The driver was a heavy, bespectacled Sikh, wearing a cobalt-blue turban. His Fiat smelled of curry. He frowned at the note, and said, in Portuguese-accented English, "This place, sir . . . do you know it?"

"I'm in a hurry."

"Maybe you should go to a different place. It is not just a bowling alley for games."

I leaned forward. "It's what? A *bowling alley*? I thought it was a restaurant or bar."

"Oh, in one place, yes, but in the other rooms . . . bad things! People get hurt. If you are hungry, my cousin owns a nice pizzeria. He puts real tomato sauce on the pies, not ketchup, like the other places, and there are no rats and . . ."

"Just go."

The driver worked gears and pulled his smoke-belching Fiat into the busy cobblestone square as church bells pealed 11 P.M.

Who is she? I thought. *Is this connected to Eddie? Is she connected to what we were asked to find? I never met any Izabel Santo. What does she want?*

I also wanted to make sure that Anasasio was really gone, so I turned to check if any headlights were following. I saw two, yellowish, a block behind, spaced widely apart, and high, the left one shining weaker than the right. Anasasio's Land Cruiser was equipped with bluer headlights. So this was

72

not him.

The yellow headlights made the first turn after we did.

The yellow headlights made the fourth turn as well.

Six

There were no streetlights by the river. The driver pulled to a halt before an eight-foot-tall iron gate and whitewashed wall topped by razor wire. We idled behind a Dodge Ram truck. Its driver stuck a hand out the window to wave at a camera angling down from above. The gate swung open. The Ram surged forward. The gate slammed behind it as a pair of headlights turned a corner behind us, left one weaker than right. The headlights pulled over, and shut off.

To reach Rondon Street we'd passed through descending layers of civilization: private home area to shantytown to warehouses to mud road, the red surface turned slick by a tropical downpour that lasted five minutes and stopped as quickly as it had begun.

The Sikh said, "I'm not going in there. I will drop you here." He let me out and drove off.

I smiled up at the camera and waved like the previous driver. The gate did not open, but dogs began barking behind it. I banged on the steel. Up the street, no one had exited the silhouetted vehicle. The steel gate creaked open, and a lean, shirtless man blocked the way, holding a pistol at his side. His eyes bulged as if he were drugged, and glitter — multicolored sequins — stuck to his muscled chest. The guard couldn't decide if he wanted to party or shoot. His white capoeira pants — Brazilian jiujitsu clothes — were worn loose, above Reeboks. He had the sinewy frame of a habitual drug user. The dogs sounded closer. The man's pupils seemed to vibrate. I didn't understand the words he spat at me, but the challenge was clear.

"I want to go bowling," I said, thinking how stupid it sounded, hoping it was code, like "tea" during prohibition.

"Boliche?" he said suspiciously, stepping forward.

That was close enough, so I nodded.

"United States?"

"Yes. USA."

He snapped out an order and raised both hands in pantomime. *I need to frisk you.* I glimpsed another guard, shotgun over his shoulder, in the shadows, holding two

Doberman pinschers on leashes. The compound was larger than it had looked from the street, lit by portable floodlights powered by a roaring generator. It was nice inside and big. There was a horseshoe-shaped parking area packed with four-wheel-drive vehicles: Toyotas, Jeeps, pickups. I saw three buildings set at least fifty yards apart, including a central main house, generously two stories high, antebellum style, with colonnades, as if in Mississippi. I saw candles flickering on a veranda, tables, a waiter with a tray, couples dining, as if it was a country club. A club with guards.

To the left across a lawn was a long, low building that might actually contain a bowling alley. A third, squarish, hulking structure seemed more warehouse, except I watched a man and woman, arms entwined, disappear into it, passing two women in halter tops and tight dresses shimmying out. There's not a city in the world that doesn't provide a location for the rich and the violent to meet on the common ground of dissolution. In Kabul it had been a converted warlord's mansion; in Baghdad, an underground bunker once used to store arms, now a bar, whorehouse, casino.

Is Rooster even here? I thought as I felt rough hands move up my thighs and into

76

my crotch and squeeze.

The guard stepped back, and a sickle moon appeared. I followed the slope of ground — gravel path and manicured lawn — toward the buildings and black river. At night it seemed clean. It would look filthy in daylight.

The note that Rooster shoved in my pocket said he would be here with the Indian.

On the curving river was a long dock and outboard boats tethered to pylons like horses. Approaching running lights meant more customers were arriving. Hip-hop music blasted from the warehouse. This place was an Amazon version of San Francisco's Barbary Coast, offering an evening of heightened sensation: gambling, cocaine, a blood fight or a sirloin steak.

Pick a building and look for Rooster. The fine restaurant is a less likely destination for a miner. The whorehouse will be more likely. I hope Anasasio isn't here.

Behind me, the gate swung open and a vehicle drove in, its left headlight flickering. Whoever had followed me had access here without being frisked. To get the best view of who got out, I bent to tie my shoelace in a shadow, to see two people exit the vehicle and walk toward the main house/restaurant, arm in arm.

One small, a woman. One a large man. I bet it's the people from the hotel.

The woman's hair fell below the shoulder. She walked on her toes, light. I saw no camera, but she had a large shoulder bag. The man towered over her in a tropical floral shirt that fell loose over his hip, where, if he was armed, would be his weapon. They were looking around, so I ducked into the "bowling alley" door.

Holy shit, I thought, walking in to the crash of pins.

It was a real bowling alley, all right, but nothing like the twenty-lane Bowlmor that I used to go to in high school. No cluster of preening eighteen-year-old football players or giggling cheerleaders, eating burgers. No retirees from Sunny Acres. No Tuesday night ladies' league, shrieking with glee at a strike or pounding the polished floor at a gutter ball. No Red Sox game on TV.

Keep moving. Find Rooster.

This bowling alley might have been designed by Hieronymus Bosch. In one lane were a dozen roaring miners, in flip-flop sandals, throwing gutter balls two at a time and snorting cocaine. In another, three women in halter tops drank beer, while a man sprawled on the floor, passed out. Mir-

78

rored spheres rotated on the ceiling. Red and emerald lights crisscrossed the faces of a mob by the bar, downing cachaça or drinking from long-necked beer bottles. In lane nine, two middle-aged couples bowled and chatted as if none of the other stuff was going on. Suburb meets hell.

I didn't see Rooster, but I spotted four Federal Police, in unbuttoned uniforms, bowling in lane two, and guzzling beer from bottles. One man was the officer who had grilled me when Eddie disappeared.

There was no Rooster in the men's room, or in a long hallway where I passed a room inside of which I glimpsed men playing cards, and another housing a man with a hand scale at a small table, weighing gold dust while a guard looked on and two grungy-looking men never took their eyes off the scale. Miners changing gold for cash.

No Rooster in the bar area, where the TV showed a CNN news alert from the U.S.: *Miami shootout with terrorists.* Normally that would have stopped me, but not tonight.

Outside again, the moon was sickle shaped, misty, and anemic. I heard macaws scream in the trees lining the path, and the moans of a couple enjoying themselves in the bushes. The river smelled of diesel fuel. I saw, upriver, the public wharf from where ferries left to head north, where Rooster claimed that Eddie had disappeared.

"Joe! Is that you? Joe! My good friend!"

Anasasio, coming up behind me, was grinning.

"You changed your mind! You came!"

He was drunk, showered, scented with cologne, and wearing a white button-up guayabera over chocolate-colored trousers. A gold watch now, instead of silver. He threw his arm around me, breath more alcohol than carbon dioxide, but then he frowned. He was the last thing I needed here.

"How did you find this place, Joe?"

"You said Rondon Street, so I asked the taxi driver if there was a good spot there to have fun."

"Ah! Smart! Now we find you a sexy woman!"

I didn't want a woman and I didn't want Rooster spotting me with Anasasio, but I allowed him to steer me into the warehouse building, and a carpeted room where a half dozen women in bikinis lounged on stuffed couches, did their nails, or watched TV. The room smelled of perfume and mildew. The women managed to smile like they meant it. A range of female faces regarded us; middle-aged and painted to very pretty to much too young.

"What do you prefer, Joe? Blond? Vigorous?"

The women were as provocative as a menu in a Chinese restaurant. Frank Sinatra's voice sounded over wall speakers. *"These little town blues . . ."* A long hallway beyond beaded curtains probably led to bedrooms. A fat guard stood in a corner and made eye contact with Anasasio, and they both nodded. They were pals. Great.

"The bill is on me," Anasasio said. "My treat. Choose."

"The small brunette on the left."

"You have a good eye, Joe! I have had her many times, and she is vigorous!"

Anasasio threw his arm around a blonde in a one-piece bathing suit that accented her large breasts. Her high heels made her six inches taller than he. She stiffened at his touch, and I noted that the other women looked relieved that he'd not chosen them. Anasasio steered the blonde down the hall, behind me. He winked as he disappeared into the next room, leaving me with the small brunette.

What if Rooster isn't here at all? What if I misread the play on that boat, and the miners and Anasasio work together? What if the next person to disappear is me? Lure him to a whorehouse. Get his clothes off . . .

"I am Agatha," the brunette said in our "room," unhooking her halter top, revealing small, pert breasts. The cubicle lacked a window, offered a single bed, smelled clean, and featured a ski poster of TELLURIDE, COLORADO! No matter where you are, everyone wants to be somewhere else.

"You are shy?" she said, at a sink in the wall, waving me over, soaping up her hands. Her bikini bottom remained on.

"You speak English?"

"I just did, didn't I?" Amused, she tested the hot water on her wrist. She was pretty: violet eyes, pink lip gloss, no mascara, musical voice. She held out a terry washcloth. "Come. I will clean you."

Rooster's instructions had been to meet thirty minutes ago. But he'd not told me there were three buildings. I stopped her hand before she could touch my zipper. I kept my voice low as a shriek of feigned female delight erupted from behind the thin wall, Anasasio's room. I whispered that I did not want her to tell Anasasio what I was about to say, it was embarrassing, and she smiled, understanding.

"Ah! You like men!"

"It's not that. I have a disease."

"Show me the sore."

82

"No, when I piss, it hurts. I don't want you to get sick also." I pulled out my wallet. I gave her money. I asked her to tell Anasasio that I'd gotten over excited and finished early, grown angry, and stormed out.

"I understand. You like men," she repeated knowingly, then winked and folded away the money.

"Just tell him what I said, okay?"

"You are not alone. You would be surprised. Do you want the address of the place for sex with men?"

I took it from her and tried to look more embarrassed. If she told Anasasio this part, he would go off on a wild goose chase to the place where the male prostitutes were.

I left.

Midnight. *Too late. If he was ever here, he's gone.*

But I tried the last building anyway, ducked across the grounds and reached the mansion, stairs, and dining veranda. It was a *churrascaria,* I realized, a restaurant serving meat, lots of it, endless platters offered by circulating waiters until patrons were too stuffed to eat more. The waiters carved meat strips off the bone at your table. Serrated knives flashed to the right and left. Rooster had lied, or never shown up, or had misled me or —

I saw him!

He was at a table for four, with big plates, a candle, a bottle of wine, and a pale, soft-faced woman and another man who had a barrel chest, long, straight, rib cage–length hair, and Asiatic features of an Indian. Rooster was cleaned up, in a tennis shirt. His hair was brushed sideways, and he and the woman held hands. The Indian had a round face with a sharp nose. He was finishing a pork chop. I arrived at the table at the same time one of the circulating waiters did, offering a wooden platter heaped with charred sausages. The Indian took two. He was clearly more interested in the meal than in talking.

"I did not think you were coming," Rooster said.

"You didn't tell me which building in your note."

He grinned. "Yes, I thought of that after, but I had to write the note fast. You looked for me with the whores, yes? Because I am a miner, yes? This is Elizabe, my wife, who would kill me if I went there. She moved to Porto Velho with me from São Paulo. She makes sure I don't waste the money that we are saving for a little farm. And this is Cizinio Karitiana. He doesn't speak English."

84

Rooster's easygoing mood turned urgent when I told him that Anasasio was here. He spoke rapidly to Cizinio, who turned his impassive face to me and began to speak. Clearly, he'd been prepped. Rooster translated as quickly as any pro at the UN. Apparently, the name Anasasio got everyone moving around here. Everyone feared the union.

"The old doctor lived on the island when I was a boy," Cizinio said. "He treated us and he was kind. He asked many questions about illness. Then a year ago a different doctor came. And other foreigners, with guns. They told Indians not to come anymore. The old doctor now won't talk to us."

I asked, "How do you know the guards are foreigners?"

"They speak another language."

"My language?"

"No, but some are white, like you."

"Where did the old doctor come from?"

A shrug. "My grandfather told me there was a big war in Europe and he came after that, under the water, in a boat."

Waiters offered more sausages, steak cuts, lamb. It was a meat paradise. There was a long salad bar in a corner and a finely stocked liquor bar and a line of people waiting for tables, the men wearing cowboy hats and boots and billowy shirts; women in tight jeans, Texas-style clothing. Elizabe was in a print dress and had a pile of sliced onions and red tomatoes on her plate. Cizinio was the only Indian present that I could see.

"Cizinio, you said the old doctor used to ask many questions. About what?"

"Malaria."

"Did he say why he was interested?"

"He walked in the forest and collected mosquitoes, too."

"What questions did he ask about malaria?"

Cizinio chewed, thought, looked impassive. "Oh, where the worst places were to catch it, which stretches of river were most dangerous."

"And now you say sick people are being kidnapped?"

"I don't *say* it. It is happening. Why don't you people ever believe Indians?"

Suddenly I felt a familiar sensation on the left side of my neck, as if an insect had landed there. Any Marine who has ever been on patrol knows the feeling. *You are being watched.* I turned and saw only diners at first, but then, at a far table, as a waiter passed, someone looked away. There sat a small woman with coppery wavy hair, and a larger man. They had a wine bottle

86

before them, and plates. But their posture was not the easy kind employed by a relaxing couple, or the rigid kind when a couple is arguing. They stared into each other's eyes. The posture was almost right. But almost isn't right.

"Are you listening to Cizinio?" Rooster said.

"Say again, please."

Cizinio finished his sausage. A waiter was approaching with another platter. "The boats bringing sick people come in the night. One time I was fishing nearby and heard screaming. The guards shot into the water, chased me away."

"What kind of screaming? Like someone was angry? Or like someone was hurt?"

"Hurt."

"Is there a way for me to get on the island?"

Cizinio thought that was funny. "Yes. Get sick. And men will kidnap you."

"Can you take us there?"

"No. I must get back to my *draga*," Cizinio said. "And get more gold."

I started to protest that a man's life could be at stake, but Rooster placed a restraining hand on my arm. "It is not what you think," Rooster said. "His son is sick, at the hospital. He runs a terrible fever. He is only ten years old. Cizinio needs gold to pay doctors. He's already lost one child to tuberculosis. The doctors work harder for gold." Rooster rubbed his thumb and forefinger together in the universal language for bribes.

I'd been here long enough to know about local health care — public for slum dwellers, private for the rest. I asked, "Is his son at the poor people's hospital or the rich one?"

"You must pay even at the poor one if you want real care. You must pay nurses, too. This is not the law but the practice. The more you pay, the more the doctors work. Don't doctors have the gold fever in your country?"

"In a way."

Despite my fear for Eddie I felt a stab of guilt and regarded the Indian in a new light. I'd come to a foreign place and made assumptions. Rooster just wanted a nice dinner with his wife. Cizinio was torn with fear over a child. "Rooster, please tell Cizinio that I am a doctor and I will see his son if he wants. I don't want gold for it. I don't want information for it either."

This time when Rooster translated the chewing stopped and the face swung up, and the brown eyes regarded me like I was a person, not a wall. Cizinio's thoughts moved beneath the surface like a fish swims out of sight. I knew that even in the early twenty-first century, there were more than fifty uncontacted tribes — spotted from the air — left in the Brazilian Amazon. The second they were contacted, they started falling sick.

Cizinio put down the fork. He had a speck of red sausage on the corner of his lip. At last I saw emotion, just a spark, in the eyes. It was confusion.

"Cizinio asks why you would do this?"

"I know what it is to worry about someone you love."

"Cizinio says that the doctors at the hospital always ask for money. As soon as he gives it, they want more. Sometimes they say, like you, that they don't want it, but when they get to his son, they change their mind."

"I won't change my mind."

"Cizinio says he cannot help you. You must understand this. Examining his son will get you no different answers."

"I understand. Let's go to my hotel and get my medical bag, and then we will go to the hospital, now."

Cizinio sat back. Then he tilted his head so as to look over the balcony, and I fol-lowed his gaze and my pulse sped up. Below,

Anasasio was standing on the path with three policemen. Anasasio was gesturing with urgency, and the policemen split up, one heading for the parking lot, one for the bowling alley, and one for the building in which we sat.

I turned to glance across the balcony. The man and the woman who had been in the corner were gone. Then I saw them, below, walking toward Anasasio.

Rooster said, reaching for his wallet, "Cizinio says you should not go back to your hotel tonight. He says that we should leave, now. He says he believes you. Otherwise those men would not be after you. He says that if they find you, maybe you will be next to disappear."

SEVEN

Tom Fargo was sealing the fifth pipe bomb, as he thought of them, when the doorbell rang. He froze, standing in the red light of the darkroom. He expected no visitors, and the doorman was supposed to alert him if one showed up. He made sure that the cardboard tube was sealed, retrieved his loaded Sig P226 combat pistol from the overhead shelf, racked the slide, locked the door behind him, and walked quietly but swiftly into the sunlit loft, toward the front door, without getting in front of it. If it blew inward, he'd be on the side.

If the FBI is here, they will have ordered the doorman not to call up. Combat vests on, they'd be prepping like the U.S. Marines who used to come into villages back home.

Tom Fargo's pulse raced.

He told himself that God would not allow his efforts to fail just as he was to start a new attack. The first planting had occurred days ago, and results should hit the city as early as tonight. If so, by tomorrow, New York news announcers would be leading their programs with it. Later would come the national news and the world.

"Who is it?"

"It's me! Rebeca!"

He did not relax, because soldiers might be with her. They might have told her to knock and trick him into opening up. He peered into the spy hole, heart hammering as fast and hard as it had five years ago, in combat, when he crawled over boulders and through rocky wadis with brother fighters, face camouflaged with dirt, dun-colored rags blending in with thorn bushes, as he moved to ambush U.S. Rangers. The feeling was adrenaline, not fear . . . the same sensation that had preceded his shooting of the female American diplomat in Rio.

Dr. Cardozo had told him after that, *Your passport has been used innocently and regularly since you came to us. Anyone checking your movements will think you've been traveling in Europe for the past six years. A rich kid killing time. Your idea is sound. We want you to contact your mother. You will go to western Brazil for a few weeks, train, and return to the U.S.*

Tom leaned into the peephole and saw her

smile, which looked hopeful. There was no guile in Rebeca, so the expression told him that he was, for the moment, safe. Relief came as a warm feeling in his knees and a throbbing at the base of his neck. Allah could protect you only so much. After that, you helped yourself.

She must have seen his eye in the hole. Voice muffled, she called out gayly, "We're having a party tonight. Greg won a big commission! You have to come, Tom!"

Magnified, her face was elongated as in a fun house mirror, but the smile was at odds with the busted blood vessels on the right cheek, a sullen patchwork of purple. It wasn't love he felt for his neighbor's girlfriend, or attraction. It was worse. Sympathy. She was smart and funny and had a good job as an engineer advisor on the new Panama Canal. He could not fathom why she stuck with Greg. Tom Fargo put the gun in a drawer by the door, swung it open, and kept his gaze off the bruise. But it was hard.

"Can't come, Rebeca. I'll be out riding tonight."

"You live half your life on that bicycle," she responded playfully, disappointment plain on her face. She was tiny, with a dancer's taut body, blue-black hair in a bun, muscles toned from yoga and weekend 10K runs to raise money for wounded U.S. veterans. Her Battery Park firm paid her a good salary. She could have dated a thousand guys who desired her each day on the street. But she stuck with the jerk across the hall.

"The city is peaceful from a bike," he said. "Our club rides around all summer. Night rider. That's me."

"Can't you make an exception tonight?"

"I'll try to get back," he said. But he had deposits to make.

She probably knew he was lying, but didn't make an issue of it. "Five questions, then," she said, grinning.

"I'm busy just now, Rebeca."

"Pshaw! Asking takes only sixty seconds!"

He sighed. She was studying for her U.S. citizenship exam, and had asked him to help her prep. There was something perverted about it that he enjoyed, as he prepared to attack this place.

He asked, "What is the supreme law of the United States?"

"The Constitution! Ask something harder."

"If the President can no longer serve," he said, considering that soon likely, "who takes over?"

"The Vice President?"

"What major event happened on September 11, 2001?"

"Terrorists attacked the World Trade Center," she said, the grin dying as she envisioned it. "All those poor people. It must have been awful."

As if his tongue moved by itself, he heard himself say, "What happened to your face?"

The hand that rose to her cheek was small and dainty, and she wore a white gold ring on the mid finger and a thin silver watch and pearl necklace. She tended to dress in tight-fitting dark-colored business suits during work hours, black or gray, that made her look professional but sexy. Tom Fargo was not like many men with whom he'd fought in the Caliphate. He was not offended if women showed parts of their bodies in public. In summertime Rebeca often went barefoot and wore white shorts that showed her skinny legs. She usually smelled of coconut shampoo and lavender soap.

"I fell while walking Cleon," she said. "What a klutz."

"You should teach that dog to heel."

"I will! We'll have a lot of food at the party. And live music. Greg knows the band. So try to come, okay?"

He'd seen her around the building but

never spoke to her for the first three months he lived here. Then he'd been out running one day on the Brooklyn Heights promenade, finishing a twenty-miler, and he'd looked down to see the tiny woman matching his gait, moving her twiggy legs faster to keep up, not panting, grinning, his cap reflected in her sunglasses, her round, cocoa-colored face flushed, her almond/black eyes merry beneath a red sweatband.

"You live across from Greg. I'm Rebeca," she said.

After that, a word exchanged in an elevator. A chance brush in the fruit market on High Street. The week he got a terrible flu and the doorman must have told her because she started ringing the bell and leaving quarts of steamy specialty soups on his mat: Tuscan Beef with Polenta, Vietnamese Pho Rice Noodle with Beef. Then the night when she and Greg wandered into the shop he managed in Park Slope, during an opening of Nicaraguan art, and Greg pretended not to see him, while Rebeca made conversation.

After that he'd started noticing her on the street more, in a bike shop, the shoe repair place, the seafood market. Had she always been there? Or had his antenna incorporated her into what he paid attention to?

"There will be single women at the party, Tom. Maybe you'll meet someone."

"I have a girlfriend in Ohio." He'd never been there.

He'd told her that he'd moved to New York to "give photography a try." "That's what I use the darkroom for." That his trust fund came from wealthy parents, which was how he afforded to rent a loft on his shop salary. She knew nothing of the fallback apartment in Queens or the cash in the darkroom, or the Subaru. Or how none of it had come from a trust fund but from opium sales or gold smuggling.

"Many rich, spoiled children, a whole society who never grow up, live in New York," Dr. Cardozo had told him. "They pretend to be artists. They spend their nights in dissipation. Your background makes you perfect for this role."

Now the apartment door behind Rebeca opened and Greg the architect came into the foyer, smiling as if his party had already started; bulky guy, ex–rugby player at Penn, but these days more fat than muscle. Dark haired and handsome, he carried himself with confidence. His pink button-up shirt hung loose, shirttails over cargo shorts. His tanned, sockless feet were encased in Italian loafers. At thirty-eight, his hair was thick and wavy and his false bonhomie made him likable for the first nine minutes in any social setting. He was a self-made man who confused romance with control. In this society he had to keep up appearances with women to be respected, but he reminded Tom of the brutes in the villages who used religion to harass: hit women, rape them, or worse. Tom knew what he was seeing, and it was something primitive and dark that lived in all cultures, in different ways.

"It's the Cycle Man!" Greg put his arm around Rebeca's shoulder and she flinched. Greg always called him *Cycle Man.* Like they were buddies. The architect dwarfed Rebeca, was four inches taller even than Tom, who was five eleven, but Greg would not have lasted three seconds in a fight. Greg said, "I told her you'd be out pedaling. What's the deal, Cycle? Where do you go?"

"All around." Which was true. "The club pedals all night." That part was not. He traveled alone. Sometimes on the bike. Sometimes in the subway. Sometimes on busses. Learning all the different routes for attack or escape.

Greg didn't care about the answer. He asked, "Did you see all the cops in the subway this morning?"

Tom Fargo's heartbeat went up, but he kept the tension off his face. "Cops?"

"I've never seen so many down there. They're opening packages right and left!" Without invitation, Greg brushed past Tom and strode into the apartment, past the hand that had risen fractionally toward his neck. A wall of windows overlooked the Brooklyn Bridge's magnificent cathedral-style arches and latticework of cables and walk and bikeway running along the center span.

Greg said, "I saw them shove a guy up on the wall this morning, some Muslim kid. *What's in the knapsack?*"

"How do you know he was Muslim?" Tom asked softly.

"You know what I mean. I'm not preju-diced. Dark. Pakistani. I work with these guys. Hell, I drink with them, well, the non-observant ones. Calm down, Cycle! I didn't know you were so politically correct!"

Greg put his arm around Rebeca and steered her away, and she glanced back, smiled . . . *Greg's awkward but he means well.* The hand fluttered toward the bruise, then stopped.

Tom went back to the darkroom. The air vibrated in here with need, blood, humidity, and there was a swampy smell from all the

99

life. On the heavy worktable were plastic trays and liquids and special foods, reflected in the glass terrariums that he'd emptied for this attack. Temperature kept at eighty-one degrees.

There were seven packages and tubes of varying sizes on the table, wrapped and labeled. *At least a thousand bombs, but not bombs — adults — in there.*

He needed to hurry.

Cops in the subways . . . try a different route.

The first tube was addressed to a framing business on 5th Avenue. The six-by-six-inch box to a medical lab on 3rd. The fancier box — *flowers?* — was allegedly going to a condo penthouse on Park Avenue. But the labels were lies. Inside the packages, plastic lining contained wet rags to keep in moisture, and adults and larvae lived in double-walled plastic bags. Petri dishes were stuffed with wet paper toweling, and on the toweling, rafts of tiny eggs. You needed to leave eggs because the adults would spend their whole lives within a mile of where they hatched. If he wanted to infect various spots around the city, with regularity, he had to make a separate deposit in each one.

The egg rafts he cleared from pans covered by plastic sheeting, filled with tap water.

From other pans he took hatched larvae, swimming and wriggling.

He fed his wards every third day, crumbling a small bit of food between two fingers for larvae. The adults got infected blood. Larvae grew in three stages, molting every few days, and then rising to the top and molting one last time, into pupae. Morphing into things that could kill. They swam by abdomen, moving in rapid jerks.

After this attack I'll need a new shipment. I'm using the last of what I have. But the supply should be here by next week.

"I'll hit them with what?" he'd asked Dr. Cardozo, frowning, when he'd learned of his full assignment. Before that he'd envisioned explosives. At first the truth made no sense. "That's what all the fuss is about? *Mosquitoes?*"

But Cardozo had seemed happy at his doubt, as if it confirmed his hypothesis that the Americans would react the same way at first, not seeing the danger.

"You will spread a ramped-up disease that has destroyed empires and still kills millions around the world," the biologist said. "Our *Anopheles gambaie* look identical to the ones that bite Americans every summer day. But yours have been changed. Two thousand people died in the World Trade Center, but you can kill many more. Each female lives for weeks. Eight hundred females to a package. One thousand eggs per hatching. You figure it out."

"Just females are infectious? Not the males?"

Dr. Cardozo had graduated from Duke University and smelled of Irish Spring soap and grew his own mint for tea. They'd met in a modest cream-colored villa on the outskirts of Rio. And later, in Porto Velho, Dr. Cardozo said, "No metal detector can detect an insect. No dogs can sniff them. By the time the Americans figure it out, thousands will be infected."

Tom had started to grow excited.

"Tom, right now our enemies see mosquitoes as you do, as a nuisance. When they realize what is happening, they will come after you with everything at their disposal. They will turn their country upside down to find you, and finding you," Cardozo said, "they will kill you."

"Inshallah."

"The Americans have a peculiar expression: *weapons of mass destruction*. I've never understood it. They mean nuclear weapons or chemicals. But isn't a plane that drops bombs and destroys villages a weapon of mass destruction? A machine gun that mows down civilians? They play with words! Well, we will give them a new weapon of mass destruction. It will be something they see every day."

Tom frowned. "But what if the insects get into a plane that flies to an Islamic country?"

"They will spray their planes to prevent this."

"What if an infected American flies overseas?"

"That might happen, but only a few times. Once the panic starts, they'll close their airports. I'm surprised you didn't ask the other question. About you getting sick."

"If you want me to stay on the island for weeks, and work with the insects, you have a way to protect me."

"Very good! An existing drug prevents infection, and you will take it. But there isn't enough of this drug to go around. You see? The panic?"

"I want to watch it up close."

Dr. Cardozo poured more tea and showed genuine sympathy. "After what happened to you, I understand."

"You on the bike," the cop ordered Tom. "Pull over!"

It was too late to turn around. He cursed

himself for letting his thoughts drift as he approached the Brooklyn bridge, and not seeing guards sooner. They *never* stopped bikers and pedestrians on the bridge, but six of them watched him approach: two Army Reservists with M4s, two uniformed cops, and two auxiliary cops in wilting white shirts with stupid-looking gold badges, looking more like office workers dressed for Halloween. The auxies were inconsequential because they did not carry arms. One cop selected passersby and sent them to a folding table on the bridge bikeway, manned by the second cop, who examined bags. The reservists, weapons unslung, stood watching, probably pissed off to be standing in ninety-degree heat, in what they regarded as one more useless terrorist drill.

Dismounted, Tom moved one step sideways as if to turn away, but saw one reservist nudge the other. Riding off would run him into the spotter cop. Or they'd get on their radios.

Three people waited in front of him in line.

Two. At the moment the table cop was arguing with a hefty German tourist who objected to his opening of her box of lingerie.

Stupid, arbitrary catch! All kinds of other

people flowed around the table, allowed to pass. Three kids who looked like gang-bangers walked by, laughing. Their pants were worn so low at the hips that Tom saw the crack of underwear beneath their jeans. A man with his face wrapped in gauze passed. He looked ten times more suspi-cious! A trio of Muslim women in head scarves. Two fat guys drinking from bottles in paper bags, but the cop had stopped a bike messenger! He didn't care about illegal drinkers today.

"Next!"

The *bombs, but not bombs* were in a canvas messenger bag, hung around his shoulder. Tom's frayed cap showed the New York Mets logo. The David Wright jersey was identical to ones worn by thousands of fans. The bike was a thirteen-year-old Can-nondale hybrid, with thicker tires for tra-versing rougher streets. Like many mes-sengers, Tom carried a thick steel chain around his neck, and a heavy bike lock. He could kill with them in several ways. If he had to attack, he'd go for the reservists first.

Allah, make the police wave me on so I can do your bidding.

"Sir, open up your camera case, please."

"Ma'am, please unzip the portfolio."

"So! Bike messenger! What's in the

tubes?"

The cop looked young, black, fit, and ready.

"Open it up, please."

"I'm not supposed to do that. They'll fire me."

"Well, one of us is going to open it. So! You or me?"

Tom saw the face with special clarity. He reached back, touched the heavy chain, judged he could take out the cop with the first swing. But there would be witnesses. And the soldiers. The tube was on the table now.

I will go down fighting. I will take as many of them with me as I can.

He pulled the chain off his shoulder, as if the weight bothered him.

The cop popped the metal tube top, peered inside, holding the tube up to catch the light. Tom had the Sig Sauer behind his back, under his shirt. If things went bad there would be a hundred witnesses, photographs, descriptions. Sweat broke out in his armpits. The cop began inching the rolled-up lithograph out. It was a cheap copy of an old Spanish drawing of two galleons anchored off a Guyana jungle beach. The poster was too short to take up the entire tube length. The tube had a false compartment on the bottom. Packed with insects.

The cop pushed the drawing back in and closed the cap. "You know why we picked you, Mets?"

"No."

The cop grinned suddenly, like it was a big joke. "Go Yanks," he said.

Tom resisted the urge to swing the chain in the man's stupid face. "Screw the fucking Yanks," he said.

"Testy, testy," the cop laughed. Tom mounted up and pedaled past the men and onto the wide walkway taking him over the East River. One Police Plaza and the great towers of Manhattan were ahead, the afternoon sunny, traffic normal, and he thanked Allah for safety, reaching the island itself.

First stop was a shut-down gas station near Elizabeth Street, off Canal, *closed for remodeling,* where a row of discarded snow tires leaned against the rear brick wall, filled with rainwater.

Two stories above that were the open windows to one of the city's premier Chinatown restaurants. Many famed athletes ate here, as did politicians, entertainers, and fashion models. Around the corner was a street where hordes of tourists passed each day, shopping at open-air stands. More than five thousand people would pass this spot at dusk each day.

He shook out a bag filled with larvae into the water in the tires. He shook out eight hundred adults.

Next stop, Midtown, and an open trash Dumpster beside a new hotel under construction, a block from Times Square. The Dumpster had two inches of water on the bottom. He mixed in a bag of adults and then opened a tube of larvae and shook it out. The larvae would mature in one to three weeks.

Third stop, the Upper West Side and the busy 96th Street IRT Station, which fed up to 40,000 passengers a day into the red line that traversed the length of the borough. He carried the bike onto the platform. After a train passed and no one remained on the platform, he tossed an open ziplock over the side, into rainwater on the tracks. New Yorkers were pigs who used the tracks as trash cans. The baggie fell with a splash, and he watched a mosquito emerge. In two hours, at dusk, a little swarm would rise out and buzz and fly onto the bare arms and legs above the tracks.

For the rest of the afternoon he and a thousand real bike messengers traversed the city; over the Queensboro Bridge to Astoria, where he left a deposit in a quiet eddy in the East River, a hundred yards from a public swimming pool that several thousand people visited each summer week, mostly kids. The pool stayed open at dusk.

He was exhausted by late afternoon, and taking a break in a bodega, buying iced tea, he saw a Channel One News broadcast: *Terrorism drill is over.* The subway was clear now. He rode the One train up to Riverdale, a pricy suburban neighborhood in the Bronx. The streets here were shaded by oaks and lined with well-kept Tudors, ranches, and split-levels. Here was the old Dodge Estate and several private schools catering to the sons and daughters of the city's elite. Getting off the elevated train, he rode the bike to a low-income home for the elderly on busy Riverdale Avenue: a faded yellow brick final stop for the men and women who sat staring at passing traffic in cheap folding chairs outside, forgotten by their families.

Dr. Cardozo had told him, "The cameras will go wherever outbreaks occur. Spread it everywhere. Make none of them feel safe. Once the panic begins, a single mosquito in a subway, a house, a park . . . will set them off. Go with God."

EIGHT

She stirred as her ancestors had as far back as forty-six million years ago, at dusk. Her food source then was dinosaurs. Now it was mammals. But food was still blood.

One by one, she and her sisters rose into the air from the pond, a shadow mass, each unit so small that in fading light it was almost invisible to the crowds streaming into New York's Central Park. PHILHARMONIC CONCERT TONIGHT!

Sheep Meadow was filling with people. Already seven thousand early arrivals for the 7 P.M. start claimed lawn space with blankets or planted flags, or flew colorful balloons so their friends could find them in the crowd. They opened wines and champagnes, unwrapped cheese, put out grapes and breads and hummus and cold cuts, their Zabar's picnic baskets filled with food.

Expected crowd tonight: twenty-three thousand. This was New York at its finest, where the high and low mixed; the super-rich, from townhouses off 5th Avenue, and illegal immigrants; kids from Harlem beside kids from Park Avenue; Wall Street titans and Bowery vendors; whole extended families; parents and kids, cousins and grandparents, five blankets to a party. Here to eat. Talk. Listen. Lie out on a hot night.

She wobbled along on air currents formed by heat rising off baked pavement and breezes off the rivers. Her compound eyes were covered with tiny lenses called ommatidia, which could pick up the slightest movement. The eyes, atop the head, were photosensitive and could detect changes in light so minor that if a hand came swatting toward her, she'd flee. She took in oxygen through slits in her abdomen. Her antennae, long and feathery, contained receptors capable of locating a human breath, a single plume of carbon dioxide, 110 feet away. She was a hunter who tracked sweat, perfume, or cologne, and she approached her victims using two sets of wings, large ones for buoyancy, and mini-wings for direction, giving her a busy appearance, four wings moving at different speeds.

Her saliva contained an anticoagulant, to keep blood flowing in victims, and natural painkiller, to keep victims from realizing she'd just poked a serrated needle, called a proboscis, into their skin.

She would keep feeding, going from victim to victim, until her abdomen was full.

Below, a record crowd poured into the park from 5th Avenue on the East Side, Central Park West on the other, coming out of the subways, getting off busses. Beneath a rising quarter moon, as the violins warmed up, she dropped and landed on an arm, sensed a slap coming, rose away, circled, returned. Blood flowed into her as an infectious protozoan swam out, and into the dangling arm.

A woman's voice nearby said, "You've lost contact with Joe and Eddie, in Brazil?"

A man protested, "I'm doing the best I can, Chris."

The arm jerked violently. Dislodged, she flew off, and, still hungry, landed on another person's ankle.

Hundreds of people were being bitten as the stirring notes of the *1812 Overture* began to play. Candles glowed. The moon rose higher. The night was perfect, or so the audience believed.

The encore — *An American in Paris* — ended at 10 P.M. the music had been sublime, the orchestra playing at a level that exceeded even their normal five-star skills. The temperature had been hot but not oppressive. The park smelled of trees and grass. The traffic on normally busy 5th Avenue had even cooperated, fewer horns sounding, and the passing busses had been quiet hybrids, not the old diesel models. The crowd oozed from the park in ten directions, hailing cabs, getting on subways, strolling along the East Side's tree-lined streets.

Among the randomly infected were a Deputy Mayor, a fifth grader from a Chelsea day school, a pregnant thirty-year-old from Greenwich, Connecticut, who had driven in with her husband to meet old college friends. A knee replacement specialist from the hospital for special surgery had been bitten. So had a former high school football star and OxyContin addict who'd fallen asleep before intermission, the CEO of a Paris-based perfume company, the Congresswoman who had introduced the orchestra to the audience, and an Albanian doorman from the Bronx.

Honey, you have bites all over the back of your neck!

Back home, a few of the bitten smeared on soothing calamine lotion.

Those little buggers seem to like your

114

cologne, Ed.

It would take a day or two before the fevers hit, and joint pain, the squeezing in the intestines, then the sudden convulsions, the black urine, and the quick deaths.

It was just a few mosquitoes, honey. Stop complaining. Don't be a baby. The itching will stop.

NINE

The double-deck ferry rode so low that only four inches separated the gunwale from the Madeira. Like other passengers, Rooster and I strung hammocks from hooks in the ceiling for the open-air trip. Every foot of deck seemed crammed with families, chickens, crates, and hammocks. The once-a-week boat, Rooster said, stopped at jungle landings, rubber-tapper outposts, and *fazendas,* remote cattle ranches. The schedule had us arriving in New Extrema at dawn, eight hours from now, but we were already late.

And now I had a bad feeling that I had just been recognized. A heavyset ferry crewman stared at me from across the deck, and turned away quickly when he realized I looked back. He sped up the stairs from the lower deck to the pilot house. This river boat trip was turning out to be the slowest rescue mission in history. A gamble that Eddie would even be on the other end, still alive.

"It was smart not to go back to the hotel, Joe," said Rooster, from his hammock.

"No roads lead to New Extrema, Joe. No airplane strip."

The sand flies were out, biting. Some would carry leishmaniasis. The mosquitoes had subsided slightly after the sun went down. The pilot steered by floodlight, sweeping it in an arc, then shutting it off for some nutty reason, chugging us into a dark so thick that we seemed to be floating. *On.* I saw something big and alive churning up brown/yellow water off port. Off. *On.* I saw silhouetted trees crowding both banks and the pink dainty hands of a sloth in top branches, where the creature blinked back.

"Joe, if we would have hired an outboard, it would be faster, but we might have put ourselves in the hands of the same men who take the sick miners. Bad idea."

No help was coming from Washington. I'd called Ray by sat phone to beg for any aid at all; satellite shots of New Extrema, pressure put on local authorities, FBI files on drug smuggling or terrorist connections in western Brazil.

"Ray, you asked us to look for a training camp. This might be it," I said.

"No, I asked you to pay attention to potential terrorists. Not to missing gold miners. I'm very sorry about Eddie. I really am. But I have a meeting now."

If it had not been for the Indian, Cizinio, last night, we might not have even gotten this far. We'd avoided Anasasio and the police when Cizinio paddled us off in a dugout. Then I'd kept my promise to him, forced my worry for Eddie from my mind, gone with Cizinio and Rooster to the public hospital, a humid, ill lit but surprisingly clean place. Visiting hours were over but the nurses admitted a foreign doctor. Nine-year-old Abilio Karitiana — Cizinio's son — lay twisted like a polio victim with eight other pain-racked children in an isolated ward, coughing up bloody sputum, vomiting, legs twisted with pain. A crazy combo of symptoms: chests filled with fluid, like pneumonia; intestines racked with spasms, like food poisoning; dark urine hinting at kidney failure; hearts galloping at dangerous rates.

One boy had died an hour before, the night doctor, a young guy named Bracamonte, had told me.

"How are you treating them?" I asked.

"The penicillin isn't working. It may be a bad batch. Sometimes we get counterfeit drugs. Which is why we ask patients for money, to buy the real thing." Dr. Bracamonte sighed. "I spend half my salary on medicines. The patients think we keep the money for ourselves."

I judged him honest. He showed a familiar helplessness that I'd seen in dedicated professionals elsewhere in the poorer world, men and women hampered by bad bureaucracy or lack of supplies. *Wilderness medicine* meant assisting doctors saddled with out-of-date instruments, expired pills, busted X-ray machines. Rooster kept translating as I interviewed Abilio. The boy was underweight and shivered with fever and gripped his father's hand as though if he let go, he would die.

"Abilio, thank you for talking to me. Did you eat or drink anything before you got sick? Maybe something tasted wrong to you?"

"No."

"You're sure?"

The head shook weakly. The eyes were huge with fright but the voice remained steady. "We ate fish from the river. We ate tapir, but it was cooked. We ate rice that we got from FUNAI, the Indian agency. It all tasted fine."

"Something you drank, then?"

"Just water, boiled, like doctors said."

119

"Maybe you went somewhere new. A mine. A ranch," I said, wondering if the kids had been exposed to a chemical used for deforestation, construction, mineral processing.

"Only to see *Shrek,* Doctor."

I didn't get it at first. I thought he'd said a Portuguese word. I asked Bracamonte what *Shrek* meant and he smiled despite the boy's pain and told me, "It is the American film. You never heard of *Shrek*?"

"The *movie*?"

"We watched it at FUNAI," Abilio forced out. "It was funny. There was a green man. Animals sang songs and talked in the movie. I laughed very much."

"Did all the kids who got sick go to the movie?"

"Yes."

"Were adults there, too?"

"They were at a government meeting about the new dam. Only children saw the movie."

"You liked the movie?" I asked, not to learn a clue, just to keep him talking while I figured out more questions. But sometimes the wrong question gets the right answer.

"The donkey was funny! It was cold in the room from the air conditioner. So cold! That old conditioner was making so much noise that it was hard to hear the singing donkey."

I sat back and let my eyes rove over the children. Blankets were thrown off some, who were sweating. Or piled on cold ones, who shivered. The ward smelled of vomit. Abilio had just said something important. About the movie. What was it? The animals talked, he said. No adults were there, he said. And then I saw it. The disparate symptoms might have just fallen into place.

Cold, he'd said. Cold!

"Old air conditioner," I said softly.

"And noisy! Clackclackclackclack!"

"Dr. Bracamonte, do you have a microscope in the hospital? Can I see his sputum or blood? Can we also get someone to scrape dust off that air conditioner?"

The hospital had no electron microscope, he said, but their compound-light unit would provide a 2,000 magnification. In a dimly lit lab, fifteen minutes later, I peered down at Abilio's sputum and saw something inside it looking like churned-up chopped meat from a hand grinder, pinkish strands. I sat back on the stool, breathing rapidly. An hour later the same pink strands showed up in the dust brought back from the AC vents at FUNAI. That the doctors here had missed the symptoms was not unusual. This particular disease is misdiagnosed even in developed countries 90 percent of the time. In fact I'd only thought of it because bioterror seminars always feature presentations on biodelivery systems, and airflow systems — ventilation shafts, cooling towers, AC — top the list.

"It's Legionnaires' disease."

The rare illness is often misdiagnosed because the diarrhea — not normally part of pneumonia — throws clinicians off. And Indians in recent contact with the modern world would be particularly susceptible. Legionnaires' was named in 1976 after it killed several American Legion conventioneers in Philadelphia, spread by a hotel vent system. The good news was that if you catch it early, treatment is available, and different for children than it is for hardier adults.

"Penicillin doesn't work on this," I explained to Dr. Bracamonte. "You used the right drug for pneumonia, but not for what they have."

Bracamonte told me that the recommended drug for children stricken with Legionnaires' — azithromycin — was unavailable in Porto Velho. I got on the sat phone and woke Stuart in New York, at 4 A.M. I told my boss that we could improve "local government relations" if he sent down some crates of the drug. If there are two words that Stuart responds to instantly, they are *government relations.*

"They will be there tomorrow," Stuart said. "How are things otherwise, Joe? Any word on Eddie?"

"No."

When I hung up, a grateful Bracamonte told me, "While you were on the phone, two men from the miners union were asking about you. They are thugs. They had your photo. One of them said he is a friend of yours, but I did not believe it. I told them you were not here. I hope I did right."

"Thank you. You did. I was never here, okay?"

That night, Cizinio let us sleep at the Indian House, the publicly maintained hostel open to any tribal member in town. It was a hard dirt compound ringed by a clay wall and it offered visitors simple dorm buildings with bunk beds along three walls. We spent the hours before dawn squatting before a campfire as Cizinio traced maps of New Extrema and the island in the dirt, beneath the southern stars. He'd not come with us, he said. He'd stay with his son.

"The guards are usually by the dock, *here.* Two of them. This is where they will many times buy Indian artwork, blowguns, or pottery. But then they send us away. There is a stream *here,* in back of the island, where there are no guards, but there are biting snakes and sand that you sink into, unless you step in the right place."

"Cizinio, do you know where I can get a gun?"

"You need gold for that."

"I have it," said Rooster helpfully.

"I'll pay you back," I promised. "My money is at my hotel, in the safe."

Rooster's plastic vial of gold dust got emptier at a shanty where an emaciated, cigarette-puffing, coughing man nicknamed "Hulk" sold us an old, well-oiled Brazilian-made Taurus pistol, wrapped in rags. It came with thirty rounds of .40-caliber ammunition. I racked the slide. When a water truck went by outside, its muffler broken, I fired into a tree. The pistol pulled slightly to the left. But it worked fine.

Rooster also paid for the boat tickets (we had to wait until dusk to leave), rice, hammocks, mosquito netting, and rain ponchos, in an open-air market near the Indian House. I felt lousy about the next part but not bad enough not to do it. Since my medical kit was at the hotel, at a side door to the hospital, we bought stolen antibiotics; tet and sulfa . . . from a fat, furtive attendant who Rooster knew. Yesterday I'd helped save patients here. Today I was robbing them. But if Eddie needed care I wanted to be able to provide it. *For everything I steal, I will send five times the amount back from the U.S.,* I promised myself.

If I get home.

But Eddie comes first.

"Your brother might not even be on the island, Rooster. And if he is, things might get violent."

"If you risk going, I can, too."

"If you knew that your brother might be on that island, why did you wait so long to check it out?"

Rooster blushed in embarrassment. "I was afraid. But you are so determined. You made me brave."

Now the weekly ferry chugged into a darkness as thick as nonexistence. The lights of Porto Velho had long ago fallen behind, steady ones for electric light, flickering ones for firelight in shantytowns. On deck, riders played dominoes or guitar music. A woman unwrapped beans and rice from a foil-covered plate for her family. It smelled good.

The river looked calm and black and I saw a pink fin glide on the surface. River dolphins turned into men at night, the story went, seduced women, and lured them back

125

to the deep. Folktales were facts here. Spirits flew among shadowed trees. Karitiana shamans saw ghosts in the mist. I was a fool to believe that Eddie had been taken.

"That man is staring at you," said Rooster.

That's when I saw the crewman, frozen, on the stairway leading to the upper deck and pilot house; a big, curly haired man, mouth open in surprise, and he turned and scurried off, glancing back as if to confirm that I was there. There was no point going after him. A confrontation would create a scene, and there was no way off this boat.

Someone could have shown him my picture. If the union people or police are really looking for me, they could have easily spoken to the crew before we left. I think it would be a good idea if Rooster and I take turns going to sleep tonight. We need to switch off standing guard.

I watched a roach the size of a mouse run beneath my hammock. The ferry panted to reach a speed that could not have exceeded four miles an hour. Every once in a while a smaller, fast-moving flying boat came up from behind, as if to catch us, and my heart seized up, but the boats passed, heading for New Extrema. Bored, people in neighboring hammocks struck up conversations, and in this casual way I learned some history about the outpost ahead.

"It started as a collection point for rubber during the boom in the 1800s," an old man — a retired priest — told us, sharing Rooster's coffee. "Back then the only place the world got rubber from was Brazil. But rubber trees cannot grow commercially, on plantations. They fall victim to a fungus, so attempts to make rubber farms failed. In nature rubber trees grow with great separation, as natural protection. So the *negocianos,* the businessmen, needed people to harvest rubber for tires and rain ponchos and boots. They tricked poor city people into the jungle, lied to thousands from São Paulo. They said that rubber grows in great balls that could be plucked from trees. That the Amazon was a paradise and that they would grow rich picking rubber. They lent these people money, and the uneducated slum dwellers flooded the forest. They bought tools on credit and trekked into the jungle. They built shacks to live. By the time they knew they had been tricked it was too late. They could not go back."

"They were stuck here," I said, appalled.

"The only way to pay their debt was to harvest rubber."

"What happened to them?"

"Thousands died of malaria, starvation, and snake bites. The few who lived could not read or add, so the merchants cheated them, paid just enough to keep them alive, but stole the rubber. In Manaus lived rubber millionaires. They built an opera house and sent their laundry to Portugal, filthy rich people; until British sailors stole some rubber trees from our jungles and planted them in Asia. There's no fungus there. Trees can grow on plantations. Their rubber was cheaper and the Brazilian market collapsed. The millionaires went broke. The opera house rotted. But the tappers are still there, eking out a living, walking the forest, sticking little tubes in the trees, harvesting rubber in drip cups like photographs I saw of maple farmers in the United States."

The man nodded sadly. "These days, in New Extrema, all that remains are some poor tappers, or smugglers who bring gold across to Bolivia, and drugs back in."

Rooster handed the man a tin plate containing a mass of sticky rice and cooked vegetables and bits of grayish meat.

"You sleep first," Rooster said, patting the pink mosquito net hung over his own hammock. "Seven hours left."

The engine coughed, broken. We drifted to shore.

"Give us an hour to fix it," a crewman said.

At 2 A.M. we started off again, just as I saw another fast-moving light coming up on us, on the river.

"Police," Rooster gasped.

But it turned out to be another flying boat, two figures on board as it crossed our searchlight. One man steered. The other was slumped over. The man at the tiller waved but the other man did nothing. He might have been sleeping. Or ill. Or dead.

That boat gave me an idea. I will hire a small boat and visit the island. I will tell the doctor there that I'm a visiting physician from the U.S. A courtesy call would be normal. If they let me on, I'll figure out what to do.

A whole day had wasted away and another dusk was coming. The sky was gray with misty rain. At 5 P.M. the mosquitoes swarmed. I saw them crawling on my mosquito net, masses of black against pink. I saw one enter the net through a dime-sized rip. I crushed it, saw from the blood on my thumb that it had already bitten someone else.

In Wilderness Medicine, I teach my students, be patient in remote areas. Don't expect things to work as they do back home. Go with the flow unless there is an emergency. Understand that concepts of time are different.

It was impossible to follow my own advice.

Rooster was shaking me. I must have slept, and the sun was high and we were moving again.

Rooster whispered urgently, "She is here, Joe."

"Who?"

"The woman from your hotel, and the restaurant. She is on the upper deck with her companion. I think she saw me, too."

The boat chugged around the nine millionth bend, which looked the same as the first one. The trip was taking forever. Rooster's anxious look turned to puzzlement as he watched my expression. "Joe, you are pleased?"

"Well, if she's here, maybe we're in the right place."

But between the crewman who'd recognized me, and the woman, all my ghosts were coalescing in the same place.

I started for the stairway to the upper deck, to confront her. The boat would be perfect for this. *She's not police, or she would have approached by now. She's not union or she wouldn't have stayed at my hotel.*

The Brazilian-made Taurus beneath my shirt had a blue finish, and a .40 caliber, fifteen-round capacity. Pulling it out on this boat would guarantee a radio call to the Federal Police by the Captain. It was useless here.

"Maybe she is here by coincidence," Rooster suggested.

"You don't believe that any more than I do."

"Maybe she doesn't know we're here."

I laughed.

The upper deck came into view, and with it, another crowd like the one below, hammocks strung, noise, crates, dogs, music. I saw the woman and her male companion. They reclined on their hammocks, drinking from liter bottles of water, by a pile of stacked crates. The man spotted me first and rose almost lazily and said something and her head swiveled sharply in my direction. He was the one blocking direct access. He was large and muscular and wore soiled khakis and moved with light-footed grace for a big man. His eyes, as I closed, looked sleepy beneath rectangular eyeglasses. *He's protection, she's the boss.*

The woman leaned back and pulled something from a knapsack and I tensed but saw it was a camera, which she aimed at me. I saw no weapons. Then again, they couldn't see mine. Rooster waddled so close behind me that I could hear his quick, hard intakes of breath, and smell garlic. He was too close for me to back away fast if something happened.

Snapsnapsnap . . . she was taking photos.

Close-up; she was slim and dark, and looked to be in her early thirties; fit, not pretty but arresting, sexy in some violent way. The skin was naturally dusty, café au lait. The body looked hard as a rock climber's or gymnast's. She had eyes the dirty green of the North Sea, two fathoms down. The cheekbones were sharp, nose thin but not knifelike, mouth a generous surprise and hair thick, curly and shoulder length, wild, colored somewhere between copper and cherry. Terrific posture. *Castizo,* I thought. A mix of mestizo and European. I saw a white, arced, penny-sized scar below the right eye. It should have marred the attraction. In her, somehow, it added challenge.

People on deck suddenly pointed beyond her, calling happily to their friends. Look! Finally! New Extrema!

Her hands fluttered up, patted the air as if to say *Calm down, boy!* The lips curved as if amused but the eyes were hard. Khaki undershirt top. Tropical-weight painter's pants and lightweight boots. She held the camera tightly, slightly lowered now.

"It took you long enough to see us, Joe Rush," she said in English, with a Brazilian accent. "Keep your voice down. I will take your picture."

I smelled Avon Skin So Soft, repellant of choice among Amazon travelers, even the toughest men.

"Stand still! What I want to know," she said mockingly, snapping shots, "is what kind of moron goes to another country and can't speak the language? Ambassador to China who can't speak Chinese. CIA in Baghdad can't speak Arabic. You have no idea what these people are saying about you, do you? Not a clue."

"*He* knows," I said defensively, nodding at Rooster.

"You think so? The passengers see you're together so they talk about chickens when he's around. Everyone on this boat except you and that *pessoa, incompetente,* knows what's going to happen to you, and they're afraid to tell you, because then it would happen to them. They're even taking bets." Her eyes flickered left.

I looked. Most passengers eyed the approaching landing, but the one or two faces that looked back at me showed the sick fascination marking onlookers at a traffic accident. The eyes you see staring before

133

you pass out, the gapers torn between wishing you well, and wanting the entertainment of being the audience for your pain.

The woman told me, "The Captain got a radio message about you and then he sent crew to look for you. Get it? The union, the police, the Captain . . . connected. If you get off this boat in New Extrema, you'll be killed, Joe Rush. *Emboscada.* Our time-honored frontier assassination." She glanced at the sun meaningfully. It was starting to sink. The faint moon was up already, ghostly above treetops, like a cataract eye.

"Ray sent you?" I said thinking, *He came through!*

"Who the hell is Ray?" She shook her head like a fifth grade teacher disgusted with a lazy student. "You people make me laugh. You shut us out. You lie. Although I admit, I might have not figured out about New Extrema if not for you."

"Who are you?"

"Oh, you don't *like* it when friends don't share information? You're *frustrated*?" Considering the force in her, I was surprised at her diminutive size. Her head barely reached my chest. She was barely five feet tall. Only now did I see that her contempt was cover for rage.

"Look, whoever you think I am," I said,

fed up, "I'm not. And whatever you think I know, I don't. So give me a break and stop talking in riddles. Who are you? And him?"

The landing coming up was dwarfed by forest. It looked like an afterthought, and could be wiped off the earth in the blink of an eye, the usual eventual fate of flyspeck settlements in this part of the world. This place had been falling apart since the moment of its creation. I saw a dozen squarish hut-like buildings, cinderblock walls, tin roofs, two rooms at most; and meat-scented cooking smoke rose from a stovepipe chimney. There had to be adults here but I didn't see any, odd, because probably the once-a-week ferry arrival was a big local event.

Maybe they'd been warned to stay away.

A red dirt path meandered from the concave dock up the mud bank toward the forest . . . and the somnambulant air was underscored by a few chickens pecking, a mud-coated pig rooting, a skinny dog sleeping, a couple of paint-faded outboard boats and a dugout on the bank, and twin bare-chested, barefoot Indian boys grinning as the ferry coughed like an asthmatic and eased sideways and sooty smoke roiled out the top. *Sleepy* didn't begin to describe this place. Dead was more like it. But the woman had just told me that killers were here. Which made the ratty buildings and massed trees all potential ambush points.

"Stay on the boat, Colonel. Go back."

Eddie must really be here.

I shook my head. "Now who's the naive one?" I said. "You're telling me if I leave, I'll be safe?"

She said nothing. Then, reluctantly, "You have a point. See those guys by the railing? They were taking bets on how many hours you'll last. Ten to one . . . not 'til tomorrow."

The boat bumped the dock. Whatever it is that constitutes instinct, every Marine knows that you ignore it at your peril, and the woman's dirty green eyes blazed with passion now. As if to tell me, *You fucked up my plans, too.*

I thought back, *There's no way I'll leave this place before finding out about Eddie. He would not leave if it was me, so goddamn you, CIA.*

The gangplank lowered and a few riders filed off, but most would stay on, bound for other settlements. I noticed one little girl holding a liter-sized empty beer bottle as a doll, whispering to it, and glancing back with curiosity at me, having heard what her parents were saying about me, clearly wondering with those big eyes if Joe Rush would even make it all the way ten feet to shore, before shotguns blasted out from one of those buildings ahead.

I told Rooster that I was getting off here, but he was going back to Porto Velho, and I got no argument! Rooster, pale and trembling, just nodded. He was a good man, and his bravery was used up.

Somehow, that talk — my protecting Rooster — made the woman answer me finally, and identify herself. It was a shock. She wasn't CIA at all.

TEN

The ambush came in the middle of the night.

Undercover Brazilian Federal Police Captain Izabel Santo reached to wake me at 1 A.M. but I was up, having heard the scraping outside. I stopped her hand before it touched my shoulder. In the dark I rolled from the unzipped sleeping bag and gripped my Taurus. The two special-assignment cops and I had practiced moving around the hotel room in blackness, the Brazilians fast-crawling to a corner, me swinging up into the latticework roof support. To turn on the bare bulb would have sent a crack of light beneath the door, alerted any attackers. But the light probably didn't work anyway. No electricity did in New Extrema after 11 P.M., when the municipal generator went off, and jungle noises flooded in.

"You're police?" I'd asked Izabel on the boat, amazed, hours ago. "Investigating your own people?"

"You don't have internal investigations in your own country?" she'd snapped.

"Why are you on this boat?"

"Because we followed *you*. You and your friend show up, and you are clearly not just doctors. You work with Anasasio, a crook. You go to the gold rush, where there are smugglers. At first I think you are smugglers, too, but now I see that if these people — these *filhos da puta* — are after you, maybe you found what we're looking for."

Posing as magazine reporters, Izabel said, she and Sublieutenant Nelson Salazar had been taking photos of smugglers paying off local police.

Having a raging argument while trying to look casual before a boatload of curious strangers can be difficult. She called me a *fool* and a *suicide* and kept insisting that I stay on board with Rooster, sail past New Extrema, and perhaps my cowardice might keep us alive.

"Maybe you work with them," I said.

"Maybe you are an idiot, Joe Rush."

"Eddie is my partner. Would you leave yours?"

She argued — hissed — that I wouldn't do Eddie any good if I was shotgunned to pieces. That maybe Eddie was not even here. That if I would just give her a day or two, she could call Brasília, *people she trusted,* and arrange for a chopper full of SWAT fighters — her own unit — to arrive.

"Eddie is my best friend."

Rooster had looked relieved to be leaving. I liked the guy. He was a miner, not a fighter. I did not want his death on me. He'd done enough by getting me this far.

Izabel had given up. *Go ahead and get killed, Colonel. Be one more casualty, because we will not help you.*

But just before the boat pulled off an hour later, I was surprised to see her and Nelson come down the ramp, knapsacks on, cameras around their necks.

"Don't say anything, damn you," she snapped, as they walked past and Rooster waved good-bye from the deck.

We checked into the only "hotel" in town, a modular collection of four cinder-block pillboxes, more jail cells than rooms. After dark the Brazilians snuck into mine. We rolled up knapsacks beneath a blanket to look like me, asleep. And now the cops fast-crawled to the same front corner. That way, if they had to shoot, they'd not fire toward each other.

"I would not leave someone I loved either," she'd told me an hour ago, still angry

140

but slightly calmed down.

Captain Santo was armed with a silver-coated .45 caliber 1911 Remington. Nelson had an Imbel .45. The Remington would kick back but without muzzle flip, so it was a better weapon for a lighter woman. The stopping power of both guns exceeded that of my Taurus. I swung myself up to the ceiling-support latticework and lay, facing the door. Izabel had guessed that the attack would come from one or two people. They'd expect me to be alone.

I could only hope she was right as my heartbeat rose and I felt the salty taste of Lay's potato chips in the back of my throat. I'd not eaten them in years. But for some reason, I taste Lay's when I am afraid. A psychologist would probably say it goes back to my youth. Eating Lay's while hearing about the death of a grandparent. Or when I saw a car wreck. Who the hell remembers how these things start.

Outside, another whisper. A creak. Maybe the door had pushed in slightly. Maybe someone had tried to move it, to check the latch lock.

Two A.M. Nothing.

Maybe whatever had been outside was an animal, rubbing against the door, or wall, and it had moved away.

My turn at guard duty. Nelson snored. Izabel sighed as she slept, and her rapid eye movement was fierce. Perhaps in a dream she was already fighting.

The ceiling was low, maybe seven feet high. The walls were starting to crumble from Amazon humidity. Rooms sat on both sides of a short open-air passageway, partially covered by a raised tin roof supported by rotting latticework. Rain would blow into the corridor if the wind came in sideways. The floor was packed dirt with rat holes chewed in cinder block. Patient vermin lived here. There were no windows, and each unit was provided with a bare forty-watt bulb suspended from a noose of copper wire. The artwork — when there was light — was graffiti, in charcoal, of rubber tappers. A lone man in rags and homemade rubber shoes made slash marks in a tree with a machete, and hung a battered tin cup by a nail, to catch white dripping latex. In the next drawing, he rolled latex into volleyball-sized spheres.

Hieroglyphics in the Amazon. Next, the man, a woman, and a child carried the harvest down jungle footpaths, the balls around their shoulders. They were human pack animals. The balls were loaded on a ferry, bound for sale.

I might have been looking at cave paintings in France depicting bison hunters twenty thousand years ago. The last illustration, spilling onto the next wall, showed two men with shotguns, crouched behind a big buttressed tree in the jungle, as the rubber tapper walked back home, toward ambush. True story? Tonight's prediction? What had the poor man done to deserve his upcoming fate?

"If we get out of here alive, my bosses will lodge a complaint about you in Washington," Izabel had said earlier, as we ate a dinner of rice and beans, purchased from the shirtless, beer-bellied man who owned the "hotel."

"If we get out, be my guest," I replied. "Anyway, isn't New Extrema out of your jurisdiction?"

"My jurisdiction is Brazil."

"New Extrema is rough," I said, meaning *for a woman.*

"I led the raid that recovered that laptop, *caralho.* The one you learned about in New York from the FBI. You wouldn't know anything if not for me," she snapped with contempt, "so don't talk to me about rough."

But this furious professional was a lifeline. She'd possibly saved my life, at least for a while. In return I had made her risk greater. And when I confirmed how she had discovered my identity, my admiration for her grew.

"You stole my plate or fork in the hotel."

She grinned, and her smile was transforming, beautiful, gone. "Your prints and photo went to our lab, and from there . . . well . . . pretty stupid of your FBI to send you here secretly and not tell your DEA. When we tell the DEA in Rio that we have an American smuggling drugs here, they get back to us and say, no, no, this man, he is not a smuggler. He is a big hero in the United States."

"My people make mistakes sometimes," I admitted, weary of her sarcasm. "But you seem worried that yours will shoot you in the back."

She seemed about to explode. But then she said, softer, "Okay, okay. Let us make a truce."

A border had been crossed, and Nelson didn't like it. The big sublieutenant seemed overprotective of her. Maybe there was something personal there. I didn't ask. I didn't care.

Friends now, kind of, I thought.

Three A.M. Maybe no one was coming tonight.

Captain Izabel Santo took a turn at guard duty. I watched her silhouette in the dark as I started to doze off. She never moved. She seemed to barely breathe.

The room had a hand-operated water pump above a basin sink of mahogany — an out-of-place $5,000 worth of rare wood but, locally, junk. There was an outhouse, but Izabel said outhouses were prime locations for ambush, so no use of the stinky facilities tonight.

"Piss in your water jar, Joe America," she said.

If I thought the boat ride had been long, it was nothing compared to that night. Dawn seemed far away. If we lasted that long, the man who operated the local outboard service had promised to take me to the island, and accepted advance payment. But the look in his eyes suggested that he expected no second payment, at least not from me. The sense was that my expected fate was common knowledge in New Extrema. No one mentioned it. It was like being in an old Gary Cooper movie,

145

High Noon.

Three ten. Izabel started talking softly, in the dark. She knew I was awake.

"After I realized who you are . . ." she said, stopped, and restarted, having a problem with saying something nice. "Look, I know what you and Major Nakamura did last year in Washington. You saved thousands of people. It was on the news here. You deserve better than being left out to dry."

I tried to sleep over the sound of dogs snarling outside. I heard the two police officers whispering angrily in the darkness. Now Nelson was up, too.

There was something off in how the two cops treated each other; a coolness that I could not pin down. Again I wondered if they were in a personal relationship. Or maybe, with Izabel in the lead, this was some male/female dustup. Maybe Nelson resented a female boss. Nelson was tough to read, although he'd shown black humor when informing me — through her — that my Taurus had probably been one of the 98,000 units sent back to the manufacturer recently by the São Paulo State Military Police when it was discovered that the guns could discharge without the trigger being pulled. "Try not to shoot yourself, gringo," he'd said as he grinned.

146

Finally, around 3:40 A.M., I actually fell sleep.

Four A.M. I was suddenly awake at a scratch on the door.

Here we go, I thought, scrambling for my perch. I heard my own breathing as I lay atop the rickety two-by-fours holding up the slanting tin roof. I heard a pitter-patter on the roof. Rain. Something fast and squishy ran across my wrist as I heard squeaky protests from a corner where — on the beam — the rats probably eyed me back.

Then my attention was pulled away by another scuff outside, a bump against the door. I raised my pistol.

Oink, came a faint muffled sound.

Shit.

It was pigs. Town pigs. Rooting around out there, in the dark. I relaxed. False alarm again. SHIT!

Wait a minute. In a jungle town you don't let pigs out at night, or something will come and eat them. Back in Smith Falls you never let small animals out at night.

The door smashed inward as my gun swung up. Shotguns blasted, loud as bombs in the cramped space. BOOM . . . BOOM.

The room was lit by bursts, and in them, glimpses of the police in the corner, firing, and a shotgun barrel swinging up at me.

147

Two attackers there, one in the doorway, one just inside the room.

BOOM!

I felt the support give way.

I was falling, falling toward the floor.

ELEVEN

Sound and smell came back into the world to the pulsing pain in my back, broiling heat, rain pattering on tin, the low, long cry of a jaguar in the jungle. I was on the ground, in my hotel room. I smelled jasmine and diesel fuel, chicken shit and singed shotgun shells. And the sweet/sour post-combat odor of viscera. Turning sideways, in the light of the flashlight lying on the ground, I saw the remains of the rat that had saved me, shredded, a torn up mound of fur and blood a foot away from my face. The creature's movement had distracted the gunman. The blast had ripped through rotten roof support. I'd crashed to the ground, but the low ceiling had limited fall distance, and I'd toppled half onto the bedding below.

I'd bruise badly, but did not think myself seriously injured.

"Joe?" A whisper from Izabel Santo.

"I'm okay. Nelson?"

His voice was shaky with pain. *"Aqui."* Izabel had a flashlight, too, and its beam showed blood on the big officer's forehead, running down between his eyes. Minor head wounds can bleed heavily. But the dark mass clotting the right side of his chest was wet and evil looking. Izabel's eyes were huge in the wan light. She turned the beam on our attackers. One had fallen inward to die just across the threshold; the other had been driven back and into the open-air corridor by our multiple shots.

Make sure they are dead before looking at Nelson.

I bent over the man in the doorway. He was a stranger. Both men, I realized, had failed to cut down their shotgun barrels, which would have created a spread pattern to obliterate all life in our room. Overconfident or stupid, they'd kept the barrels long. The flashlight beam played over the face of a pale-skinned, thickly blond-bearded stranger. His kufi, an Islamic skullcap, had fallen off his head and lay bent in half on the ground.

I'd look for ID later. I moved quickly into the corridor, to see that the second attacker was Anasasio, shot four times in the chest. In death, still dressed in his Italian clothing, one loafer off, he looked surprised.

150

I stood over my ex-translator's body and felt the greatest rage seize me. There was no question now that Eddie was close. But it was also clear that whatever we did next, we had better do it fast. More attackers might be outside. Izabel hissed something that I did not hear as I rapidly moved down the corridor to stop at the door of the owner's cubicle, last one on the right. A pale-yellow, flickering light beneath the door came from a kerosene lamp, or battery power. The hammered tin door looked flimsy. No one inside could have slept through the fight.

I heard a shuffling noise in there, a scrape, a hiss.

I kicked the door in, and he sat at a table across the room. In the kerosene light he was turning to me in fear and astonishment. He was in his underwear, on a three-legged stool before a glowing ham radio. The ham was warming up. I saw a large revolver a foot from his hand, and a half-empty bottle of cachaça. A second figure reclined on his single bed against the wall and for a half second drew my attention. It was an inflated blow-up sex doll; smiling pouty lips, blue eyes, hoop earrings. The hotel owner was so shocked to see me that he rose. In his face was terror. I couldn't tell at first if he was involved in the attack. But then his eyes changed, and his hand shot toward the revolver. I pulled the trigger of my Taurus twice, and he grunted and stumbled sideways, retched, and toppled into the blow-up doll, which bounced away as if it feared being touched.

"Where's Eddie?" I demanded, as if the man understood English, as he lay bleeding on the floor.

He clutched his throat, although there was no wound there. He grabbed at my shirt. He was trying to speak but clearly had no idea what I had asked him. Blood money — Brazilian *real* that the assassins had given him — lay scattered on his packed-dirt floor.

The ham radio would be the chief means of communication from this outpost, which lacked cell towers or phone access. The gunfire had silenced all life-forms within a few hundred yards. But I was sure that all residents of the pinprick hamlet would be up, aware, maybe trembling, maybe staring at their doors, maybe praying on their knees or clutching knives or single-bore, ancient shotguns to try to protect their children. They'd be making pacts with angels.

Let me live tonight. Let my family stay alive.

I almost shot Izabel Santo when she appeared behind me, breathing hard. From her crisp movements and set of jaw it was clear she was a combat veteran. Maybe she'd been in some of those pitched battles that Brazilian feds have had with gangs in the slums — favelas — of the east. She expertly wielded Anasasio's *Cartuchos*, his Brazilian-made Remington pump-action 870 copy. All emotion had compacted into alert determination. She reacted in fractions of time. Her head flick to the left — toward town — told me that no one else was out there at the moment. The shift to the right and head shake told me Nelson was in bad shape. I was connected to her as I might be to Eddie in a fight. There was no need to say out loud that more killers were probably waiting to hear what had happened. Maybe from the ham radio. Or when our would-be assassins returned to where they'd started out. *Probably the island.*

But Nelson needed medical attention before we could do anything else.

The big sublieutenant had managed to crawl to the corpses, search them, and gather ID, like a good cop. But his leg was dragging. Flies hovered near his chest like insect vultures. Izabel was talking quietly in his ear.

Marines don't leave comrades behind.

I used on him the bandages and antibiotics that I'd stolen with Rooster from the

Porto Velho hospital. The bandage would function as a tourniquet. But Nelson was losing blood. He sagged when I slipped my arms around him. In the dark, Captain Santo and I helped him limp down the mud path to the dock. We knew what must be done. And that it better be done in the brief period of time left before the sun came up. There was no time to wait for reinforcements. We needed to hit that island, now.

The assassins' outboard boat was tied to the dock where the ferry had deposited us. They must have cut their engine in mid river, and rowed the aluminum craft ashore. I had Cizinio's hand-drawn map to direct us, five kilometers north, he'd said, to the island. *Six guards,* I think, I recalled him saying, as Izabel and I lowered Nelson and the seized shotguns and ammunition belts into the boat. But Anasasio wasn't a guard. He must have come upriver to warn his friends. The other attacker had probably been a guard, so if Cizinio was right, there would be at least five guards left.

Above the jungle silhouette came the first red hint of dawn as we chugged into the Madeira. Light would work against us. It gave us less time. The night noises were already easing, as if earth was yawning, preparing for transition. The howler monkey and jaguar sounds were gone, and dawn birds were calling. From the river I looked back to see huge winged bats, swooping against a quarter moon that brushed the treetops, seeking the caves, knotholes, or eaves in which they would sleep away the day, upside down, like logic in this remote place.

Nelson half sat, half supported himself against the gunwale, and made no complaint. His breathing sounded ragged against the engine. He had the inwardly directed attitude of those who have suffered serious injury. He was conserving strength. Izabel Santo had done everything possible for him and let him be, but I knew how hard that was. The two Brazilians were like Eddie and me. Izabel was Uno and Nelson was Dos. My respect for them was enormous. They could have left me alone in New Extrema, but they'd stayed to help.

Somewhere behind us I heard the diesel engine powering the village start up, and a single electric light shone from beneath a door. *Good thing I smashed the ham radio.* The residents would venture out now and find the dead. Were the people out there the hotel owner's relatives? His parents or children? No way to know.

But then my mind moved ahead, because a few miles upriver people would be wondering why they had not heard from their killers. *Maybe we'll be lucky. Maybe they'll be drunk. Or asleep. Or would never think that we would attack.*

Cizinio had said, *There is a dock on the south side, and always two guards posted.*

He'd said, *There are no guards on the back side of the island, but there is mud that you sink into.*

The stars were out. Two feet of mist covered the river. We seemed to float through the bottom of a twisting canyon, the walls of which were a solid mass of trees. Overhead, a meandering slit of night. We must have gone five kilometers by now, yet there was no island. The river widened, the banks fell back. The smell was rot and vegetation and fresh oxygen so thick that it seemed to clot your lungs. The motor sounded too loud. I experienced the familiar gut clench that came before combat. Nelson's head sank onto Izabel's shoulder, not the way a man's head rested on a woman, but soldier to soldier. She whispered into his ear. Her hair was tied beneath a kufi. He sat up. He had no expression. Nelson had wanted to leave me alone in the hotel. She had made him stay.

"I see it, Joe," she said, pointing. "There."

The island was a stiletto-shaped silhouette in the middle of the river. Without being asked, Nelson lay down in the boat, so any guards would see only two figures coming their way. Only two had left.

"Two men on the dock, Joe."

The faint glow in the sky had been brightening incrementally, but suddenly a crimson streak shot across the water. Mist fell away in patches that I tried to steer jaggedly through, using just enough swerve to look natural but hide our faces. I kept the speed low. Even if the guards had night-vision equipment, the mist might provide us a few more seconds. I'd not asked Cizinio about vision equipment, and I cursed inwardly.

That had been a lapse.

Either way they'd have binoculars.

Now a garish light spread out across the water. I looked back to see the orb tip appearing barely above treetops, liquid red. I needed sun at our backs. I wanted them to see silhouettes, not faces. I wanted them to imagine for a moment what they expected, their assassins chugging back home after a job well done.

Eighty yards. Fifty. Maybe I should have given Izabel the extra day she wanted. I smelled ammonia, urine from Nelson.

Just give us one more minute . . .

With the shocking suddenness that comes in the tropics, the day flared to life like a silent explosion. There was more heat on the back of my neck. Full dawn. The sun would be directly in their eyes. I saw a long diagonal line emanating off the shoulder of a guard and the arc of the banana clip in his AK-47. The man seemed to be shielding his eyes, trying to see us better.

Thirty more seconds . . .

A harsh male voice carried over the water, in Portuguese. Probably saying, *What the fuck happened to you two? Are you drunk? Why didn't you call on the ham radio?*

They weren't unslinging the AKs yet. They were moving two-dimensional cardboard cutouts. As in target practice.

I whispered, "Ready?"

I saw, from the corner of my eye, Izabel's hands down in the bottom of the boat, touching her shotgun. We'd break out of the mist in another second.

"Now!"

I let go of the motor arm and swung up my shotgun. Hers was up, too. BOOM-BOOM-BOOM. The water was flat so there was no bounce, and at our fast moves the guards had reached to unsling weapons.

I heard the snapping sounds of an AK firing. I heard screams from the treetops. Hundreds of bats or birds launched themselves into the air.

The first guard had toppled into the water, firing at the sky, and the second had crumbled before getting a shot off. There was no way that other people on the island would not have heard the fighting. Nelson had forced himself up, his face a rictus of pain, but he held a handgun. He forced out words to Izabel as we reached the dock. "Nelson says he will tie the boat. We must run."

She was out on the dock first, and I was right behind her. We needed to get into the jungle fast. We'd be dead in seconds if we stayed here. More guards would be coming.

They have cameras in the trees. I remembered Cizinio's warnings as we pounded onto land.

There! A red light, a round lens catching sunlight, ten feet up. I shot it out and we raced past. Behind us, I could only hope that Nelson remained conscious long enough to tie up the boat, so it would not drift off.

Cizinio's voice in my head said, *The path takes a few minutes to reach the main house. Stay on the path at first.*

Floodlights burst on in the trees at the

same time that sunbeams shot down through the canopy. They angled down like artillery as I ran past a mist net — a researcher's tool, mesh so fine it was invisible to animals. It was designed to catch birds. In the net I saw wriggling life, a hand-sized tarantula attached to a bird. *Cizinio's words better be accurate,* I thought, as giant fern leaves flapped wetly into my face.

At the second bend leave the path but keep going in the same direction.

I left the path and plunged into jungle, following the upward slope of land, as Cizinio had instructed. I heard the light, quick footfalls of Captain Santo behind me, and now came alarmed shouts ahead, men calling to one another, as their voices spread out. I halted, listening. They were coming straight on. Izabel and I ducked behind the waist-high fan-shaped base of a ceiba tree. The huge trunk disappeared into the canopy one hundred feet overhead. The roots needed to be high to support such an enormous weight. Cizinio had said the guards knew the shortcut, that if they heard shots, they'd skirt the path, too. With the camera shot out, they would, I hoped, think that Izabel and I were still on the path. We waited behind those huge roots like the ambushers in the graffiti drawings back in our hotel.

Sure enough, movement, whispers, as two men came low and fast through the shadows at the base of the forest. Even with the sun up, the canopy blocked out light here, made the air cooler. There was less surface vegetation. Vegetation was thicker by the river. You needed a machete to get through there. But here the shadowy figures emerging from mist were clear, forty yards away . . . stop and go . . . stop and listen. One man gave the other a hand signal.

Izabel and I opened up at the same moment with our seized AK-47s. The guards had no chance. Both went down. One was screaming in pain, and I saw ferns waving wildly where he'd fallen. There was no sound from the second man, who'd flown backward and lay still. That made four guards down, five if I included the one in New Extrema.

Abruptly, with a cough, the screaming and fern waving stopped.

Both corpses were thickly bearded and had worn skullcaps. This place must be exactly what Ray Havlicek had sent us to find. At that moment if he had been present I would have rammed my weapon into his belly. He'd sent Eddie and me here and denied us help. He'd asked us to look for something and *we had found it* but then Ray had disappeared. *Do us a favor . . . You can call me anytime.*

I pushed Ray from my mind and into my future. We started moving again, recalling Cizinio's advice. *Stay in the same direction, follow the slope. The forest will end and there will be a lawn and the doctor's house and medical building where he used to treat us and give us medicines.*

A man's voice called out, from ahead, "Nasser?"

From behind us, from the dock, I heard three quick gunshots, *snap-snap-snap*. A handgun. *Nelson.* I heard the rapid fire of an AK-47 shooting back. I could only hope that whoever was exchanging fire with Nelson had gotten close enough for Nelson's shots to find their mark. But had they found their mark, there would have been no return fire.

Still, the man ahead of us seemed to lose heart at the sound of more gunfire. I saw ferns waving, but this time in retreat. Whoever was there had panicked, or been ordered back. He was running to the houses. Izabel and I surged forward.

A sudden thump ahead sounded like a grenade going off. But the explosion was nowhere near us.

Suddenly there were no more trees, just a sloping lawn that led, fifty yards up, to reveal what Cizinio had drawn. The one-story ranch house lay exactly as depicted, and thirty feet from it, the dorm/clinic and exam room. Cizinio's proportions were perfect. I heard another thump from the main house as the front windows blew out. I heard AK bursts inside. Who the hell were they shooting at, if not us? Gray smoke billowed out. I heard quick two-round shots, and they brought terror into my throat for Eddie, because suddenly I knew what was happening in there.

They're destroying things. They're executing people. They're getting rid of evidence.

In drills in the Virginia forest at Quantico, Eddie and I had assaulted hidden "biolabs" while other Marines playing "enemy" triggered smoke traps, smashed computers, "murdered" witnesses as they retreated, employing a scorched-earth policy that the Soviets would have envied in World War Two.

If they're panicking, there must be only one or two guards left, I thought.

"Labs" on fire, "prisoners" shot. That was all I could think as I propelled myself across that lawn, with Captain Santo screaming something at my back in Portuguese, probably, *Don't do it!*

The flowers to my right blew apart. Petals flew in the air with shrub bits. I ducked and hit the lawn and rolled into a bush, fired, and kept going, at a fast crawl. My right ankle was on fire. I'd been shot. *No, I haven't been shot, because something small is running up my leg toward my crotch. I've been stung!*

I rolled sideways and slammed my palm into my pants at whatever the hell was in there. The sensation of burning was getting worse. I saw an inch-long flattened insect drop onto the ground. Bullet ants lived in shrubs. Eddie and I had been warned about them. A half dozen bites can kill a large human. The single bite will produce pain that increases for up to twenty-four hours. The inch-long creatures inject a neurotoxin in victims that tops the list of Amazon dangers. Bullet ants, not jaguars, not snakes, not piranhas, cause more human deaths each year than any of those other things.

I could only hope that the strength of the poison inside me had crested. I was limping as I rose, and the pure, intense stabs of pain were getting worse. I thought, gritting my teeth, *You're stronger than a fucking ant.*

A shadow appeared at the window, rising

flames behind it. I fired and raked the side of the building. The shadow ducked sideways. The snout of a weapon jutted out, and a line of bullets stitched the lawn. But suddenly the AK-47 fell out of the window. Izabel was coming low and fast from the left. She'd hit whoever was in there.

Eddie . . .

I ran toward the main house while she laid down cover fire. Because now I heard screams in there, multiple voices, pleading. *Shot/pause/shot.* My heart seized up. An explosion sounded in the main building. Another window shattered, and gray smoke billowed out. At least six guards were down now and as many as eight, so who was in there, destroying evidence? How many guards were there in this hellish place?

I burst through the door.

A guard lay inside, still alive, but blood pumped from his mouth. The man wore a white *khet partug,* a long body shirt ending at the knees. His skullcap was still on. I kicked the AK away from his spasming hand.

"Sa-aidnee! Sa-aidnee!" he begged. *Please help me!* Skinny guy. Dark skinned. He had the fear of death in his face.

I shot him in the head.

Cizinio was wrong about the number of

guards. And if there are this many guards, this place is really important.

The heat was extreme and the air convoluted. The fire was intense, mahogany dining table on fire, tropical wood stairs on fire, curtains and velvet couches and Oriental rug burning, the whole world hot. *If they're burning evidence, find it, seize it, remember it.* I screamed Eddie's name and got no answer. There was no way to get up the stairs without an asbestos suit. I could only hope, as the last scream died away, that whoever had been alive up there, it was not Eddie.

The pain in my ankle had now grown into a searing mass.

Captain Santo and I moved toward the low, one-story medical building. It was on fire, too, but this fire wasn't that bad yet. The lawn was a mass of choking smoke. The pain in my leg had radiated up toward my thigh. All around us fire consumed wood, oxygen, and roasting vegetation. Marine assault teams in Afghanistan had always been made up of at least five attackers. Not two against nine or more.

There was no time to get into that building slowly. I burst in and found myself in a medical ward. And in it, a horror: two rows of single beds, containing men and women,

166

in hospital gowns, like patients, but these patients were handcuffed to iron bedposts, and all of them *shot in the head*. The blood was still soaking their bedding, fresh on their faces. I'd heard the executions. These must be the kidnapped miners.

"Jesus Cristo," whispered Izabel, coming up beside me. "Is one of these people your friend?"

I ran from bed to bed, looking for Eddie, coughing. This place was the negative image of a hospital ward; same layout, but it existed to inflict pain, not alleviate it. Hell's clinic. I saw surgical instruments collecting soot inside smashed-up glass cabinets. Normally the instruments look benign to me. Here they were implements of torture.

Find Eddie but pay attention to everything.

I saw Eddie! He lay sideways, in a blood-soaked bed, feet over the edge, mouth gaping, brain matter splattered across the pillow!

No, it was not Eddie. It was a different Japanese man. I fell against the wall in horror and relief.

The pause had situated me beside several black-and-white photos on the wall. I stood blinking at them in astonishment. The pictures curling inside heat-shattered glass were the last thing I'd think to see here.

They were *World War Two shots!* German officers sightseeing at the pyramids, with two men wearing white suits. One of them looked fifty, a European; the other was swarthier. Egyptian? Next, shots of Jews with yellow stars on their clothing, on a line, in a concentration camp. Then Adolf Hitler sitting in a chair talking earnestly with a robed cleric wearing the kind of round white turban that I recognized from Iraq. Shiite.

Hitler was leaning forward, palms open, face reasonable, if such a word could be used in his case. He was making an important point to a valued guest.

What the hell? What's the connection to this place?

When I reached the end of the ward I looked back to see fire consuming the room. A door here was closed. My leg was dragging. I pushed through the door with my heart in my mouth to see a middle-aged man in medical whites whirling toward me, holding a can of gasoline. I was in an examination room. A few beds, and human forms on them. An exam table with shackles on it. The doctor struck me as Levantine; olive skin, fleshy face and body, large nose, and furious black eyes that looked larger through thick black eyeglasses, half slid

168

down his nose. He'd been splashing gasoline on walls. He'd given up the chance to flee in order to complete the destruction. He screamed at me as fire consumed an open file cabinet, and a laptop melted and bubbled on a table. I needed this man alive. I yelled for him to put down the can. He started to throw it at me, and a burst of gunfire spun him sideways and made him dance back and smack into the wall and slide down.

Izabel Santo stood in the doorway, her AK smoking. She was panting, and the rage on her face was firelit, red. The gasoline can had sailed past me to smash into the wall and splash fuel, and now fire whooshed up on three sides.

"Joe? Is that *you*?"

I knew that voice. I couldn't believe it. Eddie was gaping at me in astonishment from one of the beds at the back of the room. He was handcuffed there, and had been hidden behind the doctor. I counted three men in all here, survivors, alive. One man burst into tears. The other screamed for help. They all looked sick and terrified.

It was hard to breathe. Eddie had lost weight and his face was pale. His croaked voice, his *actual* voice, filled me with so much emotion that for an instant there was no pain or fire or dead doctor. Eddie smiled with a kind of pain-wracked disbelief, as if he doubted what he saw, or suffered hallucinations.

"Where did you come from, Uno?"

"The key! *Where's the key to the handcuffs, Eddie?*"

Izabel moved up, gaping. "That's him? Your friend?"

"We have to tell Ray what went on here," Eddie said, as fire bloomed and beakers shattered and windows blew out and Izabel moved toward the other survivors to try to release them.

"Screw the key, One. Shoot the cuffs off," Eddie advised. He'd always been a fast thinker, Eddie.

TWELVE

White house Deputy Assistant National Security Advisor Kyle Utley's job sometimes was to sit in for his boss at meetings, take notes, and report back. He was in the White House's Roosevelt Room doing just that, eyeing the *Rough Rider* painting over the fireplace when his cell phone vibrated for the fourth time in ten minutes. The return number was his wife's. This meant the news would be bad.

"The seventy-two-hour deadline has passed, without attacks by terrorists. This false alarm was handled professionally. You all deserve congratulations," Homeland Security's Deputy Under Secretary for Intelligence and Analysis told the gathering of second- and third-tier reps from security agencies. Now that the initial alert had been downgraded, lesser officials dealt with the aftermath. Their bosses had gone on to other things.

171

"Our quiet response to the threat showed superb synergy. We avoided panic and kept the public safe."

Kyle raised an index finger to mean he was breaking, moved into the carpeted hallway, and punched in his wife's number. Angie was a lawyer for a big lobbying firm downtown, on K Street. She picked up during the first ring.

"I just got a disturbing phone call, Kyle."

Angela Utley was not a complainer, and if she was upset, there was good reason, Kyle knew. He was a protective husband, furious with anyone who would bother his wife. His first thought was that the incident related to the pissed-off plumber who had argued with Angie over a bill last week. "Who called, honey?"

"Well, that's just it! He never said his name! My secretary came in and handed me her cellular. The guy on the other end said you knew him from the New Post Pub."

Kyle felt the good mood from the meeting disappear and a hard ball of tension replace it. He fell into the hallway armchair, across from an oil painting borrowed from the Smithsonian, depicting Japanese planes attacking Pearl Harbor on December 7, 1941. American ships were in flames in the water. Smoke roiled. Sailors were burning alive.

Trying to keep his voice level, Kyle asked, "What did the caller say, Angie?"

"He told me to write everything down so I wouldn't forget it. He said that the deadline has passed, the first attack has started, and it's your fault. He said you still have a chance to limit more damage and you know how. Your fault? What did he mean?"

"I don't know."

Kyle felt sweat break out in his armpits. *The attack has started?* There was nothing in the news about any attack. No bombings. No planes down. No mobilization he'd heard of, anywhere, that could have masked a government response to an attack, here or overseas.

No, absolutely nothing coming in.

Angie's voice grew tighter. "The man said he hoped that you and I have the right medicines. He knew we have no children, and hoped that our parents would be all right. He said the usual pills should work, whatever that means. Kyle? Medicines? How did he know we don't have kids?"

Kyle thought fast. "He probably read that *Post*'s Style section piece, Angie. D.C. couples on the way up? Last month?"

Yes, the caller was a nut, Kyle told himself. The caller, as the Deputy Under Secretary for Intelligence and Analysis had suggested

173

a few minutes ago, was delusional. Maybe the caller merely imagined that there had been an attack. *Yeah, that's it.*

But if that was it, how come, Kyle thought with dread, *I have a gut feeling that bad news is about to come?* He tried to pin down the source of his premonition. It was the look on the stranger's face outside the New Post Pub. The man had seemed rational. And the approach now, reaching him through his wife's secretary, skirting possible monitoring, was diabolically shrewd.

"Kyle, who was that man?" Angie asked.

"I don't know. Was that his whole message?"

"No. He said that groups *all over the United States* are in place to begin more attacks."

Kyle felt dizzy.

"He said that the only way to prevent that is to give them what they want. He said to tell you to remember Tol-e-Khomri. What is Tol-e-Khomri?"

She was waiting for the explanation. But she knew that the explanation might not come. That was the deal they'd made at home, about both their jobs. *It's okay to ask a question about secret business, but only once. If there's no answer, drop it.*

"It is a . . . village. Angie, did he say . . .

This will sound odd, but did he tell you what the first attack, uh, *is*?"

She sounded astounded. "You don't know?"

"Just tell me if he gave specifics."

All air seemed to have drained from the White House. It was obvious how the stranger had reached Angie. Any Google search would produce her Facebook page or Twitter account, and the name of the K Street firm where she worked. After that, any scan of the online corporate directory would produce the names of employees. Easy to access a Facebook page or phone number. Next thing you know, you've reached Kyle through a back door.

"Angie, keep your secretary's phone. We'll want it."

She knew not to push things. He'd met her in a foreign affairs class at Princeton, where they'd both aspired to Washington careers. They understood the nature of secrets and how to try to keep them from interfering with marriage. That meant she needed to shut up now and answer questions. Which was easier said than done. *At first the privilege of knowing secrets makes you sexy and important to your spouse,* Kyle thought. After a while, it gets aggravating. Then maddening. Then suddenly one day you're strangers. The secrets seem more real than family.

"Kyle, he said if you doubted anything, turn on any local New York broadcast. He said New York will be covering the first attack by now. I've got New York up on my screen here. I see . . . *oh God* . . . I see lots of ambulances."

Kyle hung up fast and got the Deputy Under Secretary out of the Roosevelt Room, where he was sharing bagels with an FBI rep, Ray Havlicek, and where they were congratulating each other for not panicking over the initial threat. Together they accessed the inset wall monitors. Up swam CBS, CNN, and MSNBC. Kyle fumbled with the channel changer. Chris Mathews disappeared, and local New York One popped up.

Kyle held his breath at the sight of ambulances pulling up before a large gray hospital on Manhattan's York Avenue. The rolling banner read, *Victims brought to Cornell Medical Center.* Kyle waited with bile in his throat to hear the word *bomb.* But instead the reporter in front of the hospital was talking about malaria.

"Malaria?" said Havlicek, puzzled. "Turn up the sound."

The newswoman said, *"Health department*

officials are baffled at the scope of the out-
break. Nineteen people have fallen ill so far,
and seven have died. The city was sprayed
against mosquitoes in June, but summer is
peak times for insects. I did some research,
and malaria has not been present in New York
to any substantial degree since the 1800s.
Back then up to fifteen hundred people here
died annually from the disease. Last year New
York had only two hundred cases, and virtu-
ally all had visited tropical countries."

"This can't be it," Havlicek said. But he
sounded like he was making a wish, not stat-
ing a fact.

The reporter said, *"The strange and terrify-*
ing thing is, none of today's victims have left
the U.S. recently, I've learned. They are com-
ing in from different parts of the city. This
strain is unusually virulent. It's a deadly
mystery, playing out at area hospitals. Officials
fear widespread panic if the disease spreads."

Kyle muted the sound as the reporter
started taking "man on the street" re-
sponses. The hot dog vendor being interviewed looked scared. In the Roosevelt
Room, the lox on the side table by the
bagels was starting to smell rancid.

"Kyle? Malaria?" the Deputy Under Secretary said.

"Maybe the caller heard about this and

he's just taking credit. You know. Co-incidence."

Maybe he's in New York. If we move fast, we can get him.

Shaking his head, the Deputy Under Secretary said, "But how could you spread malaria intentionally? I thought you had to be bitten by a mosquito to get it. Right?"

"We better call Gaines at CDC."

Kyle turned to the window. The curtain was open, and he saw quick bursts of movement from insects in the Rose Garden. A dragonfly. A butterfly. Kyle realized there was a mosquito on the glass, outside. He watched it take a step on its spindly legs, fascinated. The insect buzzed back into the air. Now there were two mosquitoes there. It was impossible to tell one from the other. If one was infected, you'd not know from appearance which one it was, he saw with horror.

The little thermometer outside the window read ninety-one degrees, Kyle saw. An especially hot summer in Washington.

Kyle said, under his breath, "Bombs, but not bombs."

Five hours later there were eighty-seven known victims in New York, nineteen dead from blackwater fever and rapid-onset cerebral malaria. Then the first victim showed up at a hospital in Newark, New Jersey. *That's two cities. The threat was three,* Kyle thought.

Seven hours later the death toll topped thirty. The first case that came into a hospital in Philadelphia was a homeless veteran who'd been sleeping in a park by the Schuylkill River. By then, the national networks had the story, the White House was in a panic, and the beast down the hall, the press corps, needed blood, just like the mosquitoes.

By dusk, with malaria the lead story on all global networks, and eighty-one more ill, Kyle was in the middle of a raging argument over whether to reveal the phone threats to the news media, or keep them secret until after the national party convention next week.

Kyle argued that the news should be released, in case a member of the public might aid the investigation.

"And tell them what?" the Chief of Staff snapped. "That *maybe* we're under biological attack? *Maybe* there are cells all over the country? That we have no fucking idea who they are or where they come from? You want to explain what that would accomplish, Kyle, except to cause panic?"

"There will be panic anyway."

"For all we know your caller saw this on TV and claimed credit. There's no proof it's connected. Look, we've got the Detroit mass shooting to deal with. The China thing. The gun control. You want to announce? Then give me something positive! A hero! A clue! Something the President can announce as progress! The security agencies can do their jobs just as well if we keep this in-house for a bit. We'll send out health warnings. Try to keep calm."

"You mean keep quiet until after the convention."

A hard stare. "I mean that you calm down right now. I mean that politics is like a good marriage. You love and respect each other, but you don't tell each other every thing every minute of the day."

The only thing all present agreed on was that as the sun went down, temperatures were still eighty-eight degrees along much of the East Coast. Excellent weather for mosquitoes.

Kyle was told in no uncertain terms not to ask more about a small Syrian village with the name of Tol-e-Khomri.

He decided to try to learn more about it anyway.

Quietly, so his boss would not find out.

THIRTEEN

Rain drummed on the tent in which the Brazilian Federal Police imprisoned us on the island. The SWAT team had arrived four days ago by helicopter, after Izabel called Brasília for help. Eddie and I slept on cots, as two stern-looking uniformed guards stood outside, armed with combat shotguns. Eddie saw a doctor daily, and we were fed well, beans, fresh fish, rice, and greens, while a forensics team went over the charred house and blackened lab, the bodies of the dead, and tissue/blood samples from three other survivors that Izabel and I had rescued before the clinic roof collapsed.

The survivors — sick miners — had been medevaced to Porto Velho. Major Victorino Acosta — a bearish man with an oddly high-pitched voice — told us that they remained alive, barely, and in deteriorating shape.

"We could have questioned the doctor you killed, the guards you killed," Acosta snapped at me.

"That doctor was burning his patients alive."

"You are responsible for the death of Sub-lieutenant Salazar. You should have waited for us. You people up north, you do not own the world," he sneered.

But Eddie was alive, and I would make sure he stayed that way. Major Acosta let me use my medicines to help treat my best friend: Vermox pills against the worms that swelled in Eddie's stomach and crawled whitely in his feces. Flagyl to kill the jungle amoebas that lived in his gut. His malaria was on the wane, though. The fever bouts — shaking and burning — had stopped before I got there. Eddie told me that he'd been shackled in the lab because the doctor I'd killed was fascinated by his fight against the disease.

"You survived," I said, "because you're tough."

"He came from India, One. He said his name was Sabbir Umar. There's another doctor he'd talk to over Skype, but I never saw the guy."

Eddie also told me during periods of consciousness that all prisoners on the island had been victims of malaria. "The worst forms, Joe. That sadist harvested our blood four times a day. Sabbir Umar squatted down in the middle of the biggest natural malaria field on earth and culled out the deadliest bugs. Nature produced the killers. He harvested 'em like crops. It was a weapons program."

"But why malaria, Eddie? There are so many other diseases to work with, easier ones than malaria."

"They figured no one would link malaria to terrorists."

At first I refused to believe the next part of Eddie's story. I figured that he was remembering hallucinations, not anything real. But he persisted, reminded me of the photos I'd seen in the clinic, before they burned up. The shots from Nazi Germany.

"That doctor liked to brag while he worked, Joe. He said his work continued research that was conducted on prisoners at Dachau, the German concentration camp, in World War Two."

"What does World War Two have to do with this?"

"You never did pay attention in biohistory class. We know that the SS at Dachau experimented on Jews, infected them with typhus and malaria. We *know* they were looking for illness to spread among Allied troops. We *know* it didn't work because malaria isn't contagious. But Umar bragged that he'd had a breakthrough."

"Which was what?"

Eddie's face fell. "He didn't say."

The Brazilian cops refused to let me call Washington. As Eddie slept I kept his forehead cool. I walked him to the latrine when he needed to go. But after two days he waved off help. Izabel was gone, chewed out by Acosta for attacking the island without waiting for help. She had not argued. I think that she blamed herself for Nelson's death.

"Eddie, what else do you remember about Sabbir Umar?"

"Like I said, sometimes he talked to people on Skype. He had a laptop in the lab. They spoke Arabic, so I didn't understand what they said. I never saw the other doctor, but one time I saw another guy, different voice — a white guy, dark hair. He spoke Arabic with an American accent. He was talking about U.S. cities. I think he might have been in the U.S. I think it was about an attack."

"Which cities?" I asked, chilled.

"New York was one."

"Which others?"

"Maybe Trenton. I'm sorry. Maybe he just said *trains*. My head wasn't working right.

But after one call Dr. Umar got really furious. He told me that three of their people had died. He said the FBI had gotten lucky in Miami. But he said it wasn't over. They had a plan to make us pay."

My mouth felt dry. "Could you help an artist sketch the guy you saw on-screen?"

"The shape of the face, yes. But that's about it.

"What else do you remember?"

"Umar had a terrarium filled with mosquitoes. He fed them our blood, like a dog owner feeds pets. It was crazy. They pumped prayers over the loudspeakers five times a day. They stripped the miners of crosses, bibles, anything religious. Hard-core fanatics, Joe."

"So he feeds the mosquitoes infected blood, making them carriers."

"Yep."

There was something else important in what Eddie had told me. I could not put my finger on it, even though I went over his words again and again. It nagged me. But when nothing jumped out at me I thought that maybe I'd been wrong, or tired. Maybe there was no clue that I had missed.

On the fifth day the flap opened and Major Acosta barked that we had ten minutes to pack, because we were leaving. We were handcuffed and taken through a hard jungle rain, to the dock. We passed forensics teams still working the wreckage. Izabel was back and waited on the police launch, under an awning. She was in uniform, and wore her sidearm, so she'd survived whatever trouble she'd been in before. She was taking over control of us. Major Acosta seemed angry and snapped at her in Portuguese, and she shrugged as if his opinion mattered little anymore, as if Acosta had been overruled by a higher power. Our guards shoved Eddie and me onto the boat and untied the hawsers, and the launch took off downriver, churning white wake behind.

"You two made us quite a problem," Captain Izabel Santo said. But her anger was not directed at us. She seemed angry that Eddie and I had been imprisoned.

"Where are we going?"

"That's being decided. I am not allowed to tell more."

"Can I have my phone back?"

"No."

Eddie was white, weak, and chilled, even in the rampant heat, even with a wool blanket around him. The boat moved ten times faster than the ferry that had taken us to New Extrema. The trip back to Porto

186

Velho took only four hours. There, more cops prodded us into a Land Rover marked with a police logo, and we headed downtown. I figured we were going to headquarters, but the Rover passed headquarters and kept going, without slowing, leaving downtown, passing through the shantytown, and back onto the jungle highway.

Eddie said, worriedly, "No witnesses."

"No," Izabel said, pointing to the sky. "The *airport*. You are being expelled."

The Justice Department Gulfstream G650 idled on the runway, U.S. logo on the fuselage, and two FBI agents waited inside, banned from stepping onto Brazilian soil. The man/woman team looked as expressive as statues. *Which means we're in trouble up north. I've been on escort duty as a Marine. If you're taking home a victim, you smile, you welcome them. If you're with prisoners, you keep distant, like these two.*

"Fucking Ray Havlicek," Eddie said.

Izabel Santo surprised us, because I'd figured she was about to drop us off. But she took a small red rolling suitcase out of the Land Rover. "I am coming with you. It is part of the deal."

I raised my eyebrows as a question.

"There is some problem in the United States," she said. "It is related, we think, to what happened to you."

"What problem?"

We were strapping ourselves into leather swivel seats in the forward luxury cabin, designed to provide space for four. This plane was a comfortable prison. I saw a sideboard with drinks and refreshments. The air-conditioning worked. The floor was covered with plush pile, and there was a large conference screen on the wall, turned off. The FBI escorts disappeared into a smaller cabin in back, for aides or flight attendants.

Izabel said, "There has been an outbreak of a new, fatal malaria in three of your cities: New York, Philadelphia, and Newark. Many people are dead."

Eddie and I stared at each other. I felt bile collecting in my belly, rising hotly into my throat.

"Newark," I repeated. "You said Trenton."

"Maybe they said Newark, not Trenton. I was hallucinating then," Eddie replied.

FOURTEEN

The jet had a kitchenette and microwavable meals, and the leather seats folded back into beds. The pilots announced that we were headed to Washington, flight time eleven hours. A flight attendant served coffee and bagels and left. Ray Havlicek appeared on the screen when we reached ten thousand feet, as Izabel Santo and I drank strong Brazilian coffee. Eddie sipped a Jack Daniel's on ice, despite my warning that he avoid mixing booze with medication.

"I'm glad you're okay," Ray said.

On-screen, Ray sat behind his desk in the FBI building, the top of the Washington Monument outside his window, and the faces in a photo visible on his desk: Ray and fiancée, Chris, the public health expert, with my intern Aya, picnicking at Wolf Trap. It was a staged appeal. *He's suggesting that we're all friends. And telling us that if his career suffers, then these other people, who I care about — Ray's future family — might, too.*

"Everyone here is proud of you," Ray said.

"Don't go there," I said.

"I know you're angry, Joe." Ray looked fit in his gray suit and striped tie, his expression neutral. He'd always been an enigma to me: friendly on the surface, but holding things back. He was competent and ambitious, politically shrewd and professionally effective. He was capable of confusing national goals with personal ones, but so is everyone, I guess. If he resented the fact that his fiancée had preferred me over him once, he'd never mentioned it. He knew that his professional fate was in our hands. But at the moment this was still his plane, his staffers, his hands on the levers.

"Us? Mad at you?" Eddie said. "Why would we be mad?"

"You need to understand the big picture," said Ray. "In twenty minutes we're going to join the bioterror task force in conference. I can't tell you what to say, but you can be a huge help. What you saw, what you overheard, what you found on that island may be crucial. There's no way I can stop you from saying . . ."

"From saying how you screwed us over?" I suggested.

He sighed. "I won't try to tell you that you were adequately protected down there."

Eddie turned even redder as the plane hit an air pocket. "Even you wouldn't do that, scumbag."

"But before you make the choice, let me give you an overview. We all want the best for our country, Eddie. So I'm suggesting that we keep individual situations out of this for the present. How to overcome the big problem. How to safeguard the public. And keep rival agencies from infighting instead of cooperating during an emergency. We have a structure in place, and given the chance, other people can wreck it. You never know what other people will do. Turn something smooth into a mess."

"Don't listen to this gobbledygook," snapped Eddie. "I do agree with one thing, Ray. You turned things into a mess."

"Keep talking, Ray," I said. I despised his self-serving platitudes. But knew that they were also true.

"I made a mistake, guys. I admit it. I left you in the lurch. But ask yourselves . . . did I err in asking you to go there? *You found the camp.* Did I screw up by pointing out where the camp might be? No. I admit we thought we were looking for an embassy attack. And it turned out to be something else. *But you found it!*"

"This isn't about what we found. It's about trust. If it weren't for Izabel and Nelson, we'd be dead," Eddie said.

"Nelson *is* dead," broke in Izabel, clutching a steaming FBI logo mug of espresso in her hands. There was enough caffeine in there to fuel a SWAT team. Her thin fingers were white on the ceramic, and shook with emotion. They were devoid of rings.

"Yes," Ray said sadly. "Let me welcome Captain Santo to the U.S. I hope you will accept the FBI's condolences, for the loss of your personnel, Captain."

"It was Sublieutenant Salazar's wife and sons' loss."

Ray looked humiliated and ashamed, honest and contrite. But he faced his accusers. He had decided rightly that making threats would be a mistake. He knew he lay on the surgery table, and we stood overhead, looking down at him, judging what to do.

Ray started up again. "You weren't sent to Brazil to look for lost miners, Joe. And you know it."

"Then I guess you think we were lucky, finding that madhouse down there," Eddie snapped.

"That's not what I meant. We've got diplomatic problems with Brazil at the moment, and you know it. We're not supposed to have people there, *and you know it.* I fought for you in Washington, and fought when the Brazilians wanted to lock you away. That I didn't succeed at first doesn't mean I didn't try."

"Call me anytime," Eddie said in a pretty good imitation of Ray. "I'll have your back."

"*I'm sorry.* And there's plenty of time later if you want to get into this. But what happens now if you make a stink? What do you achieve? Maybe I'm out, sure, but maybe I'm not. Maybe you're perceived as getting overly personal. After all, I figured out a way to get eyes in there."

Eddie looked astounded. "You think you did a good job?"

The audacity of this guy!

"I think the only reason we had *anyone* there is me. But let's say Havlicek is out! Who is in? At precisely the moment when we need cooperation between agencies, *in the middle of an attack,* we're sidetracked by hearings and finger-pointing and gridlock. You've seen it before."

Ray shrugged, earnest, the truth-telling farm boy. He was George Washington admitting to cutting down the cherry tree. He said, "It's your call, Joe and Eddie. You're a key part of the work. And you'll stay that

193

way if I'm here and you want in. But if someone else takes over, or if you're perceived as going personal, who knows?"

"Is that a threat?"

"A fact."

"You'll take us off if we say anything?"

"That would be stupid. You're the best I have. You're civilians and you can leave anytime you want. *But the country needs you.* I'm saying if you open a door, you never know what crawls out. I'm asking for a chance to lay out the big picture before we get into the meeting. I know you can't be bought or threatened. Give me five minutes to show you what we are trying to stop."

"Fuck you," said Eddie.

"Okay, explain it," I said, holding back my rage.

He'd had his tech guys make a presentation, maybe to use in meetings. Or maybe he'd had it made just to persuade us. The screen divided in two. A CNN news feed filled the right side, and in it, I saw the President at a podium. On the left, shots of ambulances. Hospital emergency rooms. A New York City mosque.

Izabel whispered, *"Dio!"* Eddie leaned forward, caught his breath.

A banner across the bottom screen said,

Outbreak worsens in three states. The sound was muted since Ray would do the talking, but the President's words streamed out below.

Stay away from standing water. Cooperate with local pesticide crews when they spray. Call tip lines if you notice a concentration of mosquitoes nearby, especially the species shown a moment ago.

Ray said, "The numbers are worse than we're saying."

On the left side, a fast-moving montage. Police guarding a cordoned-off Newark hospital. Masked ambulance attendants rushing a patient on a stretcher from a Philadelphia building. The caption: *Death toll up in Manhattan. Hundreds more ill.*

"It's three times that by now," Ray said.

The President said something about a school holiday, and advised precautions for residents in infected areas. *Remove excess water collecting in cans and old tires. Wear DEET repellents of between 15 percent and 30 percent strength outside. Wear long-sleeved shirts and long trousers. Avoid being out between dusk and dawn, when mosquitoes are most active. Make sure you have screens on your doors and windows.*

"It's spread by a common anopheles mosquito that lives in the millions along the

195

East Coast," Ray said. "We believe we're dealing with intentionally infected insects. Once they pass along the illness, if another mosquito feeds on that victim, it ingests the parasite and becomes a new vector. Which gives us millions more potential carriers."

"Christ." Eddie shuddered. "My family is in Boston."

"It's not there yet."

Eddie looked relieved. "I want to phone them."

"Of course. Captain Santo! The photos and fingerprints that your people sent show that two of the guards you killed were Caliphate. Dr. Sabbir Umar — dental ID confirmed — worked for a French bio-company altering mosquito DNA as a means of controlling insect population. Joe, the blood samples you saved contained parasites matching ones recovered from victims here. And I can tell you that the timing of the outbreak coincides with certain threats received in D.C."

"What threats?"

"You'll hear more in a few moments."

"Threats by whom?" I asked, realizing that we were now talking as if we were part of the investigation, that Ray's appeal was working. The danger was bigger than complaints by Eddie and me about Ray.

Ray said, "That's what we need help figuring out. Your memories could be crucial. I've set up several meetings for you in Washington, over the next few days."

The President was back now. *"Authorities will spray all vehicles, trains, and planes leaving infected cities. If you live in those places, expect long lines at tollbooths, subways, rail stations, and airports. This is for your own good. The origin of the outbreak remains a mystery so far, but we're hopeful of learning more soon."*

Eddie looked puzzled. "A mystery? But you just said there were threats. There's a terrorist link."

"Evidently the President decided to avoid panic."

"You think those scenes on-screen are calm?"

"It's not my call."

"You're sitting on the Brazil connection!"

"Why let the bad guys know what we know? Of course there's been speculation about an attack in the press. You and I don't make policy, just recommendations. We're coming up on the conference call. What you say is up to you."

He was good. He was better than good. He had conveyed a threat without saying it. And the threat was, *Ray* was our friend but anyone else a potential enemy. *He* did not approve of secrets, but policy was out of his hands. *He* had our backs, especially since we could damage him otherwise. If we made a stink, there was no telling what would happen to us since the White House was clamping down on the news.

"You're a master fuck," Eddie said. "You know that?"

"This situation has been difficult for us all."

Eddie turned to me, the message clear in his eyes. *He'll screw us the first chance he gets, Joe. He can't have us walking around, a threat to him. He never liked you. He resents that Chris had a thing for you. He just wants to keep control. Don't listen to him.*

But Ray sat slightly more at ease; just a fraction, as if he thought that Eddie's anger, if vented in private, would not come up in the meeting.

Maybe, I saw reluctantly, Ray had a point.

"What's happening here?" asked Izabel, whose language skills weren't good enough to follow every nuance, but whose antenna for human behavior was just fine.

I told Ray, my stomach throbbing, "Okay, we start from scratch."

"You won't regret it," Ray replied.

■ ■ ■ ■

"Dr. Nakamura, are you sure you heard no references to New York, Newark, or Philadelphia?"

"No."

"At any time, were you given substances to *combat* your malaria? Is it possible that your captors sought an antidote? Or was their sole interest in cultivating your blood, worsening the disease?"

"Worsening the disease."

"Dr. Nakamura, you look exhausted. Need a break?"

"No. But thanks."

The screen now had so many faces on it that it looked like a high school yearbook page. Beside Ray, Dr. Wilbur Gaines, current speaker, headed the Centers for Disease Control and Prevention, in Atlanta. I'd worked with him in bioterror war games and found him calm and thoughtful. He tended to address problems step-by-step, favoring process over intuition. But his instincts were good. Next, Chris Vekey, Ray's fiancée and expert on on-the-ground response to biological threats. She was also our intern Aya's mom, and neither she nor I had ever acknowledged our mutual attraction. Other boxes showed observers from the CIA. White House. Army Med Command at Fort Detrick, Maryland.

"Dr. Nakamura, you said that Dr. Umar bragged that several existing medicines prevent or treat the disease."

"Yes, sir. I believe that I got sick initially because Joe and I took different antimalarials. I'm allergic to Lariam, which apparently works against this strain. The guards were taking Coartem, a fixed-dose combination of artemether and lumefantrine. That combo seems to work. I took Malarone, which doesn't."

"Pharmacies are experiencing a run on medicines," said Gaines, with a grimace. "There's nowhere near enough supply to meet demand, and even if pharma ramps up production, the gap is too big. Every doctor I know is getting calls from patients wanting prescriptions, even in unaffected cities. We had a hijacking on the Ohio Turnpike, shipments bound for New York. The drivers were shot, trucks found empty."

Chris added, "We're not even positive that these drugs work yet. We need time to see. And if they do work," she added in a depressed tone, "they need to be taken every week to be effective. Existing supplies will soon run out."

Exhausted at the meeting's end, we tried to sleep.

Over the Caribbean we breakfasted on microwaved eggs and turkey sausage, crisp wheat toast and cranberry muffins. Eddie ate double portions, trying to regain lost weight. Izabel had two helpings of banana pancakes. The Brazilian coffee was hot and strong. Then Dr. Gaines was back on-screen with Chris and Ray and a slide of an enormous magnified mosquito. With its compound eyes, and long proboscis, it looked alien, something dreamed up by Hollywood.

"She's beautiful, in a deadly way," Gaines sighed.

"You have a funny notion of beauty," Eddie said.

"I have respect. In her case, function *is* beauty," said Gaines. "*Anopheles gambaie* . . . the most delicate of mosquitoes. Legs thin, body lean. Size, no bigger than a contact lens, not like those enormous Asian tigers. Why, you barely see our girl when she's in the air."

Eddie hummed the Miss America tune. "Very romantic."

"Two predominant types of malaria infect humans, as you know," continued Gaines. "*Anopheles* carries both. *Plasmodium vivax* is older, transmitted in both hot and temperate parts of the world. Centuries ago, a huge problem in Europe and North America. But look at these places today, especially southern Europe, and you see interesting genetic changes in humans. They gave people the ability to live with the parasite in their blood. They get sick, but not fatally. So it's logical to assume that if humans had time to adapt, *vivax* malaria is a more ancient version of the sickness."

"Then *vivax* is not what we're facing now," I said.

"Correct."

"What are we dealing with?" Captain Santo asked.

I liked Gaines. He couldn't be ruffled. When he gave a briefing, he included all elements, even ones that might at first seem unconnected. He knew that something peripheral at the beginning of an investigation could be crucial later. He knew that the wrong kind of speed, *impatience,* could kill thousands. Eddie's knee was pumping with frustration. I listened hard. Gaines would get to things his own way.

Gaines said, "*Plasmodium falciparum* is what we face. It is the most deadly form of malaria, and the youngest. Evolutionary biologists believe *falciparum* has only affected humans for about one hundred thousand years. A drop in the bucket, evolution wise. The theory is, *falciparum* originated in apes and jumped to humans. Our DNA is similar enough for that to happen. But the parasite has not decreased its virulence over time. On the contrary, *Plasmodium New York* is killing faster than the usual *falciparum,* and at a greater rate. It is even younger, definitely deadlier."

"So there are two kinds of malaria," Izabel prompted.

"Actually there are many kinds. But the others affect animals. Apes. Birds. Even snakes and rodents. Dr. Umar sought the most virulent human forms."

I asked Gaines, "You're saying that this new *falciparum* has evolved, become even more deadly?"

"Not exactly."

"Mutation, then?"

"Not necessarily."

On-screen now, two mosquitoes, side by side. One labeled NORMAL and the other ACCELERATED.

They looked the same.

I was getting impatient. "Then you're saying that the malaria DNA was altered in that laboratory?"

Gaines shrugged, meaning maybe, and

Eddie snapped, "Then what's left to explain it?"

Gaines gazed out his window, at the CDC complex, containing his own labs where I knew the blood of tristate victims had been under analysis for days. Then he sighed.

"All the sick have algid malaria, the worst kind of *falciparum.* Algid multiplies like wildfire. It infects up to ninety-nine percent of victims' red blood cells. Adult sufferers in New York are dying of kidney failure and respiratory distress. Children . . ." He trailed off. He was trying not to show emotion. It didn't work. Gaines had three young children.

"Children are dying from the cerebral form. Their brains are more susceptible."

"What is different about the new strain?" I asked.

"The speed. Normally algid takes a minimum of seven to eight days between infection and onset. We're seeing something faster, since we've traced many victims to infection point. A concert. A cookout. We know when these people were bitten, and where."

"You're not making sense," I said. "First you tell us that the parasite is the same as always. Then you tell us that it's acting differently. But you shoot down every suggestion of how the parasite changed."

But suddenly I saw the answer to my own question, and it chilled me.

"No," I said, reasoning out loud, "you're telling us that a malaria attack requires *two distinct elements:* the parasite and the mosquito."

Gaines nodded as if a student had given a proper answer. "Yes. Malaria is species specific. Parasite without carrier doesn't work."

"The *mosquito* is different!" I saw. "Umar changed the delivery system! He didn't need to change the parasite. He just collected the flukes, the worst ones. He spread the net in the biggest malaria field on earth, for victims who would have died so fast they never had the opportunity to spread infection. He harvested the top killers. Then he altered the carrier!"

Eddie nodded. "And when I beat it, Umar wanted to know how." He brightened. "Does that mean my blood has an antidote?"

Gaines sighed heavily. "It's more likely that you're just stronger than most people. We'll test your blood for antibodies, but don't count on it. If there was some magical cure in you, Umar would have drained you dry."

Now I saw what looked like ancient hiero-glyphics on-screen, rows of symbols that represented mosquito DNA. But there were gaps between some of the symbols. "Normal anopheles," Gaines said. "And new ones, collected in Central Park."

I looked down from the window at Flori-da's Everglades, the U.S. version of an enormous mosquito breeding ground. Far-ther north would be Okefenokee Swamp, 300,000 acres in Georgia, and the inland waterway, the Cape Fear River in Norh Carolina, a cornucopia of Virginia, Mary-land, and Delaware rivers, harbors, and ponds, mosquito-friendly waters all the way up the East Coast.

But it was worse. Eddie and I had just spent weeks advising impoverished Amazon slum dwellers on tactics to defeat malaria, and what needed to be done here was no different. New York contained a million bodies of standing water in which insects could breed. Water in flowerpots. Water in stagnant swimming pools and old sewage drains and clogged roof gutters.

Gaines waited like a teacher eyeing a favorite student.

"But how did Umar change the mos-quito?" I asked.

"He sped up the metabolism, Joe."

Izabel asked, "How does that make the illness worse?"

"Malaria 101, Captain. The only way to get the parasite *into* a mosquito is through a blood meal. The parasite enters while a mosquito feeds on an infected person, through the proboscis, the needlelike probe it uses to suck up blood. But the only way to transmit the parasite *out* of the mosquito is through its salivary glands. And to reach those glands, the parasite migrates through the mosquito, into its stomach, then back up to the glands. Only after that, when the mosquito bites a new person, and injects saliva, does the parasite ride in."

"And this takes time?" asked Izabel.

"Normally two weeks. Hot weather, it's quicker. Cold, it's so slow that the mosquito dies of old age before the parasite ever reaches the salivary glands. That's why people don't catch malaria in cold countries, or in winter. The process is too slow. Usually."

"But now?"

A head shake. "The transition seems to be taking as little as two days. Not eight."

Horrified, I saw the implications. "So if our terrorists in the U.S. have a supply of altered mosquitoes . . ."

"And if they feed them blood meals infected with parasites," Eddie continued.

"And if the supply of altered insects is *big* enough, or they get new shipments . . ." added Izabel Santo.

Gaines looked miserable. "Then you're looking at the biggest mass murderer in history, because he can release a new batch every few days," he said.

I was thinking, *There's something I may have missed here. Something that Eddie told me. Something on the island. What am I missing?*

"It gets worse," Gaines said, which pulled my attention back to him.

"Christ, what's left?" Eddie asked.

"All the attacked cities sprayed pesticides after the initial outbreak, but still, we found some infected mosquitoes afterward, *alive.* They're resisting chemicals. Just like in Africa and South America. *It's harder to kill them.* Pesticide resistance has been growing for years."

"Super parasite meets super bug," said Eddie.

"*Dio!*" said Izabel. "You must spray and spray more!"

"We are," Chris said, "but sprays lose strength with sunlight and time. Just twenty-four hours after you spray, the chemicals begin breaking down. Plus, we've only got a limited supply of pesticide, you under-stand."

"So even if you spray widely . . . ."

"The only way we stop this for sure is to catch whoever is spreading it."

"Meanwhile, every day the death toll will rise."

In the heavy silence, Gaines's eyes shifted left, and I saw that on-screen all eyes were also swiveling. Ray's tech staff must have put through the appropriate relays. Our on-screen boxes shrank to make room for a new one, *live TV*. The President was back, in the White House briefing room.

BREAKING NEWS. TERRORIST CAMP DESTROYED.

Eddie gasped a moment later. "Hey! That's us, Uno!"

It was us, all right, in a shot taken over a year ago, at the awards ceremony at the White House. A happier occasion, as the Chief Exec handed me a Presidential Medal of Freedom. Eddie and Aya received them on that day, too, for our role in the Harlan Maas case.

The President was saying, "A joint raid by U.S. agents and our Brazilian allies de-stroyed the terrorist camp and laboratory in the jungle. It is now clear that the outbreak here of this new, fatal malaria came from that lab."

"Guess they couldn't cover it up anymore," Eddie said.

"Your 'ally' wants to hear. Be quiet," growled Izabel.

The President said, as a shot of Eddie and me in our old Marine fatigues appeared, "Two former Marine officers — working closely with the FBI — coordinated the assault."

Izabel guffawed. Ray seemed frozen.

The President said, "We will build on this success. We will hunt down and destroy any person or group behind this heinous attack. And although we are confident that we have eliminated ninety-nine percent of the enemy supply, it remains possible that a few deranged jihadists are still in the U.S. The national terrorism alert remains at red. I'm asking all federal, state, and local agencies to cooperate in the hunt for those responsible. This cowardly assault on American freedoms will not stand!"

"Working with the FBI?" said Eddie. "So *that's* what we were doing down there!"

The President said, "Colonel Rush and his team are at this moment returning to the country to remain an active part of the investigation, headed by the FBI. This group has all my confidence. They will help bring a swift, successful conclusion to this emergency."

Ray's expression was priceless. He was the one ambushed for a change. By elevating Eddie and me onto national radar, the President had just robbed Ray of his cherished control. Ray would stay in charge of the work. *But not of us.*

Eddie looked torn between anger that, as usual, we'd not been consulted before an announcement, and glee that Ray was pissed off. A power shift had just happened.

"*You* are that important?" Izabel said, staring at me.

I knew that like Presidents Clinton and Reagan, our current leader was famed for his off-the-cuff decisions. Late-night TV comedians sometimes showed diagrams labeled PRESIDENT'S BRAIN, presenting new ideas as just-formed balloons in his cerebellum, and shooting out of his mouth at the same time. Gaines looked surprised but pleased.

"*Colonel Rush is at this moment on his way to Washington, for consultation,*" the President said as Eddie scribbled a note to me.

Izabel said shrewdly, "Ah! Now I see! He makes you a scapegoat if things go wrong! Just like back home."

Eddie smirked. "Hey, Ray, Joe likes his coffee black with sugar. You better stay on his good side."

Izabel remarked, "What is the expression? Out of the frying pan, into the microwave oven?"

"Something like that."

I watched Ray's face. It was completely neutral again. I told Ray that instead of going to Washington, my "team" preferred to head straight into the heart of the outbreak, New York City. Now.

"Joe, I understand that you feel that way, but a lot of important people want to meet with you."

And you want to keep them happy, and me away from the investigation, telling the same story again and again.

"New York, Ray."

He smiled. He had to be seething inside. He listed the VIPs who I was supposed to be sidelined with, talking to. "White House. Senate Committee on Bioterror. Your story needs to be told so —"

So you get credit, which is fine if you end this thing. But you made mistakes in Brazil, and you could make more.

I told him, firmly, "We'll set up shop at Columbia University. We've got Wilderness Med there already, a whole unit trained in work in austere environments. Let us do what we're good at: tracking disease to a source."

"Not Aya," Chris broke in. "I brought her back to Washington. I won't have her in the middle of an outbreak. She's sixteen. I don't care if some medicines work. She's out."

"Of course. I didn't mean Aya," I said, backpedaling and knowing to never get between a protective mom and her teenage daughter. "Aya can help out over the phone, on her computer. From a safe distance."

"That is what I told her," Chris said, steel in her voice. "That is what *you* will tell her, too."

Stalemate. Ray saw I would not budge, and that further resistance would demean him. "I suppose," he offered, trying to limit damage, "we can fold you into one of our local groups. That might work."

"We stay on our own," Eddie growled.

Ray had to be agonizingly aware that Chris was watching. And not supporting him. *She's staring down at her desk, as if embarrassed for him, or disagreeing with him.*

And then it hit me. Someone must have gone to the President in order for pressure to be applied to get Eddie and me out of Brazil. Ray didn't have the clout. Or inclination. But I remembered now that Aya had told me when Eddie first disappeared that she was going to ask Chris for help. Ray's future adoptive daughter and his fiancée may have teamed up to torpedo him, and he probably knew it. Chris had direct access to the White House.

Eddie's eyes met mine. He saw it, too. *Aya? Go girl!*

Chris was tough and smart and had never let the frustrating history between us interfere with her professional judgment. Had Ray and Chris argued over us? Chris was hot-tempered. If she discovered that Ray had sent us down there and not backed us up, she would have been furious enough, if she thought we were in peril, to go over her fiancé's head.

If that's the case, there will be fireworks in your house tonight, Ray. Blood on the walls.

Ray made one last try to keep me out. "Joe, you know as well as I do that good communication is the cornerstone of any investigation. You can be an invaluable liaison with . . ."

"It's personal," I snapped.

"Yes, *personal*," Izabel Santo underlined, half out of her chair, staring into the screen as if into Ray's eyes.

The word *personal* hung there. To anyone else present, it seemed as if we meant that

214

we had a personal grudge against whoever had hurt Eddie and Sublieutenant Salazar. But Ray knew that *personal* included the threat to break my unspoken agreement to protect him. *Stick me in meetings at your own peril! Who knows what I might say?*

"I guess we could accommodate you two," he capitulated.

"Us *three,*" Izabel said.

"Of course. Our Brazilian guest is welcome."

Izabel Santo was regarding me for the first time with something like approval.

Then the President was gone and Ray steered the talk back to logistics as if the argument had never happened.

Eddie passed me a note. *RAY WILL SCREW US WHEN HE GETS THE CHANCE!*

Two hours later, when New York came into view, Ray was back, telling us smoothly, *too smoothly,* as things would turn out, that he'd arranged exactly what I'd asked for, my own unit. But we were only half listening, because even from the air, the view made it clear that something was wrong.

"Panic," Eddie breathed, eyeing rivers of brake lights crawling one way, at midday. Lanes heading into the city seemed empty. "Looks like half the city is trying to get out."

I was thinking that I was looking at the newest place on earth to serve as a field for Wilderness Medicine. New York has been called a jungle, and medically speaking, it was now that. In the real jungle lived creatures who spent their entire lives in the upper canopy, *like the rich in New York,* who would be the best protected. The less fortunate people here ate and slept on the streets, and, as in the Amazon, bottom dwellers would be more at risk. There were those in the middle, who ventured up and down, crossed boundaries each day: subways, offices, shops. And among them, maybe in New York, maybe in Newark or Philadelphia, or nearby, a speck, anonymous, a person or group hurting them.

Down there somewhere is the vector, I thought.

I did not mean mosquitoes.

I meant whoever was spreading them.

We will find you, I thought.

FIFTEEN

FIVE DAYS LATER

DEATH TOLL RISES IN
TERRORIST OUTBREAK

The New York Times
The death toll from black malaria, as health officials have dubbed it, has topped 1,800 with another 3,211 in serious condition in area hospitals. Most are expected to die. Panic has spread in the metropolitan area and surrounding states. Parks are empty. Thousands have fled. Children are being kept at home. "There's no way to know from looking which mosquito is harmless and which might kill you," admitted Dr. Wilbur Gaines of the CDC. Officials urge calm, and although so far only 12 cases have been reported outside of New York, Philadelphia, or Newark: "There's no way of knowing whether our aggressive

217

spraying and public health program will kill all the infected insects, or whether more will be released," Gaines told the White House yesterday at a private meeting. Customs officials are paying extra attention to shipments coming into the U.S. from Brazil. "But unless the parties responsible are located, we must regard every day as one in which a new attack may come," Gaines said. "At least, thanks to Joe Rush, we closed down the lab where these new, hideous weapons were created."

Tom Fargo caught sight of Joe Rush on TV while climbing from the subway, at 7th and Flatbush Avenue in Brooklyn's Park Slope. His belly tightened with rage. The "hero of Brazil," as reporters called him, was on a newsstand TV, being interviewed at Columbia University, where he led a special unit working with the ill, the adoring NBC correspondent said.

If not for you, Washington would have no idea what is happening. My shipment wouldn't be held up. But I am stuck here, unable to finish the job until the boxes arrive.

"I'll deliver them to your shop by two this afternoon," his freight carrier, Singh, had promised.

It was now one o'clock. Sixty minutes to go.

Tom had gotten Singh's phone call in his darkroom, as he stared at a road map on which he'd circled the next targets. Even Dr. Cardozo didn't realize Tom's true reasons for choosing them. Cardozo just cared about heightening panic. One target was as good as another to him.

All Tom had to do was load up the Subaru and drive off, *once the shipment came.* Main roads were guarded, but small ones were carrying escapees out of New York. Thanks to the new GETOUT app on his iPhone, he could instantly access clear routes. In America everything was for sale under the notion of so-called personal freedom. Freedom to buy AK-47s. Or encrypt phones so the FBI could not listen in. Freedom to post the locations of unguarded roads.

But I need those boxes! The adults can survive fifteen days in those containers, the larvae up to ten.

His shipper had said, "Customs is going through everything from Brazil. Aircraft engines. Wood. Coffee. The warehouse is crawling with agents."

Four thousand more vectors. But if they sit in the warehouse much longer, they will perish.

219

"Mr. Fargo, if we're late, sit tight," Singh had said.

Is it a trick? Is he working with the FBI? Have they found something? Do they know it is me?

Tom strolled along 7th Avenue, watching for anyone following, eyeing him from a window or parked car. His reflection in a locked leather goods shop window showed a calm man. He was not that at all.

Still, all around him, success. The street was almost empty. Windows in apartments were locked or screened. Tom passed an elementary school, normally open for summer school, closed; the twenty-four-hour-a-day Greek diner, closed. A couple walking toward him wore mesh masks even during the day. A Humvee filled with National Guard rolled past the Duane Reade pharmacy, open, but signs in windows read: OUT OF ANTIMALARIAL MEDICINE. NO INSECT REPELLENT OR MOSQUITO COILS. TRY HARDWARE STORE! Beside that, graffiti in white paint: KILL MUSLIMS! NO IMMIGRANTS!

It would only get worse, he knew.

Forty minutes left.

The White House has not disclosed my demand to the public. Maybe they're consider-

ing it, just like that fool Hobart Haines taught me.

He flashed to the old blowhard, bragging at the dinner table, bragging on drives in Colorado, in the house, or at a restaurant, a sixty-year-old mouth with legs, lecturing. *People think making deals is dirty! But we got the hostages out! We gave Iran a few guns — so what? Pressure in the right place achieves what armies cannot do. When to negotiate! When to give in! That's the question!*

Tom detoured into a fenced-in parking lot near 6th Avenue and 3rd Street. The Subaru occupied the last slot on the left. He waved at the guard booth and made sure the car started. The door panels were firmly closed, no hint of the hidden compartment beneath. In the trunk were camping supplies, disguises, a med kit, cash, golf clubs, dried food, and a clean, new MasterCard in another name.

Hobart Haines, in Tom's head, droned on. *Presidents say they will not make deals with enemies, but they do. Kennedy faced down the Russians during the Cuban Missile Crisis. But behind the scenes he pulled U.S. missiles from Turkey. Nixon said he'd never talk to North Vietnam. He sent a rep there at the same time.*

Back on the street, Tom headed for the

gallery. Every trip there was risky. The tiny shop was the vulnerable intersection point where shipments were delivered.

Thirty minutes to go until Singh arrived.

Walking, Tom saw with satisfaction that many parking spaces were open because residents had fled. Dog parks were empty. Subways ran on weekend schedules during the emergency, because many transit workers from other states refused to come in. Most pedestrians wore long-sleeved protective clothing. Tom's ball cap dropped a cloth over the back of his neck to ward off insects. He'd smeared on DEET, to smell like other people. It was easy to tell who had access to medicines, because they moved with more New York assertiveness: fast and busy. Everyone else slinking around. Some people smelled of homemade mosquito repellents flourishing on the Internet. Lavender and vanilla mix. Witch hazel and ground apples. Alleged natural safeguards that were useless.

Notices in shop windows read:

— SORRY! ALL GRISTEDES SUPER-MARKETS CLOSED.

— KNOW YOUR MOSQUITOES. LEARN TO TELL HARMLESS ONES FROM DANGEROUS . . .

— KEEP CHILDREN INSIDE AT DAWN AND DUSK.

He arrived at the folk art shop to find no FBI here. So far, so good. *If they come, I will take many of them with me,* he thought, fishing for the key, unrolling the steel grate.

Two P.M. no shipper showed up.

He called Singh, but got no answer. Probably the shipper was just running late. That was all.

Tom sat and tried to stay calm behind the cash register, surrounded by pottery, blowguns, paintings; plundered art from poor people the world over that his mother had made a fortune selling over the years, in her chain of shops around the U.S. At his back, leering war masks, mahogany boxes carved with gods of sickness or fertility. Whole cultures for sale. History for $20. Gods and devils arrayed like candy.

He turned on the TV, where Joe Rush was on television again, still at Columbia University, where his special unit was headquartered. The reporters never stopped going there. Like Rush was some sort of protective god.

"How did it feel to destroy a terrorist lab?" the journalist asked.

Everything had changed because of Rush.

Only days ago there were thousands of insects awaiting transport from Brazil. Total ignorance in Washington. And then, *because of Rush,* one of those flukes happened upon which history can turn, as Hobart used to say. The Spanish Armada runs into a storm and thus ends an empire. The chauffeur driving Austrian Archduke Ferdinand makes a wrong turn, backs up to change direction, and stops in front of an assassin. World War One begins as a result.

And now the accidental discovery of a lab in the jungle threatened Tom's plan.

Singh the shipper was ninety minutes late. Tom told himself that in New York, everything runs late even normally. The Verizon repairman doesn't show up. The subway halts between stops. The Governor of New Jersey shuts down the George Washington Bridge to take vengeance on a rival. Tom looked up to see taunting news footage from the Amazon, another sickening replay showing the martyrs in New Extrema, bodies in the jungle, because of Rush.

I'd like to just go up to 116th Street and wait for him to come out onto Broadway and kill him, he thought as his cellular rang and his heart leaped with hope that it would be Singh. But caller ID told him it was only Rebeca, trying to reach him for the second time in an hour.

He didn't answer.

The reporter on TV asked Rush, "How did it feel to kill the terrorists?"

I knew those men. I prayed with them. I ate with them and recited poetry with them.

And then suddenly a voice called out, "Hello?" almost at the same time that the front buzzer sounded. *A customer?* Tom spun to see a stranger advancing into the shop. He realized with a sinking feeling that he'd seen the man twice over the last hour, passing outside, once going east, once west.

"You're in trouble, sir," the man said, as his hand disappeared behind his back.

Tom slid open the drawer behind the counter, hidden from the man's sight. Inside lay a Sig Sauer 9mm pistol.

"Trouble?" he asked as the man's hand came back into view.

The ID said NEW YORK STATE DEPART-MENT OF HEALTH. The man was slim, fit, young, clean-cut, like a gym rat or under-cover agent. Military haircut. Shiny black shoes. Lightweight khaki jeans below a neat, tennis-style olive drab shirt. The clipboard meant nothing. The guy could be wired up. The soldiers could be outside, out back, on the roof.

"You're the only shop open on this block," the man said, seemingly more as an observation than accusation.

Tom shrugged good-naturedly. His Sig Sauer lay six inches from his hand. "Gotta make money."

"Not a lot of customers out."

"Tell me about it," Tom groaned.

The astringent smell of DEET rolled off the man. You needed to apply the repellent every eight hours for it to work. It blocked mosquito taste and smell receptors, confused insects, caused them to fly away, not feed.

"Been in this location long?" The brown eyes flicked to a batch of blowguns jutting from a tall vase in a corner. They'd been stocked with insects a month ago, when the last shipment arrived.

Tom's heart seemed to be beating louder than the man's voice. *It's an adrenaline problem, not a fear problem. Maybe he's really who he says he is.*

Tom replied, "We leased the property twenty-five years ago. The neighborhood was worse then, rent low. Then it went sky-high. But we're locked in for another year."

"Did you know that you left a flowerpot in the alley out back, collecting rainwater? Mosquitoes can breed there. Surely you've seen our advisories about that."

Tom felt air come back into the world. His hand moved back an inch in the drawer. "Sorry. I'll empty it right away. Thanks," Tom said.

"That's not all. Your rain gutters are full of leaves. Standing water, sir! You must have seen the notices!"

"I'll clean them right away," Tom said.

The man eyed him distastefully. *Are you making fun of me?* He looked annoyed, but that was good. If he was federal, *annoyed* wouldn't be his telegraphed emotion. Tom watched the guy's hands. He was not wearing an earbud. The man glanced outside, but the street looked empty.

Why isn't he writing a citation?

The inspector, if that's what he really was, began wandering around the shop, peering at displays. His right hand scratched his lower back, and came back, again empty. Tom knew the trick. Do it twice and the quarry relaxes. The third time, bring out the gun.

"Venezuela, huh?" The guy held up a wooden death mask, to be worn at an Amazon funeral. A leering face.

"Orinoco River area," Tom said.

"Go down there a lot? To Venezuela?"

Tom nodded. "On buying trips." He tried

to sound casual. "I guess I'm lucky. I had a supply of malarial medicines already because I take them when I go south."

The man put back the mask and drifted to a large clay urn containing blowguns from Rondônia. The man raised a blowgun and peered inside. He sniffed it. Tom felt the steel of the Sig brush his fingers, in the drawer.

"Ever shoot one of these?" the guy asked.

"No."

"Go to Brazil a lot?" the inspector asked casually.

"Beautiful country." Tom nodded. "Hot."

"Do Indians really use these things? Still?"

"They shoot darts coated with curare, anesthesia, which they extract from a fish. Get hit with one of those darts, it'd paralyze you," Tom replied.

"A fish?" the guy said, looking surprised, and suddenly innocent. "No kidding."

"All kinds of natural poisons down there," Tom said. "Touch a certain frog, you stop breathing. Touch a caterpillar, your heart stops minutes later. Osmosis."

"Lots of malaria there, too," the guy said.

"Tell me about it."

"Ever get it? Malaria?"

The man moved closer, and laid his clipboard on a shelf. Was he freeing up his hands? His eyes flicked outside, to the street. Microphones were so small now that they could be in a shirt button. Hell, a *camera* could be in a button. There was no way to know if the guy was alone.

"I got the symptoms once," Tom said, which was true. He'd been on that island learning how to keep the insects alive, feed them, pack larvae. He'd instructed the guards on what artwork to buy from Indians. Not baskets. They were too permeable. Ceramics. Anything with hard surfaces and space inside.

Tom said, rubbing his intestines, "I got the stomach pain. Joint pain. But I never got really sick." He shrugged. "I had the blood test but the doctors found no parasites. Probably I just had a cold."

The guy put down the blowgun. Then his eyes went up to the TV, muted now, still showing Joe Rush and the Asian guy, Nakamura. Watching them, the inspector oozed hope.

"I remember those two on the news last year, when they ended the outbreak in Washington," the inspector said.

"Real American heroes," Tom said.

Suddenly the man slumped. "I just hope someone figures this thing out. I mean, all us inspectors got antimalarial medicine at the department. But my mom and sisters don't have any. So I shared with them. There's not enough for all of us."

Tom realized that there were no microphones here. No agents. This man was who he said he was.

The guy sagged against a table holding cheap wooden boxes from Ecuador. "Midtown South almost had a riot two days ago at a drugstore on Broadway. A rumor spread that the pharmacist was selling his supply to friends."

"It's bad all over," Tom agreed. "I say bomb those ragheads back to the Stone Age."

"Well, I hope you sell some merchandise today," the inspector said. "And clean your gutters. The forecast is for rain. I'm supposed to give you a citation. But let's just call this visit a warning, okay? I'll be back."

The buzzer sounded when the man left. Tom felt the ball in his chest ease. Rush was gone on the television.

Singh is two hours late!

Someone was coming around the corner. A woman. Tom saw who it was and cursed. *Not now,* he thought as the door opened. He had to get rid of her, but then he saw the blood on her face and his equilibrium fell away. He had no idea why she had such an effect on him. He had no problem killing strangers, but a trickle of blood on her cheek put him into a paroxysm of rage. *She doesn't even wear long clothing against bites, like everyone else. She's dressed normally.* Her coffee-colored legs poked out from beneath white tennis shorts. Her sneakers were pink. She was a child wandering across a battlefield. *Why isn't she home like everyone else?*

Now Tom saw spots of blood on her leg.

"There was a riot in the subway," Rebeca said.

"I was on my way to the citizenship test study group."

"Hold still while I clean out this glass, Rebeca."

"We're going over Civil War history," she said. "Abraham Lincoln against Douglas debate. Slavery."

"This will hurt."

"The subway was half empty. Then it got stuck. The lights went off and we were sitting there. At first it was okay. But in the dark a girl started shouting, 'Something bit me!' Everyone went nuts!"

Tom envisioned riders screaming and banging at the windows, piling up by the door linking cars. It was the sort of thing he wanted to happen. It was what he'd prayed would happen. He just didn't want Rebeca there when it did.

She said, "We were trying to push into the next car, but the people there kept us out. They were afraid that if we came in, so would mosquitoes. Then the train started moving again. The light came on. You know what? It turned out to be a horsefly in there! Not even a mosquito. And then I got to study group and it was canceled."

He looked at her face and tried to control himself. Another blood stain lay directly over the black-and-blue mark, still fading, left from last week. Clearly, she guessed his thoughts.

In a tiny voice, she tried to lie. "It wasn't Greg."

He watched her eyes brim.

"I know you know," she said.

Tom said nothing. *Stay out of this.* She took his silence for condemnation, which it was, but not of her. He thought, *A big American who hurts innocent people. Who thinks he can do anything he wants all over the world. A brute who destroys weaker women and children . . .*

She said, "He's been under pressure. He has bills to pay but he's lost clients. He had a few drinks that night. He's kind and generous when you get to know him."

"It's none of my business," he said.

"He supports kids in Haiti, sends checks every month."

What Tom should have said — he knew — was nothing. What he heard himself say was, "Rebeca, you're smart and pretty. You're kind. You could be with a thousand guys who would treat you better."

She clearly appreciated it, but shook her head, defending Greg. "You don't understand. When I met him I was a cleaning girl at his office. I'd been in the U.S. for two months. I lived with six girls in a tenement. I slept in a bathtub. He *talked* to me. He was the only one who was nice. It was a long time before we were together. He only changed recently."

Because he liked you better when you had no money and slept in a bathtub. He wants to feel big, and if you achieve things he feels small. That's who they are.

"He stuck with me during my bad time, and now I have to stick with him in his," she insisted, chin up, eyes down.

"Yeah, I see that," he said, looking out the window, watching for the damn delivery truck, but suspecting now that it was not going to come today. It had been delayed.

Or stopped by the FBI.

Rebeca was saying, as if from far off, "Sometimes I think he is irritated when I talk to you. He acts like you're a threat to him, and I tell him you're just the friendly guy across the hall."

"That's me," he said. "The friendly guy."

"Oh my God! I'm sorry! I forgot because of the subway! I didn't come here because of that. I came because Greg wants to have the locksmith break into your apartment!"

Tom Fargo stared into her face, stupefied, controlling the stupendous rage coursing inside him with the greatest effort. He could only hope that his face betrayed none of the fury. The emotion froze his intestines and dragged razor blades down his throat. He could not have heard right. He could not imagine his neighbor hiring a locksmith to break into his apartment. This could not be happening.

"Locksmith?"

"He called me an hour ago, angry. He said everyone in the building got the notice that there will be an exterminator in the building today, to spray against mosquitoes. He says everyone has to leave a key with the doorman but you didn't, and the exterminator can only come today. So if you don't open up Greg will have a locksmith do it,

234

and you will have to pay the bill."

"You forgot to tell me this until now?"

"I'm sorry. I was upset because of the subway!"

"He can't do that," Tom said.

"Greg said that in an emergency the co-op board can break into an apartment. You know, for a plumbing leak. Or police issue. It's in the building bylaws."

Did I lock the darkroom? Is there anything outside the darkroom that gives things away?

"The exterminator is in the building now?" he asked. "What is Greg's number?"

She called her boyfriend, and Greg picked up instantly, furious. "This is exactly what pisses me off about renting units to outsiders, Cycle," Greg complained loudly, over the line, as if other people listened in. He was being the building "Captain." The co-op board leader. "You were given a copy of the bylaws when you moved in. You must have seen the notice under your door last night. You were supposed to leave a key with the doorman. The locksmith is here. This is a health issue. We need to get in! We're out of time."

"I'll come home right now, open it up myself."

Greg started lecturing, pompously. "Cycle, this is the difference between a responsible

235

property owner and a temporary renter. You need to pay attention! And obey rules, which are clear." Tom heard Greg, voice slightly fainter, say to someone else, "Eduardo, break in."

"Understand the rules?" Tom repeated, thinking fast.

"That's what I said."

"Like laws about beating up women?"

"Eduardo! Hold up a second, okay?"

The silence on the other end became breathing; Tom saw Rebeca go crimson, and he heard footsteps over the line, as if Greg was walking away from whoever he had been performing for. Sure enough, when the voice came again it was softer.

"What did you say, Cycle?"

"You heard me. Rules? Let's see what the police do with the *rules* when they hear about Rebeca."

Tom Fargo was in an anguish of rage. If Greg busted into the darkroom, he'd see the insects, the breeding pans and equipment, the maps, the prayer mat. It would be over in minutes.

But then Greg said, "How fast can you get here?"

"Oh, I can take a cab. Fifteen minutes."

Silence. Then Greg said, softly, and with hatred, "Eduardo will spray apartment 506 first. Hurry."

Tom Fargo took Rebeca by the elbow and went outside and locked up. There was no way to wait for Singh now. On 6th Avenue, a few unmarked gypsy cabs were usually trolling, drivers charging five times the usual fare during the emergency. Bloodsuckers. As a black Chevy pulled to the curb Tom caught sight of Singh's silvery delivery truck, R.R. SINGH & SONS, TRANSPORT SPECIALISTS, rounding the corner, heading for the shop, which they would find locked.

Rebeca was crying softly, humiliated.

He called Singh from the backseat of the car. No answer. Maybe he could have the boxes delivered to the co-op. He tried again. No answer. He tried five minutes later. Singh's voice mail was full, a brand new recording said.

Unfortunately, we just got a call that our trucks are being recalled to the spray center, and will probably be there all day tomorrow. Your shipments will not be available for at least another day.

Which meant Tom was stuck here. Unbelievable!

He would have to live with a delay.

Handle this emergency. You can do this, Tom Fargo thought. *Just keep your head.*

All because of Joe Rush!

SIXTEEN

Eddie took each death even harder than the rest of us, probably because of what had happened to him in Brazil. We slowly took off our surgical masks. The nurses slumped, and one started crying. The dead girl on the bed was a fifteen-year-old high school track star who had been bitten at home in Riverdale, after leaving her bedroom window open. The insect that killed her was probably still free.

Eddie and I had been on shift at Columbia-Presbyterian Hospital for the past seven hours.

"I told you Ray would screw us over," Eddie grumped.

"He's a good investigator."

"He'll be accessible anytime? Call him on the special number? We haven't gotten through in days. That assistant of his is as helpful as an automated operator."

"He gave us our own unit, Dos."

"As a way of telling us to fuck off," Eddie said, as we waved off reporters in the waiting room. The vultures were counting up each new death, ratcheting up fear. The whole world was waiting for the next attack. The FBI had no new clues, reporters claimed.

It was an hour before I would finally realize what I'd missed noticing in Brazil.

"Ray's revenge," Eddie said as we dressed to leave. "If we're not at the hospital, he buries us in minutiae."

I wanted the med work, but five days after we'd arrived in New York, Ray had sidetracked our investigation the rest of the time with public appearances and paperwork: tax forms for staffers; office requisition forms; reimbursement for expenses; signature required if a federal agency employs a minor, our intern Aya.

"You can still put yourself under another group," Ray had told me when I actually reached him for fifty seconds, days ago.

"That won't work."

"Then when you finish at the hospital, the Mayor requested that you do a few more interviews. People listen to you. There have been attacks on Muslims. Calm 'em down."

"A few interviews? They never stop," Izabel grouched.

Izabel had been assigned a desk overlooking Broadway, but was rarely there; a ghost disappearing into the city, or keeping up with her police contacts in Brazil. Eddie had recovered swiftly. I was glad to have him back. Aya, pulled back to Washington by her mother, worked for me remotely from a cubicle at the FBI.

"I'm monitoring Customs reports coming in from Brazil, like you asked," she'd told me. "There's thousands of them. The agents here treat me like I'm eight years old. The interns are stuck in the basement. The other kids are doing stupid stuff. Getting coffee for agents."

"Aya, did you ever see a movie where a cop acts dumb on purpose, to get information?"

"What does that have to do with this stupid place?"

"And this behavior works for the cop, right?"

"So?"

"So, if people treat you like a kid, play the kid. If they underestimate you, that's a tool. Who cares if other interns have dumb jobs. Keep on those Brazilian shipments. You find things that even trained investigators miss."

Silence. I could almost hear the slow smile spread on her face. Only God knew what

240

she was imagining. Then the imaginary smile was gone as she dove into the next subject.

"That Brazilian policewoman was on the news with you."

"Izabel is a member of our unit. Use her name."

"Do you like her? The interns here say she's hot."

"I like everyone we work with."

"Really? You mean Ray Havlicek, too?"

"I like him. He and I just disagree sometimes."

"Do you like that Brazilian woman better than Mom?"

"We're not having this discussion. Your mother is engaged to Ray. I think you should accept it."

"On ABC you held hands with that Brazilian woman."

"That was during a funeral service for victims. Everyone there held hands. Goodbye, Aya."

Thirty-one minutes before I realized what clue I'd missed on the island, we were in the back of an NYPD unmarked Chevy, being driven to my next talk. The city was too quiet. Spray trucks were not out anymore as pesticides were used up. National Guard troops protected a mosque. Restaurants were closed and parks empty. Many pet owners were not walking their dogs at dawn or dusk anymore, or they paid professional walkers seven times the usual rate.

"Joe, you're a doctor," Ray had soothed. "That's what you do best. Give the talks. You really think I'd let you run around and mess up real investigators? You don't know a subpoena from a suture. You sidelined yourself when you demanded your own private unit. You and your damn ego, Joe. Don't blame me for that."

"Izabel Santo has a hell of a figure," Eddie said, as we headed across town on 96th, made a left on West End and a right on 88th. The Riverside Park area housed some of the Mayor's wealthier supporters. Detective Jamal al-Azawi, our driver/liaison, was a tall, balding man who'd been told to provide any assistance. The NYPD was a good ally, happy to have us there.

"Izabel? Stop it, Eddie. I just went through this with Aya."

"She's an animal, Joe. Up at four A.M., works out two hours a day. Did you see those calf muscles? No wedding ring. No engagement ring. You ought to see the way she eyes you when you're not looking. It's been two years now for you, Uno. A man has physical needs."

"Eating and sleeping."

"Also, notice how she stopped pestering us for a gun?"

I sighed. "She has a gun, Eddie? How the hell did she get it?"

"She's out half the time in the foreign neighborhoods. How the hell do you think she got it?"

He was right, I realized. If she'd stopped asking, she was armed. And who was I to stop her? She'd provided weapons to me in Brazil.

"Where is she today, Dos?"

"Brazilian neighborhoods again. Newark yesterday. Astoria today. Restaurants. Social clubs. Churches. Garages. We're still trying to figure, what connects those three cities? New York, Philly, and Newark?"

"They're close to one another. They're linked by rail lines and multiple highways. I wonder if we've got one group moving around. Not several."

"Izabel's been trying to get her guys back in Brazil to track down that Indian, Cizinio, and ask more questions."

I did not tell Eddie about the talk I'd had with Ray concerning Izabel, and accusations against her back home. I was protective of the person who'd saved Eddie and me.

"There's some concern about Captain Santo," Ray had said.

"Concern?"

"Look, I know she saved your ass down there. But she's a problem for her own people. I checked. Turns out she was assigned to Rondônia after being sent away from the east. She may have been involved with the police death squads."

I'd started. I'd heard a little about these, but Ray knew more. "Death squads?"

"Secret groups that operate in the favelas, the slums, taking out gang members, drug runners. Big scandal there. She's under internal investigation, and so was the officer with her, Salazar, the one who got killed."

But if Ray had sought to make me less sympathetic to Izabel, he'd accomplished the opposite. Because I had done exactly what she was accused of, a couple of years back. There was a man dead in Norway, and another in Russia, because I had murdered them. They kept me up at night sometimes, as a breeze coming through my window in Massachusetts, a silvery slit of moonlight that shouldn't be there at 2 A.M. It's nothing, I'd think. Natural. But deep inside I believed it was them, and I knew that I would hurt them again if I had another chance.

A good friend of mine, the dean of the National Cathedral in Washington, once asked me if I believed in God. When I said I did, she told me, "Well, if you believe in God, then you don't have to play God. What a relief."

"That's an excuse for doing nothing," I'd replied.

And so I'd told Ray, "I don't care what she's done. Izabel was with us when you were four thousand miles away."

"Fair enough. But you're responsible if she screws up. Can't you give her busy work, keep her off somewhere?"

"Is that how you handle people you want frozen out? Give them shitty work?"

I had to hand it to Ray. He stuck to his principles. His voice went low and angry. "Joe, grow up. You're not trained in handling crime scene work. You haven't the slightest idea how easy it is to fuck things up so a perp goes free on a technicality that you never knew existed. You demand autonomy. Pride, Joe! You got your unit because of threats, but you're damn right I keep you three away!"

My reaction upon hearing his accusations against Izabel was curious. Both Eddie and Aya had — in their own way — underlined her as a desirable woman, but it was Ray who put me over the line.

Death squads? Joe Rush, what's the matter with you? You hear that and then you pay more attention to her?

But the answer was easy. I knew which side she served. I'd seen it up close.

I'd been a one-man death squad, too.

When she came back to the office that night I noticed — in a different way — how her rump swayed when she walked, how she seemed to move forward on her toes, with a kind of eagerness, head high, shoulders back, posture superb. Her perfume seemed more interesting, and the way her long, wild, frizzy hair framed her heart-shaped face and made her glow. I felt a surprising stirring — the kind that I thought was dead. I'd not slept with a woman since my fiancée was killed two years ago. I'd not dated anyone, or acted on any slightest interest, if I felt it. I'd turned away Aya's mother. I did not want to be responsible for anyone else getting hurt because of me.

I did not want *soft.*

But that evening I was shocked that something in me had relaxed. I didn't do anything about it. But I knew I felt it.

Go figure, I thought.

"I'll keep an eye on her," I told Ray. I hadn't, though. Izabel would use her lan-

246

guage skills here, and contacts back in Brazil, use them her own way.

Twenty minutes before I saw what I had missed in Brazil, *the clue,* I groaned inwardly, seeing the crowd waiting for Eddie and me outside a Riverside Drive apartment building. The co-op was one of those prewar edifices housing people powerful enough to arrange with city hall for a private speech. Trees lined 89th Street. So did well-kept brownstones and a couple of redbrick apartment buildings. Any pedestrians out were walking toward the corner building where Eddie and I would give our talk.

Another waste of time, I thought, wrongly.

There was an ABC News van outside, antenna up. We pushed our way through the throngs fanning onto the sidewalk and around parked cars. The doorman beamed at us. The lobby was done up in Elizabethan decor: dark wood paneling, marble floor, multi-bulb chandeliers above overstuffed furniture on which sat more elderly residents, clapping, or holding canes. Rows of metal folding chairs held middle-aged and younger people: lawyers, publishing, or Wall Street types, applauding *the heroes of the Amazon* as we made our way to a long folding table by the elevator. I shook hands with the president of the block association. He thanked us for taking time from *fighting the scourge* as my eyes rose above the crowd to the lobby decorations. It took a moment. I felt it coming.

And there it was.

I froze, my tired resentment turning to astonishment.

Eddie sensed it. "One?"

The co-op president was saying, "Colonel Rush and Major Nakamura will tell us how to better protect our loved ones. And give us a heads-up on the latest progress in tracking down those responsible for this heinous attack."

"One, what are you staring at?"

Eddie followed my gaze to the wall decorations. It was all folk art. Early Appalachian style; handmade quilts and paintings showing maple farmers in Vermont making slashes in trees, *like rubber tappers did in Brazil.* Pouring the syrup into tin cups, *as rubber tappers did with latex.* In one cracked oil, a trio of Mohawk Indians smoked pipes as early colonists planted corn, and an ox stood by, its tail swatting insects away. Flies probably.

Maybe mosquitoes.

"Shit," I said, my voice magnified by the microphone.

Eddie covered the mike with his palm. People in the audience laughed uneasily. The condo president stared.

"The artwork!" I said.

"And?"

"Cizinio said the guards were always buying art from the Karitianas. After the lab was set up, Indians were barred from the island but the guards kept buying art!"

"So?"

I looked at the ox's tail in the painting, swatting flies. "You told me they were fanatics, praying ten times a day. Jihadists, Eddie! We saw what they did in Iraq. Churches? Tear 'em down. Statues? Use sledgehammers. And send the pictures over the Net. They destroy other cultures. They don't collect souvenirs. They're five thousand miles from home. So why buy vases? Cizinio said there was even a man there telling them which work to buy."

The audience was getting restless. I held up a finger — *wait a moment, please* — and dug in my pocket, pulled out my cell phone, and pretended that I was receiving an important call. I walked away from the table and microphone. I moved my lips as if talking to the caller, clicked off, and returned to the table, where I announced, "Something just came up. We have to go."

249

Ray was not happy when I actually reached him. "Joe, I thought you said, when you declined to come to Washington, that you'd already told us anything relevant."

"This just came up."

"Maybe it would have come up earlier if you sat down for debriefing. But that was not for you, was it?"

"Why don't we make the best of this new information."

"Customs is already going through everything coming out of that area, including art. So we're covered. I'm more concerned with what else you missed. There's a reason why we have procedures."

"Ray, this could be important."

Ray Havlicek swore under his breath, said something like *could be.* He said he had to go. He'd check out what I'd told him. He clicked off.

SEVENTEEN

"Open the door to your apartment, Cycle," Greg snapped. "Now!"

It was intolerable — Tom Fargo seethed — that the grand plan's fate could come down to this; a pompous neighbor and a bored exterminator, a stupid rule about keys. He fought to appear calm outwardly. There had to be a way to keep these people from fumbling their way into his darkroom. He inserted the silver Medeco into the slot and heard the dead bolt slide open under the eyes of Greg and Greg's mortified girlfriend, Rebeca.

The exterminator needs to leave this building safely. Greg's cleaning lady comes weekly. Was she here yesterday? Or is she coming tomorrow, meaning bodies would be found?

Tom smelled DEET on the exterminator, a big-bellied man in a brown uniform with his name stitched in beige thread on the chest, LOU. Greg's musky cologne was cloying. He wore a lemon-colored V-neck sweater against the AC, white tennis shirt, khaki shorts, loafers, and no socks. The lock clicking open snapped like a 9mm slide being cocked.

If I kill Greg I have to kill the others.

Tom feigned a smile as the door swung open. The late-afternoon light was lovely, the enhanced crimson that comes from sunlight steeped in pollution. In slanting beams, dust motes floated, a fly buzzed. Thankfully Tom always kept his Koran, prayer mat, and DVD sermons in the darkroom.

All I need is a day, to receive the airport shipment. Once that happens Tom Fargo disappears.

"I'm off at five," Lou said, pumping spray along the living room baseboard. The pesticide canister hissed, and the acrid odor filled Tom's nostrils. It was four fifty-one, only nine minutes before the guy could quit.

I never thought when I didn't give the doorman an extra key that anyone might actually break into my apartment.

Greg had looked furious when Tom and Rebeca arrived in the taxi; Rebeca remained subdued, fearing an even greater explosion. Now Lou disappeared into the bedroom as Greg muttered, "I warned the board to ban rentals to strangers."

"Oh, no harm done," Tom remarked.

Greg was working himself up.

The exterminator moved into the bathroom, and Tom heard cabinets opening. Greg spun on Rebeca, index finger wagging. He was clearly talking to Tom, not his girlfriend. "The board needs to stop sublets! I'm putting it on the agenda next month!"

The exterminator will reach the darkroom in a minute. What would a real New Yorker do to stop him? What is acceptable behavior here?

Tom pushed away fear and considered how people treated one another in this belligerent metropolis. They shouted, cursed, and argued; in taxicabs, subways, shops, bars. Their impotent threats reminded him of the little Amazon anteater, a two-foot-high creature puffing its chest up and hissing to keep enemies at bay, all bluff.

Greg turned on Tom. "You're not supposed to change a lock without the owner's permission. Didn't you read the co-op rules you were given? They're written out, plain as day."

"I will after this. Sorry."

The steel tap on Greg's right shoe drummed an angry cadence on the concrete floor. Sunlight reddened Greg's scowl. It was clear to Tom that his neighbor had not forgotten being humiliated earlier. Tom's threat to call the police — tell them about Greg hitting Rebeca — had worked when there were only two of them talking. But Greg's need to look important might not withstand more embarrassment, especially in front of his girl.

As the exterminator tried the knob of the darkroom, Tom felt a fist clench inside his stomach.

"Uh, this is locked," Lou said.

"Oh, that's just a darkroom," Tom remarked. "No need to go in there."

"I'm supposed to spray the whole apartment."

"It's sealed. I'm really not comfortable with how that stuff you're spraying might interact with my chemicals. Why don't you just go? It's five o'clock. You look beat, Lou. I bet you had a long day."

Tom heard Greg's breathing change beside him, go quicker. The man seemed to pull himself up. "You asked us to wait for you and we did," he sputtered. "You said you'd open up."

"Well, I did that, didn't I? Believe me. There's no insects in there," Tom said. "Let the poor guy go home."

Lou chuckled instead of being appreciative. "You sound like Mrs. Vanderfield in

9A. *This apartment is clean!* Then I go in the bathroom. Man! Roach city! Like, gimme a break!"

"Open it, Tom," Greg said in a low voice.

"I'd rather not." Tom had no choice. Belligerence was the only option left. "I paid for this place. It's mine until Zhang comes back." He folded his arms.

Greg stepped back, astounded at the tone, and, in turn, on his face, Tom saw anger and rage. It was now clear to Greg that Tom had never intended to cooperate. Rebeca looked from man to man, sensing explosion. Lou just checked his watch and sighed.

"Either open it or I go, guys," Lou said.

Greg was unaccustomed to being challenged, in his precious job as co-op board "Captain," at his firm, or in his home. He demanded of Tom, "What do you have in there anyway?"

Tom jutted his face forward, so his breath would hit Greg's nose. Bullies respond to threat. Outrage was acceptable in New York, original home of resentment. *All I need is another day.*

Tom mimicked Greg's tone. "What's in there? Who the hell are you? None of your goddamn business. I don't owe you explanations. This is my apartment as long as I pay."

"You can't talk to me like that."

255

Tom met the glare full on. "Go to a movie or something. Cool out."

Greg's eyes narrowed and his chin thrust forward, like Mussolini's. He was quivering. "You're no photographer. I never see you with a camera. What the hell are you doing in that darkroom anyway?"

Lou held up his hands, backing away from the group. "Whoa! I'm not getting in the middle of this. I'm outta here."

Greg spun on the man, going shrill. "You're supposed to spray all the apartments! We paid for that! I'll call your boss! You don't just walk off a job during an emergency!"

Lou made a face, *yeah, yeah, you're tough . . .* and turned to Tom, both palms up in sympathy. *You have to deal with this asshole? I feel sorry for you.* Lou told them, "On 9/11 I quit at five. The day the Martians attack I'll quit at five. And my *boss* is my cousin Bernardo. So good luck."

Let it go, Greg, Tom thought. *Turn around. Walk into your apartment. Shut the door. Save your life.*

And then, after a tense moment, he saw that it was going to happen. He saw Greg catch himself, go still, probably trapped by his bottom-line problem, that Tom had threatened to tell the police he hit Rebeca.

Did he want everyone in the building to know that? The cops? Greg squeezed his eyes shut. He was digesting shame. He rocked back and forth on his heels. When the eyes opened the combat was gone, replaced by an impotent hatred.

It's going to work. He's going to turn around. He'll probably take it out on her. But that's her problem.

But then — just at the wrong moment — Rebeca spoke up, trying to make things better. "It's just one room, honey. Don't make a big deal out of it, Greg."

Tom sighed. It was over.

Lou was gone; probably by now the exterminator had reached the lobby. The three of them were alone. Greg stared into Rebeca's face and his posture straightened. Tom felt a slow drumbeat of inevitability. He felt as if he watched the scene from the future, and time was catching up to what he knew he must do.

Greg demanded, "What's in that room anyway?"

"I told you. I take pictures."

"Pictures my ass. Is it drugs?"

Tom shook his head with an exaggerated grin, as if to dramatize the absurdity of the suggestion, "Sure, Greg. I stashed drugs there. Fifty tons of cocaine."

Greg smiled thinly, on the hunt now. "Porno? Naked kids on the walls? I never see you with women. Or even guys. Or anyone, actually, except my girlfriend." He ignored Rebeca's restraining hand on his arm. He stepped closer, so that his handsome jaw seemed to hang an inch from Tom's face. Tom smelled tuna fish on his breath. Greg said, "I warned the board what would happen if we let strangers stay here, like we're some cheap Airbnb."

Tom Fargo felt a deep calm take hold.

Rebeca managed to draw Greg away, took him by the arm, and practically pulled him into their apartment. Greg looked back with malevolence and calculation as the door shut. Tom sighed, then slammed his door as if he, too, had retired to his residence. But he stayed in the foyer, listening to the arguing behind Greg's door. He was familiar with the buildup from rage to action. He'd seen it too many times. The language was different here, but the outcome would be the same.

Greg's voice said, "What's he doing in there anyway? What's so secret in that room, Rebeca?"

"It's about privacy. That's all."

"What is it between you and Cycle?"

"Nothing. I keep telling you that."

"You defend him all the time."

"He's my friend, honey. He has a right to privacy. They even teach that in citizenship class, in America! The right to privacy!"

"You're pathetic." Tom heard a sudden scrape of a table pushed across a floor, and had a sickening vision of a big man shoving a small woman into it. Greg's bully voice was drenched with disdain. "You meet someone for ten minutes and suddenly they're your best friend. You don't know this guy! He works in a shitty souvenir shop, so how could he pay cash to rent that unit? I ought to call Zhang overseas and tell him what his damn tenant is up to."

"Greg, don't make it worse. Please."

Slap!

Tom heard quiet crying behind the door. The sketches on the foyer walls, the be-wigged British barristers, were caught up in their own cases.

Greg was saying, "I ought to call the police! Call 911. Then we'll find out what's in there, all right."

The crying got louder. Tom sighed.

Greg said, "Did you hear what he said to me? How he talked to me? I think he was going to get violent."

"Honey, he wouldn't do that. And you're too *nice* to call the police." She had a tal-

259

ent. She really did. She somehow always said the wrong thing at the wrong time.

"Don't tell me who I am!" Greg said.

"I didn't mean it that way. I know you make up your own mind. I'm just saying . . . Oh, Greg . . . please . . . please don't . . . I'm sorry. I won't talk to him anymore!"

Greg suddenly sounded slightly mollified. Now that someone was hurt, his needs had been soothed. "I didn't mean to get mad at you, babe. I've been working hard and we lost that client. And then Cycle goes and lies and the police really need to . . ." he was saying as Tom turned away, opened the door of his apartment.

The heavy darkroom door swung open. The 9mm lay in the third drawer from the top, the silencer beside it. He stood staring down at it. He liked Rebeca. He really did. She was like a sister.

Tom Fargo quickly walked back across the living room, the heat of the setting sun on the side of his face. The roadways of the Brooklyn Bridge were almost deserted out there. The cold gazes of the British barristers on the foyer walls watched him rapping on Greg's door. He heard approaching footsteps. From the heavy tread he knew it was Greg, and Greg would know, since no doorman had called up to say he had an outside visitor, that Tom was at the door. Maybe Greg thought that Tom was back to apologize. Greg's ego was big enough for that to be true.

Tom kept the gun at thigh level in case Greg looked into his peephole. But Greg just swung open the door. Tom looked into a face that had probably always reflected the certainty that the world owed it things.

"Now what?" Greg said.

Tom shot him in the head — *spppppt* — and Greg fell to the side, flailing, a look of astonishment beginning to reach his eyes but never making it. The big body crumpled into a glass table, knocking a framed photo of Greg and Rebeca — happy nightclub scene — onto his thick pile. Gray ooze pumped from the black, round wound.

Rebeca was not in sight. She was probably in the bedroom, crying, or the bathroom, treating the latest bruise. Tom called out, "Rebeca?" He walked into the rear of the loft. She was not in the bedroom. She was in the bathroom, the door open, and he saw two Rebecas when he stopped outside. The face in the mirror. And the back of the head in front of it. She'd been applying a wet rag to her cheek. To the most recent blow.

She looked confused, making eye contact

with him in the vanity mirror. And embarrassed. "What's the matter?"

He shot her in the head, too, as she was starting to turn.

He never should have befriended her. He never should have done it. The calendar affixed to Greg's refrigerator told him that the cleaning lady had last come five days ago. Rebeca's office was closed during the outbreak. Greg often worked from home. With luck days might go by before anyone found out the pair were dead.

Tom dragged the bodies into the bedroom. He stuffed a rag over the crack in the door when he left. That way, when the bodies started to smell, it would take longer for the odor to reach the foyer. He turned the air-conditioning lower all over the apartment. Cold would slow decay.

I had no choice. I'm sorry, Rebeca.

Tom cleaned his prints off surfaces he'd touched and went back to his darkroom. He systematically cleaned away all traces of the insects. The pans and equipment and the smashed, incriminating laptop went into a black garbage bag. He used Clorox wipes to eliminate any chemical traces. He worked diligently, attentive to detail. Two hours later, he used a rear hallway fire exit to take the bag to the basement, and out the side entrance of the building. There were no security cameras down here, and no one saw him exit onto the street.

Anyone opening the bag — a cop, a bum, a garbage man — would find nothing useful or incriminating. On the street, trash was being collected with extra zeal during the emergency, to keep water from backing up.

Tom went back upstairs, smiling at the doorman as if nothing bad had happened. He double-checked his apartment to make sure all traces of illegal activity had been erased. As he worked, he thought back to the old man in Colorado, to Hobart's nonstop lectures. A voice in his head said, *Deception is a key to success. Always make the other guy think you are doing one thing, when you are actually up to something else. In World War Two, the Allies built an entire phony army out of plywood, in England, to make the Germans think that the invasion of Europe would come at Calais. When the invasion came at Normandy, the Germans were not ready and lost the war.*

Tom used one of the half dozen remaining encrypted phones to call Cardozo in Brazil. Once again their talk, on the surface, was mundane, about a sick aunt in Oregon. But *Oregon* was the code word.

Oregon meant, *It's time to divert the FBI*

away from the East Coast.

As he worked, the words of Hobart Haines came to him, guiding him, but not in the way that Hobart had intended.

Make the other side think you are bigger, stronger, smarter than you really are.

Tom knew that someone in Brazil should now be alerting a sleeper somewhere in the United States. Tom would not know where, or who, only that the sleeper was far from New York. The sleeper might be a student, or housewife, or any sympathizer. The sleeper would be directed to make a phone call to Washington, get a message to Kyle Utley, and say words that Tom had written, but the sleeper would not know why. The sleeper could not damage Tom, even if apprehended. He or she was completely expendable.

The diversion will hopefully give me more time.

It was 9 P.M. now.

He was helpless until he got the damn boxes! Maybe they would come tomorrow.

Hobart Haines had said, over and over, *If you're going to do something big, try to make your opponent think you are planning something else.*

EIGHTEEN

Izabel Santo knelt and lit another candle, and the flame flickered to life. Saint John the Divine — near Columbia University — is one of my favorite cathedrals in the world. The ceiling is high and magnificent, a Notre Dame in New York. The stone buttresses anchoring the nave stand as thick as California redwoods. The soaring ceiling inspires and awes. The vast interior and events held there — solstice celebrations, New Year's concerts, student weddings, or Senatorial speeches — offer up the best spirit of a diverse city, and draw people from all religions. Saint John is an inclusive place.

Tonight it was filled with people praying for sick loved ones, or protection for those so far spared.

"Twenty candles," I counted as she rose and crossed herself. I hoped they did not represent lost love, but who else do you light candles for, if not those who you miss?

"They are for men and women that I killed, Joe."

I must have looked surprised. She said, in a flat voice, "They were evil. Their souls are not in heaven. When they see the flames they are attracted to a church where God reminds them of what they did, what they lost."

"You don't think evil people go to hell?"

"What is being lost forever if not that?"

At 10 P.M. we had stopped in while strolling from office to dinner. A seedy-looking man on the front steps had tried to sell us "fresh malaria medicine," then backed away when he saw my face. Eddie had gone back to Stuart's apartment, to sleep, he said, but I think he just wanted Izabel and me to be alone. Eddie the matchmaker. Saint John dominates a hilly area on Manhattan's Upper West Side where, back on Amsterdam Avenue, we passed the cathedral's Alice in Wonderland sculpture garden, and bronzes of Alice and the Mad Hatter, eternally watching each other, eternally healthy. A convertible BMW pulled up beside us, filled with laughing young people, blasting music. Many of those who had malaria pills were as oblivious to fear as tourists in a malarial country. They went on with life.

Izabel's frizzy hair fell against her bare

shoulders, in an inverted V of coppery waves. Her eyes were a burnished dark green that highlighted the mocha skin and single gold-link necklace around her slender throat. She wore a black top with spaghetti straps, fitted white jeans, and cork-heeled sandals with rainbow straps at the toes. She carried a lightweight cashmere sweater against air-conditioning. She smelled of musk.

Her nearness created a fluid weakness in my groin, a stirring in my chest. It was not a romantic feeling. It was more of an animal waking up after a long sleep. Over two years had passed since I had chosen to be alone. This all felt quite strange.

"It is good to take a few hours off," she said as we strolled beneath hundred-year-old oaks. A blinking airplane, high above, moved west over the metropolis. It would have been sprayed with pesticides between trips.

"Look, Joe." She held out her wrist. Beneath the mosquito that had landed on it, I saw the small pulsing motion of life beneath her skin. "Killer? Or not?"

She smashed the insect with her other hand, leaving a smear of blood, hers, perhaps, or a prior victim's. What remained was a pinprick mass of mashed-up membranes.

"My people have located Cizinio, Joe. They're making drawings of the men who bought art from the Indians, and of the man who Cizinio said came there and directed buying."

"When can I see these drawings?"

"Probably faxed tonight. Or tomorrow."

"What have you learned in the Brazilian neighborhoods?"

She shrugged. "Nothing yet. But tomorrow I will zero in on Indian folk art shops. Who collects it? Who ships it to the cities that were hit so far?"

"Aya is working on that, too, on Customs lists."

"Yes, I spoke to this girl." Izabel smiled admiringly and wryly. "She is very passionate," she remarked.

I glanced down into the heart-shaped face, and sensed that what she had meant was, *She doesn't like me too much.*

"She's sixteen. But she is very smart, Izabel."

"You had sex with her mother?"

I halted, startled by the directness, although I shouldn't have been by now. I shook my head. Why not answer? "Aya wanted us to get together but it never happened," I said.

"I see. Because of you? Or the mother?"

"Both," I lied. It had been my decision.

"And Chris — Aya's mother — is engaged to Ray Havlicek?"

"Yes."

Izabel nodded as if some mystery had been cleared up. "So we can conclude that all the bullshit that has happened to us is a result of this situation?"

"Ray is a professional."

"Are you telling yourself this lie, too, or just me?"

I laughed. Business over. She slipped her arm in mine, her shoulder brushed me, and her hip grazed me, quick as thought, clear as intent. The few taxis on Amsterdam Avenue seemed to float through heat-convoluted air. The restaurant, Miss Mamie's Spoonbread Too, serves the best fried chicken I've ever eaten, candied yams, and sweet tea in mason jars, so sugary that it hurts your teeth. It's a small, homey place frequented by neighborhood and university types. OPEN! WE WON'T BE DEFEATED BY FEAR, a sign in the window said.

A few restaurants had reopened over the last few days as the infection rate slowed, although none offered outdoor tables. We sat beneath the blowup black-and-white photo of the ex–fashion model who had founded the place.

269

The restaurant was only half filled. Clearly, a couple by the front door recognized us, from the news. But in New York celebrities are left alone. Privacy is a gift given by this rambunctious city to celebrities. And at the moment, our TV appearances put us in that category. Our table was small and we sat very close.

"Are you married?" she asked, then laughed when she saw my reaction. "You think Brazilians are too direct?"

"I'm not married. I was, years ago."

"Then your fiancée was killed after that. I know. I am sorry."

"Me, too." Someone must have had a handheld TV on nearby. I heard a news broadcaster. *"Here in San Francisco it's hard to believe there's an outbreak elsewhere. Life goes on. But the question in some minds is, are we next?"*

She picked up a piece of corn bread and buttered it. She ate in small bites. A dab of butter remained on the corner of her mouth, by a freckle. She said, "Nelson and I worked together for four years. He wanted to be my lover. I tried it once with him. But it was uncomfortable. He was energetic. But he wanted to be more involved."

"You don't have to tell me this."

"Why not? What shall we talk about, then?

270

The ten thousandth conversation about malaria? You know as well as I do what is going on between us. Or not."

I sighed. I said, "Yeah."

She placed her hand on top of my wrist. "We are on a crucial investigation, and it is always best to give your body what it needs. It needs to eat. If you do not sleep, you are not fresh. Why is this different? I can't do anything with Eddie. He is married. To sleep with a married man is against my belief. Joe, if you think that every single waking minute is a moral question, you should be a priest. And not live as a regular man."

"You won't sleep with married guys but you shoot them."

"You do that, too."

"Very romantic."

She laughed. I laughed. Neither of us wanted romance. *Something in common.* It felt as if months had passed since I'd laughed in a way that made my stomach muscles ease, even at the same time that other muscles tightened. The waitress laid down heaping plates of golden crispy chicken, and mason jars of sweet tea. The cook had doubled our portions. This was a gift of respect. The couple by the front door was now taking photos of us on their phones.

Okay, so maybe the city doesn't give privacy so much.

As I ate, my skin felt alive in a thousand different places. I drank the sweet tea, yet my throat remained dry. The way the overhead light hit the contours of her bare shoulders. The way the coconut smell seemed to roll off her long hair. The way the little freckle by the mouth moved up and down when she was chewing. I could feel my nostrils flare with lust; my fingertips were numb, and inside my knees was the sensation of hollowness. We ate in silence, but with a hungry relish. She told me about growing up in the favelas of Rio, in a one-room concrete shack with a tin roof. She told me about the way gangs had run the favela, and how it was only recently that a woman could work for the Brazilian Federal Police. She said that she had to be tougher than the other cops, the men, and that she had been assigned to work in her own old favela. She said, as she licked the bones clean on a wing and asked the waitress for one of the huge pieces of banana cake sitting under glass, on the front counter, that those favelas were war zones, and in war zones, "you must do special things or you lose."

Izabel had a small body that demanded

lots of fuel.

Ten minutes later we were back out on the street.

"I'll walk you home, Izabel."

"Good, Joe. Yes. Very good."

She had, I thought, been right on every level. Out there at this moment was a group seeking to kill thousands of people who I had sworn as a Marine and as a doctor to protect. *You must do special things.* I had done them in the past. I would probably do them again. Why be a hypocrite and pretend otherwise? Eddie had not done these things. Nor had Stuart or my old boss, the Admiral. But Izabel had done these things. She was like me.

The apartment that Stuart had arranged for her, a one-bedroom walk-up in a brownstone, lay on Riverside Drive with a third-floor view of the edifice of Grant's tomb and leafy Riverside Park. She did not turn on the lights. She did not offer me a drink. We both did nothing at first except stand at the window and gaze out at the elms and quietly parked automobiles and the massive general's tomb and beyond that, the strip of park. We were not delaying. I think we were savoring the immediate future.

"I saw a small boy out there last night, at two A.M.," Izabel said. "Then I thought I saw a man with him, with a beard. Smoking a cigar. Wearing a uniform. But not a uniform I recognized. Neither person had protection."

I turned to her.

"They looked up at me. It was foggy and then suddenly they were not there any-more."

"You saw this?"

"I see these things sometimes," she said. "Do you?"

"You saw the boy and the general?"

"Maybe only a grandfather and a child, at two A.M."

I peered out and wanted what she said to be true. Because across the street from the round rising edifice of the general's final resting place is a child's grave, one of only three publicly protected single grave sites in the city. The tombstone names a boy who fell to his death in 1797. He is called *the Amiable Child.* In my brief stint as a part-time visitor to the neighborhood, during strolls, I had seen colorful balloons or bright flowers that some residents still leave at the grave of the boy, as if his spirit relishes pres-ents, as if his pain can be assuaged, centuries later, by recognition or love.

Had Izabel actually seen the boy and the general? It shook me. Because she was telling me that she, like I, sometimes wondered at 2 A.M. whether those who are no longer physically with us still populate a thin space between the past and present. That they travel somehow; maybe scientists call them nanoparticles. That they try to visit, and that they occupy a category without a label; they represent a triumph of spirit over known fact.

I don't know which one of us moved first. I do know that when my arms encircled her, the body felt surprisingly small, the arm and belly muscles hard. The moon glittered on mica flecks embedded in the general's mausoleum. There was no blanket on the bed, just sheets. In the heat, I guess, she slept in the nude. Her eyes remained open and smiling the whole time, and the muscles in her belly clenched in slowly, and then faster, and then in a circular pattern that made me want to cry out in pleasure, made me grit my teeth to keep from release.

I was behind her, thigh to rump. Then, on our sides. Her hair was wet at the tips, and those tips were in my mouth. Later, when we woke and started up again, the moon was in a different quadrant of the window. Her tongue tasted like banana cake. It had been too long since I'd done anything like this. The next time we woke up, it was almost dawn and a hawk was on the railing outside, looking in.

When it was over I felt as if the fluid that had pumped out of me had built up for two years and now there was once again space in my head to fill up. I looked into her beautiful eyes and saw pleasure. I knew that what we both felt was not romantic attachment, only the filling of mutual need, and that was more than enough. What is so bad about that? Because we were two assassins, who had shared choices. We were killers who had used each other to armor up so we could go out into the world and fight again.

Aya called as we exited the brownstone and walked toward the office, 9 A.M., on a sullen late July day. Grant's tomb stood gray and mist coated and half shrouded in a humid fog that resembled the spray from a pesticide container. The Amiable Child's grave was a small plot contained by a black picket fence, across the grassy median strip from the monument. A trio of joggers passed, in shorts; *they've got medicines.* An ambulance screamed by, heading toward Columbia-Presbyterian. *Malaria victim?*

I felt a surge of irritation seeing Aya's number on my screen. It was as if the teen had been spying on Izabel and me, and was calling to catch me out. It was stupid to feel that way. But I did.

"What?" I snapped.

She sounded hurt. "Why are you so grouchy, Joe?"

"Sorry. Bad night. What's up, Aya?"

"I found something funny."

I halted, and so did Izabel. This morning she wore white, tight jeans and a tight-fitting V-necked white T-shirt, and she carried a V-necked cobalt-blue cashmere sweater over her arm, against air-conditioning. Her hair was pulled tightly in a bun. The earrings were gold studs. She smelled of coconut body lotion. The Nikes would allow her to move quickly in an emergency. If she had a gun, like Eddie believed, it would be in the drawstring leather bucket bag, which could easily hide a pistol.

"What?" I asked Aya. Her words ran together in excitement as she answered.

"I didn't go home last night. There's cots set up on the fourth floor here. Agents use them. I found an extra. Mom's in Newark and she said I could stay."

"And?"

"They gave us dinner at eleven: roast beef and beets, which I usually hate. But these were pretty good."

I sighed.

"You'd think the FBI would have better food, but it was like the high school cafeteria. Then I was talking to Clara? She's the girl next to me? She used to work in a shop that sold souvenirs at the mall?"

"Aya, get to what you found."

"I am! You asked me to go through Customs lists, stuff coming in from Brazil. But a lot of other people are doing the same thing. So I thought, after Clara was talking about shops and how they work, why not do something extra?"

"And?" But I gave the kid time now, because she was good. And she got to things her own way.

"So I got the list? There's like thousands of items there? Like, in a million years, you could never open all the crates and boxes. Like, there's a billion dollars' worth of all kinds of stuff."

"So what did you do, Aya?"

"I worked it backward. I went online and made lists of places in New York, Philadelphia, and Newark *selling* stuff from Brazil. Advertising online. Like, I wasn't just looking at Customs forms for incoming. Like, I tried to match shipments and destinations, backward and forward."

"Don't say *like* all the time."

"Anyway, I found this funny thing? Like

this one shop? In Brooklyn? That advertises Indian stuff from Brazil? But Customs has no record of anything going there *from* Brazil. So how can they sell stuff if they never get it?"

I felt my breathing slow. "What's the name of the shop?"

"It's like a chain? There's a bunch of them around the United States? It's called NizhoniYee. That means *beautiful* in Navajo. Because the first shop sold Southwest stuff, then they branched out. Your voice is different this morning, Joe. Are you all right?"

"It's just the connection."

"Can you use this information?"

"It's definitely something to look into. Worth a shot."

"I did good?" she asked eagerly, like any sixteen-year-old.

"You did great, Aya, as always."

I felt her grin. "Will you tell Mom that? So she isn't mad because I stayed here all night?"

"I thought you said you had her permission."

Silence. "Kind of. Well, I thought I did."

I sighed. Considering what we could have been fighting over, this was easy. "Sure. And *you* find out everything you can about that shop. The owner. Contact information. But *don't call the shop.* Don't call anyone. Do it all online."

"Why not? I found the place!"

"Did you hear what I said?"

"All right, but you should visit there."

"I will. Today if I can. I'll head out, take a look."

And I would have that morning, I really would have gone out to Brooklyn to scout the place, except when Izabel and I got to the office, the man from Washington had shown up. He said he'd been trying to reach us for days, but that his phone messages had gone unanswered. This made sense, since we got hundreds of them each day, and lacked support staff to sift through them. He showed us ID identifying him as a Deputy Assistant National Security Advisor. He was in his early thirties and seemed smart and lacked the demanding aspect that I had found marked too many men and women once they received high-level designations. He seemed more burdened than self-important, and I liked him immediately. He'd taken the 6 A.M. train up from D.C. this morning, in order to reach New York when our office opened.

"I want to tell you a story, Colonel."

Kyle Utley said that he wanted to ask us about the island in the jungle.

"Did anyone ever mention a place called Tol-e-Khomri when you were there?" he asked.

NINETEEN

"Why did he come to me?" Kyle Utley said.

He'd walked in without official fanfare;
no demand for a briefing, no black car pulling up outside. Just a lone figure arriving
hat in hand on a private mission. Kyle Utley regarded me with fatigue-reddened eyes
from a steel-backed chair as steam spiraled
from disposable cups of coffee that Eddie
had fetched from the diner below. On the
sides, Greek warriors from the time of the
Iliad wielded spears, fearsome weapons in
the Bronze Age, useless in the age of AK-
47s, satellite surveillance, bacterial war.

The man from Washington had dressed in
a casual style that conflicted with the agony
on his face; pressed khakis and a dark blue
jacket, open-necked collared shirt, rubber-
soled Bass shoes. He laid a thin manila
folder on my desk. The edge of a black-and-
white photo protruded from the edge, but
there wasn't enough visible to know what it

showed. The label on the folder said TOL-E-KHOMRI.

Utley said, "I keep asking myself, is there a crossover point? Did I ever meet him? Or even see him before? It was like he was gloating at me . . . like it was personal with him."

Eddie leaned forward on his desktop, weight on his palms, palms on his blotter. I'd pulled my chair up close, and Izabel stood, arms folded, staring at Utley as if he were a suspect, which is what he was to his own people, he said.

"Everyone at the office treats me differently since it started," Utley said. "I guess I'd do the same if he had approached them. The FBI's interviewed my wife, parents, neighbors. Staff meetings? I'm out. And the questions! Did I ever meet the guy before? Have I had previous dealings with Jihadists? Did anyone approach me and I kept quiet about it? They're in my computer. They ask about college. Did I attend certain meetings at Princeton? Was there something I didn't say when I was vetted for the job?"

"Was there?" Izabel asked coldly.

"No."

"Nothing like sympathy from your own side," Eddie said.

First impression, he was candid. And

283

burdened, fast aging; the thick brushed hair tinged with gray at the tips, the crow's feet by the brown eyes deepening. He mentioned that he was fifth-generation government service with diplomat ancestors going back to the Spanish-American War. If his career ended, so would that chain of proud family history.

Utley said, "I would have been one of the people you'd have briefed had you come to Washington. So I figured I'd come to you. Maybe you saw something in Brazil, something that may help."

"Have a Danish," Eddie said. "There's cheese and blueberry. You look like you could use some energy. Then let's go over Tol-e-Khomri again. And see your pictures."

"Thanks, but I'm not hungry."

His career is over by way of association. He'll always be the point man for the worst attack on U.S. soil since 9/11, unless he figures out how to help. His name will be synonymous with destruction.

I said, "The pictures, Kyle."

"Dr. Nakamura, you're sure that when you were on the island, no one mentioned Tol-e-Khomri?"

"I don't think so."

Utley looked at the closed file, reluctant to open it even though he'd come with it,

284

and he glanced meaningfully at Izabel. "Need to know, Colonel Rush. You and Major Nakamura have the clearance to see this. But Captain Santo is, er, not in that category."

He turned to Izabel, expecting her to leave, and she shook her head. Utley turned to me, waiting for me to order her to go. I shook my head also. She wouldn't have gone anyway. Eddie explained to him, "Look, she stays. If it weren't for her, Joe and I would be dead. And you'd know nothing about Brazil. You came this far. You've already said more than you should. So don't be stupid. Technically, we're ordered to cooperate with her. Any fallout is on us."

Utley sighed, visibly weighing infractions. But in the end he had come too far to stop now. He opened the file. *The lesser of two bad choices.* I saw with surging interest that the top shot was an aerial. From a drone, reconnaissance plane, or satellite.

Kyle said, "Like I said, it's the name of a Syrian village, but also the name of a refugee camp in southern Turkey, where the people from that village showed up."

I was eyeing a tent city, a sprawling mass of quickly thrown-up tents, lean-tos, shacks, and latrines, miles in diameter. Troops patrolled outside a fence. Smoke — choking cooking-fire smoke — made it harder to see details. A convoy of dump trucks snaked in through a front gate, past sandbags, packed with human cargo. I saw tethered goats. I saw a line of women with buckets for water on their heads. I saw a water truck and Red Cross and Red Crescent tents. Thousands of displaced people, desperate ones, were there.

"People fleeing fighting to the south. People trying to get to Europe. More coming every day," Kyle said.

Next shot, this time a close-up, more trucks, except the passengers were exclusively men or boys.

"They're not all so innocent," Kyle said. "Some pretty bad guys are mixed in there, too. They came to disrupt."

I saw more photos. Life in the camp. A ditch into where men and boys urinated. A shower facility marked in Arabic, WOMEN. Except a lot more women lined up outside than the facility could hold. Refugees standing four deep, a quarter mile back, waiting to eat, or lying listlessly in sleeping bags beneath lean-tos. The sense of building pressure coming from the photos. The sense that two-dimensional images could not hold all the need. I saw angry people, massed, yelling at the soldiers. Fists raised. Signs waving. Hate. *Let us out! Feed us! Let us leave this place!*

"The jihadists pushed it, encouraged it," Utley said.

Watching the inevitable progression to outburst was like sitting in a silent movie, as it rolled out frame by frame. I saw the first AK-47. It must have been smuggled into the camp by the jihadists. I saw a Turkish soldier on the ground, screaming in pain. A tent was on fire. A Humvee was smoking. A section of fence was trampled. Women threw rocks and bottles at retreating troops.

"They took over the camp for some hours," Kyle said. "When the troops came back it got pretty bloody."

In my hand, people were now running away from the fence. I saw clumps of earth bursting upward, and a body in the air, its limbs folded at impossible angles. The face seemed detached from the shoulders, as if it had materialized from dust. Another face rushed toward the satellite eye so swiftly that the cheek muscles were pulled back as if by g-force, as if the man was an astronaut. Concrete blocks flew in the air, light as Lego pieces.

"Jesus Cristo," Izabel Santo said.

The riot and aftermath unfolded, and life

became death, structure disintegrated, tent fabric became cinders, geometry disassembled into atoms of blood. The soldiers were inside the camp again. The settling dust revealed overturned cooking pots and burned Humvees and the truncated base of what had been a Quonset hut a few hours before. I saw a field of untouched beans, and a small boy, naked, screaming, urinating without realizing it, beside a shredded, smoking cotton chair that lay sideways as if it had fallen to earth from outer space.

I saw bodies, wrapped in blankets, in a row.

"Dr. Nakamura, Dr. Rush, you're sure that no one mentioned this place when you were in Brazil?" Kyle asked.

"Sorry," said Eddie.

Utley's sigh conveyed lost hope. He'd known before boarding the train that his quest for answers was long odds. His hands seemed to move by themselves, turning over more photos. In the next one light was grayer; either clouds had rolled in or time had passed, dusk approached.

Utley said, "During the period when the troops evacuated, these next images occurred."

More vehicles arrived; a couple of Land Rovers and a Ford Escape. Running toward the wreckage, jihadists left vehicle doors open. One fighter was down on a knee, the body of a woman bent backward over it as he cradled her in his arms. Her right leg, poking from a singed chador, looked obscenely bare. The man's stricken eyes were upturned as if he knew a drone was there. He cursed God, drones, cameras. His scarf had fallen off. His face was white, his beard dark; the shaking fist pantomimed rage or retribution.

The photo quality was so good that I saw tears streaming. Next shot, the face was closer; it lurched toward me by sidestepping time. The countenance was weathered, in a place where heat and sun suck away human juice. I saw squint lines at the eyes; sunburn and goggle marks disappeared into beard; teeth that were cared for. The close-up was so good that I saw a small gap between the front top incisor and the tooth to its left. Just a bit of extra space.

Kyle said, "We believe this man may be an American."

Eddie looked up sharply.

Utley nodded. "There are more Westerners there than we care to admit. The dumber ones, low IQ, failures at work, are easy to track through the Web . . . we have a list. But smarter ones stay away from the Net

289

now. Some have been recruited; others find their way to a certain village in Turkey, a certain inn in Pakistan. They surrender their passports. The more sophisticated groups have started keeping those U.S. or European passports active. They hope to send the owners back home after training. These traitors are told to tell their families back home they're in the Peace Corps. Or backpacking. Believe me, the disinformation is top quality. Postcards sent to families from vacation spots. Phone calls home. Dad and Mom think little Bobby is on a beach in Thailand, because he says so. His passport has a stamp to prove it. But he's in Jakarta. He's in Brazil. Colonel, the bad guys are wising up."

Eddie nodded, seeing it. "Why waste a fighter on the battlefield when you can slip him home, do far worse damage, and get lots of PR, all over the world?"

Kyle Utley looked miserable. "One rumor is they're being coached by an American who knows D.C., how it works."

"Rumor or fact?" said Izabel.

"That's the problem, trying to understand, isn't it?"

"This guy in the photo is one of these people?" I asked. "He's the one who approached you?"

"I wish I knew," admitted Kyle. "All I

know is, the man who threatened me mentioned this place. He was American, I think. See the tooth, in front? The gap?"

"It's the same guy?"

"I said I'm not sure. Maybe I just want it to be. My boss says it's wishful thinking," Utley sighed. "And my guy looked different, except for the tooth. He had an Army tattoo. This man doesn't." Utley picked up a Danish, stared at it as if he didn't know what it was, and put it down. He said, weakly, "I hoped you might help somehow."

"Why not make the photo public? Say he's a person of interest? *Have you seen this man?* If he's here, like you say, back from there, someone might recognize him."

Utley shook his head and his lips tightened. I could see what he'd look like when he reached age sixty. "The FBI won't do it. They've listed hundreds of people as persons of interest. Their tip lines are overflowing. They're getting three thousand calls and e-mails a day. 'It's my neighbor.' 'It's the guy from the 7-Eleven.' 'It's the Pakistani student in the dorm.' So if there's no hard reason to add more names, they don't. Besides," he said, in a lower voice, glancing at Izabel, *in for a penny, in for a pound,* "Americans are involved in defense at the camp, so it's touchy. If these shots got out, they'd be worth ten thousand new jihad recruits. Congressional hearings. Who failed? Who screwed up? Careers down the drain."

He was right about the secrecy. I'd done things myself, things you get medals for, but the kind of medals that — after they are pinned on you — are removed, boxed up, and locked away in a safe. We want our heroes to relieve us of moral choices. They take credit. We get to feel good.

Utley started to say something else but caught himself. It was the first time he'd done that. *So he has secrets, too.* He said, subject changing, "I should never have walked out of that bar. I should have just finished my burger."

"Thanks for your time," I said, standing, extending my hand to shake, letting him know he was to leave now.

Utley looked startled, Eddie surprised, as he had not caught Utley's lie. But as far as I was concerned, Utley was here to share, and if he was going to conceal things I had no use for him. Eddie thought I was treating the man harshly. But Izabel Santo smiled at the corner of her mouth.

"Up until this minute you played it straight," I told Utley. "I appreciate that. Whatever else you're sitting on, I'm sure you have a good reason. Good luck."

"We can talk about other things."

"No, sir. I don't believe we can."

Utley blew out air. He saw that our meeting was over unless he revealed what he did not want to say. But he did not stand up. *He wants to tell us.* He looked at the floor, thinking, and it was Eddie who picked up on what Utley wanted us to do.

Eddie asked him, softly, "Something else happened in that camp that we need to know?"

Utley did not respond at first. Then, slowly, a faint head shake. It was okay to tell us what had *not* happened. This was an old D.C. game, and I knew how to play it. *I never told you this. This didn't come from me. Technically, I never told you a thing.*

I guessed, "You left out something the man said. Something important."

Utley rose and went to the window. He looked down at Broadway. He said, "People are starting to walk around out there again. It's funny how fast things can go back to normal."

So he'll shake his head when we're wrong, and talk about bullshit when we're right. Just like he probably does with journalists, to confirm or deny a story.

"The man ID'd the group he works for,"

Eddie guessed.

Utley shook his head, just a bit.

"The FBI has a lead you're not telling us," said Izabel, getting into the spirit of things.

No.

"The administration is doing something else that you're not revealing," I tried.

Utley kept staring down at Broadway. He remarked, "Are the sandwiches in that deli across the street good?"

Silence. *So the White House has some other strategy. But what?*

"Navy Seals raid?"

No.

"Rangers? Secret mission?"

No.

"Well, it can't be negotiations," I said.

Kyle Utley turned away from the window and gathered up the sweater he'd left by the chair, and all the photos. I reached out and took from his hand the close-up of the blond man's face. The rage so profound that an eight-by-ten space could not contain it.

But Kyle had not shaken his head. Negotiations?

"I need that photo back please, Colonel Rush."

"You showed it to us, so why not give it?"

"It's not for distribution."

"Agreed."

"Do you know what happens to me if they find out I gave this to you?"

"The same thing that will happen if they find out what you told us. It's not like your career is going anywhere anyway just now."

Wordlessly, we both turned to Eddie, who nodded. Then we regarded Izabel, who hesitated, frowned, and nodded, too, in agreement. *The photo — this meeting — stays secret.*

"Keep it," Utley said. "Technically, I'm not even supposed to have these photos. I had to work to get them."

"I still do not understand something," said Izabel. "You told us you have no idea who threatened you. So how can anyone be negotiating with them?"

Utley headed for the door. He'd taken this as far as he could.

I said to his back, reasoning out loud, "We're threatened with an attack, *unless we give them something.* And then we're 'negotiating.' So this must mean . . ."

I cut myself off as I saw it. The cold sensation started in my chest and spread outward into my throat.

"We're giving them what they demanded?"

Kyle Utley sagged. And turned. This time the head shake was almost imperceptible. It was like he was fighting off five generations

295

of secret-keeping DNA, and the best he could manage, if he used all his willpower, was a two-millimeter movement of his skull. Why couldn't the guy just say it?

"They are close to giving in," Izabel guessed.

Kyle Utley blew out air. "I think so. They're panicked. I think if there is one more attack, they'll give them what they want."

I heard his light footfalls fading on the creaky floors of the old building. I heard the *ding* of the elevator arriving, and the *ding* of the doors closing again. Eddie was standing now, Izabel Santo frowning.

"Now what do we do, Joe?"

I eyed the jihadist's photo. I had no idea if it was relevant. I named a general I knew at the Pentagon, a top analyst at the CIA, a crackerjack woman tech genius I'd worked with at Defense Intelligence, a facial software guru in the bowels of Customs Enforcement. Each of them would have access to different lists, names, codes, and priorities. Each owed me a favor. All were, in my opinion, long-term reliable. And despite recent rules designed to coordinate the efforts of intelligence agencies, only a fool would rely on a single route to find something out.

"You know damn well what I'm going to do," I said.

"We promised not to share it," said Eddie.

"And he said Washington is about to give in. Dos, we're an autonomous unit. The President himself ordered us involved. Utley said no one in D.C. takes him seriously. If we don't consider avenues that others ignore, who will?"

"And Utley?"

"I like him." Meaning, *I hope he survives this all.* But I hoped the nation got through it, more than any one of us.

Eddie said, "Something bad is coming and I know it. No one's taken claim for this. No one's been caught. There's no way they just sank into the woodwork. I keep remembering that laboratory. Every day I'm thinking, *When will it come?*"

Izabel said, "Let us get to work."

We spent all day into early evening on the photo, and by nine that night had run into all dead ends. Facial software came up empty. No match at Customs, at CIA, or at Army Intelligence. Nobody I spoke to knew anything about a refugee camp or Syrian village called Tol-e-Khomri. The files on fifth-columnist Americans came up blank. I guessed that I'd hear from a furious or frantic Kyle Utley sometime tomorrow, when the blowback reached him. *Too bad.*

"Well," said Eddie at ten, as we sat around an Italian meal delivered from Carmine's, huge platters of chicken, sausage, and calamari, "Kyle said it's probably a dead end. I guess it is."

"What do we have tomorrow?" said Izabel Santo. I felt her foot touch my ankle under the table. My tiredness vanished. I felt a hard stirring in my groin. My body needed food, and sleep, and it needed Izabel Santo. Anyone who thinks that sex is not sustenance is crazy. My fingertips were tingling. I allowed myself to feel the anticipation because I knew there was no romance in it, no love, promise, or future, just animal need. It was like gravity. We were two planets in close orbit. We were about to crash and burn each other up.

Eddie said, "The hospital. And probably ten more tax forms to fill out. But maybe we'll get lucky on the photo. I gotta tell you. This quiet. I hate it. Something more is coming very soon."

"I'll check out that art shop," said Izabel. "In the morning."

"I'm going to go back to the office," said Eddie.

"I'll walk you home," I told Izabel, and

over my shoulder, as we left, saw Eddie's approving smile.

Aya's call came after midnight, jerking me out of one of the deepest sleeps I'd had in months. Izabel was up instantly, the moonlight on her sculpted shoulders, the sheet crumpled by her narrow waist.

I saw the incoming number and shook my head with irritation and also admiration. The kid was perfect for our unit. She worked tirelessly and she stayed on problems long after others would have given up. She even had the evasiveness down, an instinctual feel for how to ignore instructions. It was hard to get mad at this, since half the time I did the same thing, I thought.

"I did exactly what you said," she started out, a clear indication that she had not, or she'd not bring it up.

"Aya, do you know what time it is?"

"Of course! But I need to tell you something! See, you told me not to call anyone and technically, I didn't."

I sighed. Everyone I talked to seemed to be throwing the word around today. *Technically.*

"Meaning what?" I asked.

"Well, me, Aya Vekey, I can't make phone calls because you ordered me not to. Aya would never make a call. But Megan Luchs can."

"And who is Megan Luchs?" I asked. Izabel got out of bed and, mouth dry, I watched her sway toward the bathroom, and the light go on. The room smelled of musk and sweat, bedding and perfume.

"Megan Luchs is a customer looking to buy Brazilian art for her mom's new house. Her mom loves folk art."

"She's you, in other words."

"Technically, you told me that I can't call."

"Aya, just tell me what you did."

"Well! *Megan* called the shop in Brooklyn but kept getting a machine, so instead of leaving a message, she looked up the chain headquarters. Remember I said there were stores in different cities? There's a website!"

"So Megan looked up the chain."

"And it turns out that it was founded by an old woman: she's like maybe fifty, her name is Johanna Fargo, and she lives in Denver. And there was a number on the website for headquarters. It's there, too."

"Which Megan called."

"And I was surprised because Ms. Fargo herself answered! She was very nice and asked me, uh, she asked *Megan* questions about high school and what she likes to do, hobbies, what college Megan plans . . ."

"Get to the point," I said as the bathroom door opened and Izabel came back to bed. The moon gleamed on the muscles of her abdomen, the small breasts, the hollow in her throat, her small white teeth. She cocked her head. *What's up?* Being with her here was not like sleeping with a wife, or a girlfriend. What we had was raw and exhausted, friendship and solace amid confusion, a few moments of forgetfulness grabbed when we were too tired to work anymore, in the middle of too short a night.

Aya said, "Ms. Fargo said she knew who ran the Brooklyn shop, because it is her son Tom!"

"Her son is Tom Fargo."

"She's proud of Tom. She said he was away for three years, helping people overseas in the Peace Corps. And recently, he came back."

I started to feel a tingling in the back of my neck.

"She said that Tom backpacked around in South America after that, but finally came home and took up her invitation to run a shop. She said he used to help her in the first shop, when he was a boy. So he knows the business. She said that the Brooklyn shop is probably closed during the emergency, but Tom is in New York because she just talked to him the other day."

"She spoke to him on the phone . . ."

"His cell phone."

"Did you get the number?"

"I didn't ask, Joe. Sorry."

I sighed.

Aya said, coyly, undoubtedly grinning at me in triumph, "But *Megan* got the number. And the address where the bills go, a private mail service."

"Damnit!"

"I didn't call the number, but I did look up the name Tom Fargo in New York, and guess what? I found three who have driver's licenses. One is eighteen and the others are in their sixties. So it's not him. Then I looked up property owners and found four, but one was a woman, Tomasina, and one was ninety, and the other two were the ones with driver's licenses. Same in voting rolls. Not him. No other Tom Fargo paying electric or water bills. The New York City income tax people *were so nasty* and wouldn't talk to me when I called! The lady said I sounded like a kid and was it a phony phone call!"

"Imagine that."

"It's not funny. How come this person has no records in New York?"

"Did you or did Megan check the Peace

Corps?"

"Yes," she said triumphantly. "Only one Tom Fargo was in the Peace Corps in the last four years, anywhere, and he came from Mobile, Alabama, and is sixty-one years old, a retired nurse. I was going to wait to tell you tomorrow. But what if it's important?"

"You did right. Aya, do you ever sleep?"

She giggled. "I'm sixteen," she said. "Not ancient like you. I don't need that much sleep."

On the night table lay the photo that Kyle Utley had left with us. Of the bearded jihadist raising his fist at the sky.

Aya gave me Tom Fargo's cell phone number. By now Izabel was back in bed. She lay her hand on my thigh and snuggled close the way animals in the wild will sleep together. I had my arm beneath her neck, a human pillow. Her warmth made me drowsy. I held the slip of paper with the number in moonlight. The AC was on, the window down against insects. It was hot outside. By now, days after the initial spraying, any mosquitoes recently hatched would be out in the park.

"He lied about the Peace Corps," she said.

"He has no address we can find?"

"Nothing in New York. No phone bills. Or any bills. No address or voting registration or city ID. I'll keep poking around."

I punched in the number for Ray Havlicek, and, at 1 A.M., got a voice message. I tried his assistant and got the same thing. I left detailed messages for them both. I thought a moment and then found the business card for Detective Jamal al-Azawi, our driver, and called his scrawled home number. He picked up after the second ring.

"The commissioner told you to render every assistance?" I asked.

"Yes, sir," said the rapidly wakening voice.

"Does that include tracking a phone number?"

"I don't see why not."

"Can your guys tell me where a particular phone is at any given moment?"

"That's tech stuff, sir. I think it depends on the phone. New phones are harder. But I got guys I can call."

I gave Jamal the number, and he said he'd wake people up. No problem. Happy to help.

There was nothing else to do until morning. Then I'd have Jamal drive us out to the Brooklyn folk art shop. But morning was hours away. Jamal was a good cop and I liked him. The locals seemed more cooperative than Ray Havlicek, or perhaps they were just more desperate. Maybe, I thought, dozing off, we'd get lucky. Maybe an answer would come from the conjunction of a visit from a burdened D.C. bureaucrat and a phone call from a teenage girl. My eyes began to close. My breathing was becoming more regular. Izabel Santo's smooth muscled leg twitched and moved on top of mine as she slumbered. Maybe she was chasing a suspect in a dream. Maybe she was running for her life.

What I suspected was that, at that moment, in Washington, men and women were getting ready to give a group of murderers whatever it was that they wanted, whatever goal they had been killing to get.

TWENTY

The driver carrying the shipment from Brazil was an Irish-born immigrant without papers named Sean Cross, a twenty-year-old high school graduate from Cork, who dreamed of someday being a doctor. He'd taken a vacation in the United States, fallen in love with a poet named Julia who he met in Washington Square, and stayed on for a year to woo her, and then another year, after she left. He was a bad driver, paid cash off the books, and was thinking, as he narrowly missed hitting a parked car in Park Slope, that he probably should not have come to work today, because his hangover was bad.

He was certainly not thinking about his high school health class until he spotted the fat gray rat dragging a half-eaten pizza slice across 6th Avenue ahead, backing the meal toward an open sewer grate.

"Fucking ugly rat!"

He swerved violently to try to hit it. In back,

as a result, a box in which Amazonian pottery was packed slid three inches to the right on a wobbling pile and almost toppled. Sean hated rats. Several lived in the walls in his East Harlem tenement. They were dirty and disgusting and they carried disease. Watching the pizza slice flop into the sewer in the side mirror, he recalled the voice of his old high school public-health-class teacher in Ireland. He had no idea that the process the voice was describing was — at that instant — happening in the back of Sean's truck.

"During the Middle Ages, a few tiny mutations in a bacteria," said the voice, "killed two hundred million people, sixty percent of Europe. The equivalent number today would top a billion."

Sean saw in his head the map of the ancient world that his teacher, Mr. Colgan, had unrolled over the blackboard.

"The year 1347," Colgan said in his smoker's rasp.

At the bottom of the map, a dotted line extended over land from China to Turkey, and with a sketch of a wind-driven merchant sailing vessel below, another dotted line showing the sea route from Constantinople through the Bosporus, and Black Sea, and into the Mediterranean.

"The rats on board carried fleas. And in the

307

gut of those fleas lived a bacteria called *Yersinia pestis.*

"If the fleas bit a sailor, the man became infected," Colgan said. "Within days, victims sprouted buboes the size of peaches in their groins and armpits. Then came high fever and violent vomiting of black blood. Terrified mariners named the disease Black Death.

"When the ship reached Genoa, the rats left, and with them, the fleas," Mr. Colgan added in the hushed voice of a good Irish storyteller.

"Within hours of docking, probably a merchant was bitten by a flea near the waterfront. Peasants in a quayside market were bitten; maybe the woman who sold fresh fish, or a cook buying supplies for a count's dinner; a gypsy fortune-teller, a passing knight, at an inn that the rats invaded," Mr. Colgan said.

"A quarter of those infected began to die."

On the map, the dots left Genoa and, like rats, branched out across Europe. More dots went east.

"In 1348, the disease reached Pisa, Italy. A year later, Marseille, Spain, Portugal. Germany by 1349. Russia in 1351," Colgan said. "And then it got worse, because our little friend *Y. pestis* changed. And so did the flea."

"How?" Sean asked, from the front row.

"Ah! A few tiny changes over time reconstituted the bacteria. Almost invisible alterations, so small you needed an electron microscope to get any idea that it was there at all. It's funny. Ten million years can go by while something alters. But then one day the effect happens, and a year later thousands are dead!"

"Tell us the change!"

"Imagine the male flea, *Xenopsylla cheopis,* so fragile looking that it seems translucent when magnified. The microscope light shines through! And then, a few alterations and a common bug that lives in your gut morphs into one of the biggest mass murderers in history."

Sean looked at the GPS on his dashboard. He was now only one mile from the drop-off point, a folk art shop. Someone named Tom was supposed to meet him there.

Mr. Colgan had been the one who inspired Sean — before he got distracted by love — to want to become a doctor. The ex-Jesuit spent summers volunteering in a TB ward in Manila before becoming a teacher. He kept the students on the edge of their seats with his tales. He'd said, "It was only in 2014 that Poinar discovered original plague bacteria in a twenty-million-year-old flea, trapped in amber. That ancestor of *pestis* is named *Y. pseudotuberculosis,* still around today. Catch it and you suffer thirty minutes of diarrhea, nothing worse. *Pestis,* on the other hand, kills in sixty hours."

"What changed *pseudo* into *pestis*?" Sean had asked.

"Three small changes created a plague! One. *Pseudotuberculosis* in its original form killed fleas! Yes! Fleas could not carry it! So our first change was the elimination of a single protein, called urease, that kept fleas from carrying plague. A small genetic mutation stopped *pestis* from making that protein. With the protein gone, fleas became vectors. They could now carry the bacteria."

"And the second change?" Sean had asked.

"Again a tiny mutation, this time to a gene that encodes a protein that dissolves blood clots. The gene is called *pla.*"

"*Pla?* What do blood clots have to do with it?"

"*Before* the change, even if a flea bit a human, even if it transmitted the bacteria, the body would clot blood by that bite, to stop the bleeding. This clotting trapped the bacteria, kept it from spreading. So although the flea carried disease, it could not damage a new host."

"The mutation stopped the clotting," Sean guessed.

"Good! With clotting gone, the bacteria could spread into the victim's lymph nodes, and start multiplying. One bacteria became a hundred, a million. All a victim had to do was sneeze to pass it on."

"Wait a minute," Sean had said, puzzled. "I thought you said the disease was transmitted by a bite. Now you're saying a sneeze could transmit it?"

"That's the third change that happened; a last mutation changed one amino acid in *pla,* and made the bacterium contagious from coughing or sneezing. Much easier to transmit. The bubonic plague became the pneumatic plague, more virulent, ninety to one hundred percent death rate, fevers, headaches, pneumonia. Spread by aerosolized particles, it devastated a quarter of the world's population."

Sean shuddered, remembering the rat he'd seen a few minutes ago, and he wondered whether the process that had been horrifyingly described to his class back in Cork could ever happen again. No, he reasoned. It couldn't. Because in the modern world there was better medicine, equipment, and preparation, so something as small as the mutation of a single protein could not do the kind of massive damage that his old science teacher had riveted the class with, on a foggy day, years back, when the teacher told the tale.

Sean had no idea that the opposite had oc-

curred twelve feet behind where he was sitting. No idea that there were insects packed
inside the cargo carried in his truck. No idea
— as he brought the truck to a halt in front of
a small folk art shop, and went to the back
and caught sight of a box teetering on top of
the pile — that inside it was something that
could wipe out a quarter of the human population on earth, if it got out.

Sean got into the truck fast, and stabilized
the box.

Inside were thousands of female anopheles
mosquitoes and larvae that carried virulent
malaria, the original kind that could be transmitted by the bite of a mosquito only.

But one mosquito carried a genetic altera-
tion in the malaria parasite. In her, just as in a
flea/bacteria combination a thousand years
ago, a tiny parasite could be transmitted by
coughing, sneezing, or kissing. Even by an
infected man breathing into your face on a
subway, during evening rush hour.

No mosquito necessary to transmit this variety. Which meant that the single insect carrying this new variety was capable of starting a
chain reaction sweeping across earth. Even
the men who had genetically altered the
insects in the shipment were unaware of the
existence of the mutated parasite inside one
of them.

The men who had created the disease that Tom Fargo was spreading had thought they could control it. But if the new variety got out, no one could control the spread.

Like the pneumatic plague, this was aerosolized.

Sean remembered the closing words of his biology teacher, as he watched the door to the Nizhoni Yee shop open, and the man who ran the shop come out, happy to see his shipment from the airport finally here.

"Mutation is, by definition, always a surprise."

TWENTY-ONE

We were stuck in traffic on the Brooklyn Bridge, on our way to the art shop, crammed in the middle of a honking mass of delivery trucks, taxis, and autos. Nothing moving. Progress stopped dead.

"There's some kind of demonstration on the Brooklyn side," our detective driver Jamal informed us. "Community groups claim that Manhattan got all the spray and medicine. That no one cares about them."

"That's ridiculous! Spray supply just ran out!"

Jamal shrugged. "To me, this traffic is normal." He put on the siren. It helped us move two feet ahead.

"This is normal?" Izabel shook her head. "I would not want to live in this insane place."

She held in her hand a fax from Brazil. The artist's sketch of the man who had visited the jungle island.

314

The day was broiling, and with no fresh attacks, some New Yorkers were going back to work. Some shops and offices were reopening. Wall Street brokers were back at the nexus of world finance, at our backs. Airports open. And a few more supermarkets.

"How far to the shop, Jamal?"

"In normal traffic, seven minutes."

"And in this?"

A shrug. Jamal mercifully shut the siren off.

"Could be thirty, could be fifty."

At least Ray Havlicek finally answered his phone.

The head of the national manhunt to find the attackers was in Evanston, Illinois, a suburb north of Chicago. He was two blocks west of the campus of Northwestern University, off Lake Michigan, on Lincoln Street. He was crouched behind a Bureau car, outside a private home surrounded by FBI and Evanston police. He wasn't the on-the-ground commander, or he wouldn't have picked up.

"Turn on CNN if you can," Ray said.

On Eddie's iPhone I saw it from a network copter; the leafy oak-lined street, the target, a two-story-high yellow Victorian home, with its wraparound porch, gables, and tur-

315

rets. A bird feeder on an upstairs porch. The stupid ceramic gnome on the front lawn. The snipers lying on the roof of the brick colonial home across the street.

"Who's inside the house, Ray?"

"The house is divided into apartments, evacuated except for one. Two males. Chemistry majors from Belgium. Looks like the big break, Joe."

"Is that you, Ray, behind the black car?"

"Damnit! I told my guys to move the cameras back!"

I saw Ray, crouched, looking around, shouting orders.

Then he was back. "Talk fast, Joe. Your message said important."

FBI tracks malaria threat to Illinois, said the rolling banner crossing the bottom of Eddie's mini-screen. *Foreign students threaten to blow themselves up.*

"Does CNN have the story right, Ray?"

"For a change, yes. *What do you have for me?*"

"How'd you find the students?"

"They made a mistake. They made a threat call to someone in D.C. last night." I envisioned Kyle Utley. "They mentioned things they'd only know if they're involved."

"Like a refugee camp named Tol-e-Khomri?"

316

Silence. I heard sirens, and a bullhorn in the background. But I couldn't hear the words. Ray's breathing came over the line, quick and hard.

"Where'd you hear that name, Joe?"

"What difference does it make?"

"Do not mention it to anyone! Say you hear me."

"How about the man with the gap in his teeth? Is he in that house, too?"

Ray's anger came across the line as a sharp, sour buzzing. "Damnit. If you're trying to impress me, congratulations. Talk fast. What do you want?"

Taken beside the array of firepower in Illinois, the story I told sounded flimsy even to me, my alleged evidence thin. Maybe we were wrong. Maybe the folk art shop in Brooklyn was nothing more than a store. That the men in Illinois had barricaded themselves in a house was proof that they were involved in something. All I had was a story about ceramics coming into the country without any record at Customs, and a vague sketch from Brazil, a face.

"That's it? The whole thing?" said Ray, unimpressed.

"His name is Tom Fargo."

A sigh. "Fine. We'll put it on the list of

five thousand other names we're checking out."

"We're heading over there now."

Ray said, "Good. Wait! Something is happening!"

Jamal broke free of traffic, moved thirty feet forward, and braked behind a smoke-belching appliance truck with cartoon elves on the rear door. SAME DAY SERVICE. Izabel Santo was turned from the front seat, staring at the screen in Eddie's hand. I saw the angle suddenly shift. Instead of the FBI at the house, I saw a pack of newspeople, across the street, grumbling, leaving. Ray had ordered the cameras turned away from the house.

"They're about to assault," Eddie said.

The aerial shot went sideways as the news copter left.

I heard the magnified sound of bullhorns ordering the men inside to come out, hands up.

"Sound diversion," Eddie said.

I imagined SWAT guys moving in through a rear garden. I imagined them with a battering ram and assault rifles, moving onto the front porch. Over the iPhone came the faint but unmistakable *snap-snap* of M4s firing.

Then one of the cameras showed the

house again, only from a straight-on angle. *The camera crew must have talked their way into a house across the street.* Eddie and I had assaulted homes in Iraq and Afghanistan, and my heart was in my throat for the safety of the attack team. We heard the muffled report of an explosion. The camera violently shifted to show a carpet. The FBI must have realized they were being filmed and found the cameraman. No, wrong, because the shot adjusted and I saw the house again, from across the street. The front door was open, and flames erupted from inside. A black-clad FBI agent lay on the lawn. A figure appeared in the doorway, singing, right hand up, holding something, torso bundled up under his shirt. *His thumb is pressed to a detonator.*

He blew himself up just as shots drove him back.

"Ray?"

Ray had hung up.

The front doorway was now gone, a jagged oval of hanging wood bits and plaster. The upper windows had blown out.

Eddie sighed. "Well, Ray got 'em. Should we turn around and go back, Joe?"

"I hope you're right. But we keep going."

We crawled forward and reached the source of the two-mile-long traffic jam. The chanting demonstrators blocked all lanes but one. Their waving signs read, GOVERNMENT LABS KILL OUR CHILDREN WITH DISEASE; RELEASE SPRAY SUPPLY; MAYOR DOESN'T CARE; TEAR DOWN WALL STREET; and FUCK THE RICH. Six-lane Flatbush Avenue was clear ahead. We finally sped up.

"Six, seven minutes," Detective Jamal al-Azawi said.

Aya called, on the way, with news.

"Joe, I did what you said. I tried to get anything more I could find on a Tom Fargo."

"Did you sleep at the Bureau again last night?"

"Don't start with me. Mom asked the same thing. She's still in Newark and no one else is home so who cares where I sleep as long as I do? You said that a good investigator never gives up. You said it! Gives one hundred and one percent!"

"They go home at night after that."

"Did *you* go home last night? I bet you didn't."

Actually, I'd gone to Izabel's apartment, so this line of reasoning was counterproductive. I heard my own testy voice, as demanding as Ray Havlicek's, short-tempered and exhausted. I wasn't her father. I don't know why I felt responsibility for her. I calmed

320

and asked, as if speaking to any adult researcher, "What did you find out, Aya?"

"That's better! I found an address!"

"For the shop? You already gave us that."

"No. Different! Maybe where he lives!"

I sat up straighter. We were on Flatbush now, moving at a brisk clip toward Park Slope. "How?"

"Well," she said, bragging now that she had my attention, "*first* I had his social security number. From his passport. So I cast the net, went to all databases."

Which, at the FBI, she'd have wide access to. "And?"

"And it turns out he bought a car when he went back to visit his mother last year, in Denver, after he was overseas. So he needed to register it. His car is a six-year-old yellow Subaru. I have the VIN number. Colorado license plates are green and white and they show the Rockies, but don't have a slogan."

I was smiling. "No slogan."

"Don't make fun of me! Maybe you want me to stop."

"Sorry."

"He got a ticket! A parking ticket, in New York! I have this friend, see? Her name is Grace? She moved to Washington from New York when her parents divorced? Well she told me last month that there are all these stupid parking laws in New York, like, you can't leave your car on blocks for more than two days in a row, like, because they clean streets. Like, if you don't move your car or sit in it double-parked for like *hours* you get these expensive tickets, over a hundred dollars. And he got one!"

"He got a ticket," I repeated, very alert now.

"The ticket doesn't say his name, because the person writing the ticket wouldn't know that? But it has the license plate? And the address where the car was? So I thought, *last night when you wanted me to waste time sleeping,* that maybe the address will turn out to be where he knows someone, or even where he lives?"

"Didn't your mother tell you not to make statements like they're questions?"

"You sound like Mom. You should date her. You have a lot in common. Like telling me what to do. If you want to be my step-father, marry Mom. Otherwise stop it!"

"I give up."

"Anyway, LIKE, I decided to check the address, and it turns out that address is a co-op building."

Aya gave me the address of the building.

"I got a phone number for the building."

"I told you specifically not to make phone

calls, Aya."

Sweetly, she said, "I didn't. Don't I always do what you say?"

"Yeah. Always."

Aya giggled. "Okay, *now* I'll go get some sleep; that is, if a certain someone thanks me for all the effort."

"Thank you, Aya. I mean that."

"You're welcome," she said, and hung up.

Izabel Santo mused, "Maybe that whole thing in Chicago is a . . . How do you say it? A trick? A diversion!"

We looked at each other.

"I have no idea. Keep going," I told Jamal.

The folk art shop was closed, even on a weekday morning at 10 A.M., even though the hours open sign on the grated-in front door said opening should have been half an hour ago.

"Other shops on this block are open," Eddie said.

Across the street, I saw a hole-in-the-wall diner, a leather goods shop, a Thai restaurant, a candy store/newsstand, a shoemaker. Next door to the art shop on one side, a Comfort Sofa shop, showing couches in the window. On the other side, a drugstore, Duane Reade.

As Izabel waited at the art shop, Eddie

and I split up and visited the other stores, asking questions and hearing the same answers that I got from a cranky, mustached man named Ian Crossgate, manager of the convertible sofa store.

"Do you know where Tom Fargo lives?"

"Is that his last name? I know Tom's the first name, but I never knew the last."

"Do you know where he is this morning?"

"He was there when I got in at eight, getting a delivery. I guess he went somewhere after that."

"A delivery from where?"

"How do I know?"

"Did he have a car here?"

"I had a car and got sick of paying tickets! The Mayor wastes our taxes and then sends fascist ticket agents to steal more, ticketing our cars! No! I didn't see any car! Tom's probably too smart to own one."

I pulled out the blowup satellite face shot that Kyle Utley had provided. "Is this man Tom Fargo?"

"Him? That guy has a beard, and Tom doesn't."

"Pretend there's no beard."

"Pretend? Whaddaya mean? The whole shape of the face is different. And this guy is Muslim. I can see from the hat. Tom's

Christian. And Tom has a scar on his face, I think."

I frowned. "A scar?"

"Wait. *Does* he have a scar? Lemme think. Hey, Ivan! You know that guy Tom next door? Does he have a scar on his face? Or was it the guy who used to run the place?"

Ivan didn't remember any scar.

I thanked the manager of the sofa shop. I thanked the manager at Duane Reade. Eddie thanked the people at the diner. None had helped. Izabel was leaning against a parked station wagon when we got back to the art shop, shaking her head. *No Tom.* At 11:50 A.M., the shop remained closed.

"Let's try the condo Aya told us about," I said.

Detective Jamal reminded me that I was supposed to be at Cornell Medical Center giving another talk, in half an hour.

I sighed. "Cancel it."

The building in front of which Tom Fargo's car had been ticketed turned out to be a onetime pretzel factory converted to lofts. The brick had been sandblasted, a glass lobby added. The remodeling was stylish, and residents would have a great view of the Brooklyn Bridge. The co-op sat down a cobblestone street from one of New York's premier restaurants, the River Café, on a barge, which offered a five-star view of the Manhattan skyline.

We had to wait a few moments in the lobby while the doorman chatted with a short, sweaty Hispanic woman who — from the talk — appeared to be a cleaning lady, and was complaining about broken air-conditioning on the A train. She was headed upstairs to "Mister Greg's apartment."

When the doorman turned his attention to us, his polite expression became more animated.

"I recognize you! My God! You were with the President on TV! I have a cousin who lives in Barrow, Alaska. He said you stopped an outbreak there two years ago!"

His name tag read MAURICIO. The lobby seemed quiet and had potted palms under an old blowup photo of Ebbets Field, onetime home of the Brooklyn Dodgers. I'd noticed outside that signs posted on poles warned drivers that streets here were cleaned on Mondays and Wednesdays between 9 and 11 A.M. *Move your car during those times.*

"We're trying to find an old friend of mine, a man named Tom Fargo," I said.

Mauricio shook his head, disappointed that he could not help. "Sorry. There's Tom

Wilson in 4B, across from Greg's. No Fargo."

"Wilson, huh?"

"Nice man. He runs an art shop."

"Do you mind looking at this photo? Recognize him?"

Mauricio's open expression became worried, concerned, even before he glanced at the photo. "Does this have something to do with the malaria?"

"Not at all. It's a personal visit."

Mauricio looked at Eddie's face, and at Izabel Santo. He had an intelligent face, but even someone with limited intelligence would have seen through my lie.

Mauricio studied the photo carefully, held it far from his face, pulled it close, frowned, looked sick.

"Why is he screaming?" he said.

"He lost a loved one."

"He has a beard. And that hat is different. The only thing like Tom Wilson is the little space in the teeth. I can't say if this is him."

"Is Tom home now?"

"He's not an old friend of yours, is he?"

Detective Jamal held up his shield. Mauricio said, at once, "I didn't see him leave this morning, but I can call up to see."

"How about if we just go knock?"

"I have to call first. Rules. Sorry."

Jamal shook his head. "No, you don't have to call up."

We were moving across the lobby when the elevator door opened and the Hispanic woman — the cleaning lady — rushed out, screaming that there were two dead bodies in Señor Greg's apartment. That Señor Greg and Rebeca were up there in a back bedroom, lying by a roaring air conditioner, their blood soaking carpets, their blood on floors and walls.

TWENTY-TWO

Every mile heading inland took Tom Fargo farther away from safety, a harbor where he could steal a boat, the border to cross into Canada. Pittsburgh — site of the next release — lay five hours west, he reckoned, as the Subaru cruised smoothly along Interstate 80, through Allegheny Mountain passes and the Delaware Water Gap.

Soft targets. Targets filled with people who are just as guilty as the politicians and generals.

The vectors slept in their travel cups, inside the doors. National forest rose on both sides of the highway. Tom felt as if his vehicle formed a protective capsule of inevitability around him. He was aware of other cars yet felt invisible to their occupants. These people had wound him down like a spring. They'd worked on him for years. His actions now were the natural consequence of their casual, endless brutality.

Emergencies are always like this. In one city, panic. In the next, a few miles away, people eat ice cream cones and laugh at comedy movies. Pittsburgh tonight, next stop tomorrow. I have enough supply for one last release after that. The best one.

He was in a clock running backward, having scouted the infection route months ago, zigzagging through America's heartland, appraising parks, lakes, ponds. Here an Iowa state campground, where thousands of people gathered in summer, eating cotton candy or watching draft horse pulls, *feeling safe.* Here a quiet eddy beneath a Mississippi River bridge, by a beach where people lay in the sun. Hobart Haines had helped him pick the targets. Tom wanted these people to fear the very air they breathed. Hobart had said, *Make them think that TODAY might be their last one. You'll get people to do what you want.*

But Tom's confidence turned bitter as he recalled that for all his progress he was crippled in his mission. Back when he'd scouted the land, he'd assumed he'd have a regular supply of vectors. And that other attackers would be ranging through the South, hitting other targets.

330

Now there was just him and three thousand remaining insects BECAUSE OF JOE RUSH.

I can still make them think there are many attackers. Billions of mosquitoes live along the East Coast. The Americans will fear that my mosquitoes will breed with theirs. I will make them pay.

Pittsburgh, eighty miles.

The CD broadcast a sermon, recorded by another American he'd met overseas, a convert who had seen truth and gone over to the right side also. *"Fight for the sake of God those who fight us, but do not attack them first."*

Tom said, out loud, "I did not attack first. They did."

"God does not love the aggressors."

"All I wanted was to be left alone."

The GETOUT app had made New York Departure easy, directing him from Brooklyn to Eastern Parkway and the Jackie Robinson, avoiding the silvery Whitestone Bridge. "Heavy NYPD action there," the message warned. "Try the Throgs Neck Bridge instead."

In America, nothing was coordinated anymore. Not politics. Not justice. Not friendship or even safety.

Route 80 grew more congested as he approached Pittsburgh. He'd dismantled his GPS to discourage electronic tracking, in case the federals figured out who he was. His hand-scrawled directions exited him onto two-lane Pennsylvania State Route 8N in Hampton Township, and then, as his heartbeat rose in anticipation, past fast-food restaurants and signs saying 2 FOR 1 BURGERS and new subdivisions with names like Indian Lakes and suburban Hardies Road. He entered a public parking area for North Park. On a pleasant summer dusk the seventy-five-acre lake shimmered. Canoes formed silhouettes against the sinking sun. Joggers enjoyed trails. Picnickers cheered a softball game. A poodle fetched a Frisbee, veering around riders on road bikes. No one challenged the lone man with a knapsack walking casually into the state forest, carrying a plastic container swarming with vectors.

The picnic area was just as he remembered, hidden from the main trail. It abutted the blue lake, and mosquitoes were out at this time of day. No one else was by the shore as he knelt down, and opened the container as easily as if it contained potato salad. He watched his mosquitoes fly out. It was like seeing a swarm of bombers take off from a military field. The wings were the jet rotors. The vectors would hone in on human sweat or perfume like a smart bomb is programmed to veer toward targets.

The swarm dissipated, going this way and that, a few lighting on a lily pad, some heading off toward the trail, others drifting sideways on a breeze toward joggers who had appeared and retreated into the forested path.

Tom wedged the container into a muddy nook filled with cattails. There were still a few sluggish insects inside. He stood and brushed off his pants, and ten minutes later he was back in the Subaru, his radio tuned to an all-news station as he left the park. *"FBI sources in Chicago confirmed that the two men killed in a standoff — and who made a threatening phone call to Washington — had ties to a jihadist group."*

Tom smiled. The diversion had worked!

"A car registered to one of the men was found with a booby trap inside. Fortunately the bomb did not blow up. It had been rigged incorrectly."

Tom grinned because the bomb had intentionally been rigged not to work, so the agents would find planted "evidence" left in the glove compartment of the car.

"Maps identifying future targets were found

in the car. A massive manhunt for associates of the Illinois attackers is under way through- out the Midwest."

Tom laughed. No attacks were planned there.

Reaching I-80 again, he felt a small stab on his wrist and observed a mosquito there. Not one of his. It was bigger. A tiger mos- quito. He let it feed. Then it was sucked out the window by a breeze.

In two days people in Allegheny County would start to get sick, among them, he hoped, some of the special people who had caused him to choose Pittsburgh as a target.

Tom headed east and south. He carried dried camping food, granola bars and jerky, fresh water in gallon containers, and an empty bottle to piss in, if he decided to avoid stops. Four hours later he pulled off the road in West Virginia, ate a ham sand- wich, used the public restroom, and slept six hours, curled on the front seat.

Refreshed, he headed off again.

Even if the police find the bodies in New York, no one will connect me to the outbreak. I am sorry I had to kill you, Rebeca. I will pray for you.

The radio announcer said, *"In other news, White House spokesman Jack Ickel today an- nounced 'mission accomplished' in Tunisia in the effort to contain Islamic militants. Ickel said local governments are now strong enough to mop up on their own. Military aid will be diverted to humanitarian purposes."*

Tom pounded the dashboard in jubilation. *They gave in! They actually gave in! Hobart Haines was right!*

He had promised Kyle Utley to stop the attacks if the U.S. capitulated. *Now the plan's succeeded on multiple levels. Panic and death. Profit for the cause. And now that Washington gave in we can blackmail them or bring them down by releasing the information.*

Back in Brazil, Dr. Cardozo was trying to create more vectors. *If that happens we will send teams to hit the enemy in Germany and France, London and Russia!*

The promise to Kyle Utley had always been a lie.

I'm not going to stop until all vectors are out.

He'd rejected Washington as a target. He preferred to sow fear in other cities, to have America blame their leaders for the problem, not sympathize with them. He skirted the capital on the maze of surrounding highways, a man-made capsid of tar protecting human bacteria. The D.C. Beltway spilled him onto I-95 in Northern Virginia, last stretch of East Coast megalopolis.

Urban congestion dropped away. Thick forest rose up on both sides of the highway, and traffic sped up to seventy-five miles an hour. He took the Richmond bypass and three hours later crossed into North Carolina. The road went from six lanes to four. Everything looked more rural. A grassy median strip separated northbound lanes from south. Billboards jutted above pine forest, showing ads for log cabin homes; a shop that sold fudge; Pilot brand gasoline. He smelled pine sap and pig farms and freshly mowed grass. Visit the mothballed battleship *North Carolina* in Wilmington, he was advised. A gray state police car passed, lights flashing, its trooper ignoring Tom, not even glancing at the biggest threat he'd ever be near.

An hour and a half later Tom exited I-95 at the I-40 cloverleaf turnoff and steered west toward Tennessee.

Six hundred fifty thousand people lived in Memphis, on the Mississippi bluff. The rock and roll birthplace. The barbecue capital of the U.S. In summers, vacationers swelled the population on any given day to over a million.

Tom saw the Colorado license plate on the mobile home in front of him; the white and green, the outline of the Rocky Mountains. His head began to hurt. His gaze drifted down to the familiar, proud red bumper sticker.

I TOOK THE COLORADO CHALLENGE!! I FOUND COLORADO CALM!!

From inside that camper ahead, a small boy looked out at Tom from the back window. He made an imaginary pistol with his fingers. He "shot" at Tom. He looked about six.

Tom couldn't believe his reaction. After all these years he realized he was crying. He felt the tickle of a single tear on his cheek.

He did not want to look at that kid. He sped up and passed the camper. That boy was heading toward Memphis. The boy's parents might stop there to enjoy a meal, view, motel. That halt might kill them.

Tom pressed down on the accelerator, and the mobile home receded in his rearview mirror.

He thought, drying the tears with a wrist itching from the mosquito bite, that the kid had looked familiar.

He'd looked like Hodge.

The world condensed for Tom. Some people mark past years by seasons, by jobs, or by marriage. Tom divided his youth into periods corresponding to the men with whom his mother had slept at the time.

Tom thought back, transported.

Five-year-old Tom Fargo lies in his single bed in the two-room pine cabin and smells wood fire, ponderosa pine, and aspen forest outside, and a whiff of rum from the bedroom, behind the closed door. Mom and Doug are fighting in there. Mom's boyfriend drinks heavily some nights. And when Doug gets loud, so does Mom.

"You have no self-control. Like a goddamn dog!" Mom screams.

Tom lays wide-eyed, terrified. Doug has never hit him, or Mom, but he is big and scary when angry. Normally everyone likes Doug, especially women. "They give bigger tips," Doug says with a wink when he and Tom are alone.

Tom's bed is in the living/dining room in the company cabin. They all live just outside the Pike National Forest, one hundred feet from a ring of larger cabins housing clients who pay a lot of money to come here for two weeks at a time.

"Switch off the computer and reconnect with nature. Join us for a once-in-a-lifetime experience led by professional guides! Hear your heart beat in the magnificent Rockies! GET COLORADO CALM!" the brochure says.

But Colorado calm is for clients, not their guides, Doug and Mom. Tom's mom is a petite twenty-two-year-old from Denver, who got pregnant when she was sixteen, barely finished high school, and left home. Doug, twenty-five, is charming, funny, a storyteller with clients. In public, Mom and Doug are always smiling. But inside the cabin where they live for six months a year — the other six they live in Mexico — fights erupt.

"I saw you kiss that slut," Mom screams at Doug.

"So what? We agreed to do what we want. It's not like we're married, babe! Or like I'm his father!"

"Tom, don't tell clients about the fights," Mom pleads with Tom.

Mom is "excitable," Doug explains when they're hiking, alone. Mom "doesn't understand guys." There are no other kids around, and Tom is too young to go to school. Doug is usually fun. He shows Tom how to love the forest, how to start a campfire, track a bear, fish for trout, find healthy mushrooms. How to climb freestyle on rocks.

"Guys stick together! Let's pick some wildflowers for your mom! It's that cranky time of month for her. Someday you'll understand."

Doug's a six-foot-four, shaggy-haired, muscled giant who smells of moss, mushrooms, and marijuana, wears T-shirts outside even when the temperature drops to forty degrees, and says he used to be a Navy Seal.

The clients love Tom. "You're our mascot," they say. They're a mixed bunch: out-of-shape Chicago lawyers, troubled teens whose parents pay the $5,000-a-week fee, adventure seekers, singles, honeymooners, all worked to exhaustion by Doug and Mom each day. Like they're paying money to go to a military boot camp.

"Climb that rope faster! Pick up the pace!"

The clients dangle from harnesses in trees, run rapids in kayaks, eat trout they cooked over open fires on sticks. Millionaires pick up trash and run miles carrying full packs. Doug and Mom are a perfect unit when working. At night, Tom hears Mom moaning or screaming and Doug grunting and farting. One time Tom walked in and the bedroom door was open. Mom and Doug formed a gigantic hump-backed shadow in firelight, jerking like camp-ground dogs when they mate.

"You said you loved me, Doug!"

Mom crying and packing her duffel bag in the middle of the night finally. "Get dressed," she orders Tom. Mom driving them away in their rusty fourteen-year-old Civic. "Don't treat women like Doug does when you grow up, Tom! Promise!"

"I promise, Mommy."

"Can you believe he slept with Cindy Carnahan? She's twenty years older than him! No more asshole men for me!"

Guru Shahid is short and chubby and thickly dark haired all over, and he has shiny blue eyes that are always smiling at six-year-old Tom through round wire-framed glasses. Shahid was reincarnated — he says — after living a thousand years ago, in India. Guru Shahid smells of curry and onions, and so does Mom's bed when he climbs out of it some mornings in the ashram, a converted horse farm on the outskirts of Colorado Springs. Shahid is able to levitate — that means float — in the air, he says, but not when anyone is watching.

"Your mother has an old soul," Shahid tells Tom. "She lived in ancient Egypt as a princess! I was lowly, a bakery cook for the Pharaoh. I loved your mom from afar."

"Shahid sees the real me," Tom's mom says.

With a revolving cast of thirty people, who have donated their worldly goods to Shahid, Tom and Mom tend the community vegetable gardens and go on Dumpster dives in town for food, because, Shahid says, "Supermarkets throw tons of useful food away. It is crime to waste it." Tom is especially good inside Dumpsters, because he is agile. Food search parties go into town at night from the ashram. The adults lift Tom over the top of the Dumpsters and tell him to watch out for an occasional rat in there, and only take food that has not rotted badly.

Guru Shahid is the only one in the compound permitted to own money, but this is because he needs to "do business with outsiders," he says. His face is rapt when he lectures the group, explaining that truth is a mix of Buddha, Siddhartha, and Kurt Vonnegut novels. Shahid receives messages from an ancient voice that calls itself "The One" and comes to him behind the barn, he says. The voice says that a great war is coming. And that only people who know "special secrets" will be saved. The voice tells Shahid that it is important to throw off "the shackles of technology," so Shahid walks around the compound naked on Tuesday nights, when he sleeps with Tom's mom. On other nights, he sleeps with other women, or, sometimes, men.

Then one night Tom wakes up to see Shahid standing by his bedside. Shahid's eyes are shinier than usual, and he licks his lips. The matted hair on his chest seems sweaty in the moonlight. His eyes look tiny with the glasses off. Shadid's hand is touching Tom's neck when the door bangs open and Tom's mother begins to scream.

"Liar! Pervert!" Mom packs up the car.

"Where are we going?"

"I don't know. He was a fraud. He's from New Jersey, not India! I can't believe I ever listened to him!"

"How come your stomach is getting bigger?" Tom asks as they drive off. "How come you were throwing up this morning? Are you sick?"

"Not sick," Mom says. "There will be three of us now. You'll have a brother or sister. Won't that be great?"

Actually, soon there are more of them. Gunther is a ski instructor in Breckenridge, where Mom gets a job in a folk art shop, selling Navajo ceramics and western paintings to tourists; real Ed Zorensky originals of cowboys in Wyoming. Navajo rugs and ceramics. Hopi beads. Tom helps out sometimes, after school. "You have a knack for selling," Mom says. "You have an eye for art." He is now twelve. Gunther and Mom have been together for three relatively calm years.

"I'm not your dad, but I'll always be here for you," Gunther says in his thick German accent.

Gunther stays up with Tom at night and helps with math homework. Gunther knows how to cook fresh venison with lime and cilantro, chile rellenos with cheese, vegetable casseroles seasoned with fresh basil. Elk steaks.

"I thought you said meat was bad for you, Mom."

"That idiot Shahid said it! Isn't this London broil delicious?"

Gunther takes Tom skiing and teaches him how to carve turns in snow, how to keep his hands out front and downhill when they traverse deep powder.

"You are a natural athlete," Gunther says. "When you and me and your mom go back to Germany, we will all live together and ski in the Alps. You will love it."

"Will Hodge love it, too?"

Hodge is almost five, seven years younger than Tom. Tom's little brother adores him and follows him everywhere, and Tom loves it. If Gunther teaches Tom something, Tom teaches Hodge. Everyone likes Hodge. Tom takes Hodge to the bunny hill and teaches him skiing. He shows Hodge how to track rabbits and read coyote and lynx scat. He helps Hodge with homework, especially on nights when Gunther and Mom have been drinking wine or smoking marijuana, and are laughing too hard or eating too much to help Hodge out.

Tom loves that Hodge is always asking him questions. Why is the pine tree green? What

344

makes the sky blue? What happens to the dog after it dies? Why are some people taller than others?

Tom also runs Ms. Kelley's art shop when Mom is away on buying trips. In school that year, he's learning about Islamic terrorists. He's assigned to read about Islam on the Internet. He stares at photos of thousands of men and women walking around a huge twenty-foot-high black cube in Saudi Arabia, on a pilgrimage, the website says. They look peaceful and happy and seem to have purpose. They don't look like killers or terrorists. They look like a big family, going to a different kind of church. It looks nice.

Hodge and Tom sleep in a room in single beds, and sometimes Tom looks over at the little lump in the next bed and feels a swelling in his throat. One time in school a bully — an older kid — hits Hodge, and Tom comes flying out of the crowd and knocks the kid down, pummels him until his face is bloody. Tom threatens to kill the kid if he ever touches Hodge.

"You're the best brother in the world," Hodge tells Tom. Nothing, no compliment, has ever filled Tom with as much happiness.

His last memories of Hodge begin on the day their next-door neighbor — a Denver real estate lawyer named Richard Gruntz —

knocks on the door and announces that he's got tickets to that night's Nuggets game in Denver. He can take six boys along with his son Josh. Would Tom like to go?

"Only if Hodge can come."

"He's a little young to stay up that late, isn't he?"

"I won't go unless Hodge can."

So Hodge can go. And Tom makes sure that Hodge gets a window seat because Hodge can get queasy on the road. It starts to snow on the way to Denver. There was a storm last night, too, and huge piles of drift lay on both sides of the mountain roads. The radio warns of ice patches. Hodge is staring out the window, excited about the game, when Tom catches sight of Mr. Gruntz pulling out his cell phone. Tom knows that a driver is not sup-posed to use a cell phone; Tom reaches to pat Mr. Gruntz on the shoulder to ask him to stop, but at that moment — as Gruntz looks down — the van skids, and by the time Mr. Gruntz looks up they've slammed into the guardrail, snapped through it. The van is plunging down into a ravine.

Tom screams, "Hodge!"

Hodge is snapped into his seat belt so when the van turns over the boy stays fixed in place. Windows shatter. The roof caves in. The mountain flashes past sideways over upside down, and the boys are screaming and Mr. Gruntz's phone goes flying and the snowmelt stream at the bottom of the ravine is rushing at them faster, closer, and . . .

CRASH!!!

Tom hurts all over. He has never hurt this much. It is hard to see because something is wrong with his left eye. Something is in it. It's hot and sticky. He's terrified for Hodge. Mr. Gruntz has the front door open. His right arm seems to be hanging, not moving, but he's getting the boys out of the van, which has started to smoke. Smoke from the vehicle mixes with mist rising from the stream, in which the half-smashed vehicle lies sideways.

Hodge is not bleeding but he's staring at Tom in terror, gagging and clawing at his face as Tom tries to unbuckle the belt. Hodge's breathing is crazy fast. Tom's head hurts badly — myfaultmyfault I made Mr. Gruntz take Hodge. It is hard to breathe or think.

But he gets Hodge out, and sees that other than the terror, Hodge is okay. He's OKAY! Tom's relief is so profound that he wants to sit down, but he can't, because two other boys still need to get out.

The front of the van flickers with fire.

He tells Hodge to wait, sit on a rock, and he runs to the van, reaches in with Mr. Gruntz, pulls out Larry Benton, and half drags out blathering Kendall Black. Both boys are bleeding and crying. Mr. Gruntz is white-faced and says, "I'm sorry." Tom shouts at him about the cell phone, and Mr. Gruntz puts his face in his hands and cries tears and says, "I was just going to check my messages." Suddenly the van bursts into flame, fierce and yellow. The blast of heat whips into Tom's face.

Hodge has fallen asleep.

No, not asleep.

Hodge is lying sideways, toppled off the big snow-covered rock where he was sitting. No breath comes from his mouth. His little hands — gloves off — are twisted near his throat, as if he'd clutched at it. There is hardly any blood. No big injury. Tom sees the smallest, silliest-looking cut on the side of Hodge's neck. He tells Hodge to wake up, open his eyes. He shouts it. He grips Hodge by the ski jacket and shakes him. He is still screaming as Mr. Gruntz pulls him off, and then police are there and putting out the fire and firemen are helping the boys climb up the ravine, and a stranger, a woman, is dragging Tom up the hill toward an ambulance and all he can do is scream, "Help Hodge!"

Later he will learn that Hodge drowned. The cut in the neck came from glass driving into his trachea, piercing an artery, shooting blood into his lungs. He drowned just as surely as if water had flooded in there. What Tom had taken for panic had been choking. The boy drowned on his own blood while Tom was trying to help the others.

"You could not have saved him, son," the doctor says. "Do you hear? Say that you heard it. Look at me. Tom!"

Later a police detective comes to the house and tells Tom that Mr. Gruntz says he never used his cell phone in the car, that Tom must be mistaken. The detective explains that the police have a way to check if someone was using a phone at a particular moment. Gruntz never made a call.

"He wasn't using it! He was starting to! He told me!"

"Maybe you just think that! Everything happened fast."

"You killed Hodge!" Tom shouts at Mr. Gruntz, in the hospital. And at the funeral. Tom waits outside Mr. Gruntz's condo and screams, "You murdered Hodge," whenever Gruntz walks in or out. He tells anyone who will listen what Mr. Gruntz did to his brother. He calls up a reporter at the newspaper and tells her, too. Mr. Gruntz doesn't look sorry about it anymore. He looks mad. And the detective comes back and tells Mom that if Tom doesn't stop bothering Mr. Gruntz there will be "consequences," but Mom is in no shape to do anything but cry and smoke dope and sleep.

Gunther doesn't know what to do either. He takes Tom to a church to talk to a priest, a compassionate-looking older man with gray hair and a bald dome on top. The priest listens to Tom, and almost seems like he will cry. The priest tells Tom that God does things that look mysterious, but actually have a purpose.

"You mean God killed Hodge?"

"I mean that we can't understand God because his ways are complicated."

"It's not complicated! Hodge died!"

"Let me read you something from the bible."

"I don't want to hear the bible! I want you to tell me WHY HODGE GOT KILLED! YOU DON'T KNOW WHAT THE FUCK YOU'RE TALKING ABOUT!"

"Watch your language, son."

Gunther announces a month later that the house is "no fun" anymore. "You must both get over this. Bad things happen. I will be moving back to Germany next month."

Mom tells Tom that they're leaving Brecken-ridge and moving to Denver, to live with his grandparents and "have a more serious life."

"I thought you said my grandparents were dead."

"To me they were. I need to grow up now and they can help. You'll like them. We both

350

need to change. No more drinking. Or dope. I've gotten a job in a gallery in Denver. And, Tom, I promise you, I mean it, no more men."

Tennessee Welcomes You, the sign read. Tom was in the mountains now, past Asheville, and the land descended and rapidly flattened. Once it had supported tobacco farms or dirt roads funneling slave-grown cotton east to the ocean, west to the Mississippi.

I-40 traffic slowed as he reached the outskirts of Memphis. He exited the highway by the Mississippi waterfront. He passed the big University of Memphis Cecil C. Humphreys School of Law. The revived neighborhood offered upscale souvenir shops and cobblestone plazas, and he saw crowds of tourists wandering about on a lazy weekend. No malaria fear here! Cars bore license plates from many states, so Tom's Colorado one blended in. The city had the vibrant feel of a place where the population was exploding. Working from his hand-drawn map, he got turned around for a few minutes, made a wrong turn, entered a commercial zone . . . Hooters, Pancake House . . . . and passed into something more calmly residential, with fine old antebellum houses and blooming trees where moss hung from two-hundred-year-old branches that once shaded Confederate troops. He turned the car around and headed back toward the waterfront.

No more men for me, Mom had told him. *I swear it this time.*

She'd been honest about it.

Until Hobart Haines came along.

Tom reached the waterfront, and the wide, muddy Mississippi River. Crowds flowed toward the landings and park abutting the waterway, or back to the restaurants and greenways. Tom saw the tall white twin stacks of the riverboat *Queen of the Mississippi,* docking by the busy Beale Street Landing. He passed a brewpub and an old tobacco exchange converted to souvenir shops. A summer arts festival was in progress. When Tom had scouted this place it was practically empty, but now streets were packed and there were stages set up for bluegrass bands.

Tom strolled the paths along the riverfront, growing frustrated. There were too many eyes here. He could not risk a release. The last thing he needed was for some stranger to see him freeing mosquitoes. He had a lie prepared if that happened — *I'm with the University, studying them* — but only a fool would risk using it.

Also, unlike New York, where people avoided eye contact, here passersby nodded hi. A crowd had gathered to hear a popular North Carolina folk singer, Philip Gerard, perform his new hit song, "Robert Johnson and the Devil."

Tom Fargo almost fell as a drunk bumped into him, apologized, and lurched away. Giving up, he remembered the name of a city park, his fallback point, a small lake off Wolf River, a wetland Mississippi tributary just a few miles north on State Route 51.

Tom made it back to the parking area and strolled toward the dead end where he'd left the Subaru. Cars were packed into diagonal spaces like horses tethered to poles two hundred years back.

As Tom approached the Subaru he slowed and his heartbeat rose. He spotted a couple of blue-and-white city police cars there, blocking his way out.

It can't be for me.

There was a small crowd. One police car was parked so close to the Subaru that it almost touched it. Another vehicle — a Chevy Tahoe — had apparently backed into his door. The Subaru's driver-side door was bent in; worse, he saw with horror, *there was a rip in the door where the impact had taken place.*

Inside that door were the mosquitoes.

Tom started to turn away but spotted a fat woman standing with one of the policemen, pointing Tom's way. He had a feeling that the busybody was telling the cop that the Subaru was his car. Maybe she'd seen him park. The larger cop was coming toward Tom. It was too late to turn away now. Too late to come back later when there would just be a note or ticket on his car.

"Is this your car, sir?"

The woman gripped the other cop's arm, clearly insisting, yes, that's the man. The officer before Tom had a jarhead haircut and attentive stare and seemed quite fit. There were too many people here to start a fight. Even if he were inside the Subaru, it was impossible to drive off with cars blocking his way. Could he ram his way out? He told himself that what he felt was not a fear problem but an adrenaline problem. *Control the adrenaline,* he thought.

"Yes, sir!" he said, acting indignant, glaring at the trio of teenagers by the offending Chevy. "What the hell happened here?"

"They hit your car, sir. They actually called us to report it. I know one of those kids. Relax. May I see your license and registration? You're from Colorado, I see."

To protest would only make the cop suspicious. Tom reached for his wallet and remembered it was in the car. He would have to open the glove compartment to get it. But the Sig Sauer was there, too. Then he saw something that froze his blood.

A small dot, a mosquito, was climbing out of the Subaru's driver-side door through the rip in the metal.

The impact must have busted a carrying case.

A second insect appeared. There were more than three thousand insects in there. What would happen if hundreds of them began crawling and flying out?

"The registration is in the glove compartment," Tom said, heading for the passenger-side door, hoping to distract them from the rip on the other side. They were all watching him.

Which will I come out with? he asked himself, opening the compartment. *The registration? Or the gun?*

TWENTY-THREE

"Get us into that apartment," I ordered the police locksmith. I was in a black rage over the twenty-four-hour wait for a search warrant. I couldn't believe that judges had denied our request, even after the dead bodies of Tom Fargo's neighbors had been found, murdered, across the hall.

"Goddamn liberal judges. He never came home. Never came to the shop. No sign of the damn car." Eddie mimicked the reason for the delay. *"There's no proof! No evidence! You can't just break into any apartment near a crime scene."*

With us in the foyer was Detective Jamal and an NYPD canine handler named Kovics and his four-year-old German shepherd, Dorothy. Yellow crime-scene tape hung off the door across the hall. Forensics crews had left, and the bodies were long gone. The dog was trained to detect chemicals in which mosquitoes are shipped.

Sucrose solutions vary in taste and flavoring. Manufacturers add lemon or caramel to enhance taste. Dorothy would also allegedly alert to the smell of Parafilm, which to humans has no odor at all.

Dorothy strained at her leash as the eyes of the British jockeys in the lithographs on the wall seemed to watch the locksmith pull out the Medeco. My anger was a steady drumbeat in my skull. In the Marines I'd never had to deal with search warrants.

"I'm going in anyway," I'd told Jamal yesterday.

"No, you're not." With two uniformed officers, he blocked the way. "Not without probable cause."

"Two bodies aren't probable cause?" Eddie asked.

"That's like saying anytime anyone is killed, police can enter any residence within a hundred yards."

"Well, why can't they?" Izabel asked.

"I'm frustrated, too," Jamal said, "but I see the point. I grew up in Bed-Stuy. If open entry was the rule, I would have spent my whole childhood watching cops turn our apartment and neighbors' places upside down. Sir, if you go in, I've been ordered to arrest you." Jamal had folded his arms. He didn't like it. But he meant it. At least he looked miserable over it. I gave him credit for that.

Finally, Jamal located a seventy-six-year-old judge who wrote the warrant, not caring if the entry was declared invalid later. The judge told us, "If you find something, this will reach the Supreme Court. I always wanted one of my rulings to do that. Better late than never."

The dog handler was a small, athletic man, and ex-Army. As the door opened, he ordered Dorothy, in a high, squeaky voice, "Play the game! Go, girl!"

Dorothy ran in. If she found a person she'd bark and corner him. If she found a body she'd bark. The apartment was sunny and immaculate with high ceilings and no sign of life or struggle. Dorothy's claws made scraping sounds on the bare floor or were muted by throw rugs. I heard her excited breathing as she ran from couch to coffee table to corners.

Nothing.

Dorothy disappeared into the bedroom.

She came out. Nothing.

The bathroom.

Lots of South American folk art hung on the walls. I saw a painting of Brazilian rubber tappers in the forest, reminding me of people I'd seen on the ferry in Rondônia.

We're close. I saw clay vases, crudely made, marked with yellow and black geometric patterns similar to ones I'd seen in the market in Porto Velho. I saw blowguns mounted in glass and a headdress with beads and parrot feathers. The apartment was a mini-gallery. The coffee table offered colorful photography books. *From the Amazon.*

Dorothy stopped before an interesting oddity in the place, a thick closed door blocking entrance to a built-in room-within-a-room, clearly not part of the original layout. Just a square enclosure in the middle of the loft. Musical practice room, maybe, to shield neighbors from noise. A soundproof cave where a drummer could bang away.

"Or a darkroom," Izabel speculated.

Dorothy lay down in front of the door and stared at it, ears straight up.

"She's alerted," Kovics said.

"It's locked."

Eddie said with caution, "Rigged to blow?"

We regarded the room from two feet away. I asked Kovics, "Is Dorothy trained to detect explosives?"

"That was her original job."

"Which does she smell now? Explosives

or chemicals?"

Kovics leaned down and rubbed his knuckles over the dog's head, roughly. He scratched inside Dorothy's ears. The dog never shifted her gaze.

"Good girl. Find the boomboom," Kovics said. "Where's the *boomboom*?"

Dorothy immediately stood and, door ignored, began searching again in the rest of the apartment.

"I think we're okay here," Kovics said.

"You think? Or we are?" Eddie said, taking a step back.

"Call the bomb squad," demanded Isabel.

Dorothy was moving along the baseboards, sniffing, a four-footed, living divining rod.

Kovics nodded with a confidence that Eddie did not feel. "If there were explosives in there she wouldn't have left."

The locksmith breached the room as Eddie moved back. The inside had been cleaned out. Wire shelves were empty. The block tabletop was shiny bare. There was a corkboard with puncture marks from tacks. I smelled Clorox and Lysol. Someone had gone over these surfaces with double care.

"Nothing here, so why lock it?" I mused.

Dorothy was back again. She'd found no explosives in the apartment. Inside the darkroom she lay down, long nose pointed directly into the shadow beneath a counter. Her ears were straight up. Alert!

"Good girrrrrl," Kovics said in the high, squeaky voice, rubbing Dorothy's ears.

"How can she smell anything over Clorox?" Izabel asked, wrinkling her nose, crouching down to see what was under the counter.

Kovics bristled at the slight. "Dorothy has two hundred twenty-five million olfactory receptors in her nose, to your five million. She can smell a body twenty feet below an ice-covered river, and differentiate between human blood and a squirrel's."

Izabel Santo's feet were sticking out from beneath the worktable. She grunted and her sneakers scraped the floor as she pushed back into view. She held up a ripped scrap of paper. On it, blue labeling: PARAFILM M LABORATORY FILM.

My breath caught. This was the "false skin" used in the shipment of mosquitoes, the film laid over their carrying containers, blocking exit, but allowing them to feed through the surface on stored blood.

Eddie rocked back on his heels. These days he unconsciously massaged his arm that had been injured in Brazil when he was thinking.

"You did it, Tom," he said.

Jamal used the siren and dome light on our way to the art gallery. This time, he easily obtained search warrant permission on the way. The break-in team met us at the grate. Inside, Dorothy made a beeline to the basement and alerted in front of a wooden box stamped RONDÔNIA, inside of which we found a half dozen Indian-made ceramic vases. The pattern on the side was familiar.

"Uno, I think we just found the carrying cases," Eddie said. "Now where's the goddamn *guy*?"

This time when I called Ray Havlicek he came on the line immediately. He was still in Illinois, where the search for contacts of the dead terrorists was under way. FBI agents were questioning other students who had taken classes with the dead men, workers in a Northwestern University lab, and a cousin in prison in Joliet. When I explained what we'd found, Ray's breathing slowed audibly. He whistled when he heard about the Parafilm.

"So! Two groups at least! Chicago and back East."

"He's disappeared. I think we should go public, ID him. Anybody see this guy? Or car? He's wanted for questioning in relation to the attacks and two murders in New York."

"I'll run the idea past the Director."

"We should announce it now, Ray."

"It's a little more complicated than that."

"What's complicated about it?"

I heard him exhale. "We're dealing with lots of parts. The East Coast cell doesn't know you found the thread. So sure, we look for Fargo; talk to the mother. But go public too soon, we risk alerting the whole group."

"There could be more attacks in the meantime."

"Yeah, always the question. *Balance.* Give me a little time. Meanwhile, we're on Fargo. Good job."

An hour passed. Two dozen agents arrived at the shop, along with a van filled with lab technicians.

"The Director and the Attorney General are figuring out how to handle this," Ray said, when I reached him an hour later. "Hold tight. We're quietly distributing information. He gets stopped for speeding, even noticed on the highway, we have him. His name is available on certain lists."

"*Available* isn't the same thing. And what does 'certain' mean?"

"Do you want to panic these people just as we get an idea of who they are, Joe? Send them underground?"

"They *are* underground."

"Look at the big picture for a change."

"Then fill me in on the part I don't know."

"I'll share one thing, Joe," he said. "The Peace Corps has confirmed that Tom Fargo never joined it."

"I told you that hours ago!"

"Just sit tight a little longer."

"We sitting tight?" Eddie asked when I clicked off. I'd had the phone on speaker mode, so we could all hear Ray.

Izabel said, "Well? What now?"

TWENTY-FOUR

"Look at the car door, Ma! Mosquitoes!"

A small boy had spotted them. An eight- or nine-year-old kid wearing glasses, standing at eye level with the gash in the Subaru's door. The kid was pointing. Onlookers turned to stare. They saw what Tom saw; mosquitoes clustered around the gash where the larger Chevy Tahoe had rammed into the side of Tom's car.

"Ma, you said mosquitoes are dangerous!"

The cop in front of Tom glanced down and left and saw it. Another insect crawled from the hole. Tom had, at most, seconds before the looks of amusement or incomprehension turned to something far more dangerous. For the moment the accident was forgotten. The group focused on Tom's door.

The boy pulled at his mother's hand, tried to get her to leave. "You said they're bad! They make people sick!"

Whap!

Tom felt the torn metal slice into his palm as he smashed the mound of crawling insects. One or two escaped, took to the air, wobbling off, absorbed into dusk. The folk music from the landing seemed to grow louder. The faces of the onlookers had gone slack. They'd been assured by authorities that there were no more mosquitoes here. Memphis was considered, so far, a disease-free zone.

He let his anger show, raised his voice above the murmur around him as he demanded of the cop, "Don't you people spray in this town?"

The policemen had clearly been given instructions on how to soothe away fears of visitors to their city. The cop went automatic, spewed forth platitudes. "Sir, the health department has been spraying for days."

"With what? Water?" Tom demanded, moving his rump over the gash in the door. He realized with relief that the onlookers had assumed the most logical explanation, at least for a moment. That the vectors had been attracted to something on the door. Sap. *Something.* It had not occurred to them that inside the door were containers swarming with vectors. It was too much of a leap to think that Tom was driving around, releasing them.

Some bystanders were moving back, away from the accident. They'd seen infection zone news and been warned to avoid mosquitoes on news programs, at schools, at work, in newspapers. Panic was close to the surface, even here.

Tom snapped at the cop, louder, "This place is dangerous! How do I know those mosquitoes aren't infected?!"

He imagined hundreds of insects inside the door, crawling in the dark. He grabbed back his license and registration from the policeman, snatched the scrap of paper that the other driver offered, containing a home and insurance company number. The second cop was talking with urgency into his neck mike. Tom saw the man's lips form the word *mosquitoes.* The closer cop now turned to soothing onlookers. Clearly, both men had it impressed upon them to reassure visitors that their local waterfront was safe.

Several people from the crowd were now in their cars, pulling off. Someone was taking photos of Tom's car with a cell phone. He wanted to grab it away.

"I *told* you we shouldn't have come," he heard a woman snap at her husband. The man took her arm. They walked off.

Everyone was looking around, nervous, for more mosquitoes, peering at their bare arms, toward the trees and river. Danger could come from any direction. It was so small it might be invisible. Then, as if Allah himself helped Tom, the air — at dusk — began swarming with gnats.

"Something bit me," the little boy cried.

"Those aren't mosquitoes. Those are gnats," the larger cop explained.

"It's in my shirt!" a man called, slapping at it.

"They're just gnats!"

It was no use. People were rushing off, to their cars, away from the riverfront. Tom saw the alarm spreading. Former gapers stopped strollers or bikers and pointed back toward the accident. *Mosquitoes there!*

Tom heard a crunching sound of metal hitting metal. He saw with satisfaction that a hundred feet away, two cars had backed into each other. The cops hurried toward the fender bender. No one watched Tom anymore. He climbed into the Subaru and started up and his lips formed a prayer: *Thank you, Allah.*

Tom joined the stream of cars exiting the lot. He headed toward his backup release point, hoping that only one container had opened inside the door. He imagined that insects were flying out of the hole in the door. But as he calmed and got farther from the river he realized that the hole had merely presented him with a different opportunity. Any insects escaping would still be hungry, would feed, would be attracted by perfume or human sweat. Driving, he was releasing the things to attack anyone nearby. Pedestrians. Dog walkers. Diners at outdoor restaurants.

Tom's Subaru was like those vans back in Brazil from which biotech companies released genetically modified mosquitoes — sterile ones — to breed with local insects and kill the populations off. Those vans cruised around, windows open, as thousands of sterile male mosquitoes flew out. In Brazil the strategy halted disease. Here the opposite would occur.

Tom pulled into a closed Shell station, up to the air pump, as if to fill his tires. No one was watching. He pulled out the interior door panel and saw with relief that only one of the containers inside had opened, and only a little. Hundreds of mosquitoes crawled and flew in the space inside the door. He waved them from the car. They left in a small cloud that would not be visible from more than ten feet away. The cloud diminished as the vectors took off, many headed across the two-lane road, toward an open-air Mexican restaurant. Since the evening was hot, at least two hundred diners sat outside, enjoying margaritas, chimichangas, salsa dip, and happy talk.

Within a couple of days, some of you will be sick.

The release had not been planned, but it had worked.

Clouds were rapidly obscuring the moon. Heavy clouds.

The visit had been a success.

Back on I-78, Tom accelerated to check whether the car functioned normally after the accident as the first drops fell. There was no shimmy. No pull to left or right. Any damage had been cosmetic. And the last remaining sealed container still hung inside the door, ready for use.

Five hours to the final release point, 383 miles away, tomorrow night.

That final release point would be especially sweet. Even Dr. Cardozo did not know the real reason Tom had chosen it.

Tom headed east and then south, crossing into rural Mississippi.

He turned on all-news radio, which reported heavy rain ahead, and even a possibility of tornadoes. The sky was suddenly roiling with rapidly moving clouds. The road lacked streetlights. His headlights probed dark. A first fat raindrop struck the glass, and a sudden gust buffeted the car. The rain, when it hit, came on in a wave. Suddenly it was hard to see.

"We now go to New York live, where the NYPD Counterterrorism Unit is about to make an announcement. New York's Police Commissioner has just introduced Colonel Joe Rush, of the National Bioterror Task Force."

Rush again, Tom thought with fury.

Ahead, the wind was tossing branches off roadside trees. A sheet of paper went flying past. A bird was trying to fly straight, but went sideways. A man walking on the roadside fell down, raincoat flapping. Tom had never seen weather this bad come up so fast.

"Thank you, Commissioner," Rush was saying. "In conjunction with the New York Police Antiterrorism Unit and the Brazilian Federal Police, we are asking for help in locating a person of interest in our investigation. We are seeking a man named Thomas Fargo."

Tom Fargo almost drove into a ditch but straightened on the four-lane road. It was hard to see in the downpour. He came up fast on a big lumber truck with a DONALD

371

TRUMP sticker on back. He slammed on the brakes and slid but kept control. Heart hammering, he crawled through violent hail, trying to comprehend what he was hearing. He understood why the New York police might want to talk to him about the murders of his neighbors. He could not fathom how Rush had gotten his name or connected him to anything else.

Rush is a jinni, a demon.

The hated voice said, "The passport photo you see is Tom Fargo, wanted for questioning in connection with a double murder in Brooklyn, and to the bio-attacks. Fargo may not be in New York. This is his car. And license plate. The information has been distributed to police across the country, but we are also asking you to help. If you see this man or this car, call the 800 number on your screen. Detectives are standing by."

Ya Ka-lib! *Those Memphis cops will remember me.*

Rush said, "I want to stress that Tom Fargo is a person of interest only. He has not been convicted of a crime. He may simply be traveling, unaware that we need to talk to him. I will take questions now."

Those cops will remember the mosquitoes and check their report and match up my car! And the people in the crowd took photos!

372

Tom turned on the defogger. Sending up sheets of spray, he drove through a four-inch lake covering a depressed area of road. Back when he had scouted the way east, months ago, he had often seen police cars on the side of this road. Speed traps. He had no way of knowing whether such cars lay ahead, even in the storm. He had to get off this road and get rid of this car. He needed to find a big enough town for that. He had no idea how long ago the initial alert from the NYPD had gone out, whether it had been distributed in Mississippi, whether cops here knew about him.

Allah, make the storm shield me.

The radio was getting staticky. He was almost out of range of the station. But the press conference wasn't over. He switched channels and heard snatches of Christian radio, gospel music, Broadway show tunes, *Annie,* a commercial for a Triple-A league baseball game. He hit a clear station out of New Albany, Mississippi. Rush was back in the car. Rush would be in cars all over the country. And on TV screens in bars and restaurants and in millions of homes. Tom's photo, car, and license plate would be on-screen, too.

Tozz Feek, Tom thought, cursing in Arabic, fighting an urge to hit the accelerator just as he spotted a shadowy rectangular shape . . . Mississippi state police car . . . parked in the grassy median strip. Tom passed before the cop as a sheep passes the slaughterer. Tom looked into his rearview mirror. All he saw was rain streaking the back window in sheets. And then he saw headlights two hundred yards behind him. But he didn't see revolving dome lights. Was the car closing in on him a civilian one, or the cop?

Allah, I do your bidding. Make me invisible for a little while longer.

Tom did not see the headlights anymore. Suddenly the immense rear of a tractor trailer truck loomed inches from his grill. He swung the wheel and rammed his right foot into the accelerator and took a chance on passing the slow-moving truck. He had to reach the next town before the Memphis police spread information on him, *He was here an hour ago* . . . before cops in Mississippi dispatched squad cars to intersections and roads. He was whooshing past the heaving truck on a hill. Headlights rushed toward him. He hit the brakes and fell back *too late* but then jerked the car into place just before another lumber truck sailed past, heaving rain off the immense logs in back. The driver sounded his horn in a long, angry protest.

On the radio, Rush was taking questions from reporters. It was clear from the shouting that the journalists were excited. Tom pictured a briefing area at One Police Plaza, Rush at a podium, detectives there, too, reporters standing along walls and crammed into rows of metal folding chairs.

An NBC reporter, a woman, asked, *"Colonel Rush, is Tom Fargo an American-born terrorist?"*

"He is a person of interest only at this point."

"Can you be more specific?"

"We believe that items found on his property are related to the transport of mosquitoes."

"Colonel, why isn't the FBI making this announcement? Why is it coming from the New York police?"

"We've coordinated with them," Rush responded tersely.

"Colonel, if the FBI shared your feelings, wouldn't they as lead investigators be here, too? Do the FBI and NYPD disagree over whether Tom Fargo is involved?"

"It's all the same investigation," Rush said doggedly, but Tom Fargo saw that the reporter might be right.

"Colonel Rush, do you disagree with the direction that the FBI has taken in Chicago?"

"No. Does anyone have a question about

Tom Fargo?"

"Would you characterize the different priorities as a fight between the NYPD and FBI?"

"The country is facing an unprecedented emergency. We're trying to locate someone who may help save lives. I find your insistence on looking for differences between law enforcement agencies disgusting," Rush snapped.

"So you admit there are differences?"

Rush was silent for a moment. Tom could feel the man's anger over the miles. Rush's urgency was like a radar probe sweeping invisibly over the atmosphere. Rush snapped back at the relentless NBC reporter, "Have you taken your antimalarial pills this week?"

A pause. Then, taken aback, "Yes. Of course."

"Well, two hundred million Americans don't have access to them. So sit down and shut up and run the story. And if you want to be useful, put the goddamn photos of Tom Fargo on your news bulletins. Next?"

Colorado license plates were green and white. Mississippi plates were light beige or white. Tom's plate might as well be a beacon shining out from the car.

Tom was moving at forty miles an hour, ten below the speed limit, but in the storm it felt too fast.

WELCOME TO NEW ALBANY, MISSISSIPPI, BIRTHPLACE OF WILLIAM FAULKNER. GATEWAY TO THE TANGLEFOOT TRAIL!

The rain, as he turned off the main highway, fell harder. Ahead a fallen tree half blocked the road. A power line was down. He passed what looked like a small campfire but saw it was a sparking wire. Home lights were off.

The better part was that what showed in his headlights told him that New Albany was a tourist town, judging from signs advertising a Hampton Inn, Miss Sarah's Inn, Magnolia Knoll Guest House. There were signs for July baseball games in the Cotton States League. William Faulkner was NEW ALBANY'S FAVORITE SON. In the wild storm, traffic was almost nonexistent, which meant that any car out would be more noticeable to police.

The periphery of the city looked similar to others Tom had scouted in the Southeast. The land was slightly rolling and green, forest once, the air perfect for mosquitoes. Mississippi and Alabama had been two of three U.S. states worst afflicted when malaria was rampant in the country. It wasn't until the 1940s that the disease was eradicated in the Deep South, by DDT.

It's back, he thought, driving past a utility truck and men on a telescoping ladder, in the downpour, wearing yellow slickers, working on restoring power. The town had a spread-out feel. He passed empty strip malls and closed-up gas stations. The roads were mostly two lanes wide, with a middle turn lane by shopping centers.

He knew what he was looking for but not where to find it. He drove by the feel of neighborhoods, figuring that what he needed would not be downtown, *too geared for tourists and business,* and not in a wealthy residential area, but somewhere in between. He was looking for a no-man's-land of strip malls and low-end swap shops, hockshops, and, he hoped, auto-repair shops. He'd noticed in his zigzag route east earlier this summer that these areas marked most American towns.

He passed a Walmart and Food Lion with big, empty parking lots, car dealerships, a seafood restaurant, a raised rail bed where freight slow-rolled by. He saw a Sonic restaurant. It was too risky to go into a bar — if one was even open — and ask directions.

Come on . . . come on . . . It has to be here.

He was on Bankhead Street, a main drag, when he saw a red dome light racing toward him in the rearview mirror. An ambulance passed, heading for an accident, or taking victims to a hospital.

More lights came up behind him.

A police car shot past, following the ambulance.

There! He saw it, with triumph and relief!

The repair shop was wedged between a Pep Boys and a Kentucky Fried Chicken. He made a right turn into a small parking lot, beneath the BOB BENTLEY'S FOREIGN AUTO sign. His mom used to go to a shop like this for car repairs, leave her Nissan overnight, with keys above the visor. Tom did the same thing when in his late teens, before going overseas.

The layout here was classic, a lot in front, filled with domestic and foreign models to be repaired, or ready for pickup. A narrow driveway looped him out of view, behind the shop. More cars were parked here in a potholed dirt area, backed against a brick wall, in the storm.

I can't be seen from the street here. It's Saturday night, and this place probably won't open until Monday morning, thirty-six hours from now.

The shop was locked. There was no way to know if there was an alarm or camera.

But in the old days, in Colorado, lots of drivers left their keys in their cars. Also, he'd seen a small lockbox by the front door, chained to the brick. A sign above it said, KEYS.

I need a car. But it can't be one that will break down two miles from here. I need one that's been fixed already, or needs something small.

Tom backed the Subaru into a narrow space between a twenty-year-old Jeep and a new Toyota 4Runner. He stopped before his rear bumper hit the wall. The Subaru was now dwarfed, partially hidden by larger cars. Tom exited the Subaru, ignoring the rain that instantly soaked him.

He opened the trunk and toolbox and removed a large Phillips-head screwdriver and knelt in the mud by his front license plate. The first screw he tried to turn was stuck.

Shit.

Tom applied pressure. Nothing. Rain blinded him. He hit the screw to loosen rust. He tried again. The screw moved a little. He tried hard. He got the screw off.

Tom went around to the back of the Jeep and unscrewed its Mississippi license plate more easily. He affixed the plate to his Subaru. Now, if a police patrol came by, the officer would see a Mississippi plate.

Hurry. Find a car to steal.

The nearest car, a Smart car, tilted sideways due to two flat tires. Beside it was a Chevy Malibu, *locked,* and a blue Hyundai Sonata, *locked,* and then a Volkswagen Passat, *locked. Forget looking for keys in the visor.*

Tom went back to the Subaru, froze at a loud *cr-aack,* and saw, above and behind the brick wall, a tree falling in the wind. He wiped rain from his eyes, and took a pry bar from the trunk. He strode to the front of the shop. There were no headlights on the road. But that could change in a moment.

At the shop's front door Tom listened for barking, in case there was a dog inside. He did not want to risk an alarm unless he had to. He knelt beside the lockbox. Like a lumberjack, he raised the pry bar and began slamming it into the padlock guarding the box. The back hinges of the box gave way before the padlock. He reached in. He found three sets of keys and more keys inside envelopes, along with notes from their owners.

Floyd, she keeps stopping dead at lights, said the note with the first key. Forget that one.

Floyd, it still makes that noise when I go more than 30 miles an hour. Ball bearings? said the second note.

Not that one either.

Change the oil.

That one. The key chain said HONORING VETERANS. Tom stood with rain pounding his face. He went out back and pushed a button on the key fob and heard a loud *beep* from his left as headlights on a Ford flicked on and off.

He needed five minutes to transfer the vectors and supplies: med kit, guns, golf bag, suitcase, from the Subaru to the Ford. Suddenly he saw twin lights stabbing into the lot. A car was coming. He crouched down between two vehicles. Had a patrolling cop spotted the smashed-in lockbox out front? Was it just a bored officer on routine patrol? Had someone seen him and called the cops?

Tom pushed against the side of a Jeep as a car crunched and squished into the back lot.

Allah, help me.

The white searchlight showed rain sheeting down as it stabbed out, car to car. It illuminated the sliding twin rear doors of the shop, and the forms of cars on hoists inside. A car door slammed. Tom heard a grunt.

382

He heard boots splashing in puddles. He saw the reflection of the cop and flashlight in the window of the shop. The cop stood still now, listening. But the only thing to hear was wind. The parked cars sat as still as animals frozen in fear.

Tom realized that he had left the Sig Sauer in the Subaru. It would be visible, sitting on the seat, if the light stabbed that way.

The light shut off. He heard the police car roll away.

Ten minutes later he was on the road again, driving back toward the highway. The Ford's fuel gauge indicated a full tank of gas, enough for the four-hour trip. The sky ahead lit up with an awesome display of lightning, troposphere to earth, an inverted, bare tree of electricity, electric trunk and branches, snaking down like a trident at anything living in a flash of white that left its imprint on his retinas. Frozen in the glare were swaying trees and rooftops and bouncing power lines. Tom felt chilled from the rain. He coughed suddenly and violently.

Was he getting sick?

"Just a few more hours," Tom said to himself. Normally he would have fed the insects by now, but he wanted them hungry. He wanted them to feed when he released them tomorrow at a very specific place.

When he found an all-news station, Rush was gone from the airwaves. But Rush had, tonight, recruited a hundred million people to help him find Tom.

In Islam, Tom knew, the story of the biblical flood was regarded as real. That was the feel here, now; of punishment, of rage and revenge.

Tornado warnings . . . get inside, the radio said.

Trees had snapped or bent sideways, a branch tumbled across the road like a tumbleweed, a bird flew past at eye level but backward, a cardboard box sailed toward him and away as if sucked into the air by a spaceship. He hydroplaned through a lake in the road. Had there been a tornado here? He traveled inside a ghost corridor of smashed pine trees, trunks snapped like toothpicks, debris rolling in the road, a flapping metal sign, ERNIE'S BAIT & AMMO, unattached to any shop, just sitting in a tree.

And in the next flash of lightning, the accident he was about to plow into. The cypress tree lying three quarters across the road, blocking it unless he went around on the grass. The sparking power line, writhing and snapping. The silver sedan must have collided with the overturned semi. The truck lay in a V shape, cab going one way, container the other, driver's door open, body lying half in and half out, as the dome light strobed and buzzed in the rain.

He saw smoke or steam rising from the long trailer in back. Dry ice? Liquid oxygen? Something explosive?

Tom didn't know and did not want to find out.

He needed to get around the damn thing, but he did not trust the soggy median strip to hold up the car. He slowed, tapping the spongy brakes, risking the road edge. A figure stood in the rain ahead, waving at him to stop. It looked like a boy. Tom needed to get around the kid without forcing the car into the ditchlike median strip. He didn't want to run the skinny kid over but saw he had no choice. There was no other way around. He hit the accelerator, but the wheels spun the car sideways. He was sliding into the ditch. Then the wheels caught at about the same instant that there was a violent smacking sound on his window.

A man loomed there. A man with a gun, shouting at him, to stop. Right now. NOW!!

There was no way to speed up, to get away.

Tom took his foot off the accelerator, heard thunder, heard his own breathing, heard the stupid ad for a comedy show on the radio, heard the kid open the back door as the man opened the front one. The gun was now two feet away, pointed at Tom's face.

"You were going to goddamned drive away and leave my family here."

"That's not true."

"Shut up. Get out. Get out now and help Wayne carry his mom into the backseat, you hear me?"

The man was at the breaking point. He must be from the car that had collided with the overturned truck. The boy would be his son. The injured woman would be his wife. They'd been standing here waiting for help, and Tom had tried to drive past them. Tom had no illusions. This man was on the verge of firing.

"Sure, sir. Sure. Let me help your boy there."

Tom. Good Samaritan Tom.

"I ought to shoot you, mister," the man said.

"I'm sorry, sir. I really am. I didn't see you."

"Don't give me that!"

"She's hurt. Let me help. Let me get her into the backseat, sir. She needs medical attention."

"You're damn right she does. You're taking us to the hospital, in New Albany."

Back where I just came from, Tom thought, dragging the semi-conscious woman through the storm by the arms. Tiny thing. Cotton dress. One shoe off. Blood on the chest. She wore a hijab, a soaked head scarf, so *she is a Muslim. An American Muslim. What a joke.*

"Just get us to the hospital" the man said. "And keep this car steady. And pray that my finger doesn't squeeze down, because I know you are the asshole who was ready to drive right by my wife and boy."

TWENTY-FIVE

The FBI contingent rushed in as the press conference was ending. Ray Havlicek — still in Chicago — must have called his New York office when he heard what I was doing. *Stop Rush right now!*

Eddie quipped as I left the podium that Ray had not moved this fast on anything, ever, so I should be proud. I'd finished answering the last question, so it was too late for Ray to stop the alert from getting out. The reporters — sensing conflict — looked like hungry animals, watching prey. The lead agent, a tall blond man, led the police commissioner into a back hallway as his staffers spread out like security guards at a rock concert.

Their faces were expressionless, but their posture and coordination screamed of disapproval. This was a polite raid.

"Hey, Dr. Rush, I see that the Bureau and NYPD are getting along just great," quipped the wiseass NBC reporter, Vicki Ponte, grinning, in the front row.

Temperatures in the room had been turned down to discourage mosquitoes. The usual New York–crowd odors of sweat, perfume, or cologne had been replaced by DEET or Avon Skin So Soft. Insecticides floated through office and prison ventilation systems throughout the city, and the effect had accelerated the draining away of repellent supply elsewhere across the country. *If the terrorists hit another city, casualties will be astronomical,* I thought.

The NBC reporter sidled up to me. "Anything you want to share, Colonel, before they shut you down?" She gave me her card. "Coordinated investigations? Give me a break!"

I sensed the worst when I reached the police commissioner, still huddled with the lead agent, nodding in agreement, steadily and unhappily. The agent turned to me, disgust on his face, cell phone extended. "Mr. Havlicek wants to talk to you, sir."

Ray's voice was dead, flat, enraged. "You couldn't wait even a few hours, could you, Joe?"

"I'm not sure we have a few hours to wait, Ray."

"You're out," Ray snapped. "Hand in your

389

credentials. Clear out of Columbia. Go home to the woods and take Eddie with you."

"I'm working in New York, Ray. I'll stay in New York."

"Oh, I think you'll find that your new friends feel otherwise," Ray said. "They'd prefer to keep their federal aid. Because it all disappears: roads, schools, cops, too . . . if you stick around in any capacity. Also, on a personal note, you should be ashamed. You had Aya sleep at the FBI? Work around the clock? Christ, she's sixteen."

"That was her idea. You ever try to stop Aya?"

"Pshaw! You don't pay attention to the President. Or to me. But a teenager leads you by the nose? Give me a break."

"If you did your job, I wouldn't have to."

"You think this is personal," Ray said. "You're wrong. There's no denying you made a big contribution. You found Brazil. You ID'd Fargo. I'm not blind to it. But there are other considerations. Tell you what," Ray said, and for a moment I thought he was reconsidering. "You want to stick around? Then help out on the tip line. It's important? You diverted detectives for it? Great. You and Eddie work the phones. *Tip line! Joe Rush here!*"

When I said nothing Ray made a mocking sound. "Oh? NOT so important anymore? I didn't think so. Let other people do the shit work. It's all bright lights for Joe. And if you want to tell everyone I didn't back you up in Brazil, be my guest. Also, Izabel Santo is going home, on the nine P.M. Varig flight out of Kennedy."

I swallowed my pride and said, "Aya loves being an intern. Don't take it out on Aya because of me."

"Oh, I'll keep her on. Just not you." Ray sighed. "Besides, if I hindered her getting into college, her mother would kill me."

"You're covering up something."

"Go back to the woods. I'll say you've gotten sick. You're taking time off. You'll stay a hero, Joe. See? Don't worry. I know what's really important to you."

He clicked off. The police commissioner was a good man, and he looked mortified, furious. He'd conferred with the Mayor while I was being chewed out by Ray. "I feel lousy about this, Joe. You have our gratitude. You saved lives. You'll always have a friend at the NYPD, and in my home. But for the moment, you won't be working with us. Anything else you need? Ever? Please let me know."

TWENTY-SIX

"You're out? I won't work with Ray!" Aya Vekey snapped at me over the phone. "I hate him!"

I was in Izabel Santo's apartment, sitting on the bed, watching her pack for her trip home. Men in their underwear look clumsy and half dressed to me, but half-dressed women seem provocative. Eddie was at Columbia, cleaning out our office. Jamal had shaken my hand, thanked me, and been reassigned. "You did good work, sir," he said.

"Aya, you're only hurting yourself if you quit. You love this work. The internship will help you get into college."

"I'll get in just fine, Joe!"

"You need to get used to having Ray around. He's marrying your mother whether you like it or not."

"Don't tell me what I have to do. No one tells you!"

When I sighed she softened. "Is it my fault this happened? Because I slept at the office? I started it?"

"It has nothing to do with you."

"Well, I don't understand how you *find out all these important things and helped them* and instead of making you a hero, Ray *fires you.*"

"Don't quit as a favor to me."

She hung up.

"I like her," Izabel said. "Fiery."

Tom Fargo was out there somewhere, moving around. He was out there and by now had probably heard my announcement, and might have gone to ground. But the news was now spread to every police department and federal agency in the country. I did not regret what I'd done.

"Come to Brazil with me," Izabel said, folding the last pair of jeans into her bag. "Help us track the people who set up that lab in the jungle."

"I don't speak Portuguese, remember? You're the one who said it. *What kind of moron goes to another country and can't speak the language?*"

She straddled my knees. She smelled great. Her arms went around my neck. Grinning, she said, "Hurt your feelings?"

I laughed.

"Come for a week or two, to a place where you'll be . . ." she said, brushing my cheek with an index finger, "appreciated."

"After."

"Because you might be needed here? Because you might think of something? You won't give up?"

"It's my nature."

Outside, it was hot, even for summer, and Riverside Park was still and green in the streetlights; Grant's Tomb a looming edifice, and the tiny grave beyond it, the little fenced-off resting place of the *Amiable Child,* lay whitish in moonlight. At the window I looked out. A man and boy walked out there, with a dog. I imagined that they were the Amiable Child and dead general, eternally guarding the ground where they had been laid to rest. Still alert.

Izabel and I kissed and started making love. She'd just put on her travel clothes but slipped them off easily. But there was no lust to it, and no love either . . . it was just something to do. Our hearts were not in it, so we stopped.

"Rain check," she said, dressing again.

Eddie and I would drop her at the airport and then Stuart and Allison had invited us for a late dinner at their apartment. I planned to go over my notes after that. Izabel was right. Even fired, I might think of something.

When the doorbell rang I figured that it was Eddie, come to fetch us. But the voice on the intercom belonged to Vicki Ponte from NBC News, always the pest.

"I got a phone call for you, Colonel. Can I come up?"

"How did you know I was even here?"

"Major Nakamura. The call I got? It was from a man who phoned the tip line but got the runaround. He figured I'd know where you were. He reached me by calling my boss. Get it? He had access at NBC. You'll want to speak to him."

Annoyed but intrigued, I hit the buzzer. Vicki was probably still working the FBI/NYPD split angle, weaseling her way in here to try to get a sour grapes quote. But at the moment, I was not particularly busy.

And when Vicki walked in she surprised me. She came alone, no camera. She did not mention the FBI. Her eyes went from Izabel to me. She said, holding up her smartphone, "I can reach him now. He told the tip line detective that he would only talk to you. The detective says no, tell me. But he'd seen the press conference. He'd seen the FBI take over. He was afraid to talk to anyone else."

"Why? Why afraid of the FBI?"

"He'll tell you himself, I guess."

"This man had your private number?"

"I told you. He called our anchorman. See? He had Lester's *private number.* And Lester called me."

"Meaning he's important."

"Meaning let's make a deal before I call him back."

"No," I said, sounding like Aya.

"Hear me out. If something comes of this, give me the story. That's fair. If you meet him, I come along."

"In other words, you *don't* know what he has to say?"

She looked annoyed. But then confident. "He said I can come if it's okay with you."

I said nothing. Vicki Ponte insinuated herself further into the apartment. She sat down, like it was her apartment. She said, "Well, which do you like better? Not making deals? Or not finding out?"

"In Brazil we would make you tell," Izabel Santo remarked.

"Good thing I'm not there. Believe me," Vicki said, "on the way here I had my guys check him out. He's no lightweight."

"Okay. I agree. What's the name of this important man?"

"He's retired State Department. *High up* State Department. His name is Hobart Haines," she said.

TWENTY-SEVEN

Jetblue flight 1024 to Albuquerque was delayed due to bad weather over Ohio. Otherwise I never would have made it on time. Eddie dropped me at Kennedy, that deteriorating madhouse of an airport, after letting Izabel out at the international terminal.

"If you change your mind about coming, let me know," she said, and kissed me on the mouth. Eddie, grinning, said nothing but raised his brows as he started up the car.

The jet was full so I'd had to buy a Mint class seat. As Manhattan's spires fell away I turned on my laptop and tried to reach Aya. No luck. I checked news reports. No progress in finding Tom Fargo, if they were right.

Time stretches out on planes. It was impossible to believe we were moving at 540 miles an hour. Or that Hobart Haines had insisted he'd only speak to me in person.

He seemed old and paranoid. *How do I know it is really you if we talk on the phone?* But he'd managed to reach me through high-level contacts, so I was humoring him now.

I think I know where Tom is going, Haines had said.

I watched the seat-back route map, which showed a plane zigzagging west, forgoing a straight route. I shut it off. I gazed out the window at a landscape that formerly hosted malarias. The Ohio Valley — once forest, now suburbs or farms — had produced millions of mosquitoes to sicken wagon train riders. TVA dam builders in Kentucky had contracted malaria in droves. The disease had been prevalent as far west as New Mexico. In the 1880s the East Coast from Massachusetts to Florida was rampant with it. In 1942 Washington created the Office of Malaria Control in war areas, which evolved into the CDC. By 1952 the East Coast was clean.

I hope my trip isn't a wild-goose chase, I thought as a flight attendant brought Mint class dinner: poached lobster, the luxury at odds with the emergency. I had a fold-down massage seat protected by a privacy-enhancing plastic shield, like a face guard on a level-four mask.

"Do you mind if I ask you a question,

Colonel?"

My neighbor, a big dome-headed man in his forties, sipped his second Grey Goose martini. People who need permission to ask a question invariably have an unpleasant one in mind.

My neighbor had eyed me disapprovingly from the moment he'd seated himself. He'd clearly recognized me but followed the New York tradition: Don't talk to your seatmate until time lapses in a flight. Initial silence marks you as acceptable. New York rules. What a place.

He was robust looking, in an open-collared shirt and yellow V-necked cashmere sweater. He smelled of good cologne, so he took malaria medicine or believed he'd never catch the disease. He'd been reading stock market reports over his dinner of herb-crusted monkfish and white wine.

"Ask away," I said.

"If you don't mind, why is the *government* wasting money sending you people first class?"

There was an unpleasant edge to the words *you people.* He probably regularly ranted against "big government," although I suspected he loved it enough when it came to corporate bailouts. I didn't have time for an argument. I just told the truth. Which was better than the way I'd treated Vicki Ponte, sending her home for a travel bag, then bolting to the airport, leaving her behind.

"I'm paying for the flight, sir. Not Uncle Sam."

He blanched. "You?"

"Why not? My trip. My dollar."

He had the self-awareness to turn red with embarrassment, grace enough to apologize by asking if he could buy me a drink, even though they were free. I was not interested in fellowship, but, contrite now, he wanted to talk. *Hell, it kills time.* He told me that his name was Robert Packer and he was the president of a hedge fund in Stamford, Connecticut. He was on his way to Albuquerque to meet with an important client. I didn't care. He asked the purpose of my trip. I just said, "Family." This was true, but not related to my family at all.

I almost married Tom's mother, Hobart Haines had said on the phone. We were over Texas, the pilot announced.

"What did you just say, Robert? My mind wandered."

"I was asking what you learned about the investments."

"What investments?"

"You know! The fund? The South Ameri-

401

can one that poured all that money into drug companies that make antimalarials, two weeks before this whole mess began?"

I turned to him, my pulse picking up. Maybe this was one more silly rumor. But maybe Mint class travel had not been a bad idea after all. No one had said anything to me about suspicious investments. Ray just said that I didn't understand the big picture. He'd never explained what the big picture was.

"You don't know?" Robert Packer looked surprised.

"I just track disease."

"Well! I talk to brokers all over the world every day. We all know that the FBI's checking out money that went into drug companies — Capper, Poong-Koman, Humbles — before the outbreak. Whoever did it made billions. By the time everyone else got in, those stocks had hit the roof."

"These firms are in South America, you said?"

"Argentina and Brazil, I think."

"Do your, uh, friends know if the FBI found a connection between the outbreak and investments?"

He looked puzzled. "I was asking you that."

"We're compartmentalized," I said. "The

left hand never knows what the right one is doing."

"But that's ridiculous."

"Tell me about it. Excuse me, Robert. I have work to do."

I e-mailed Eddie and asked him to check on the alleged investments. And then Izabel, asking her to check brokerage firms in Rio or São Paulo. *Might be nothing. Might be big.*

I tried Aya again. Still no reply. I dozed, dreamless. Suddenly I was awake and we were landing. Robert Packer waved goodbye in the terminal. I rushed outside with my carry-on bag and got in line for a yellow cab, whose driver shook his head when he heard where I wanted to go.

"Santa Fe? That'll cost about three hundred eighty dollars. There's a shuttle bus, though. A lot cheaper."

I handed over four one-hundred-dollar bills. "Big tip if you hurry up."

The one-hour ride felt like five. The dawn sky was starting to lighten. We passed the twinkling lights of desert towns beneath white morning stars. The moon was a huge reddish crescent that looked closer to earth than it did back East. It seemed that it might strike the horizon. Climbing, the highway passed an Indian casino's neon sign. The number of trucks on the road multiplied with daylight, as if they were animals emerging after sleep.

I tried Aya again, and checked news, to read with gratitude but alarm that police in Memphis had just announced that Tom Fargo had been in their city yesterday. Positive ID.

So the news conference worked.

My excitement turned to dread as I watched a mom and her son — he looked about eight — being interviewed.

"I saw mosquitoes flying out of his car! There was a hole in the door!" the boy claimed.

Next came clips of police roadblocks near Memphis, and along rural roads in nearby Tennessee and Mississippi. Every officer in that tristate area had been provided with photo kits and sketches of Tom Fargo, the ones I'd shown at the conference, and which now flashed on-screen.

He's driving around releasing mosquitoes, I thought.

Ping! *E-mail from Aya! Finally!*

But I didn't open it because the cab had left the interstate and was turning onto Hobart Haines's red-dirt, suburban road, on the outskirts of Santa Fe. It was narrow enough for two cars to barely pass if they risked ruts on the side. Properties were large. Driveways snaked to half-hidden one-story homes. The land was arid; arroyos, dry runoffs from violent downpours, depressions sprouting cactus and thorn shrubs, wet leaf hackberry, quince, and peachleaf willows. The cab threw up dust. The sky was pastel blue and smeared with a single dagger-shaped cirrus cloud facing east–west.

"Tell me what you know now," I'd urged Hobart Haines, on the phone. "It will save time."

"Face-to-face is better, Colonel." The voice had been hoarse, and hesitant, as if the man was sick. "I was a diplomat. I don't want anything for myself. I don't want publicity. I saw the FBI shut down your press conference. So! Just between me and you."

His property began at a cattle guard fence, which swung open by remote control after I phoned to tell him I was here. The house was almost invisible from a hundred yards off because it blended in, built into the mountain. Or, more accurately, it seemed to be emerging *from* the mountain, as a low mass of steel and concrete that jutted into the morning chill. The angular construction might have graced a 1960s architecture magazine. The steel deck — and figure in a wheelchair — was accessible from a staircase or deck-level sliding picture windows. The view would be downhill to city and valley. I smelled sage, pinyon, and coffee as I got out of the cab, and asked the driver to wait.

"Waiting costs more."

"Then you will get it," I said as a woman came down the steps from the deck. Filipino, I saw. In her late twenties. Short and slim, in denim jeans and matching lightweight jacket, long black hair falling free to her narrow waist.

"I'm Josie. Hobart didn't sleep, waiting for you. He is sorry he made you come so far, but he did not want people listening in on the phone."

"He's sick?"

She considered the question, a gentle intelligence in her face. "He is . . ." She searched for a word to describe his condition. "Lonely."

Her boot heels made snapping sounds as we mounted the deck stairway. A big house, an old man, a private nurse. *Money.* Haines looked shrunken close-up, and I smelled wool and age over the sharper odors of bacon and coffee. I saw a green oxygen canister beside him; unused but ready if he started to wheeze. The house seemed solid, and its sharp angles challenged a notion of deterioration. The figure looked as if a good wind could sweep it away.

"Colonel Rush, thank you for making a long trip."

"I hope it will be worth it, sir."

Haines nodded as Josie set up folding tables and put steaming coffee mugs on them. He was a soft lump beneath a Pendleton blanket, a red stocking cap on against the morning chill. The eyes were watery blue. The voice was hoarse. I imagined Tom Fargo — at this moment — releasing thousands of vectors by a river, park, field.

"I want to tell you a story, Colonel."

If regret had human sound, it would be the voice of Hobart Haines.

An outdoor fireplace/oven sent mesquite smoke across the deck. Josie was putting down, for me, scrambled eggs with peppers mixed in. Crispy bacon. Tabasco sauce. For Hobart, oatmeal and a small spoon, for tiny bites.

"I was sixty-three years old when I met Annie. Tom's mom."

The coffee was chicory flavored, and revived me. The heat was extreme from the oven, yet the onetime State Department star did not seem to mind. The rising sun glared off his wire-rimmed glasses. Regret is acid in the human heart.

"I'd retired. Never married. I'd inherited my parents' home in Denver, and Annie moved in next door." The right side of his face smiled. The left side remained fixed. *He's had a stroke.* He said, "I fell for her but I was . . . well . . . inept in social matters."

"Shy," I suggested.

"It's funny," he said in a way that suggested he did not think it funny at all. "In my work I'd always been good with people. I could walk into a palace with a Saudi prince who hated us and come out with an agreement. I knew how to threaten, back off, walk away. You'd think a good negotiator could do a simple thing like court a woman."

"No one ever said that's simple."

"You're kind."

Curbing impatience, I said, "Tell me about Annie, sir."

"She was very beautiful. She'd lost a son. She was struggling to get over it. Working in an art shop. Extra protective of Tom. When I saw his photo on TV yesterday, I thought, *I was afraid something would happen, but this is even worse than what I feared.*"

"What did you think would happen?"

But he would get to things in his own way. He grasped the little spoon but did not use it. "Annie wouldn't admit it, but Tom was wounded. He'd been dragged around place to place, lived with a succession of worthless father figures. He'd lost his brother in a car crash and blamed himself; lost faith in everything; a quiet kid who spent a lot of time alone. No friends. Hours hiking or on the Net. Annie told me — later on I mean — that she'd gone into his room once and he was on his computer, on an Islamic website. He was seventeen then. More coffee?"

"Keep going, sir."

His eyes closed. I wondered if he had fallen asleep. But then he resumed talking.

"You don't wear a wedding ring, Colonel."

"I'm divorced," I said. I did not mention Karen, my fiancée, who had died a few years ago.

"I bet when you courted your wife, you did all the normal things. Flowers. Romantic weekends."

"Oh, I think in courtship anything you do is normal."

"I didn't want to drive her away, tell her that Tom was in bad shape. I wasn't his father. I was the old guy next door, who fixed things, drove them around if her car was broken. The harmless eunuch who listened to her talk about men who wanted to take her out. I just," he said, "talked."

"I don't understand."

"Why should you? Ineffective diplomats! A writer once described us as *men in their underwear, dancing with brooms.* I did what I did best, talk. Pontificate. Educate about good things in America. I actually thought I could get closer to the boy by telling him things I'd learned in my career." He laughed self-mockingly.

"Good things about America?"

"We'd take drives. Annie had ignored the kid for years, so she insisted that we do things together. I told him about Iran when we were at Pikes Peak, on a picnic. I talked about how to balance threat with action. How to fool the other side in negotiations. How even presidents fold to threats behind the scenes. *We traded arms but we got back hostages, Tom. It's important to know how far the other side will go.*

"Other guys talk baseball or take a kid fishing. I took him to Los Alamos to see where the atomic bomb was born. Tom just sat there. He never complained. I thought he enjoyed it. But on the day he exploded, I saw that I'd fooled myself."

"Exploded?"

"It was the week she said she'd marry me. The happiest I ever felt. For six hours."

I felt as if the second hand of my watch was a razor, scraping my skin as it cut away time. I wanted to shake him and demand to know where he thought Tom Fargo was going. But you let a person get to things their own way, because often you learn more if you do.

"I'd proposed the night before . . . had a few drinks and built up courage, and she'd shocked me, actually said yes! She said I made her feel safe. She said the boy needed a reliable man. She didn't love me, but she respected me and that was enough. We were going to tell him at lunch. Annie worried how he'd react. She'd promised him over and over, no more men, and broken those promises."

"You were nervous."

He smiled, and I saw what he'd looked like when he was younger. He'd been handsome. "I wanted his approval."

"That makes sense, sir."

He sighed. On the blanket, his crablike fingers were scratching at the fabric, bunching it.

"I was nervous so I talked. The craziest thing started it. I looked up and saw fighter

411

jets on maneuvers out of Colorado Springs. Suddenly I'm launching into a tirade about defense contractors. How the company that built those jets made parts in different congressional districts, to influence congressmen there. As if the kid could care! I'm going on about how diplomats want peace, generals want peace, but contractors want equipment used so they can sell more. Annie is squeezing my hand, wanting me to stop. And out of the blue, in the middle of this, Annie turns to Tom and blurts out, "Honey, Hobart and I decided to get married."

"And Tom blew."

"You're damn right. I was terrified. He was screaming so loud that I could barely drive. He's calling her a liar and a fool and demanding that I stop the car and let him out. He's out of control. Someone ought to kill the contractors, he says, get a rifle or bombs and go to all the factories, blow them up. Make an example of one company. He's ranting about Muslims killed by those planes. It's all mixed up. *You're going to marry him? YOU TOLD ME THAT HE'S AN OLD MAN AND YOU HAVE NO INTEREST IN HIM!*"

"Sorry," I said.

"I knew even before she told me that we

were not going to get married. I actually had to stop in the next town. He wouldn't ride with me. She wouldn't leave him. And she'll protect him *now*, you know. She'll never help you find him. She'll never do anything to hurt that kid again."

"He's not a kid anymore," I said, knowing that the FBI had been to see Annie. Hobart was right. She'd paid for Tom's car. She'd given him a job. She didn't care, she'd told Ray's agents, if they arrested her. She'd not say anything to harm her son.

"Hobart, if that's what made it fall apart, it would have fallen apart anyway," I said gently.

"I know."

"Where is he going?"

"Didn't you hear what I said? The cities where he's released insects? Have you found what connects them? New York? Newark? Now Memphis. Look for a defense contractor with operations in those cities. He's doing what he said. Making an example of one company. Find other places where they have branches, wait for him there."

Doubtful, I said, "That was an awfully long time ago. You think he's still that way?"

"Well, he's here, isn't he? Attacking us, isn't he? He went over there to join them and came back, didn't he? Do you have a better idea? He's targeted one company. Figure out which one."

I heard a boy screaming in my mind. *I don't care about your stupid lectures. Someone ought to blow everyone up.*

Regret smells like an old blanket, mothballs and sage, shoe polish and pinyon; it sounds like a hissing oxygen tank on a deck in New Mexico.

Haines said, "Ten years later I met my wife, Cyn, and fell in love. This house was Cyn's. Cyn died of cancer five years ago. She left the place to me."

"Things worked out," I said.

"I was lucky in the end. But you never forget the first one. I keep thinking, what if I gave Tom the idea?"

Josie was back, hands on hips, looking down at Hobart with caring disapproval.

Is it possible what he's saying is true, or did I just hear rambling fears from an old man who is out of touch? Is it conceivable that the boy who Hobart Haines knew grew into a man who has targeted one company?

Josie piped up. "You need to sleep, Hobart. And you should go, Doctor. Your driver was a thief and I sent him away. My friend will take you to the airport and charge you nothing. I will fill a thermos with coffee. And a sandwich for the plane."

Check it out, I thought. *Fast.*

TWENTY-EIGHT

Tom Fargo forced himself to look meek and afraid, but he was waiting for an opportunity to kill his captor. He headed back toward New Albany, in the wrong direction, away from his final target. The gun in the hijacker's hand hovered six inches from his stomach. The man leaned close in the passenger seat, the boy and woman in back, her head on her son's lap. The sky was black, and rain pummeled the windshield so hard that the wipers barely helped his visibility. The headlights — on high — cast a pathetic glow extending out a few feet.

The smell of blood and wet was ripe, and the car hydroplaned through water, sent up twin shafts of spray.

I can't drive them to a hospital. Or even into a town. By now Memphis police will have probably distributed the photos of me that kid took with his cell phone.

Tilting power lines seemed about to

topple down on them. Masses of electric cables disappeared like writhing water moccasins into streams overflowing across the road.

"We're going too fast," Tom said.

"I ought to blow your head off," snapped the man. Big guy, black, mid-thirties, with gray, short wooly hair and a thick beard and black-framed glasses. The man wore a skullcap. Of all the people to stop Tom, a *Muslim*. A brother, wearing his weekend going-to-dinner best; checkered button-down sopping cotton shirt and soaked khakis stained with his wife's blood.

"If Tina doesn't make it, you won't either," the man growled.

I could have released the insects anywhere. I could have let them out of their containers in a dozen places between Pittsburgh and here. But I passed up that opportunity. I wanted to release them in a specific place.

He had no illusion as to what would be coming toward him, from town. No way state and local police had not been alerted by Joe Rush's press conference. Maybe they'd not recognize the Ford. But they would be stopping cars, checking drivers.

It can't end like this. Give me courage. If my mission has your favor, show me a sign.

The woman moaned. Her hijab had slid

off her head to wrap her shoulders like a scarf. Brown plain dress. Spittle on the lips. One shoe off. Tom had glimpsed the unconscious moon-shaped face when they laid her down. The boy cried silently. The woman had voided herself. The purplish stain gluing dress to chest told Tom she'd probably been thrown forward by the crash, hit a door or steering wheel or piece of glass.

Fear is an adrenaline problem. Conquer it and convince them you will help them. Get that gun moved away.

Tom made his voice tremble.

"My brother, may I tell you something?" he said.

"I'm not your damn brother!"

He gasped, "Please! I've been driving since yesterday! No sleep! My father! He's in the hospital in Florida! He has cancer! I need to reach him, and when I saw you in the rain I didn't think! . . . I was wrong not to stop!"

"Watch the road, asshole."

Tom jerked the car sideways and straightened at the last second. The swerve pushed the man against the door. But he remained in control. Tom glanced at the glove compartment. Inside lay his pistol. A fleshy ripping sound seemed to come behind, from inside the woman.

Tom recited, in a quavering voice, *"You will not attain true piety until you voluntarily give of that which you love. Whatever you give, God knows of it."*

The boy's gasp came over thunder. "You're Muslim?"

Tom said, *"Those who expend their wealth right, openly or secretly, their reward awaits them with the Lord."*

The boy said, glancing at his dad, "Poppa?"

Poppa growled, "Just drive and shut up."

But Tom did not shut up. *"To walk with my brother for his help is better than keeping to the mosque for a month.* Put down that thing. It's freaking me out."

The gun, a big Smith and Wesson 629, a bear defense gun, stayed up. NEW ALBANY, 15 MILES. Tom did not need the guy to like him, just to hesitate. In town would be police, nurses, patients. Tom imagined himself carrying the woman into the hospital. He imagined people staring, turning to an overhead monitor broadcasting national news. He saw his face on the screen as Joe Rush said his name for all to hear. Tom made himself tremble.

"Stop shaking," the man with the gun barked.

"I can't! You're scaring me!"

419

He tried to think. What lay ahead that might help him? Had he seen turnoffs or rest stops? He could not recall. He'd concentrated on driving earlier, not on the sights.

Tom pleaded with the man, piteously. "Please! It might go off by accident."

"I saw your face when you tried to get past us. You knew what you were doing."

"Poppa?" the boy called in terror.

"What?"

"I think she stopped breathing," the boy said.

The man didn't turn around. But he shifted closer to Tom, and Tom smelled bile on his breath. Raspberry . . . gum or candy, maybe, and sweetish pipe tobacco.

"She'll be okay," the man tried to reassure his son.

NEW ALBANY, 6 MILES.

Lightning flashed on a sign: a yellow triangle with a black cross on it. An intersection was coming up.

"Poppa. I can't stop the bleeding."

Tom volunteered, "I know first aid."

"She's alive. And tough," the man said. But he'd given Tom what he needed. Confusion. Fear. A chance.

"Look, you have the gun," Tom said. "She needs help *now,* before we get to the hospi-

420

tal. Let me make it up to you. Stop that bleeding."

"Poppa? The blood!"

"Please! Let me help," Tom urged.

"Keep going," the man ordered, but there was less rage in him now. Tom took a chance and started braking.

"What are you doing?" the man demanded.

"We need to help her now." *We!* "We need to pull over for a minute." *We!* "There's no time!"

The intersection was coming up, and Tom glimpsed — far ahead — a series of red flashing lights, meaning ambulance or police. The man and boy had been looking at the woman, and they'd missed it. It would mark another accident or downed tree. Or worse, a roadblock. An upcoming curve in the road hid the flashing lights. Only Tom had seen them.

"Do it fast," the man said, but now there was more despair in his voice than anger.

Tom coasted onto the gravel shoulder. He did not know if the vehicles ahead had been coming toward them — if they were they'd be here in moments — or had been stationary. The Ford stopped with a jerk. There were no lights visible and no traffic behind them. When the hijacker turned to see his wife, Tom's hand came up off the steering wheel and he drove the side straight and true into the man's Adam's apple, crushing the larynx.

The gun went off but fired into the seat. The boy screamed. Tom had the man's wrist in hand as the man clawed at his throat, eyes bulging. The woman had toppled from the boy's lap. It was easy to pluck away the gun.

Tom shot the man in the face, jerking him back. He spun and shot the boy, too. The woman remained unconscious.

The rain battered the windows and streamed down. Tom pressed down on the accelerator and rolled twenty feet to the intersection, then turned onto a small feeder road. It was black and deserted, farm country. He heard sucking sounds from the back. The woman still lived. The boy could not possibly be alive.

He pulled over a quarter mile later and got out. The grass was mowed here, and there was a wire fence along the road. A pasture maybe. A ranch or farm. But he saw no lights. No homes. He was in a bubble of darkness.

Tom opened the passenger door and dragged the man out. He was big and heavy, but Tom was filled with adrenaline. He toppled the body into a roadside ditch. Then he did the same with the boy. The woman was breathing fitfully, eyes shut, twitching. The rain smashed into her as he dragged her through the grass. She rolled down onto her husband and son. Had she seen him? Had she regained consciousness for a moment and seen him?

She had not seen him. She might live if God smiled on her.

Tom left her lying with her men, barely alive.

He drove back onto the highway. The rain had lessened enough so that he could see, in the direction of New Albany, that the flashing red lights were now arrayed in a line across the road, blocking the route into town, or out.

Roadblock. But he'd avoided it.

He kept the headlights off because those cops might otherwise see his car turn around, head the other way. The feeder road carried him across the median strip. The car smelled of shooting and blood, and the backseat was soaked and shredded from the bullet. Padding lay everywhere. He shivered from cold, rain, or adrenaline loss. But he was free again. As long as no one stopped

him, no one could see the evidence in the
car.

Allah, keep me safe until tomorrow night.

He turned south again, and east. He
needed only a few hours to reach the correct destination.

Where I will release the last vectors, he
thought.

Against a very specific foe.

TWENTY-NINE

New Mexico state police and health officials had set up way stations at the airport. Security lines leaving terminals were slower moving than ones going in. IF YOU ARE COMING FROM AN INFECTED AREA, STOP AND HAVE ALL LUGGAGE EXAMINED. IF YOU FEEL ILL, ALERT AUTHORITIES, signs read.

I'd switched my return ticket to an earlier flight with a Washington, D.C., stopover, and, waiting for boarding, found a seat in a quiet area to convene a group meeting. Eddie's face swam up on the left top of my screen.

"It's in Pittsburgh, Joe. Five infected."

I fought off twin senses of anxiety and letdown. I'd flown across the country and now knew about as much as I had before I left. Hobart Haines was an old man with a far-fetched theory. It was hard to believe that Tom Fargo was carrying out some idea

425

he'd spewed forth as a kid. That Haines, driving around with the boy, years ago, had created a future terrorist, pulled the psychic switches.

Haines probably exaggerated his own importance. It's what old men do when they look back.

Eddie said, "The Pittsburgh victims remember being bitten two nights ago, at a park."

Beside Eddie was Stuart, in his office. We were meeting thanks to the Wilderness Program's encrypted system, as we were frozen out of the FBI's. Reduced to the status of fretting civilians, we got our news like most people in the country, from the press.

Stuart said, "That park was sprayed earlier, Joe. But it was crawling with mosquitoes. Amazonian variety, from the DNA."

I told myself, *Just because Hobart's theory is old doesn't mean you don't check it out.*

Izabel Santo had not answered my summons. She was either in the air, or asleep back in Brazil. Aya occupied the lower left-hand box and had a pugnacious look on her face: lips tight, eyes hard, probably because I'd not returned her call earlier. Mostly she looked hurt. I reminded myself that my intern was only sixteen.

"Where's the Brazilian?" she asked, uttering the nationality as if it were a curse, refusing to use Izabel's name. I said Izabel was gone. "Good," Aya said. "She's like, slutty!"

I noticed a dozen travelers and airport workers clustered beneath an overhead monitor, watching shots of police roadblocks around Pittsburgh and Memphis.

"Ray was right about one thing," Eddie said. "Cops all over the country are being flooded with 'sightings' of Fargo. And the tip line! Over five thousand calls."

Stuart nodded morosely and looked left, out of the monitor. Probably on *his* screen Eddie was on his right. Eye movement in teleconference is deceptive. Stuart said, "People are calling us, too. Phones ringing off the hook. *I saw Fargo in London! In L.A.* Nashville announced that they caught him, but it turned out to be someone else. Maybe Ray was right about not diverting personnel."

"What did you learn from Haines?" Eddie asked.

I filled them in. "He's had no contact with Tom or Tom's mom for years. It was all theory. But it's worth checking defense contractors," I said, eyeing Aya, who would be the main one to do it. "To see if one of them has branches in the cities that have been hit."

"Even if we find him," Eddie grumped, "he's just one guy. What about the other jihadists?"

"I'm not convinced there are others yet."

"You can't believe it's just one guy!" Stuart said.

"If it's different groups, how come the first infections were all near New York? He's had time to get to Pittsburgh and Memphis. It's possible that he wants us to think there are more attackers than there really are."

Eddie shook his head. "What about Chicago?"

"There were no *cases* in Chicago, Eddie. Just threats. I'm just saying, if it's lots of groups, why aren't outbreaks more widely spaced?"

"Christ, he could head from Memphis to Saint Louis. New Orleans. The whole goddamn Mississippi River area. At least there's crappy weather there. Everything's shut down. Tornadoes, Joe! Maybe the storms will slow him down . . . unless he's already dumped the car. Hell, what if he's flying?"

"If I were him, I'd dump the car," Stuart said.

"Aya? Would you like to add anything?"

"Oh, someone cares what I think finally?"

Here we go, I thought. "Aya, I didn't call you back before because I was busy with Haines."

"You told me to work with the FBI! You said help Ray, not you!"

She was looking away, off screen, pouting.

"That was for your own good, Aya."

Her lips twitched. I realized that she was trying not to cry. Aya said in a choked, accusatory voice, "You didn't tell Stuart to work with Ray. You didn't tell Eddie or anyone else in Wilderness to work for Ray. Just me."

"Aya!" But she was right. If she hadn't refused that order, she wouldn't be with us now. I felt sorry for Ray suddenly. He had to deal with her teenage emotions all the time. But I was angrier at myself. It was my job to remember that she was young. A team leader has to be aware of the strengths and weaknesses of people who work for him. I'd treated Aya as an adult if I needed her, but as a kid when I did not. Not fair.

"I made a mistake," I admitted.

Aya's lips were quivering.

I said, "My bad. My fault. Aya, we don't have time for this now. You're with us, okay? So act like it."

She nodded. She composed herself. I admired her guts. The adult expression was back, a look of moral superiority. Aya said, with an air of drama, "Joe, what if the *whole story* you told me about that refugee camp, Tol-e-Khomri, is wrong? What if things I learned *on my own* are the truth?"

"What things?" I said.

"Maybe it's better that I can't access the FBI system anymore. Because maybe all the official reports I saw when I was an intern were wrong," Aya answered.

"What did you do?" Eddie asked with attentive amusement.

"I accessed jihad sites from home. I mean, the Bureau keeps a list of sites and chat rooms that we — I mean *they* — monitor. If you're working there you steer clear of them unless you're assigned to watch them. But I wasn't there anymore, and I knew which ones were real ones. So if Ray wants to arrest me now he can just do it! I can't believe my mother even dated him for more than . . ."

"Aya," I prodded, to keep her on track.

"Well! I know those sites are propaganda, like, lies, like, accusations to like get jihadist recruits."

"What did you see?" I resisted asking her not to say "like" all the time. My semi-parental authority was a bit limited just now.

"I'm just saying I know they lie. But *you said* to look for things that are different. *You said* never assume that something that sounds crazy is wrong. You said sometimes information is in plain sight but people don't see it, so *always check out even crazy stuff.*"

"All right. What did you see?"

"Well, you know that story you told me about terrorists taking over that camp, during a riot, months ago?"

Kyle Utley had told us that. "Yes."

"Well, the story I saw was that the riot had nothing to do with terrorists. It had to do with food."

"Food?" Stuart and Eddie repeated at the same time.

"Donated food. From America. The bloggers said that America was trying to poison refugees."

"That's ridiculous!" Stuart burst out. He had many contacts in the humanitarian field, and Wilderness Medicine often worked with NGOs in refugee camps.

"I'm just saying!" she said. "They *said* refugees died from eating food from America. That they ate canned hot dog chili sauce and got botulism! That's what triggered the riot. The poisoning was covered up."

"There was nothing about botulism in the

reports from the State Department on the riot?"

"They blamed terrorists."

I asked, "Did you find any material supporting the blogs? Camp officials? Press reports? Anything?"

Doubtfully, she said, "No. But remember, I'm frozen out of official stuff now, so how could I check? I saw photos. I know they can be doctored, but I saw them. One was the man from the satellite shot. Tom Fargo. In plain sight."

I realized that my flight was being called to board.

Aya said, "In the photo, he held a dead child on his lap. He was screaming. And doctors were trying to calm people. And Turkish soldiers were there, too."

Travelers lined up at the gate showing boarding passes. The airline agent was trying to complete the process quickly, so that the plane could leave.

I thought, *Is it possible that we got reports of poisoning, and ignored them? Well, we had reports that Osama bin Laden was dangerous for years before we took them seriously. Reports that ISIS was a menace long before we paid attention. Yes, it's possible. But did it happen?*

Stuart made a mocking sound in his

throat. "American companies don't go around poisoning people, Aya!"

"Maybe it wasn't on purpose," Aya said. "Maybe it was an accident! If it was, those jihad killers would still say it was on purpose. It's what they do."

"Hot dog chili sauce? Give me a break!"

But the kind of food was not important. Eddie and I had worked out of aid relief camps in East Africa. I remembered huge tents there filled with donated material bound for South Sudan; mounds of bicycle parts, jerry cans for fuel use, candy bars, 110-pound bags of sorghum from Kansas, baked beans, thirdhand clothing from Minneapolis, vegetable stew donated by a company in California, boxes of useful items beside boxes that had found their way there for no better reason than that they enabled donors to get a tax write-off. Expired tetracycline beside brand-new penicillin shipments. Eyeglass lens cleaner beside rice to keep people alive; battery- or solar-powered radios beside math textbooks, old bathrobes, new sweaters, last year's stylish shoes. Anything and everything had been donated. Useless junk and valuable commodities. Canned peas from Israel. Canned beef from Ireland. Boxed soy milk from the U.S. The truth was, certain companies wrote off tens of millions in tax payments annually by donating products overseas. It was no reach to imagine that an expired or dangerous product got in there, by accident or oversight.

Why not hot dog chili sauce in the mix?

"I'm sure the FBI checked this out already," Stuart said. A good-hearted fellow, it was hard for him to conceive of an aid effort harming people.

I said, as the gate area emptied of passengers, "It can't hurt to check. As long as we're looking at defense contractors, why not food companies, too? See if there's a chili maker with facilities in cities where outbreaks occurred."

Stuart rolled his eyes. "You're grabbing at straws."

"Do you have a better idea?"

Aya looked triumphant. "I looked up Mideastern food. People there like spicy. That chili sauce is spicy. Maybe they put it on rice or flatbread they eat."

Eddie piped up, thoughtfully. "A lot of these companies are actually part of bigger conglomerates. What are you thinking, Joe? That Haines educated Fargo about big organizations? Years later, he goes after the parts?"

"I'm just saying check, that's all."

Aya looked pleased with herself, especially after I told her I was proud of her.

"Thanks, Joe."

Once my plane reached ten thousand feet, the captain got on the intercom and announced that passengers could use computers. I checked on defense contractors first, as Haines had suggested, tried to match up companies with infected cities. I tried "weapons manufacturers," "military suppliers," "defense industry," "military bases." It was a flawed approach because any classified stuff wouldn't be available on Google. But a flawed approach was the best I could do right now.

I found nothing. *Maybe one of the other people on the team is having better luck.*

Next I tried to link affected cities to a specific military branch; a base; Army, Navy, Air Force, Marines.

Nothing.

The flight attendant asked if I wanted a drink. I accepted a vodka. I typed in, "hot dog chili sauce," to see what came up.

Within seconds I was looking at a dozen brands of sauce, that came in jars, cans, even squeeze bottles. Up swam ads for sauce. And ratings in a national culinary magazine. Sauces had names like Uncle Ed's and Terrific Value and Rochester's

Best. Sauce makers were spread across the country, from northern California to Texas, Wisconsin, New Jersey.

I tried to match a manufacturer to all the infected cities.

Nothing.

Well, good try, I thought.

I finished my drink, and the flight attendant was back with a lunch menu. I wasn't hungry. Back at the keyboard, I dropped the city names and just called up chili makers, to read about them. Eddie had been right. Uncle Ed's was a subsidiary of a larger Kansas City company called Great Foods International. Rochester's Best had been bought, four years ago, by Fresh Unity Food and Beverage. Terrific Value, available in big-box stores, was owned by a French conglomerate based in Paris. Small companies had been consumed, so to speak, by bigger ones.

Okay, then, try to match the conglomerates with cities that have been infected.

It's funny sometimes, because you can spend weeks on a problem, frustrated, trying to figure the answer. The problem seems like it will beat you. You don't sleep. You can't stop running over possibilities. You grope in the dark and tell yourself to give up. And then suddenly something, a person, a sentence, a photo, changes everything as if a floodlight has come on.

A small ping told me that Aya was trying to reach me. I could see the first words of her message in capital letters. "I FOUND." This time I went to her message right away. She and I had hit the same point simultaneously.

"Fresh Unity Food and Beverage is one of the eight largest manufacturers and distributors of processed food products in the U.S., behind Coca-Cola, Anheuser-Busch, Kraft, and Smithfield, with sales topping $19 billion last year."

She'd forwarded a *Forbes* magazine article.

"Fresh Unity grew from a small Arkansas poultry processing company in 1906, founded by the George Riverside family, which still controls a majority of stock. Fresh Unity's mission statement, taken seriously by 'employees who want to rise,' CEO George Riverside IV has said, 'is to give back to the world as much as we take.'

"Fresh Unity is now headquartered in New York and annually donates an immense tonnage of food to trouble spots and needy people around the world."

I realized that the vibration that I had taken for the throb of engines was the accelerated beating of my heart. The flight attendant was passing with lunch. Aya had forwarded the "subsidiaries" list.

It took a few minutes of crisscrossing, but we found the connections together, on the online annual report, and they stunned me.

"Aya, Fresh Unity's chili sauce is manufactured in Pittsburgh, with beef processed in Memphis. The trucking company that transports the sauce is based in Philadelphia. The airport for mercy flights is Newark. Corporate headquarters, New York City."

Which links every infected city. Five out of five. That's a 100 percent correlation.

Reading, I felt my lips form the names of other cities in which the conglomerate owned businesses. "Galveston for fish processing. Saint Louis for beer. Soft drinks in Columbia, South Carolina. Pork from northern Florida. Processed chicken from Little Rock, Arkansas."

At least five cities here are within easy driving distance of Memphis, in all directions from it.

As I read, my mind wandered to those immense supply tents that Eddie and I had seen in northern Kenya, and the chartered planes landing on that aid base daily to disgorge tons of supplies. Most were donated by public-spirited organizations. But some came from cynically minded people or groups taking advantage of tax write-off laws. It was not hard to conceive of someone in a company, or a policy itself, sending expired or unsalable food on a supply plane, instead of into the trash.

I stared down at the map of company locations that Aya had forwarded. Tom Fargo could be in any of those cities. Or getting close to one.

"This is it! Yayyyyyy!!!!!!!" Aya typed giddily.

I agreed. It looked logical, hopefully solid. We were wrong, though. Quite wrong.

THIRTY

Half the streets seemed to have the same name in this ridiculous city. Tom Fargo drove along commercial Peachtree Street, passing Peachtree Lane, Peachtree shopping center, Peachtree apartments, and a Peachtree hotel. The least imaginative person on the planet must have come up with these names.

From the highway, at dawn, Atlanta had loomed in the distance, its downtown towers jutting up, sparkling as the storm cleared. There was nothing gradual about the change from country to city. Not like up north. There, rural became suburb and suburb gritty outlying city. Roofs got higher, colors browner. Atlanta sprouted all at once, a mirage: Bank of America building, One Atlantic Center, Marriot Marquis Building.

Oz of the Southeast. It seemed to epitomize all the brash overconfidence of the nation.

Tom Fargo steered down Ponce de Leon Drive, made a right on Ponce de Leon Street near a Krispy Kreme shop, and entered suburban Druid Hills, near Emory University. After the escapes of the night he felt as if he floated forward in a capsule of inevitability. He was almost serene. The homes were quiet and well kept, the styles reflecting more lack of imagination; faux antebellum beside McMansion or Greek Revival. Lawns were extensive. The air smelled of magnolia and dogwood, knotty southern oaks, and the few old surviving pines that may have avoided Sherman's fire.

He smiled when he saw clouds of gnats flitting in morning mist. Good! Either insecticides sprayed here had lost potency, Atlantans did not think themselves in danger, or the pesticide supply was, as in other cities, used up.

Airbnb, the terrorist's best friend.

The house he'd rented with the Seth Pryce credit card — bills sent to a Brooklyn PO box — looked out of place even in the patchwork neighborhood. *Architect's dream home,* the ad had read. Set between a fake Cape Cod and mini-Tudor, the three-story tower looked like boxes piled atop one another, with a sharply slanted roof slathered with solar panels. The skinny tower

441

reminded him of a rook in a chess set. There was a single aquarium-sized porthole-style window set into the cinder block front. He saw a circular metal staircase through the window, as if in a lighthouse. Lush flower beds surrounded the attached two-car garage, sitting there like a motorcycle side-car.

Three bedrooms. Quiet. Private. No smokers allowed.

Between the heated lap pool in back and screened-in porch, he found the rock garden and "Druid cairn," three flat stones atop one another. He'd arranged for the key and garage access to be beneath the top one. He'd paid for four nights and a stocked refrigerator. Inside, a note in feminine script — *Eat hearty, friend!* — along with foods he had requested: store-brand hummus, bread, deli turkey, olives, eggs, and milk. The air was cold and the house smelled of air freshener. *Oregon Forest.* There was a wide-screen TV and blowup photos of a family, dad, mom, and kids, touring ruins. The Parthenon. The Sphinx. A site in northern Syria he recognized, as Tom had helped dynamite that particular Roman temple. The family played Frisbee at Peru's Machu Picchu. They were probably, at the moment, gamboling through ruins somewhere else.

I'll stay inside until tomorrow.

Tom felt his tension draining into exhaustion. *Check the mosquitoes.* They looked sluggish. He'd fed them before leaving, and they were supposed to easily survive a couple of days without food. But he didn't like the way they sat there. He got the last container to a top-floor master bathroom, set it on the granite sink, replaced the plastic cover with Parafilm and got out the blood meals. He didn't want to feed the mosquitoes too much, as he needed them hungry. A dozen insects flew up and attached themselves to the film.

Then he fed himself and sipped hot, sweet mint tea.

He took a shower, prayed, and unloaded the car, inside the closed garage: suitcase, weapons, golf bag.

Finally, he stretched out on the master bed.

He would stay here, invisible, all day and night, until tomorrow morning.

I can leave once I release the vectors, but this time I want to watch. I waited for this. Then I can get back to Brazil. Maybe Cardozo has made a new batch by now.

He dreamed of Tol-e-Khomri as the sun rose, full and hot. Neighbors mowed lawns. Children passed on bikes, outside the porthole. Tom began to sweat and moan.

The bombardment signaled that the main attack would begin soon. Mortar rounds travel slower than sound, and the high-pitched whistle was caused by air rushing over the fins. The melon field began splitting apart. The fighters crouched in the ravine by the village shoved cotton in their ears. Animal parts — a sheep, a donkey — flew into the air and into the village well, which crumbled, the stone sides falling in.

"Get your families out," the commander ordered his men. "In the refugee camp they will be safe."

Tom's brother fighters took turns hustling their loved ones away from the line, a mile back, to the Roman-era road that led north to the border. The land was arid here in a way that surpassed Colorado, with rugged mountains and wadis in the distance, but the angles were soft, blunted by time. Limestone outcrops protruded as if they were the calcified skull of the planet, worn smooth by rain, sandals, donkey hooves. He'd found an old Roman winepress once, a museum-quality wheel made of raw stone. His sneakers crunched over clay splinters from pottery fashioned a thousand years ago. A few weeks back the fighters had seen a lone sheep charging them but at wolf speed, which was impossible. Then they'd heard small boys laughing. The boys had tied a sheepskin over a dog as a joke. It had been funny.

Now Tom told his wife, Sakina, as they reached the road, "I will come and get you after the fighting is over."

Sakina clutched their infant son, Ayman, to her breast.

That this far-off place felt like home was a miracle. He'd not previously known that such a powerful sense of belonging could exist. It had certainly not existed in the U.S. He'd expected to find prayer and austerity here as he made his way overseas, following website instructions for incoming foreign fighters. He'd gotten what he expected. But he had not expected poetry readings, too, and fellowship. The sports events and arranged marriage. Or that on his wedding day, he would learn that Sakina had chosen him, not the other way around. She'd seen him from her house. I want him, she had told her dad, his commander, fifty-year-old Mohammed al Ricki, who wept with emotion at invocations, or while singing a cappella jihadist religious hymns, as the use of instruments was illegal. Mohammed was called He Who Weeps. But he did not weep when they fought.

Life here when there was no fighting was

affectionate and playful. There was basketball and storytelling. Tom felt lucky because in other villages the commanders were brutal in the treatment of women. They encouraged rape; captive teenage girls married by Imams temporarily, so they could have sex with fighters under Sharia law. Birth control mandatory. Girls locked up all day, used at night.

But Tom had come for justice, not sex. He'd made that plain when he volunteered to fight. He'd been questioned by three men . . . one from London . . . before being sent to this unit, which had a high percentage of foreign fighters. In photos released by the Caliphate on the Internet they looked terrifying in black balaclavas, raising their AK-47s into the air. But with balaclavas off they became individuals: fat Mahmoud al-Hamsi from Saudi Arabia, complaining about toenail fungus and telling his dreams each day; Amin Saedi, a Belgian nineteen-year-old butterfly collector, who carried a tooth-cleaning twig called a *miswak,* and wore nonalcoholic perfume; Abdel Regeni, the skinny philosophy professor from Macedonia, half blind in his left eye, who favored Pakistani gowns and flak jackets; Martin Blake, from Toronto, an ex–drug user convict who had gotten religion in prison, and boomed out Ahlam al-Nasr's poetry at night.

"Shake the throne of the cross," he'd recite.

446

"Extinguish the fire of the Zoroastrians. Strike down every adversity, and go reap those heads!"

Now lines of civilians and disguised fighters headed north on the blasted-up highway, on foot, on a donkey, on a white horse. A parade of vehicles sent up steady exhaust.

The Americans and their paid allies were coming. Tom had refused to fight Americans when he volunteered. "I'll fight anyone else," he had said. "If you don't like that, I'll leave. I came here for God. Not to kill Americans."

Up until today, he'd not hurt them.

Tom watched his wife and baby climb into the dump truck. Normally it conveyed militia, but today all he saw were head scarves and frightened female faces. He had not conceived, when his marriage was arranged, that he would find love here. It had not occurred to him that his trip would bring him home.

She left in the parade of terrified civilians, hidden fighters, and jury-rigged conveyances: a bicycle with a wooden milk-crate seat, a Volkswagen pulled by mules, a horse cart with a windshield attached by bungee cords, hauling boxes of pilfered U.S. Army self-heating meals.

That night the main artillery barrage started, and in the morning men to the left and right of him in the ravine lay still. Sullamed, the

447

Somalian, blown to pieces; Martin Blake, screaming for his mother; Abdel Regeni, a rat running out of his body, dragging a piece of red intestine.

Tom knew he was going to die as the enemy moved forward. But the high-quality Iraqi equipment never matched their will to fight. The Kurds opened the assault, coming hard on the right. The Sunni militia advanced on the left. The Iraqis, center, were sluggish, even prodded by the Americans. Iraqi soldiers hid behind their Humvees. As the attack faltered, Caliphate reinforcements arrived.

Then the Iraqi troops pulled back and their allies had to do the same. A sure victory had turned into a rout, and the fighters thanked God for another day of life.

Afterward, it was easy for Tom to get over the border, to fetch his family back. The Turkish guards had been bribed, and knew if they stopped fighters, they would be attacked.

In a dream, Tom remembered the refugee camp, the smell of pit latrines and unwashed bodies, gasoline generators, the mountain of discarded food cans, the medicine and viscera reek from Red Cross and Red Crescent hospital tents. Hobart Haines peered out of one tent, dressed like a doctor. Gunther the ski instructor out of another. Hodge lay beneath an overturned van, blood gushing from his mouth.

"People got sick after eating," Hodge told him, in the voice of a middle-aged French doctor. "Your wife was one of them. I am very sorry. She is dead."

He woke and squeezed his eyes shut and tried to escape back to the camp. He could still feel the clammy cold of Sakina's skin on his cheeks, and saw the tiny face of his son, blue. He lay in the double bed in Atlanta and smelled refugees. His son, Ayman, had been trampled during the riot.

Tom swung his legs out of bed, said his morning prayers, facing east. *They made me this way.* He did not mind that today or tomorrow might be his last on earth. He'd known from the first that his life might end here. And if he got out, and made it back to Brazil, he would trust God to determine whether Cardozo would keep him alive, now that he'd been identified by the Americans. But nothing succeeds like success. Tom would take the chance.

Maybe Cardozo would send him back to the Caliphate.

Tom Fargo sat at the woman's dressing table and shaved his head, careful not to cut the skin. He would have preferred

449

dentistry to plug the gap between his teeth, but the over-the-counter resin would work for two days before it crumbled. He patted his skull dry and fitted on the $4,000 wig, bought with cash in a Rio shop that served the city's millionaires; industrialists and oil folks, models and TV stars. The wig, Swiss virgin hair, gave his head a wiry look. "This makes your chin weak," the "hair advisor" had protested when he bought it. "You are more handsome than this! This makes you look plain!"

"I like it fine," he'd said.

From the eyeglass case came brown-tinted lenses, also bought in a Rio Zona Sul boutique. He examined himself in the mirror.

No one will be looking for me there, anyway. No one will associate one more guest with the man on TV.

In the bedroom Tom hung up the two sets of clothes he would need tomorrow. Lightweight sharply creased lime-green trousers. Short-sleeved pink Lacoste shirt and white Reeboks. Brooks Brothers pressed dark blue sports jacket and crisp gray slacks and loafers. On a night table he laid the printed invitation that he'd received in *Seth Pryce's* PO box, its words in gold script.

Come celebrate with us!

He'd need to carry weapons and ammunition. But hiding them should be no problem, considering where he was going.

In Atlanta, a perfect sunny day, hot, skies clear. For tomorrow, he saw on TV, the forecast was the same.

The announcer grinned. "Wear sunblock today! Protect yourselves, my friends!"

THIRTY-ONE

In the old days, only a year ago, Eddie and I had no trouble getting into places if we needed to ask questions. We showed ID. We worked for a national agency. If we met resistance, the Admiral or an FBI official made a call, and we got in, fast.

I'd figured that now that we were off the task force, it would be harder to see important people, but I'd not accounted for Stuart's status in Manhattan. As head of the Columbia program, he moved effortlessly through social strata accessible to me until now only by threat or ID.

"We're here to see Chairman Riverside," Stuart told the lobby guard. "We have an appointment."

The glass tower occupied a corner at 6th Avenue and 50th Street, a block from Broadway. The sun-drenched atrium featured artwork commissioned in the 1920s by a railroad titan who hired a Mexican communist to paint murals on his walls.

All around us, in vivid colors, Spanish conquistadores slaughtered Aztec Indians, who morphed into white-clad farmers ridden down by Emperor Maximilian's French dragoons. The French were replaced by Mexican soldiers, shooting at Zapata's peasant uprising. On the fourth wall impoverished railroad workers lay tracks in scrub desert, then trudged home to shacks where peasant women rolled tortillas and fried beans, and small children slept.

Maybe tortillas were the connection to the food company. Frozen tortillas were a product line.

The elevator that whisked us high above the city featured an inset TV showing Wall Street news; stocks of makers of insecticides and antimalaria medicines were up, up, up. The door opened directly into a waiting room featuring a striking canvas, a cubist Picasso copy.

Stuart nudged me. "It's not a copy, Joe."

Up until now I'd appreciated Stuart's medical knowledge but in security matters, thought him naive. He was a do-gooder, and I admired him for that. But hours ago I'd watched him pick up a phone and get through on the chairman's private line to a secretary who said that George Riverside IV was busy. Stuart responded pleasantly, "Tell him that this is important, not a social call."

I stared at Stuart. *Social?*

"He's a big donor," Stuart said now as we sat in a glass waiting room, sipping bottled water. "Allison and I sit at his table at the Explorers Club dinner every year. You should join, Joe. Tarantula appetizers. Yum!"

"I'm not a joiner." I figured we'd have a long wait.

"Haven't you figured out yet that it's not about that?"

"What is it about, then?"

Stuart smiled with his mild blue eyes. Except now those eyes were looking more savvy. "Joe, two kinds of people join the Explorers Club. Those who do things. And those who want to be *near* people who do things. They donate money. They bankroll expeditions. Nice folks. They adventure by proxy. The truth, Joe? They don't just donate to a cause. They donate, you might say, to envy."

"And they envy you?"

Stuart shrugged. He disappeared for months into the wilds of New Guinea. He worked cholera outbreaks in Haiti. He was a soft-spoken presence who'd spent four months on the Orinoco in search of a lost Russian expedition once. He'd contracted so many tropical illnesses over the years that he ate a restricted diet. It had taken him almost a decade of hard work to convince Harvard to start up the first Wilderness Program. Columbia had followed.

How the hell did I ever underestimate him, I thought, *just because his business card lacks the word* Government?

Stuart said, "I do it because I like it. I like them. But that doesn't mean there isn't value in it. So join. Every bit helps."

"Stuey!" a voice exclaimed as a man rushed into the waiting room. "Where the hell were you Monday for squash?"

"The FBI was already here, asking about Tol-e-Khomri!" Riverside told us, minutes later, in his office.

"Oh, we know that," Stuart lied. "We just want to go over a couple things again, Legs."

Legs? I thought. *Squash? Stuart?*

Riverside looked to be a fit white man in his mid-forties; lanky and broad shouldered, strong jaw, intelligent eyes, oddly dirty fingernails. He'd made sure that we knew that his desk was made of sustainably grown tropical hardwood, and he'd personally served us sustainably harvested guava juice bottled by his company. ONE DOLLAR OF EVERY PURCHASE GOES TO SOUTH PACIFIC

FARMERS! the label said. George was showing off. The company sold pork rinds, jelly candy, and beef jerky, too.

Stuart told me, "George is pigeon-toed, Joe, but he moves around that squash court like a cockamamy animal."

George laughed. "That's because you run me ragged, Stuey. No rest for the weary, Joe."

"Oh, you're far from weary, George."

I wanted to shout questions as George and "Stuey" laughed. *The FBI had been here?* Eddie and I were used to coming in and firing out questions. Instead, in the last few minutes, I'd learned that George and family enjoyed the Broadway revival of *Porgy and Bess,* that a fellow squash player nicknamed "Hands Christian" had broken a leg while skiing in Chile last week, that Stuart and his wife should "come along on the Rainforest Alliance trip to Ecuador. It will be fun on that little boat in the Galápagos. We donate there, you know. Preservation."

"Speaking of your good work, George . . ."

And finally, we were talking about Tol-e-Khomri.

George told us, "Two agents showed up, as I recall, after terrorists shot up that camp. I gave them our report on what happened. I had Bob Welch up here. He's in charge of our charity work. He spent hours with them."

Stuart asked, "Do you remember the report?"

"Not every detail. Why?"

Stuart glanced at me. *Pick up the ball,* he meant.

"Well, sir," I began.

"Call me George, please."

"George, there's a correlation between the black malaria attacks and cities where you operate."

The color drained slowly from George Riverside's face. He looked at Stuart as if hoping that Stuart would disavow what I'd said, but Stuart nodded. The link was clear if you thought about it. But Riverside had not thought of it until now. Maybe he operated in so many cities that the correlation had been hidden. Maybe the fact that the attacks had not been directly against his people, but whole cities, had disguised what they were really about.

"Surely this is a coincidence," he said.

"Maybe," I said. On the walls were photos: His wife and two boys holding tennis racquets. An elderly woman in a beach chair, who had Riverside's longish face. A shot of an aid plane landed in a dirt field in Sudan. A shot of the opening of a new high school

457

for single mothers in Nepal. George Riverside picked up the receiver on his desk
phone.

"Honey, get Bob Welch up here, will you?"

I must have looked surprised, because he
said, putting down the phone, "Honey is
my secretary's name."

"Oh."

Seven minutes later a sweaty-faced
middle-aged man entered, wearing an expensive pin-striped suit that did not hide
his pear shape. His balding pate was sun-
burned. His lips looked rubbery, and his
oddly small hand, in mine, was moist. The
deep, cordial voice was confident, the voice
of someone else. Either Bob Welch was a
self-possessed man with a sweat problem,
or a nervous man with a radio host's voice.

"I found the business cards the FBI left,
sir. Agents Mathew Friday and Roberta
Weir. I also brought the file."

"Tell the story, Bob. Leave nothing out."

Dots of moisture beaded Welch's upper
lip. Possibly he was cursed to sweat all the
time. He seemed more cooperative than
fearful, more toady than secretive, excruciat-
ingly aware of the proximity of the chairman.

"Yes, sir." The story rolled out, pretty
much along the same lines that I had heard

from Aya. The food arrived without incident. It was successfully distributed with several tons of other supplies. There was no indication of trouble in the camp, then suddenly guns were going off, refugees were screaming.

"Later on the jihadists blamed it on us, but believe me, there was no problem with that food."

"You were there then?" I asked.

"No, that was Christine's job. Christine Mahin."

"Is Christine here now?"

Welch shook his head. "She was so upset by what happened — afraid for her life that day — that she quit. She was with us for six years and did a great job. But she and her husband want children. Visiting trouble spots is a young person's job."

"Did Mahin follow up on the poisoning report?"

Welch nodded vigorously. "Of course! They'd blamed us! Christine was scrupulous. She checked with the doctors. They'd tried to find food residue in the empty cans, do tests. But everything was destroyed in the riot. Terrorists! They use any excuse to rile people up!"

"Where is Christine Mahin now?" Stuart asked.

Welch glanced at Riverside as if confirming that candor was what George wanted. George nodded as if to say, *What are you waiting for? Tell them what they want to know.*

"She left months ago. She's with the NGO that runs that camp now, working stateside. Revolving door, sir. People go from companies to NGOs and back. She's in administration. The only travel she does is to and from her desk."

"Where?"

"Oh, I got a Christmas card from her. She went south," Bob Welch said, and finally smiled as he passed the problem on to someone else. But he was still sweating as he held out a copy of the report. The manila folder was moist.

"She's in Atlanta, Georgia," Bob Welch said.

THIRTY-TWO

The Druid Hills Country Club had changed management a year earlier, the sign at the entrance said. The magnificently kept clubhouse (established 1912) and links lay just off Lullwater Road, only half a mile from the house in which Tom Fargo had spent a comfortable night.

Tom arrived in an Uber, so his stolen car would not sit in the parking lot, visible to all. He'd walk back to the house when he was finished here, tonight. His chatty driver rolled them down a wooded access road to stop at a guard shack. Eric Englert was the name tag on the guard.

Tom showed his invitation through the back window. "I'm not a member. But I have an eleven A.M. tee time and was told that guests for tonight's gala can get a round in first."

"Sure thing, Mr. Pryce. Go right in."

Hobart had taught Tom to use first names

461

when talking to people. It made them friendlier. "Eric, I was told I can leave my clothes for tonight in the clubhouse."

"Yes, sir. Just tell them inside. Have a nice round."

In a widened pocket of his golf bag were the insects and his pistol. The pro teamed him up with three players here for tonight's event: Jerry, a retired corporate pilot; Eddy, the vice president of marketing at a soda company; Howard, a divorce attorney. Howard was the oldest but most athletic, Eddy was a cigar smoker in his thirties, and Jerry smelled of alcohol at 10 A.M. "I'm not flying planes anymore, so if I want an eye opener, I have it. Played here before, Seth?"

Tom pretended this was like those diplomat meetings that Hobart used to describe. *Chitchat,* Hobart called it.

"I'm a duffer, put on earth to make you look good."

Howard and Eddy smiled but clearly didn't want the fourth man slowing their game down. Jerry roared, "I've heard that one before. Next you'll want to make bets!"

Tom laughed and despised their garish clothes, expensive watches, and costly clubs, their air of prosperity and casual indifference while elsewhere people suffered. The assumption of the good life was so American. These people destroyed anything deemed inconvenient as they blundered across earth. Tom heard children splashing in the clubhouse pool.

Eddy winked. "Not worried about mosquitoes, are you?"

Howard said, "There's not been a single case in Atlanta. That's what I told my wife. Plus, we take Lariam."

Jerry nodded. "I think this manhunt near Memphis? For that Largo guy? Or Fargo? Whatever? It's bullshit. This whole outbreak will turn out to come from a government lab."

Tom was grateful for his practice golf sessions on that jungle island and in Manhattan. In Brazil, sometimes low balls skipped across the water. "You're a natural athlete," the golf pro had told Tom at the Chelsea Piers range, in New York. There a huge cage had prevented balls from flying into the Hudson River. The city spewed toxic waste and sewage into the Hudson. But drew the line at golf balls.

You're the ones who need a lesson, Tom thought now.

He'd tied the golf bag onto the electric cart.

"Tee up, Seth," Jerry said. "By the way,

watch out for sand traps on one. And water in the rough off Lullwater, especially after the recent rain, I heard."

Tom eyed a catering truck pulling into the parking lot, and the maroon-jacketed waitstaff setting up tables for eight for tonight's gala, on the stone patio overlooking the course. He noted large planters below the patio. They were filled with water from last night's rain. He wondered if it might be possible to put the insects in the planters.

Tom asked the guys, as if nervous, "Do grounds crews spray against mosquitoes here?"

"Ah, don't listen to those Chicken Littles at the CDC," Eddy said, pointing to a series of rooftops three miles away. "Those guys get paid to scare you. All they accomplished by spraying was to kill off every bat, dragonfly, and bird within twenty miles before they ran out. If we ever get a real outbreak, nothing will stop it. Want to worry? Worry about the pond on hole two."

Tom drove his first shot straight and true, almost three hundred yards.

"I knew it!" cried Jerry happily. "How about a little wager?"

Three and a half hours later, on the eighteenth hole, he pretended to poke around in the dense juniper and bushy cleyera trees for a lost ball. He emptied the last container of nine hundred mosquitoes in a little standing pool of water, emerged from the trees, took a one-stroke penalty, and hit his next shot onto the fringe of the green.

"Nice shot, Seth!"

"Guess I'm just lucky today," he said.

THIRTY-THREE

Eddie started to shiver in the car. Malaria parasites can hide out in the liver, go dormant, and even after medical treatment sneak back into the blood years later. Until then, the patient thinks he's beaten the illness. As Stuart drove us back toward La-Guardia Airport, to make an Atlanta flight, I saw Eddie's clenched fists. He was fighting the fever, willing it away.

"I'll go alone," I said. "Get to the hospital."

Eddie shook his head. "No."

"Eddie, I'm just going down for a few hours. It's probably unrelated. A double check."

"I've had fevers before."

"Not like this. And you know it."

We reached the Delta terminal, and I climbed out and looked back at Stuart, who spoke to Eddie as if to a child. "Neither of you will get any work done if you're sick on the plane. Check in with Joe from the hospital."

"Shit." Eddie looked yellowish.

In the air, I tried to keep my mind off Eddie and on the report on Tol-e-Khomri. It was thick, thorough, and made no mention of infected food. But reports are distilled observation. Even the best ones discard facts. Good reporters choose the right facts to eliminate. Mistakes happen if wrong ones get left out.

"We conclude that at least a dozen jihadists hid amid refugees with the goal of creating havoc in the camp. No evidence points to company culpability or infected food." Signed: Bob Welch and Christine Mahin.

Back at Fresh Unity, as George Riverside sternly grilled Welch, I'd wondered if it was an act.

"Is there anything you're not telling us?" Riverside demanded.

"Absolutely not, sir."

"If there is, you've got five minutes of amnesty. Onetime offer. If our product made people sick, even accidentally, even a possibility, I want to know."

"Sir, we shipped over four thousand cans and only thirty people got sick. There were no expired cans in the warehouse. No way to check one hundred percent because any

467

food residue burned. What can I say? It's impossible to reconstruct totally. Christine assured me, no link."

"Don't let her know that Dr. Rush is coming."

"I promise. I won't."

"Bob's reliable," Riverside assured us, after the man left. "The sweating? He picked up a bug a few years ago in Uzbekistan. Wreaks havoc with body temperature. He sweats all the time. He's honest, that Bob."

Is he? I thought. *Are you?*

Stuart reported by e-mail that Eddie was vomiting by the time he checked into Columbia-Presbyterian. He was in the malaria ward. His relapse meant that this new malaria might be tougher than originally thought.

Then Stuart's news got worse. "There's breaking news about Kyle Utley. A problem in Washington."

I turned on seat-back NBC, to see the correspondent who I'd ditched in New York. *Washington whistle-blower accuses Administration of dealing with terrorists.* With the reporter was Kyle Utley, in the studio, in suit and tie, looking unhappy. I'd liked the man, and was surprised at my anger at the word *whistle-blower*. After all, I was a whistle-blower, too. I'd released news about Tom Fargo to the world.

Joe Rush, hypocrite. Go figure, I thought.

NBC: You personally received a threat from Tom Fargo?

UTLEY: Yes. Then he called my wife and made a second threat.

NBC: The FBI knows this, you say?

UTLEY: I told them immediately.

NBC: And now you allege that the White House's diversion of military funding was a capitulation to jihadists?

UTLEY: That's what they demanded.

The reporter looked triumphant.

NBC: But just to be straight, you have no proof that the diversion wasn't planned anyway, as the White House insists. *You* say jihadists played the White House for fools, since attacks are still going on. *They* allege that you're lying because you are about to be fired.

Stuart e-mailed me as I watched Utley flailing around before cameras. The message read, "Havlicek is at Congress, to testify. The investigation's stalled. I can't get through to anyone. You're on your own, Joe."

Atlanta is one of the twenty worst cities in

the country when it comes to mosquitoes, according to the Centers for Disease Control and Prevention. Sixty-five varieties live there. The majority are not potential malaria carriers, but larger tiger and smaller culex mosquitoes. Tigers can carry Zika virus. Culex can carry West Nile, too.

"Welcome to Atlanta," the flight attendant announced.

I studied photos of mosquitoes as we taxied. Christine Mahin was on maternity leave, Bob Welch had told us. She was probably at home, eight and a half months pregnant.

It's my custom when traveling in a potential outbreak area to ask people there if they've taken precautions to reduce the chance of getting sick. I did not like what I was hearing now. The flight attendant said that she did not need malaria pills because she "stayed inside during layovers." My seatmate had taken Lariam when the outbreak began, but his pharmacy had run out. The cab driver explained on the way to Christine's house that since the CDC was headquartered in Atlanta, he was confident that the disease would be kept away. And besides, the pills could cause bad dreams or hallucinations. His neighbor was taking herbal remedies, not pharmaceuticals. I would have thought that with so many medical experts here, there would be more medicine, more belief. Not less.

Add in delays from a traffic pileup and I didn't reach Christine's driveway for another hour. The Buckhead neighborhood, Bob Welch had said, is the Beverly Hills of the South. It was beautiful in an antiseptic way, as if a child's plastic toy set had gotten large enough to house people. Homes looked more like showrooms. The leafy trees had a sheen that, near dusk, made them seem artificial. At 6:20 P.M. the sun had another two hours until it sank away.

Local mosquitoes would stir soon, if they were alive, but most of the urgency I felt was for Eddie. After all, there were no facilities in Atlanta operated by Christine's old company. I just wanted to see her expression when we talked. But the bad part of using surprise as strategy is that the surprise happens to you if you can't locate the person who you're looking for.

And nobody answered the door of the adobe-colored ranch house set beside a two-story French provincial. I saw an envelope taped to the door with a name, *Ted,* in black. The note inside, in feminine script, read: *Ted, My neighbor has the key.*

I rang the neighbor's bell, and a slim

woman yanked the door open as if she'd been watching me from her window. Freezing air-conditioning washed out. The woman seemed to be in her early forties, friendly, and I heard a TV on inside, a cartoon children's show. Lots of shooting, beeping, and trombone music. Roadrunners falling off cliffs.

"Are you the architect?" she asked.

She had a tanned face, green/blue eyes, and wore a gold sweater, white slacks, and matching sandals. Her dirty blond hair was feathered. She held a Paul Theroux novel. *The Mosquito Coast.* The title made me want to laugh, but not in a funny way.

She said, "Christine said to tell you to check out the bedroom closets, and leave the drawings in the kitchen."

I heard more music, hip-hop now, over the kids' show. The house was a madhouse of electronics. I heard children running, the tromp of socked feet, a small girl screeching in delight and a boy yelling, in a Dracula accent, "I em Mosquito! I vill BITE you!!"

Everywhere I go in outbreak zones, children incorporate death into play. "Ring Around the Rosie" was first sung by youngsters during the great London Plague, because victims had *rings* around their eyes. *A pocket full of posies* referred to flowers that warded off disease smells. *Ashes! Ashes! We all fall down* had those long-ago children imagining corpses burning as they held hands and danced.

"Christine said she and Alan won't be back until late, from the gala. She'll call you tomorrow."

"Gala? What gala?" I asked, returning the smile.

THIRTY-FOUR

Dusk.

The hungry female mosquito rose on a column of warm air from the pond on which she'd been deposited, along with hundreds of sisters. All were capable of feeding on many mammals that lived near the golf course: raccoons, possums, dogs, or cats. But she detected something more attractive nearby — perfume — with her spearlike maxillary palp, which jutted out between her antennae.

Normally, dragonflies and bats lived in the country club woods and ate many times their body weight in mosquitoes each day. They were efficient insect control systems, but recent pesticide spraying had wiped most of them out, along with any mosquitoes that had lived here only weeks ago.

Now the sweet smells drew her and her sisters toward the lit-up building like metal filings pulled to a magnet. Their compound eyes had tiny lenses, ommatidia, capable of detecting movement. Propelled by sheer wings, they adjusted steering with smaller ones, called halteres.

She detected large forms ahead, outlined by bulky movement. The odors grew stronger as she closed the distance between woods and hot pools of electric light.

She was different than even the lab-created sisters around her. She was — in fact — the only one of her kind in the world. She carried in her proboscis a parasite representing the seed of global medical conflagration.

All she had to do for that to happen was feed, and pass the parasite on.

THIRTY-FIVE

"I can't let you inside, Sir. Sorry."

My taxi had been stopped by the gate guard at the Druid Hills Country Club. He had orders to turn away anyone lacking an invitation, and did not look sorry at all. He shrugged off my claim that I needed to talk to someone inside, and he suggested in bored tones that I contact the lady tomorrow.

"Please call the clubhouse and check," I asked.

"Can't." The guard shook his head, meaning, *won't*.

I had no ID attaching me to any official investigation. He glanced at my Wilderness Program card by flashlight, but it meant nothing to him. He accurately gauged the extent of my frustration, because he told me in a firmer tone that if I did not turn around, he'd call the police.

"What if I buy a ticket to the gala?"

"Now?" The guard looked resentful.

"It's a fund-raiser, right?" I said. "Why not?"

"Tickets cost a lot." He looked me over. Was I important? His eyes flicked to the shiny parked Mercedes, BMWs, and upscale cars in the lot, as if the ticket expense would be prohibitive for me.

"It's for a good cause," I said.

He found my suggestion irritating. But he went into the guard shack — keeping the traffic bar down — and made the call. I could not hear what he was saying but had a feeling that it was not that a friendly gentleman had shown up. I had a feeling he was saying that a pest was at the gate, trying to weasel in, possibly with a bogus credit card.

The guard looked self-satisfied when he came out.

"All tickets were sold days ago. No more spaces, sir."

It's just a few more hours, I thought, disappointed, as the cab U-turned back toward Clifton Road. *I came to see her face.* I asked the driver if he knew of a motel nearby. I'd return to the Mahin house tomorrow, ring the bell, and try again.

"There's a Comfort Inn a few miles away, sir."

I told him to go there, but changed my mind. "Pull over, on the grass." On one side of Clifton Road were lit-up houses, on the other, golf fairways beyond thick brush and trees and moonlight gleaming on a chain-link fence.

"I'll walk to the motel," I said.

"It's far."

"For exercise."

"You'll get lost."

I tipped the driver and thanked him. Shaking his head . . . *some people* . . . he drove off as I pushed into the brush. Five minutes later I'd managed to rip my jacket on a thorn bush, and get my shoes wet in a stream. A thorn tore at my face. I felt a cut open. I gripped the fence and climbed.

Tom Fargo should leave, he knew, but he could not help watching. Anonymous, he gazed at the gala around him. Until now the damage he inflicted was always distant. He deposited vectors and left. Later, on TV, he watched victims from a distance. But this time he wanted more visceral satisfaction. There was a grinding sense of justice in his belly, and anticipation was a coppery taste on the roof of his mouth.

These people killed my family.

His name card . . . *Seth Pryce* . . . seated

him at a periphery table, by the patio and open French doors. He'd be eating with food company executives who had flown in from out of state. He introduced himself to a bright young lawyer on his right from the legal division, and his wife, and to the woman on his left, from the Saint Louis beer division. Neither, they said, had taken antimalarials before coming. "I don't want to risk the side effects," the woman told him. "Besides, we're only here for one night."

People were going in and out of the doors, to the patio, to talk, to smoke, to look at the view.

A small salad sat before him, lush greens wrapped in carrot skin, topped by crushed onions, tomatoes, fresh Tuscan dressing that was the brown color of the sauce that had killed Tom's wife.

On the dance floor, a smiling man in a tuxedo lifted a microphone. "Welcome to our annual gala to benefit Food For All. We are here to honor the doctors and workers who risk their lives overseas to feed the hungry. And to honor YOU, our donors, without whom there would be no FFA."

Tom had never told Dr. Cardozo that his choice of targets was personal. This morning he'd called the gala reservations number,

479

reached an overconfident voice, and been assured that "there's not been a single case of malaria in Atlanta, so part of the evening will be outside if the weather holds."

Tom had said, "I haven't taken any medicines," and the voice had assured him, "Many guests are also coming from uninfected areas. Besides, we saturated the grounds with pesticides a week ago. The only living thing out there will be a few last golfers at dusk."

That's what you *think,* he'd thought.

Now the MC said, "Throughout the evening, we will be showing slides of our work. Those tents you see are near Syria, set up to feed thousands displaced by fighting."

A live band played oldies, and couples got up to dance. A few stylishly dressed women — bored with husbands talking sports — gyrated with one another.

"In this Sudanese aid camp, children are measured and given plastic bracelets. Blue means they are so underweight that they are fed twice a day. Red means once," the MC said.

At a table across the dance floor Tom spotted a face from Tol-e-Khomri. He stared with fascination.

"Please welcome Dr. Ravi Agarwal from

WHO, the World Health Organization."

Tom clapped and pretended to listen, but the hum of anticipation made words hard to hear. The concealed pistol was snug against his back. The speaker's self-congratulatory whine grated like nails on a blackboard. Americans converted suffering into entertainment. They did not send gladiators into arenas like ancient Romans did but pretended to care while they sipped vodka tonics and watched skeletal children on screens.

But where were the insects? Tom fretted. They should have been here. Had something happened to them? Had the vectors flown the wrong way? Tom turned this way and that, seeking movement in the air. *Where are they?*

Tom spotted a tall man walking in through the French doors, from outside, wearing a sports jacket, but it looked disheveled. The man stopped in the light and scanned the crowd, his attitude forceful. The man wiped his cheek with the back of his palm. Tom saw smeared blood there. A bolt of acid surged into Tom's belly. He resisted the urge to jump to his feet. That face had been on the news. It was the man who had destroyed the laboratory in Brazil, and announced to the world Tom's name. There was no way

Joe Rush could have traced Tom here. But he was not going away or turning into someone else.

Tom glanced around the room but saw no police at exits, no men or women in dark suits, wearing earpieces. Only relaxation on all faces, except for Rush.

Rush asked someone a question, and the person pointed toward the table at which the woman from Tol-e-Khomri sat. Rush started walking toward that table.

At that moment, Tom saw the first mosquito wobble in from outside, through the bright gala light.

I made my way toward Christine Mahin as the band played the Earth, Wind & Fire oldie "Shining Star." She was a large, moon-faced woman who looked ready to deliver her baby at any moment, swelled and sack-like in a maroon maternity dress. Her hair was up to keep her cool. A single strand of pearls lay around her neck. Tethered to her chair by pregnancy, she chatted with a man in a light blue sports jacket who held her hand. The husband. She looked up when she sensed my presence. The blue eyes were friendly, but they widened. Her hand went to her cheek. *I must have a blood smear on my face.* She took in my soiled jacket. She looked puzzled, but not alarmed.

"Ms. Mahin. I'm Dr. Joe Rush. May I speak to you? It's important."

Her confusion became recognition.

"Rush? You're on the news. I don't understand. I would have remembered your name on the guest list."

"It isn't there."

"You're affiliated with the charity?"

"Can we talk, ma'am?"

The husband was a thin man in white jeans, with banded green-and-pink socks, a shaggy haircut, artistic plastic glasses. Quirky guy, out of place. He wasn't sure whether to be protective or curious. His eyes went from my face to hers. I said, "I got your name from Bob Welch. I need to talk to you about Tol-e-Khomri."

Her mouth opened involuntarily and she started to rise but sank slowly back into her chair. The husband, alarmed, asked if she was all right. Christine nodded, but her eyes never left my face. The dance floor was clearing. Waiters were bringing chicken dinners. The MC tapped a finger against the mike. Time for more talk.

She's afraid. But I can't tell if she looks guilty.

She looked around to realize that others at her table were watching us. Between the chatter and clatter of dishes, if you wanted

483

to be heard, you had to shout or lean into a listener's ear. She did not want to shout. She grasped my wrist with a damp hand. "Can you help me up? Into the hall? Alan? Arghhhhhh," she said, trying to rise.

This is why you always ask in person and never take a report for granted. You always watch the eyes.

Other than a face at a far table who I saw staring at us as we left the room, a man who quickly looked away, no one paid us any attention. Christine walked with difficulty, puffed and sweated and wiped her brow. In the hallway the noise instantly muted. It was cooler here, with glass cases filled with golf trophies, and old black-and-white mounted shots of past invitationals, even signed head shots of the greats: Palmer, Player, Woods.

"Was it us?" she asked, straight-out, a terrible urgency twisting her face. "Was our food responsible?"

"You're asking me?"

"I need to sit. The chair. Thank you," she said, sinking down, looking up. *Tell me,* her expression said.

"We think," I said, using that *we* as if I was here officially, "that there's a link between Tol-e-Khomri and the cities where black malaria has been introduced."

Her eyes widened. "Link?"

484

I explained it. She did not know what to make of it. But it terrified her. The connections were obvious, yes, she said, "but nobody attacked the company. I don't know if anyone who got sick even worked for the company. If you have a grudge against the company, why not hit it directly?"

"The grudge is bigger than one company," I said, spreading my arms to include the club, city, state, nation. "The company? Maybe it's just a way in. He could have picked anywhere. But I think he chose locations that had special meaning to him."

She needed time to absorb it. Her husband tightly held her hand. She said, in a small voice, "But they told me it was jihadists. I didn't even hear *anything* about food poisoning until later, when it showed up in jihad blogs."

I waited.

"The UN people assured me, so did the head of the camp. And I checked! I tried to find out if our food sickened those people. It was impossible. The cans were burned up. The doctors said the deaths were from fighting. I went over our manifests. The expiration dates all looked okay."

"Then why the expression on your face?"

"It was the worst day of my life," she said, looking at her husband, who nodded at her, meaning, *Tell him.*

I pushed it. "Ms. Mahin, was the company taking tax write-offs on expired food?"

She looked down at the carpet. She looked back up, and this time I saw a glisten at the corner of her left eye.

"Not the company. One person in Memphis. *One person* was sending out expired stuff. I found other cans in the warehouse, ready to go. Damaged or expired. We fired him. He never admitted sending expired food to Tol-e-Khomri. I couldn't prove it. He wasn't making money off it. He just wanted a better balance sheet. He thought that expiration dates were stupid. Government overregulation. He'd shipped tons of expired stuff before that, without a problem."

"That's why you quit?"

"I was going to do that anyway."

"The report you signed said there was no evidence of tainted food."

She wrung her hands. "There wasn't. Dr. Rush, Fresh Unity donates eighteen million dollars a year to feeding the hungry. Do you know how many people that keeps alive? Should I have put the program in jeopardy? Lawsuits? Headlines? Every year half the board — the lawyers — want to close the program *because they're afraid of this! Suits!*

486

What would you have done if you were me?" she asked. "No proof! Too late to stop whatever happened. In the end, I wrote the facts."

"But not the truth."

But the truth was, for all my cheap moralizing, I did not know what I would have done if I'd been in her shoes. She'd found the culprit. She'd gotten rid of him, and saved a program that fed thousands of people. A program that might have been shut down otherwise. Had she done wrong?

She must have anticipated my next thought, because she added, "Bob Welch had nothing to do with it. It was my decision. That's what I told the FBI."

"When did you tell them this?"

"The last time? Weeks ago. Don't you know? But they didn't tell me about any connection to malaria. They just showed up as if they'd been looking into it for a long time. I never connected all this until now."

I said, regretting my harsh words a moment ago, "I don't know what you should have done. The man spreading this disease is filled with hate. Nothing you could have done would have changed that. He would have gone after someone else if not that company. Believe me, his people didn't develop this weapon just to use once."

"Really?" She was like a five-year-old asking for assurance that I lacked power to bestow, but she wanted the illusion anyway.

Alan Mahin massaged her shoulders, tried to calm his wife. They seemed a caring couple, and I liked them. He reminded her that anything I said was just supposition, and told her to "do the breathing exercise."

"There's no proof of this, is there?" he asked me aggressively, defending her.

"You're right, sir."

"Your jacket is ripped. You're not on the guest list. You snuck in here. You're upsetting her."

"I know. I'm sorry about that."

"We waited a long time to have this baby. She's had a bad time of it. I didn't even want her to come tonight."

"Alan, it's all right," she said. "Really. Maybe we can help him. Help people. Dr. Rush, is there anything else you need to know?"

That's when I saw the mosquito land on her arm.

THIRTY-SIX

The mosquito must have flown in through the gash in the screen, in the hallway window. It crawled on the fleshy white of Christine's bare wrist, above a bluish vein that rose into her lifeline. She didn't see it and neither did Alan. She might never feel the bite.

I felt it squash beneath my thumb. She looked startled, but eyed the crushed insect. I'd killed it without thinking.

"Sorry," I said. "Habit."

There was no blood smear, so the mosquito had probably not started to feed, and no reason to think that the presence of a single mosquito meant anything alarming. Christine and Alan didn't seem to think it troubling. After all, no one in Atlanta had gotten sick yet.

I didn't see what kind of mosquito it was.

I thanked her for her time and excused myself and went back inside. She lingered, reluctant to go back to the party, upset by talk, memory, and pregnancy. The moment I opened the door the music grew deafening. The swirl of bodies on the dance floor was thick, and the patio doors were shut across the room, except for one, still open.

Everyone smiling. Dancing. The parade of grotesque images on-screen — *our good work* — remained off for now.

It was just one insect.

The bar area was packed, and conversation lively. No one here was paying attention to anything serious as my head swiveled this way and that, search-pattern style.

I don't even know if it was an anopheles mosquito.

I walked the periphery of the room and tried to spot insects. A couple of dancers eyed me, maybe because of the rip in my jacket, or my rumpled appearance. There were millions of mosquitoes in the United States. There was no reason to assume that what I had seen was anything other than a natural phenomenon.

But then I saw another person across the room, doing the same thing I was, walking, solo, head swiveling toward the ceiling and corners, moving as I moved. Pause and look. From a distance he seemed to examine thin air. He was the man who had stared at

Christine and me earlier. Suddenly his head swiveled sharply, as if he followed the zigzag route of an insect that was too far away for me to see. Then he turned and his eyes met mine and he froze for a fraction of a second. His gaze slid away, and he slipped sideways into the crowd, as a fish seeks concealment in a school. Hide among your own.

Could it be?

Now my search pattern changed. There had been something wrong with that man. This was the second time I'd noticed him. I recognized the quickening pulse in my throat as battle instinct. Always pay attention to the invisible soldier on your shoulder. Ignore him at your peril.

The hair was not Fargo's. He wore glasses, unlike Fargo. The height was right but everything else wrong. The last place Fargo was seen is only a few hours from here. Is it possible? And if he did come here, why stay?

But then I thought, *He's been ahead of us since Brazil. The FBI isn't here. They're concentrating on other cities. No one thought to protect the people who ran that camp.*

A woman on the dance floor several feet away from me suddenly jerked away from her partner, slapped her neck, and pulled her hand away. She went back to dancing.

A second woman — nearby — waved her

hand violently before her face, as if shooing away an insect.

And then, with horror, I saw the small cloud of insects floating in from the patio, individual dots breaking off and zigzagging into the light. Outside, the shadow of a bat swooping. It might be the last survivor of the pesticide spraying, doing its job, using radar to accomplish what I'd been unable to do, track Tom Fargo's damage.

Where the hell is he?

I felt an itch and saw that one of the creatures had landed there. I held up my hand, fascinated. And I knew.

I was looking at exactly what I'd seen in microscopes weeks before the outbreak, what Stuart had shown Eddie and me in photos and artists' renderings and what we'd seen a thousand times in Brazil. Anopheles mosquitoes rest with abdomens up in the air, unlike other mosquitoes. I saw the maxillary palp jutting out between the two antennae. The perfume and carbon dioxide detector. I saw black-and-white scales on the wing.

The mosquito took off before I could slap it.

I have to get these people out without alerting him. If it's Fargo, he'll be armed. He murdered his neighbors in New York. There are more than two hundred guests here. And if I'm wrong and it's not him, the worst that will happen is that I'll make a fool of myself.

More insects flew in now. People became aware of them. Someone shut the door to the patio, too late.

Where is he?

As I rushed through the sea of celebrants the oddest fraction of a boyhood memory flicked to me. I was in row four at Horror Film Sunday at the Pittsfield Cinema. A rainy October afternoon. *The Masque of the Red Death* playing, an oldie based on Edgar Allan Poe's tale. In the story, a plague ravaged a European country. But the wealthy and powerful believed they were immune. They isolated themselves in a castle, locked the gates, and held a masquerade ball. They giddily ate and drank. But one celebrant among them — masked as death — was not in costume. By the end, all those people were infected. It was a story about self-deception, possibly the worst disease.

Pull the fire alarm. No, that won't work. All that will do is send the guests outside, have them milling around where mosquitoes are rampant. Think, damnit!

Suddenly I knew what to do.

Tom Fargo watched rush from the bar area,

through the crowd. Rush slapped one of his hands. There must have been an insect there, and maybe Rush had killed it. That left more than eight hundred other vectors here. *Well,* Tom thought, *you're probably vaccinated, unlike many people here.*

He could leave, he knew. Just walk out of those patio doors and onto the fairway, slip across the greens and out of the golf course, return to the house and drive away and get back to Brazil. There were ways, and he knew them. A certain ship that left from Galveston, a certain plane that left from beside a Louisiana sugarcane field. There were toll road highways in the air, and you could rent space from a pilot or a gang to use them. *Black travel* was as systemized as buying a ticket online. It was harder to know where to go to do it, but once you knew, getting out of this country was as easy as getting in. You sit on a bundle of contraband. No security check. Just go.

Tom moved toward the patio door. But he stopped. He looked back and eyed Rush. What was the man doing?

Rush had gone up to a man, and was talking urgently to him. He'd not spoken to that man before. What was he saying? Tom had seen the second man outside on the patio earlier, smoking a cigarette. Rush was arguing with the man. Rush snatched something from the man's hand. The man called angrily after Rush as he moved off.

What are you up to? You saw me. I know it. Why are you leaving?

Tom felt a surge of hatred. If it had not been for Rush, the lab in Brazil would have kept producing vectors. The FBI would never have identified Tom.

But then he felt something almost worse, and it was blame. *He never could have found me if I'd picked random targets, like I told Cardozo I was going to do.*

Rush pushed out of the room as if casually going to the bathroom. He did not look back.

And suddenly with a chill Tom realized what Rush was doing. He began pushing through the crowd toward the door through which Rush had disappeared. "Rude!" a voice protested. "Hey!" But Tom knew that Rush had recognized him, all right. They had recognized each other. It had been chemical. Like vectors following carbon dioxide. If Tom didn't stop Rush, Rush would save a lot of people now.

Tom pushed through the door also. The hallway was empty. Tom listened for footsteps or voices. All he heard was the whoosh

of air-conditioning. Tom reached for his Sig
Sauer.

THIRTY-SEVEN

Christine and Alan Mahin looked up in shock as I rushed toward them in the hallway. They had not moved location since I'd left them, and I was grateful for that, at least. I called out that she needed to phone 911. She needed to get the police here immediately. I said Tom Fargo was in the ballroom, now, and an attack was beginning.

Alan, stupefied, did not take it in. "Don't you have a phone, Colonel?"

"Where's the fire alarm box?"

"Call the police?" Alan asked.

"Blond wig, cut curly and short. Dark-framed glasses. Dark jacket and gray slacks. He'll be armed."

As I hurried past, she was pulling a cell phone from her bag. But the couple was also walking the wrong way, back toward the ballroom, not out to the parking lot.

I stopped. "What are you doing?"

"Someone has to warn the others."

"I did that," I lied. "Get out! And don't stand around outside! Go home!"

They turned and went in the right direction, as Christine punched in numbers on her phone, and I hurried up, searching . . . but not seeing what I needed. Down a flight of carpeted stairs to the lower level. The pro shop. The locker rooms . . . *Where is it? Where the hell is . . . ?*

And then I saw the sprinkler on the ceiling. It was too high up.

I needed a goddamn chair to reach the ceiling. There had to be a chair in this million-dollar place. Inside the glassed-in pro shop I saw golf clubs for sale. And more trophies, this time for winners in junior league play.

In my pocket was the lighter that I'd snatched from the smoker's hand in the ballroom. If I could get the fire alarm and sprinklers going, guests upstairs would flee. Soaked, they'd head for their cars and homes, for dry clothes. They wouldn't, I hoped, stand around and gape.

There was no chair here.

The trophy case looked as if it would shatter from the weight of a man standing on it. But maybe the metal frame would support me. I lifted myself and managed to wobble on the inch-wide metal strip of the case. It bent but held. Teetering, I heard pounding footsteps from the stairwell, coming in my direction. But then moving away.

I heard two quick snapping sounds upstairs, muted but unmistakable. *Gunshots.* Tom Fargo was up there. Christine and Alan should have left by now, but I feared they hadn't.

Swaying, I reached for the sprinkler. The lighter made a clicking sound. It didn't light. It might as well have been a piece of flint wielded by a caveman. But then it did light. I held it up to the sprinkler, praying that the system would work, as I tried to keep my balance on the case, one hand steadying me against the wall.

RINGGGGGGGGG!

The spigot above began spraying water over me as the alarm began to bray.

Upstairs, I hoped, guests were shrieking as water poured down on them, driving them from the ballroom in a sopping rush. Hopefully any insects up there would be pinned by the flood of water.

And then, climbing down from the case, I saw a man through the spray, standing at the far end of the hallway. His arms extended toward me in a V shape.

As he fired I threw myself sideways and down, falling through a spray of shards. My shoulder hit the ground. The shots kept coming, muffled by the clanging fire alarm.

Snap . . . snap . . .

The clanging was steady as I rose and zigzagged off at a crouch, through a swinging door into a stainless steel kitchen. The appliances and counters heightened the echoing alarm. I had no gun. He'd be coming after me. I had no idea whether Christine Mahin had reached 911, whether Tom Fargo had shot her, Alan, and their unborn child.

I threw open a freezer door and left it open as I passed, pulled open a walk-in closet door and kept going. The open doors might make him think I was inside, or might block shots. There was a fire door ahead. I shoved through and into another hallway, pummeled by water.

Hide.

There was a storage room here, *locked,* and a boiler room, *locked,* and supply closet and unmarked door, *locked.* I looked back and the swinging door was opening. A foot began to come through. Ahead, another fire door, an exit. I reached the bar and pushed. Something hit the steel . . . *shots . . .* but I was through, out of the building. The water stopped pummeling me. I stayed flat against the clubhouse wall, moving behind a row of bushes. If I ran out onto the fairway, I'd be visible when he appeared.

Sure enough, he came crashing out.

Sirens now. Coming closer. Lots of them.

Fire department? Police? Did Christine get through?

Tom Fargo's silhouette stood frozen outside the building. I saw the outline of his pistol. His head was up, swiveling slowly. He heard the sirens but wanted me.

But then Fargo began loping away, onto the golf course, out into the dark. In a minute he'd be absorbed by it.

He was getting away.

Fargo diminished into shadow, and the shadow headed off toward the seventeenth green, and the fence. The shadow disappeared and reappeared. He must have run in and out of a sand trap. The shadow was now seventy or eighty yards away, moving fast.

I followed.

He had a gun and I had nothing. He was in good shape, younger than me by too many years. Politicians call terrorists cowards, but they are rarely that. They are brave. I despise them. But they're not cowards. If you don't understand your enemy, you make mistakes. Tom Fargo was running because he was smart.

I was starting to falter. I'd never fully mastered sprinting with my missing toes, and speed and distance took a toll. But then the shadow stopped, whirled, and crouched, and I knew he had seen me. I hit the ground. But no shot came. I looked up and he was running again.

He doesn't want police to hear shots. If they do, they'll move toward the sound.

I got up, heaving, running again. He pulled away.

The sprinkler system suddenly went on all over the golf course. Under the moon, arcing water created a Las Vegas–like display. Clear moon. Bright stars. A flood of water. I looked down and saw that although Tom was distancing himself, the wet grass was flattened where he ran over it. Even if he drew beyond my vision, for a little longer, I could track where he went.

Tom Fargo sped up and glanced back and saw the shadow that was Joe Rush falter. He was outdistancing the older man. The sirens were louder now, closer, and he saw red lights over the silhouetted clubhouse roof, and more above the treetops. Before shooting the pregnant woman and her husband, he'd heard her telling police over the phone to get to the country club.

Tom had been heading for the fence but turned away now, tried a new direction. If he could escape the grounds he could slow down, walk, get the car.

But he had to get off the golf course first. He ran through sprinklers, into a sand trap, and out and over a bunker and, hunched over, across a slanted green. Something moved to his left. He jerked the gun in that direction. He was astounded to see a dog-like figure loping by the rough and tree line. The coyote was playing, watching. The fucking police were here and this stupid animal wanted to have fun.

Water ran into his eyes. He kicked his shoes off, stripped off his socks. Barefoot was easier. Otherwise he might slip on the wet. If he made it out of the golf course, he'd be conspicuous, he knew, running through the streets in bare feet, clothing sopping. But he'd deal with that later. Now he just needed to get out.

He plunged into the grassy rough abutting a fairway. Beyond trees and bushes he saw the glint of chain link. But then he saw a red flashing light approaching. More cops.

Tom turned around and tried a new direction.

Running, he thought, *It's not the end. It's a*

setback. People will get sick here. I will get back to Brazil. Cardozo will come up with a new batch sooner or later.

The red lights looked farther away now. The golf course was large, so there had to be a way out. He glimpsed a new area of fence, but before he got clear of the bushes he heard the *snap-snap* of bolt cutters ahead.

Police, coming through the fence.

A possum hissed at him and hurried off with a humpbacked gait. He saw an owl staring down at him from a tree branch. Wildlife, Atlanta style.

But Rush? Rush was gone, left behind, at least.

Tom Fargo stopped, out of breath, in a corner of the golf course where two fence lines converged, beside a private home and backyard. He saw no red lights. But flashlights bobbed far behind him, hundreds of yards away, on a fairway. They were searching the grounds.

The clubhouse was no longer visible. Tom Fargo looked beyond the fence, into a mowed backyard of a lit-up colonial home. He saw a swimming pool and a trampoline, and there were slides and swings and toy guns in the grass. Plastic M4s. The kids who lived here probably shot at each other ten times a week.

Tom reached and felt chain link against his fingers. He fitted his toes into the fence. The top of the fence grew closer. There were no red lights or sirens anymore. He was safe. He was going to get out.

Made it.

Which is when the person behind him hit him, and pulled him down, hard.

I should have killed you, he thought as they began to roll, and fight.

Tom Fargo fell on top of me when I pulled him off the fence. I lost my breath as my back hit the ground. I must have struck a sharp protruding root. I felt it go in, like a spear. My back exploded in pain.

"You!" he cried.

He was a skilled fighter, and strong. I was winded but flooded with adrenaline. His weight drove that root in farther. I tried to buck him off. His gun was on the ground, out of reach. He went for my eyes and I parried, sideswiped his wrist, aimed at his Adam's apple, but it was not there when my three-finger strike arrived.

With a burst of strength I rolled left and felt the root tear out of my body. But he rode me, still on top. I could hear sprinklers hissing on the fairways. Tomorrow golfers would hit balls into these woods. Maybe, searching for a lost ball, they'd find something else.

I had delayed him and harassed him. I had followed but not stopped him. And now against his fury I felt my strength begin to diminish. I went for his eyes. His face was so close that I smelled onions he'd eaten tonight. A floodlight on the house went on, showed his shadow-banded, frenzied face above me, left eye brown, right eye blue, like a malamute dog's. A contact lens had fallen out.

His knee slammed into my solar plexus. I heard air rush out as pain flooded in. My left arm was paralyzed. Maybe if I'd been younger, this would have gone better. I heard shouting. Other voices. Coming closer fast. Fargo leaned back and saw that he would not get out of the golf course. He still had a choice. And seconds to make it. Without hesitation he reached for his gun. In the moonlight his eyes were terrible and focused, but no longer on me.

"Police!" a voice cried.

Tom Fargo's lips were moving.

"Put it down. PUT IT DOWN!"

Tom Fargo smiled bitterly. He reversed the pistol.

"Allahu Akbar! Allahu Akbar!"

His head jerked back and sideways when he fired.

At the end I'd seen bitter triumph in his eyes. That he'd denied us answers. And kept himself from the windowless rooms. That he'd managed to hold on to secrets.

I hoped, as the police reached me, and voices told me to lie still, *he's bleeding, get a doctor . . .* I hoped, looking up at strangers' faces, that there was not more to come.

THIRTY-EIGHT

She was still alive, hungry, and smelling the wonderful odors of carbon dioxide and cologne. They made her wings beat almost involuntarily, to try to reach them. All around her, big shadows were moving. Food!

But she couldn't fly because the water had come suddenly, as she was lighting on an ankle. Her proboscis had touched warm skin just as heavy drops swept her down, pushed her off, pinned her to the floor. Feeble, she struggled to rise.

Inside her, the mutated parasite — only one of its kind in the world — remained in the probiscis. It had had no chance to get out. And it had no more awareness of this than a mindless cell in a stalk of celery.

There were voices all around her.

"Who pulled the alarm? There's no fire!"

"The gala is ruined!"

She had no sense of a boot heel descending on her, or that the person above her did not even know she was there. And then she had no awareness at all.

The fireman kept walking through the country club. He knew that the police were chasing someone who had run onto the golf course. He hoped they caught the guy. He assumed the man who'd pulled the alarm was the police quarry.

The fireman hated people who pulled false alarms.

THIRTY-NINE

The new batch of mosquitoes was ready!

Dr. Nader Cardozo, thirty-eight, stood with pride and excitement in the glass-walled terminal of Porto Velho's Governador Jorge Teixeira de Oliveira International Airport, watching an Azul Airlines Boeing 737 board. Flight 34 was the daily milk run plane that circled Brazil's hinterland, its Amazon cities, terminating in São Paulo, from where international flights left the country.

Passengers jogged through misty rain to hurry up the mobile stairway. They included locals, gold miners heading for the duty-free city of Manaus, cattle ranchers going to their main residences in São Paulo, a couple of forest police — charged with protecting Brazil nut trees from being cut down — and, thanks to the martyr Tom Fargo, five newly trained ops from Europe and North America: a female hospital worker from

510

Florida, a baker's assistant from London, a former lieutenant in the French paratroops, a Turkish sailor, and a Moscow cab driver. They would release vectors in Orlando and Tampa, Marseille, Moscow, London, and Istanbul. *Inshallah!*

Nader's eyes went to the mobile baggage cart by the plane. He watched suitcases glide up the conveyer belt. A pet carrier. Then seven square wooden boxes marked FRAGILE.

I did it. I figured out how to make another batch.

It was eight months since Fargo's death, and the success of the martyr's mission: terror in the U.S., the defeat of a presidential candidate, the money transfer, and more gridlock in Congress, not to mention the stupendous profit realized by jihadists who'd invested in pharmaceuticals. Cardozo thought, *The money was a side benefit, but the whole thing even made the Caliphate money! And now, soon, more threats, more power, more panic everywhere.*

The doors to the 737 closed. Airport workers rolled away the staircase. The terminal vibrated as the jet rolled down the runway, diminished into a speck in the sky, and was eaten by clouds.

Cardozo felt the muscles relax in his neck

as he turned to Yasmine Riquera, the sexy lab receptionist, who he had brought along today. She was dressed in one of her usual fetching outfits, tight sleeveless V-necked aquamarine top, showing off toned arms and firm-looking breasts, and a hint of delicious cleavage. Tight-fitting white jeans, formfitting her fantastic legs. Well-defined ass, jutting up because of the cork-heeled sandals. Fingernails and toenails a matching peach color. And the whole mouthwatering package topped by dyed chestnut hair that accentuated her slutty aspect. His own wife was a Russian Brazilian, blond and sexy, theoretically, but after ten years of marriage, familiar.

"Dr. Cardozo, it was so kind of you to invite me to see the plane leave with our young scientists on it."

"Well, not just watch," he told Yasmine. "We're also going to lunch, aren't we?"

Yasmine giggled. They both knew what "lunch" meant.

"You are a hero fighting illness," Yasmine said.

"I wanted to spend my life helping people."

He put his hand on her rump as they made their way outside, to a privately hired Toyota Land Cruiser. Cardozo told the driver to go to the main dock on the Madeira, and "the floating restaurants." In the backseat he allowed his hand to fall over Yasmine's shoulder. She moved closer, smelling of citrus shampoo.

"The mosquitoes you make will end much malaria," she said in the semi-worshipful tone he adored.

True, up to a point. In his official, legal job, Cardozo ran the Amazon labs for Allard-Foss Pharmaceuticals, the French multinational. The two million male insects they had genetically engineered back at Colonel Rondon Industrial Park would do exactly what Yasmine said. The males were sterile. By breeding with wild females, they'd eliminate the possibility of offspring. Allard-Foss vans in two Brazilian jungle states were even today releasing mosquitoes. Company stock was soaring. Journalists visited regularly, and interviewed Cardozo, took his photo, lauded his public work.

To create the other secret 10 percent of his crop, Cardozo had labored long and hard, alone at 3 A.M., working from sketchy notes he'd made in talks with Dr. Umar, and notes made at Dachau death camp almost eighty years before by Cardozo's great-great-grandfather, a Lebanese-born SS doctor who hated the British and was a

513

follower of the Grand Mufti of Jerusalem, Hitler's Arab ally. Cardozo's ancestor had escaped Germany on a U-boat at the end of the war, set up shop in Brazil, and restarted his research, first for a Nazi group. Later — when the Nazis were gone — for liberation groups in the Mideast.

Tom Fargo thought I didn't know that he chose his targets for personal reasons. But as long as he created panic, I didn't care which targets he chose. And now the new people will carry on his work.

This thought excited him so much that he allowed his hand to brush Yasmine's breast. They had reached the waterfront. Mostly it looked seedy, a mud landing area for old riverboats, but there was also a new dock, and a half dozen small motorized craft, their drivers ready to ferry tourists or picnickers out for an afternoon pleasure ride.

Cardozo chose a larger boat with a private room. It was a mobile motel. As they chugged into the river Yasmine and Cardozo examined the cabin. She seemed to think the red walls, crisply made double bed, lit candles, and stocked wine rack classy. He'd probably fire her in a couple of weeks. You never wanted to keep them around too long. Otherwise gratitude turned to expectation, hero worship to something more human.

Cardozo got enough human treatment from his wife at home.

"Are you hungry, Yasmine?"

They chugged around a bend, and Porto Velho disappeared. They were in a wider section of river, with three or four other floating motels out here, probably hosting businessmen and girlfriends, ranchers and girlfriends, politicians and girlfriends, tourists and bar girls. Sex in the heat.

"We will dine on deck. Bring wine," Cardozo told the captain.

They ate at the little round table on the fantail. He saw a spider monkey staring at him from the branches of a tree; probably the last such creature alive within miles. Yasmine ate in small bites, tearing at her beefsteak like an animal. White teeth flashed against smooth, coppery skin.

"Yasmine is an Arabic name," he observed.

"My grandparents came from Gaza."

"Do you keep in contact with family there? I have no people there," he lied.

Mideasterners could carry grudges in DNA. Your ancestor hit mine with a rock, in a cave. Your ancestor stole my ancestor's sheep when Jesus was alive. Someday we will return and take back our land. Our home. Our water.

Lunch over, he took her hand and led her

515

down two stairs into the cabin. She smiled when he locked the door. His head pounded with anticipation. He felt himself stirring beneath his waist. Her blouse came off. She wore no bra. She looked eager, and the sight of her bare breasts drew his hands forward, as if by themselves.

"You are so very beautiful," he said.

"You murdered Sublieutenant Salazar."

Dr. Cardozo blinked. "Excuse me?"

"*Vai te foder,* Doctor! The boxes you loaded are not filled with vectors. I killed all the vectors last night. You shipped normal mosquitoes, which will be removed from the plane at the next stop. Along with your murderers."

This can't be happening, Cardozo thought as she moved toward him. Why was she smiling?

The first blow rammed into his solar plexus, doubling him over, dropping him to the deck. He couldn't breathe. She kicked him and yanked his hands behind his back, and suddenly he was handcuffed. He called out to the captain, for help, even knowing that none was coming. The door opened and the driver of the boat stood there, staring down at him but not moving. Cardozo told the man to get this crazy bitch off him. To overpower her.

"You mean her?" the man said, as if he could not understand what he was seeing right before his eyes.

"I'll pay you! A lot!"

"My name is Rooster Alves," the man said. "My brother was Alfonso Alves. Do you know that name?"

"What are you talking about? Who is Alfonso?"

Rooster shook his head sadly. "You didn't even know his name." Rooster walked back out.

The world was upside down. One minute Cardozo had been sipping wine and now he gasped for breath. The perfume smell had changed to a moldy/wood odor, a whiff of gasoline and fish and a trace of citrus on her ankles.

Yasmine said, "I am Captain Izabel Santo of the Brazilian Federal Police."

Cardozo saw a ray of hope. "You work for Major Lupo?" Lupo, he knew, could be paid to do things. Smuggle. Send patrols elsewhere. Jail a certain man.

"Major Lupo has been arrested."

"General Figerola?"

"Arrested also."

"Look, I have gold. A lot." She seemed to be paying attention to this and considering.

He felt a twinge of hope. Gold usually worked. But Cardozo realized that the boat had turned in the wrong direction. "This isn't the way to Porto Velho," he said.

"It isn't?"

"What do you want?" he said.

She bent over him. Her eyes had changed color from vibrant green to a dead color of the sea, fathoms deep. She wiped her lipstick off with the back of her wrist. She squatted down beside him and *where did pliers come from* rammed the twin handles of the instrument into his mouth, breaking teeth, making him scream.

"What I want," she said, "is names."

The boat slowed hours later, and out the porthole the bleeding, groaning doctor saw that they had reached the gold rush. He had told her what she wanted to know. She had broken his teeth as easily as if smashing a glass vase. Now all he wanted was for the pain to stop. Cardozo had identified routes of insect and gold shipments, named middlemen and police who received payments, even in Brasília, and a woman in Zurich, who worked in investments.

Captain Santo's clothes were streaked with his blood and vomit. She did not seem to mind.

Now, from the port window, he saw a half dozen mining *dragas* up close, huge, like a scattered herd of brontosauruses grazing in the middle of the river. The air roared from the nearby rapids and the industrial violence. He did not understand why they had come here. The little boat pulled up beside a *draga*. He heard many footsteps on deck. When the door opened it was not Rooster this time, but three tough-looking miners who dragged him from the cabin and hooked ropes beneath his arms. He was hauled — like a box of cargo — up onto the deck of the mining boat.

There, a grungy tribunal. Too many men for all of them to be from only this one *draga*. In front stood a man who was not dressed as a miner, but in well-worn khaki fatigues ringed with sweat marks at the chest and armpits. This man wore a khaki ball cap, with a SCIENCE logo over the green brim.

There was something familiar about the man. Cardozo stared through waves of pain. The nightmare kept getting worse. He knew this face from television.

"Help me," Cardozo whispered, eyes flickering to Captain Santo.

Joe Rush stepped forward. His face hovered, inches away. Rush, up close, looked

519

exactly as he did on television. "I promise," Rush said. "You don't need to worry about Izabel anymore."

Dr. Cardozo began to weep. "Thank you."

Rush said, stepping back, nodding to the miners, "No problem at all."

Through his tears of pain Cardozo realized that the men had formed into a line, single file: a fat, oily man behind a skinny malarial one; a potbellied, wormy one behind a red-haired one; a pitted face behind a man whose skin showed burn marks. They were poor men who had come here to make their fortunes, who lived with malaria, fear of murder, and distance from their families. Most miners were decent men.

"My son was Paulo Ninevah," the first man said, walking up, turning away. It made no sense. Cardozo thought, *Who?* The second man approached now.

"My wife's brother was Antonio Sul." He joined the first man at the rail.

— "Your people took my twin brother! His name was Lucca Barboza. He had six children and you killed him."

— "Alvares!"

— "Leitao!"

— "I am Magano!"

Now Cardozo understood and was terrified. When the names had all been uttered, the men stood there, looking, and in their eyes was a uniform finality.

Someone was throwing chum into the water, great bloody chunks of fish or eels. Dr. Cardozo heard meat hitting the river. Then a violent thrashing sound, which would be caimans or predator fish drawn to blood and easy food.

Joe Rush came close and looked long into the face of Dr. Cardozo. "I'm just a guest here." He shrugged. "They decided. But I voted, too. We all did."

Rush held up a stuffed manila envelope, already wilting in the Amazon humidity. "In here are the names of all the Americans you killed. Over five thousand people. And one name of someone you couldn't kill, my friend Eddie Nakamura. Eddie would have said to bring you back, and put you on trial. Eddie is that way. That's why he isn't here and I am. Eddie actually tried to save you. So I came alone."

Cardozo screamed when the miners lifted him off the deck. He was hoisted up by many hands in the way that a victorious soccer player is carried triumphantly around a field. It could not end like this. Cardozo screamed for anyone to save him. And then he was falling. And the water closed over his head. He surfaced. He was bleeding. He could feel the creatures converging on him even before they hit and bit.

And then he was dragged down.

The last thing he saw was Joe Rush and Izabel Santo, standing beside each other like a couple, then moving apart like strangers, Izabel watching, lips back like a wolf's. Rush, through an inch film of water, walking off by himself, as if Cardozo, Izabel, and this place itself were already a memory to him, and nothing more. Nothing at all.

ACKNOWLEDGMENTS

The author would like to thank the following people for their help in the researching, planning, and writing of *Vector*.

To my good friends and excellent writers, Jim Grady, Phil Gerard, and Charles Salzberg, huge thanks.

Thanks to Lizzy Hanson, for the advice. And to my dad, Jerome Reiss. Both of you are great at putting yourselves in other people's shoes, imagining their behavior.

On mosquito traits and behavior, thanks to malaria experts Dr. Jane Carlton of NYU and Dr. Photini Sinnis at Johns Hopkins University. Also to Dr. Gloria Coruzzi at NYU, for the contacts. Any science mistakes are mine.

To Jeff Stein, thanks for letting me crash at your home in Washington, D.C., during the research of this book. And Max Protech, my dear old friend, was kind to let me stay at his home in Santa Fe.

As always to my neighbors Ken and Ann Smith, in the Berkshires, thanks for being there during the writing of one more book in the woods. And to Dr. Robert Prezant at Montclair State University, thanks once again for an intellectual home.

In Atlanta, the stealth guerrilla researchers, Christine Mahin and Eric Englert, did a fantastic job.

Thanks to my agent, Esther Newberg. And to my terrific editor, Tom Colgan. And the team at Berkley.

Dr. Stuart Harris (the real one) heads up Harvard's Wilderness Medicine program and has consistently been willing to take calls and questions regarding different diseases in remote areas around the world. I've named a character in this book after Stuart, in his honor. The Stuart in the book is fictional, and at Columbia, not Harvard. Both Stuarts are great guys.

Wendy, once again, with love, thanks.

Malaria has been mostly eradicated in developed countries, but millions around the world fall victim to this terrible disease every year. The events depicted in this book have not happened, but mutations are always possible. At present, new, dangerous forms of the disease are showing resistance to pesticides once considered effective.

ABOUT THE AUTHOR

James Abel is the pseudonym for Bob Reiss, an accomplished author and journalist who has written extensively about trouble spots and exotic locations around the world; including the Arctic, Somalia/Sudan and the Amazon rain forest. He is the author of the Joe Rush novels, including *Cold Silence, Protocol Zero* and *White Plague.*

The employees of Thorndike Press hope you have enjoyed this Large Print book. All our Thorndike, Wheeler, and Kennebec Large Print titles are designed for easy reading, and all our books are made to last. Other Thorndike Press Large Print books are available at your library, through selected bookstores, or directly from us.

For information about titles, please call:
   (800) 223-1244

or visit our website at:
   gale.com/thorndike

To share your comments, please write:
   Publisher
   Thorndike Press
   10 Water St., Suite 310
   Waterville, ME 04901